The Silent Twin

A voice on the monitor. A law on the fridge.

A.M Jones

Jones Thrillers

The Silent Twin

First published in 2025 by

Jones Thrillers, United Kingdom

ISBN Paperback: 978-1-9192578-2-2

ISBN eBook: 978-1-9192578-3-9

Contents

Dedication   1

Act I: Unease   2

Chapter One   3
Sleepless

Chapter Two   15
The Voice

Chapter Three   29
Baby Blues

Chapter Four   45
Old Secrets

Chapter Five   62
What We Lock

Chapter Six   77
Doctor Woman

Chapter Seven   92
Ferry Night

Chapter Eight   105
Sensory

Chapter Nine   121

Knots

Chapter Ten   132

Witness

Chapter Eleven   143

Second Floor

Chapter Twelve   153

The Photo That Moves

Act II: The Fracture   167

Chapter Thirteen   168

Paperwork

Chapter Fourteen   184

The Jug

Chapter Fifteen   201

The Boy on the Bus

Chapter Sixteen   212

Static

Chapter Seventeen   225

Split

Chapter Eighteen   239

The Hall Mat

Chapter Nineteen   254

Caravan

Chapter Twenty   267

Left–Right

Chapter Twenty-One   281
Doctor Woman, Three

Chapter Twenty-Two   294
Viable

Chapter Twenty-Three   304
Blue Jug

Chapter Twenty-Four   315
When Doors Open

Chapter Twenty-Five   326
Payback

Chapter Twenty-Six   336
Ferry Burnt

Chapter Twenty-Seven   348
Breakwater

Act III - The Binding   359

Chapter Twenty-Eight   360
Contract

Chapter Twenty-Nine   369
The Boat Song

Chapter Thirty   382
Witnesses

Chapter Thirty-One   394
Two Clicks

Chapter Thirty-Two   406
The Hall Mat Only

Chapter Thirty-Three   420
Apples

Chapter Thirty-Four   432
Not a Girl — Grown

Chapter Thirty-Five   440
On My Terms

Acknowledgements   447

Also by A.M Jones   448

About the Author   449

Dedication

For both: kept; none spent.

Act I: Unease

Chapter One
Sleepless

The baby monitor crackled like distant rain.

Clara lay on her side, one hand flat on the sheet, the other pressed into the small of her back as if she could hold herself together through the night. The red LED on the base unit pulsed gently: breathing in, breathing out. In the next room her daughter made small animal sounds, the soft huffs and snuffles of a creature new to air.

"Go to sleep," Mark murmured. His breath warmed the back of her neck. He had the heavy quiet of a man who could still fall from standing to sleep in five minutes, even with a baby in the house. She envied him with a bitterness she didn't like to name.

"I am," she said, and listened harder.

Another little crackle. Then nothing. The house settled around them, old pipes ticking, the boiler muttering to itself like an elderly relative. From the street came the faraway hiss of tyres on wet tarmac. It had rained after midnight. The curtains were a darker black than the room.

"Clara," Mark said again, half asleep, "she's fine. We checked her—what—twenty minutes ago."

"Eighteen," Clara said. She knew because she had counted the seconds between breaths, because the counting sometimes kept her from spinning off.

He gave a small laugh into the pillow. "You're impossible."

"Mm."

The monitor made a sound like a throat clearing. The little red light flickered from one bar to two as if someone had stepped closer to the microphone. Clara raised herself on an elbow. Mark's arm fell from her waist to the mattress with a muffled thud.

"Did you hear—" she began.

A soft sigh came through. Breath, but not the baby's quick rabbit breath. This was older. Shaped by words. The hairs lifted on Clara's forearms.

She touched the volume button with a fingertip, nudging it up one notch. The plastic clicked too loudly in the quiet.

"Don't," Mark said without opening his eyes. "You'll wake her."

"She's asleep," Clara whispered.

"Exactly."

Clara stared at the monitor as if it might blush and confess. She could see the nursery in her mind: the cot beneath the window, the pale moon of the night-light on the chest of drawers, the soft crush of the rug under bare feet. The stuffed rabbit propped at the corner of the cot, ears at attention like a sentry who never blinked. The mobile hanging above, paper stars that moved when the air moved, that sometimes moved when the air did not.

The red LED sank back to a single bar. The machine sighed and went quiet.

***

Clara lay down again. Her body felt like it had been filled with pins. She shut her eyes and watched darkness bloom and fade in waves, like the inside of a lid when you press too hard.

When the voice came, it came from another room and from years away.

"Clara?"

She sat up so fast the mattress punched air. Mark swore and rolled on to his back, hunting for the quilt with one hand.

"What?" he said, properly awake now.

Clara's mouth had become extremely dry. She swallowed and felt it all the way down. "Did you—"

The monitor crackled again. "Clara, wake up."

Not loud. Not booming. A girl's voice, pitched low as if not to wake the baby. Familiar in the way scents are familiar, not the way faces are. It seemed to fit into Clara's ear as if the ear had been made expecting it.

Mark levered himself up on his elbows, frowning. "That's interference," he said, as if naming it would send it back up the aerial to wherever interference lives. "These things pick up taxis. It's in the leaflet."

"We don't live near taxis," Clara said. She had intended to be brisk and funny and sane; it came out thin and cross.

"We live near the main road."

"That's not—"

The monitor hissed. A rush of static. Then the soft sound of breath, as if the speaker had moved closer to the microphone.

"Clara, get up," said the voice. "I'm cold."

The red LED climbed to three bars and held.

Clara swung her legs out of bed. The carpet was cool and slightly rough under her feet; she had meant to buy a rug and hadn't. Her head felt filled with weightless water, sloshing.

"Clara," Mark said. "Wait."

She didn't. She crossed the landing on the edges of her feet like a thief and pushed the nursery door with two fingers. The night-light made a small moon of the room. The air had that sweet milky tang of a baby sleeping properly for once.

The baby lay as Clara had left her: arms flung out, one hand curled, the other open as if sifting dreams. Tiny breath, perfectly spaced. In, out. The mobile was still.

"Hello," Clara whispered to the room. She hated herself a little for doing it. "Is anyone...?"

The monitor unit by the cot was blank and well-behaved, its little green power light unwavering. It did not bear guilt.

Clara stepped closer and put two fingers gently on her daughter's chest. Rise, fall. She held her fingers there until her own pulse stopped hammering, until the rise and fall became a metronome she could borrow. In, out. She stood long enough for pins to creep up her calves.

Behind her, the hall floorboard gave the small, complaining sound it always made when stepped on wrong. She turned, biting a scream that would wake the street. Mark stood in the doorway, hair a mess of shadows, an apology already forming.

"I should've made tea," he said. "It's always three in the morning, isn't it. Whatever goes wrong."

"Who was that?" Clara asked, and it came out flatter than she meant.

He rubbed at his face, then his eyes, as if the answer might be written there. He looked past her at the cot, checked for himself without moving closer. "No one," he said. "Interference."

"You heard it."

He hesitated. "I heard... something."

"It said my name."

He shrugged beached shoulders. "Maybe it was me. You know. In my sleep."

"It wasn't you."

"Then someone's baby monitor across the way is picking up ours, or the other way round. It happens. It's in the leaf—"

"Not everything is in the leaflet, Mark," Clara said, softer than the words.

He winced. "Come back to bed."

"In a minute."

He stood there a second longer, making his own inventory of the room, as if he could find the thing that would settle the day. Then he sighed and disappeared, and the floorboard complained again on his way out. Clara looked around the nursery slowly, feeling the edges of everything with her eyes. The stuffed rabbit wasn't where she thought; it seemed to have turned its head. She immediately told herself not to be ridiculous. She straightened the rabbit and rearranged the blanket folded over the cot rail and looked at the door to the landing and felt, very briefly and very definitely, that someone else had stood where she was standing five minutes before.

She rubbed the feeling away like fog from glass. She leaned on the cot rim and watched the perfect, heedless sleep of someone who had yet to learn fear. She tried to let some of it seep into her bones.

"Ellie?" she said before she knew she was going to. The name surprised her mouth.

Silence thickened, then thinned again. The monitor at the bedside table in her own room made a small throat-noise through the open door.

Clara left the nursery light low and went back to the bedroom, carrying the monitor base unit with both hands as if it might spill. Mark had rolled to her side of the bed and was already half gone, the kind of sleep that wouldn't survive much questioning.

She sat on the edge of the mattress and placed the monitor on the bedside table like an offering, then angled herself so she could watch the screen and the doorway at once. She felt enormous and brittle. The day had been one long rubber band stretched across the hours; now, at night, it pinged and nicked at her with petty, mean little stings.

She thought of the shoebox in the loft, the one with the faded teddy on the lid. It had been her mother's; her mother had given it to her when she was pregnant. When we turned out your drawers, Martha had said, we found it tucked behind the old cot. As if the house had been keeping a promise for her.

Inside the box were tiny socks like dolls' jokes and a card with a lamb on it and a hospital bracelet with a name in ballpoint: CLARA MORGAN. And beneath it, the other bracelet. ELEANOR MORGAN. She had shown it to Mark and he had said, gently, as if to a skittish horse, It's not unusual for twins to have their own bands even if— And then he had stopped because there is no polite finish to the sentence even if one of them never needed it.

Her mother had not lingered on the story, the way you don't linger in rooms that make you feel unwell. You were supposed to be two, Martha had said, and smiled with her mouth. We brought you home. We were very lucky.

Clara had grown up with that idea like a window that didn't open: there, cool to the touch, useful for letting light in, not for letting truth out. She had put her ear against the glass sometimes and imagined weather in another place.

The monitor crackled once, twice, as if clearing its throat again. Mark snored faintly, then shifted into a quieter rhythm. The red LED climbed to two bars and hovered like a thought about to become a sentence.

Clara leaned closer before she remembered there was no point; the sound would be the same however near her ear. She felt silly and afraid and tired in a way that had nothing to do with muscles.

"Clara," said the voice, and now it was unmistakable. Not the words themselves but the shape of them. The way the L curled. The way the final A didn't quite fade, as if the speaker liked the taste of the name.

Clara's heart climbed into her throat and sat there looking around.

"Who are you?" she whispered. Her mouth felt bruised by the effort of making breath into words.

A small, almost amused sound came back. "Don't be daft," said the voice, as if she had asked where the door was in a room with one wall missing. "It's me."

Clara put her hand over her mouth because something wanted to come out of it that would wake the child and the street and the birds. Her eyes prickled. The room tilted; she set her feet wider on the carpet to keep it from sliding.

"What do you want?" she said, because that seemed like a grown-up question.

"That song," said the voice. "The one from the caravan."

Clara's stomach dropped like a lift misjudging a floor. The caravan—she hadn't thought of it in years. A damp summer in a field that hadn't decided whether to be in Cornwall or in heaven. Her mother sitting on the step peeling apples with a knife that knew every apple she'd ever peeled. A song at bedtime about a boat so small it fit in a hand. She hadn't sung it since she was seven.

"How do you—" she began. Stopped. Swallowed. "I don't sing."

"You do to me," said the voice. A small pleased hum that sounded like someone putting a hand into a pocket and finding exactly what they meant to.

Clara closed her eyes and saw the caravan's window steamed by bodies and weather. She saw two shapes between the bunks, knotting the same rope to the same pretend mast. She saw a hand the same size as hers. She opened her eyes quickly and counted the edges of the bedside table. One. Two. Three. Four. She breathed into her teeth and out again.

"Say something only I'd know," she said, surprised by the steadiness of herself. "Now. Say it."

A pause. A rustle. For a second the monitor breathed static like rain on tin. Then, in a voice that carried a smile she could see but not prove, came the words: "Mum hid the biscuits in the tall blue jug."

Clara stood up too fast and the room went white at the edges. She sat down again immediately and put her head between her knees, and was a teenager in a school corridor for three vivid seconds, hoping not to fall in front of someone who would remember it.

Mark snuffled. Turned. Slept. The little domestic treachery of it made her want to shake him until coins fell out.

When she could see properly again she stared at the monitor as if it might be a mouth. Her throat had locked. The words came through tight.

"Ellie?"

A breath like a yes.

The baby made a small squeak through the open nursery door, the kind of sound that meant a dream had turned the wrong page and then decided to let everyone off.

Clara reached for the volume knob and turned it all the way down. The red LED continued its patient inhale, exhale. She placed the monitor face-down on the table and sat very still until her pulse had learned to stop drumming behind her eyes.

In the morning she would say nothing. She knew this already, the way you know a bruise will look worse in a few hours. She would make tea and clean the baby's bottles and tell herself about interference and taxi radios and the weather. She would think about ringing her mother and not ring her. She would consider googling the words auditory hallucination and decide not to. She would put the stuffed rabbit in a different place and forget, by mid-afternoon, which place that had been.

For now she lay down and looked at the ceiling and let her eyes go out of focus until the whole house was only a shape, and behind that shape another shape, and behind that—

***

She must have slept because she found herself suddenly awake and not knowing why. The light at the curtains was grey that meant almost morning. She listened, body strung like a wire.

From the nursery came a sound like someone humming a line of a song they were not sure they remembered. It was only a bar. It was enough.

Clara sat up, grabbed the monitor, turned it over.

The red LED climbed to three. The humming stopped. A small voice began to sing in the rhythm of a caravan on a lane. The boat was very small. The sea was too big. The person in the boat promised they were not afraid.

Clara closed her eyes and did the cruel, necessary thing of being still so she would not wake the man beside her whose love had not prepared him for this and would not protect either of them if she was mad.

When the voice stopped, it did not say goodnight. It did not say anything at all.

Clara stared at the ceiling until the grey made way for a paler grey, and then for the thinnest early yellow. She got up when the birds did and went to the nursery and did not look at the rabbit.

***

At breakfast, Mark said, "You look better."

She said, "I slept," and discovered that lying at eight in the morning was easier than lying at three.

He kissed her cheek. Picked up his coffee mug. "See? Leaflet."

She smiled because people needed to be kept alive with small mercy.

The smile felt like a plaster that had lost some of its stick but was trying. When he had gone to shower, she opened the back door and let in a weather she could name. The garden had that too-green you only see in wet months. A pigeon on the fence made the stupid, comforting noises of a bird with no metaphors to carry.

She whispered into the empty kitchen, "If you're there, say it again."

The fridge hummed. The house breathed its old breath. The monitor on the table addressed its own silence.

From upstairs the baby gave an interrogative squeal followed by a satisfied gurgle. Clara put her hand on the monitor as if she could feel heat through plastic.

"Okay," she said to herself. To the house. To a girl with her voice. "Okay."

She switched the monitor off. The red LED went dark. The room felt immediately too quiet, as if someone had left.

She waited. Nothing happened. She put the kettle on and watched cold water transform into promise.

When Mark came down, rubbing his hair with a towel, he said, "What's on today?"

"Nothing," Clara said. "Maybe I'll go up in the loft. Look for that box."

"What box?"

"The one with the bracelets."

He paused. "Why?"

"So I can put it somewhere I'll stop thinking about it," she said, which sounded adult enough to pass. "Do you want toast?"

He narrowed his eyes and then decided, kindly, to let the day be ordinary. "Yes," he said. "Please."

She made toast. She buttered it. She cut it diagonally because diagonal toast made mornings a fraction less heavy. She placed the plate in front of him and sat down and let the steam from the tea soften her face.

In the quiet that followed, something unclenched inside her. It didn't give up; it rested.

***

When Mark had gone to work, when the baby had gone back to sleep, when the house had done its small daily shrug, Clara pulled down the loft ladder and climbed into dust with a torch she didn't entirely trust. She found the shoebox where she had known it would be, because houses keep faith with you even when you do not. She carried it down like a relic. She set it on the table, the same table where the monitor had sat and made a mouth of itself. She lifted the lid.

Two bracelets lay exactly where she had left them. CLARA MORGAN. ELEANOR MORGAN. The handwriting on the little white tabs was neat and bored, the handwriting of someone doing a job properly. The elastic had yellowed slightly with years.

Clara touched the one that had not been used and felt—nothing. No sense of a name stirring; no electricity; no ridiculous movie jolt.

She exhaled, long and shaky. "See?" she said aloud, to shame herself. "Leaflet."

The baby monitor, which she had switched back on without noticing, crackled once, twice. The red LED climbed to two bars as if called.

Clara's head came up as if on a string.

"Clara," said the voice, patient now, as if humouring someone who is always the slower twin. "It's me."

She put both bracelets back in the box, very gently, as if putting something to bed.

"Ellie," she said, and did not say the rest: if you are here, if you have always been here, if this is what I have been afraid of and longing for since I could make longing into a shape, then say the thing only we would know. Say it until the world stops being a leaflet.

The monitor clicked. The voice began to hum the boat again, and this time Clara hummed with it, very quietly, so no one would hear and call the wrong doctor.

When the song was done, the house did not applaud. The box sat dumb and content on the table. Upstairs, her daughter slept the sleep of the blameless.

Clara stood in her kitchen in yesterday's jumper and decided—not for the last time—that there were worse things than being mad. One of them was being alone.

She put the lid back on the box and went to make more tea.

Chapter Two
The Voice

Morning arrived like a visitor who didn't bother to knock. It slipped through the curtains and sat itself at the kitchen table while Clara tried to look like a person who understood mornings. Nappies. Steriliser. Bottles arranged in a small white army. The baby made the satisfied little piglet noises of someone who had eaten and intended to sleep immediately afterwards.

Mark moved around the room with his careful usefulness, sleeves pushed up, mug in hand. He loaded the dishwasher with the solemnity of a man doing a job with measurable results. When he kissed Clara's hair it felt like being stamped *PASSED* by a friendly official.

"You all right?" he asked. The question was soft, rehearsed.

"I slept," she said, which was true in the technical sense, the way a person sleeps on a train between stations and calls the jerks and starts *rest*.

"Good." He touched the baby's foot; the baby curled her toes as if gripping a rung. "She looks... content."

"She's a tyrant," Clara said, and kissed the small round head because that was the entire point. "A benevolent one. For now."

Mark smiled. "I'll get out of your way. I've got a call at nine."

He carried his laptop upstairs, steps quiet, as if noiselessness could be a contribution. The house exhaled. For a few minutes the only sounds were the tumble of the washing machine turning wet into less-wet, and the quick comfortable breaths of someone new who had no idea what any of this cost.

Clara made tea and forgot it on the counter until it sulked into brown cold. She made another and drank it too hot. She wiped the worktop in tight small circles and made it shine and then felt silly for needing things to gleam.

The monitor sat on the table, its red LED a patient pulse. In, out. She told herself she didn't need it while the baby dozed in the bouncer not five feet away; still, she angled it towards herself, the way you put a chair nearer the door in a room that feels the wrong size.

***

By ten she had found the rhythm of the morning: attend, adjust, admire, repeat. She carried the baby upstairs and laid her in the cot for a proper sleep, the sort with a sheet and a promise. She lingered long enough to let her eyes catalogue the room — cot, night-light, rabbit, mobile — and to be annoyed with herself for cataloguing.

On the landing she paused, embarrassed by the urge to look back to see whether the rabbit had turned its head. She didn't. Small victories counted.

In the kitchen, the fridge made a conscientious little hum and the boiler cleared its throat. Clara set the monitor on the table and stood with both hands around her mug as if hands could learn heat by example. The red light brightened for a single breath and settled.

She should have used the quiet to nap. She should have lain on the sofa and let the world be responsible for itself for forty minutes. Instead, she took a tidy stack of post from the hall table and sorted it into piles with stern names: *Important, Later, Nonsense.* She had no authority to be stern with anything. She did it anyway.

The baby monitor gave a slender fizz, like tonic poured over too much ice.

Clara looked up. "No," she told it, because sometimes you could parent objects. "Shh."

The fizz faded. The red LED kept time: in, out. It was ridiculous to feel both relieved and snubbed.

She put the pile marked *Important* on the chair and sat on it without noticing.

***

At half twelve she made lunch from ingredients that didn't want to be a lunch together and ate it with the careful appetite of someone performing normal. She scrolled through her phone and let other lives push against hers — pictures of beaches that didn't exist, babies with symmetrical hair, a recipe for a traybake that promised to change her life in twelve minutes. Somewhere a friend from years ago had posted a photograph of a boat, small, white, on water that had decided to be glass; the caption said *Cornwall with my two*, and the word *two* reached into Clara's chest and tapped a place that flinched.

She put the phone down. She turned the volume of the monitor down a notch and immediately turned it back up because fear sounded like silence now.

A lorry went by and made the glass briefly tremble in its frame. The boiler sighed. The house settled into itself in that small, decent way old houses have, as if making room for everyone's mistakes.

At one o'clock, exactly, as if the hour had been arranged in advance, the monitor said her name.

"Clara."

It wasn't loud. It didn't boom. It arrived the way a memory arrives: suddenly and with the confidence of something that knows it has always belonged to you.

She put her mug down too hard and tea leapt over the rim and made a brown comet on the table. "Who is this?" She reached for briskness and found only breathlessness.

Silence. Not the flat kind; the kind with a shape. Then, very softly, a nursery rhyme she hadn't thought about for decades, faulty in the precise way childhood makes things faulty.

Ring o' woses,
pocket full of posies...

Clara's throat closed. She saw her mother's kitchen, lino that tried to be cheerful, a chipped blue jug on the shelf that had once hidden biscuits. She saw two girls, one always half a step in front of the other, one tripping deliberately so the other could catch up and be first.

Her fingers went cold. She pushed her chair back with her knees and stood, the scrape too loud. "Ellie?" She hated the pleading in it; she could hear her own hope like a child's hand tapping a window.

The rhyme stopped. A breath. Then a small, satisfied little hum, as if someone had found a marble in a pocket they had forgotten about.

Clara crossed the room as if walking on a deck. She took the monitor in both hands, foolish, as if she could trap whatever the air was trying to do. "Say it again."

Nothing. Only the domestic orchestra carrying on without her: washing machine thud, the fridge's long vowel, a car door kissing itself shut in the street.

"Say it," she whispered, and surprised herself with how fierce she sounded. "Say it the wrong way."

She waited until the silence became embarrassing. She put the monitor back down very gently, the way you put down a glass after a toast at a funeral. Her knees felt unreliable. She sat and then stood again because sitting made the room tilt.

Upstairs, a floorboard remembered its party trick and creaked in that stupidly familiar way. The baby did not cry. The baby had decided to be kind.

Clara wiped the tea with a cloth and then threw the cloth into the sink as if irritation had heft. She laughed once, because anger without an audience needs the relief of a noise.

***

She carried the laundry up and folded it in the bedroom with an attention that would have pleased the army. Mark's shirts squared themselves into stacks. Her T-shirts made smaller stacks that made her feel small. She put the baby's sleep suits in a drawer and shut it too firmly and opened it again and smoothed the top one as if apology could be folded.

She went to the nursery door and looked in. The room had arranged itself politely: cot, night-light, rabbit, mobile. She stepped closer and looked at the window catch. It sat down and correct, engaged. She pressed the sash anyway: the window didn't budge. It was a small relief, but she took it. She had begun to collect small reliefs the way some people collect teaspoons.

She put two fingers on the baby's chest because habit had become religion. Rise, fall. Borrowing calm, she left her hand there, and when her own breath had learned the trick she removed it slowly, as if not to spill anything.

On the way out she moved the rabbit's head half an inch so it would look at the cot properly. She couldn't help herself; it helped.

In the hall she paused and listened the way a person listens when they've told themselves not to. The house breathed back. Pipes ticked. Once, just once, something like a hum slid along the skirting board, so soft she could tell herself it had been nothing if she wanted to. She didn't want to. She wanted it to be evidence.

She walked downstairs, holding both banister and argument in the same hand.

***

Mark made coffee at three as if three were a time that rewarded coffee. He leant in the doorway and watched her tidy things that had already been tidied. "How's the day?"

"Obedient," she said.

He smiled. "Is that good?"

"It's something."

He came to stand beside her, shoulder brushing shoulder. "You don't have to be brave by yourself."

"I'm not." She angled her body away to make the lie easier to carry.

His hand hovered near the small of her back and then found a polite place on the counter. "Anything... odd?"

She could say it, she thought. She could say, *She sang the rhyme with the wrong mouth.* She could say, *At one o'clock my name belonged to someone else.* She could say, *I am relieved and furious to be haunted.* Instead she said, "The washing machine's making a new sound."

"We'll get someone in."

"Mm."

He sipped his coffee and set the mug down carefully. "You know you can tell me."

"I know."

He waited. When it was clear the waiting wouldn't be rewarded, he kissed her temple and went back upstairs to his work, his footsteps making kindness of wood.

Clara stood still for a count of ten, then twenty, then to the end of a number she decided would be respectable. When she moved again she did it quietly, as if the house might think better of her if she practised stealth.

***

The afternoon dulled. Clouds pressed their faces to the windows. The neighbour's wind chime rang once with the specific malice wind chimes have on grim days. The baby woke in a mood and then, as if apologising, gave Clara a series of improbable smiles that made the world ridiculous with love.

Clara put her in the pram and rolled her slowly along the hallway, back and forth, the wheels making that cheap little rrr-rrr that vibrated harness and hip bones. She counted the passes like a person pacing out a sentence: thirty, thirty-one, thirty-two. She whispered the boat song on a breath and stopped herself, because summoning is not a thing to be done by accident.

When the baby slept again, she stood over the pram and watched the eyelids flicker. What do babies dream, she wondered; milk, faces, the bright geometry of mobiles, the astonishment of their own fingers?

She had the sudden, unhelpful thought that sometimes the newly born dream of the place they left, and felt the floor tilt a degree under her feet.

The monitor on the console table flickered a little brighter, then dimmed again, as if remembering its lines.

"Don't," she said, not sure to whom.

The hallway made its usual long sigh.

***

At half four, the doorbell rang, and the sound was so everyday that Clara laughed for real. She opened the door expecting a parcel and found nothing but air and the smell of rain. The little patch of paving in front of the step shone like something polished. For a second she had the irrational certainty that someone had been there a breath before and had slipped sideways, into the thin place between this and the next.

"Parcel?" Mark called down.

"No," she said, and tried to arrange the word as if it meant nothing at all. "Wrong house."

When she shut the door the monitor in the hall gave a single hiccupping crackle, as if someone had swallowed a laugh.

She told herself off. She told the house off as well, for parity. She wheeled the pram back into the sitting room and tucked the blanket tighter around a child who would, in five minutes, kick it defiantly away as if protesting propriety.

***

Dusk found the garden and turned everything into respectable silhouettes. Mark made a sauce that smelled of competence. They ate in a quiet that tried too hard not to be listening.

After, he ran the bath for the baby and narrated the procedure in a cheerful voice as if speaking an instruction manual aloud could keep harm away. The baby tolerated it with the deep suspicion bath-warm babies have and then rewarded them with a yawn so enormous it seemed impossible it belonged to such a small face.

Clara held her wrapped and hooded like a saint. The weight in her arms told a simpler story than the house did. She pressed her lips to damp hair and whispered, "You are the realest thing I have," and felt the treachery of the sentence even as she said it.

They put her down. They stood over the cot longer than necessary, doing that pretending-to-leave where you leave and then unleave repeatedly until the baby calls your bluff by not waking. The night-light hummed its yellow coin of safety.

In the doorway, Mark squeezed Clara's hand. "We're okay," he said, as if saying it might get it notarised.

"We are," she said, and left the room with her heart arranged neatly under her ribs.

At nine, rain arrived properly and committed to the performance. It battered the windows and then, bored, softened itself into something that sounded like memory. The house drank it. The gutters rejoiced. Somewhere, a drip began a monologue that would last all night.

Clara sat on the sofa with a book that didn't want to be read. Words skated. Sentences refused to confess. She placed the book face-down and watched the ceiling instead, where a faint water mark had decided to be a continent.

Mark watched something on his laptop with earphones in and practised neutral expressions so she wouldn't feel obliged to ask if he was
all right.

The monitor on the coffee table breathed its red breath. In, out. In,
out. She hated and loved it in equal, ridiculous measure.

At ten, she stood and stretched and felt her spine register every hour
of the day. She said she would go to bed. She did not. She went to the
kitchen and stood at the back door and looked out at the garden made
cheap by the security light, every leaf glossy and trying too hard to look
fresh.

In the blackness beyond the fence a cat's eyes gleamed for a second
and were gone. The shape of that gone left a pressure on the glass.

Clara placed her palm flat on the cold pane and made a small sound
that might have been a laugh and might have been its neighbour. Her
breath fogged a fog small enough to be a child's. With her fingertip she
drew a circle, then wiped it away before it could be a letter.

Behind her, in the doorway, Mark said, "You coming?"

"In a minute."

When she turned back for a last look, two shapes seemed to pass
each other on the garden wall — one tall, one narrow — but when
she looked directly there was only night and rain, decent and without
opinion.

Near midnight, the house reduced itself to essentials: heat, breath,
the small arguments of wood settling after a wet day. Clara lay on her
side and listened, a person classifying moths by wing beat.

She had almost drifted — that dangerous kind of almost that makes
falling asleep feel like stepping off an unbuilt step — when the monitor
made a sound like a child trying not to laugh.

"Clara," said the voice. Not a question. A statement, pleased with
itself.

She felt the now-familiar rise of cold from her spine to the back of her head, like a wave pulled through the body by wire. She sat up, slow, because quick felt like an invitation. Beside her Mark murmured and turned on to his other side, his breathing finding the new rhythm shortly afterwards like a man redrawing a map.

"What do you want?" she asked, and was surprised at the steadiness in it. As if asking clearly might make the answer behave.

A gentle breath, as if someone had leaned right against the mic and remembered not to wake the baby. Then, lower, almost conspiratorial: "Left-right."

Clara swung her legs out of bed. She moved through the doorway like a person in a film, ridiculous and inevitable. In the nursery the night-light held its small moon. The baby lay frank and perfect, hands open, mouth softened, her entire body a letter written to the word *safe*.

Clara stood at the cot and rested her palm on the little chest. She rocked, left-right, because command had become habit. The baby didn't wake. Somewhere, the house changed gear and sighed.

She looked at the window, at the catch. It was set properly. Both parts. Two clicks. She told herself she wasn't going to check it. She checked it. It held.

"Happy?" she whispered, and hated herself for the childishness, and then hated herself for hating herself.

The monitor remained quiet. The red light kept time as if it had gone back to being a machine. For a moment the absurd notion came to her that it disapproved of her sarcasm.

She leaned down and pressed her lips to the baby's warm forehead and felt the deep, blank animal peace of a child's sleep wrap itself around the edges of her. It didn't make the fear leave. It made the fear sit down and wait its turn.

On the way out, she adjusted the rabbit's ear and told herself it had merely drooped.

In bed, Mark breathed like a person who believed in physics. Clara placed the monitor on her chest and felt the faint tick of its pretend heart through the bone. She closed her eyes.

"Don't let him silence you," the voice said from the plastic, fond, amused.

Clara opened her eyes into the dark and stared until shapes made themselves and unmade themselves again.

"I won't," she said, and noticed the part of her that wanted to add *I can't*, and didn't.

She woke to a grey that tried to be kind. Rain had done its best work and left the street darker and cleaner. In the kitchen the kettle made its pre-boil tremor like anticipation. Mark came down rubbing sleep from his face in a way that made him look briefly like a boy, and the sight undid her a little.

"You look—" he began, and stopped himself from saying *less haunted*. "—better."

"I slept," she said, and discovered that telling plausible lies at eight in the morning was easier than telling the truth at three.

He nodded. "Good." He poured water over coffee as if making coffee were a ceremony that could guarantee outcomes. "What shall we do today?"

"Nothing," she said, which sounded wonderfully ambitious. "Maybe the loft. I thought I might put some things away."

He looked at her for a second too long and then chose to believe her. "I'll help."

"You have work."

"Work can wait."

She smiled at him. It felt like a small thing stitched onto a larger thing with bright thread. "Later, then."

He raised his mug in a toast to the day. "Later."

When he went to shower, she stood at the back door and opened it and let in air that smelled like a promise and a warning. The fence dripped neatly. Somewhere a pigeon shouted its idiotic belief in itself.

Clara looked at the garden as if it were a stage that might admit actors at any moment. She said, very softly, "If you're there, say it again."

The fridge hummed. The house breathed its old breath. The monitor on the table was quiet and dignified, like a person who refuses to repeat a joke.

From upstairs the baby produced a small interrogative squeal followed by a satisfied sigh. Clara smiled despite herself and placed her hand lightly on the monitor's plastic case, a silly, tender gesture that made her eyes sting.

"Okay," she said, to the kitchen, to the house, to the girl who spoke through machines, or through the plaster, or through her. "Okay."

She turned the monitor off. The red LED went dark. The room felt immediately too quiet, as if someone polite had left without saying goodbye.

She waited. Nothing happened. She put the kettle on and watched cold water become something you could hold.

Behind her, the sitting room ticked as it settled. Above her, a very small footprint of sound moved along the landing — nothing more than the house shifting a rib. She decided not to go and look. She had decided, today, to let some things be true without proof.

When Mark came down, he said, "Toast?"

"Diagonal," she said.

"Obviously," he said, and smiled, and for a minute the kitchen was simply a place where people made breakfast and nobody belonged to a story they were afraid to be in.

By ten the morning had put on a sensible face. It would not last. That was all right. Clara had begun to understand that sanity, like weather, was a thing you dressed for.

Up in the nursery, the rabbit regarded the cot with stitched suspicion. The mobile waited for air to do something with it. On the dresser, the monitor sat blank and obedient, reflecting a small slice of window and the idea of a hand that would, in an hour, reach for it.

Downstairs, in the drawer next to the cooker where lighters and elastic bands and the past go to be useful, a cheap lined notepad waited. Clara would take it out later and write: *13:00 — voice (monitor): "Clara." Rhyme (woses).* She would underline *woses* and, without meaning to, draw a small boat beside it and fill in the sail until the paper thinned.

For now she made another cup of tea and decided to believe in the simplest explanations, and the simplest explanations, sensing their chance, let her.

The day moved on with its own soft footsteps, and the house, which had learned their names, listened and didn't say so.

Chapter Three
Baby Blues

Mark had the news open on his phone, brow furrowed, toast cooling on a plate he was pretending not to ignore. The baby lay in her bouncer in a lemon-yellow sleep suit, feet bicycling, face set in that solemn, comic look of someone who was learning the rules of living and disapproved of most of them.

"You should see the GP," he said, eyes still on the screen. "Start the ball rolling."

"What ball?" Clara asked. She knew which ball. She needed him to say it so she could dislike the sound.

"The... tiredness. The voices. The way you drift off mid-sentence as if the bit in the middle doesn't apply to you."

"I'm not drifting. I'm listening to the baby."

"I'm not criticising." He set the phone down, palms up, as if to show he wasn't carrying a weapon. "It will help to talk. Postnatal stuff is—"

"Common," she finished, sweetly. "I've seen the posters."

He smiled as if given a point in a game. "Phone them after we eat."

"We're eating?"

"We're performing eating. It counts."

He offered her a triangle of toast as if it were a treaty. She took it. The baby hiccupped and made both of them laugh, the sound like a match struck in fog.

***

By eleven, the morning had been tamed into chores: nappy, bottle, steriliser, wipe-down, repeat. Clara moved through them like a careful burglar. She placed the monitor on the kitchen table, angled towards her chair, then adjusted it again because the angle felt superstitiously wrong. The red LED breathed softly. In, out.

She dialled the surgery and listened to the recorded woman explain that calls were recorded to improve service and discipline. At the end of a ringy maze a human voice appeared, bright and practical, and offered 2.40 with Dr Patel.

"That's today?" Clara asked, as if she'd been given a train in twenty minutes to a city she hadn't decided to visit.

"That's today," the woman confirmed, cheerfully pitiless.

Clara thanked her and wrote the time on the pad next to the hob. She didn't need to. The numbers would stand in the room until they were done.

"Happy?" she said to Mark, who was rinsing mugs as if they'd offended him.

"Relieved," he said, and dried his hands too carefully. "Do you want me there?"

"No." The word came out too quick. She gentled it. "It's fine."

He nodded, which meant *I disagree and will translate that into silence.*

The baby sneezed, startled by her own cleverness, and then looked deeply pleased. Clara kissed the tiny forehead because there are rituals you perform even when your faith is complicated.

The waiting room was new paint over old scuffs, posters that wanted to help and therefore accused. The television mounted too high showed a cookery programme where a woman with tidy hair beat eggs into compliance. The sound was off; the captions arrived a second late, like a friend who meant well.

Clara signed in and immediately hated her own handwriting for not making her more reliable. The baby slept in the pram, cheeks flushed, mouth arranged in a small O like a backup plan. A toddler in dinosaur pyjamas jumped off a chair again and again while his mother deployed the word *no* in increasingly decorative ways.

A poster asked *Are you feeling low?* beside a photograph of a woman whose smile looked like something stapled on. Another explained how to use an inhaler. Another showed a breast in tasteful half-shadow and told her to check it and then, helpfully, check it again.

She stared at the noticeboard and pretended not to be listening for her name.

"Clara Morgan?" sang the screen, and the polite chime tried to make it good news.

Dr Patel had a kind face that didn't overdo it. He asked about sleep, appetite, crying, panic, the shape of the days, whether the dark felt heavier than it used to. He said her name often enough that it began to sound like room temperature.

"How much sleep are you getting, Clara?"

"Enough to function," she said, and then, guilty: "Barely."

"Any thoughts of harming yourself or the baby?"

"No." She meant it with a ferocity that surprised him into a nod.

"Voices?"

She had promised herself she would not sound like a person who wanted to be interesting. "Sometimes I hear... static," she said, keeping her voice ordinary. "A voice in the static."

"Whose voice?"

"My sister's." She didn't let her voice fall on the last word. "Ellie. We were twins. She didn't... come home."

"I'm sorry." He wrote something down and she wanted to see the word he chose. Grief? Hallucination? Normal? "Memories can be loud when we're exhausted. The brain tries to stitch torn places with old thread. I'd like you to see our perinatal psychiatrist, Dr Harriet Vale. She's very good."

He slid a leaflet across the desk. A mother held a baby under a clean tree. The paper smelt faintly of damp cardboard.

"We can also talk about medication if things worsen," he went on, matter-of-fact. "It won't dull you. It won't take you away from the baby. It will give your mind a bit more floor."

"What if it is a voice," Clara asked, softly. "And not a... memory?"

Dr Patel tilted his head. "Do you want it to be?"

She had not allowed the answer room until now. The yes arrived like a bird flying through an open window and startling both of them. "I don't know," she said, truthfully. "I want to be believed. That feels greedy and childish."

"It feels human." He tapped the leaflet. "See Dr Vale. We'll put the floor in together. Come back next week."

He took her blood pressure. The cuff bit her arm with bureaucratic enthusiasm; the numbers came up smugly normal. She completed a questionnaire with boxes to tick about hopelessness and shame and fear like weather. When she handed it back she felt as if she'd sat an exam in a language she didn't speak.

On the way out he said, "If the voice says anything that frightens you, write it down. Writing turns fog into furniture."

She nodded because it sounded like a spell.

***

Rain arrived just as the bus did. People jostled and apologised in the British way that turns apology into sport. Clara wedged the pram into the buggy bay and sat where she could put one foot against the wheel, as if she could brake fate.

The windows fogged. She drew a small C in the mist and rubbed it away quickly, embarrassed by herself. Outside, the day turned the colour of washing water. Inside, the baby dreamed something proper and tiny.

Between stops she glimpsed a charity-shop window with a caravan teapot in the middle of a cluttered display. The sight made her heart trip. She closed her eyes and pressed a knuckle to her mouth. Do not summon, she told herself. Do not be summoned.

The bus sighed to a halt outside their street. The pavement shone like a confession. The pram's wheels clicked over the threshold, into the hallway that smelt faintly of milk and clean socks and old house. She breathed in greedily. Her ground.

Mark met her at the door with a hand on the pram handle that wanted to help and prove something at once. "Well?"

"Referral to Dr Vale. Next week."

"Good." His relief was almost indecent. "Do you feel better?"

"Asking makes it worse," she said, and regretted it immediately. "I'm sorry."

He shook his head. "Don't be. Do you want a nap? I can—"

"No nap." The idea of sleep made the skin on her neck tighten. "Tea."

He made it with zeal, the way he made things when he felt useless otherwise. He set the mug in front of her as if hot liquid could be a plan. "We're all right," he said, practising the sentence for size.

"We are," she said, and some small mean part of her wanted to ask *which 'we' do you mean?*

The baby coughed and then smiled, the two faces of infancy. Clara smoothed the muslin on her shoulder and felt steadier than she had any right to.

The monitor on the dresser gave a small, civilised crackle. Both of them stilled.

"Interference," Mark said quickly, as if speed could make it true.

The red LED climbed to two bars and held there, bright as a thought. "Clara," breathed the voice, fond as a secret.

Mark went very still. "Jesus."

Clara's mouth dried so fast she felt her lips catch. "Left-right," the voice added, as if pleased to find them again. "She likes the boat."

Clara didn't move. The room didn't move. Then her body remembered before her mind did: she took the baby and rocked gently left-right. The tiny body settled, face smoothing into the arrogant peace of the newly asleep.

Mark's hand hovered over the volume knob. "Turn it down," he whispered. "Please."

"If I do, will it stop?" she asked.

"I don't know."

"Neither do I."

They stood there, two adults with a machine between them, and the house watched politely. Somewhere in the plumbing a pipe tried a note and thought better of it.

Mark lowered the volume a fraction. The red LED dimmed, rebuked. The voice didn't repeat itself. The baby exhaled like a small balloon giving up.

Clara felt relief and disappointment arrive together, twins that knew how to share.

***

She started the notebook after lunch because writing makes fog into furniture. She wrote the time in the corner of the first page, underlined it, and then, carefully, *monitor — voice: "Clara", then "left-right, she likes the boat". Baby soothed with left-right rock. Mark present; heard voice.* She stared at the page until the words steadied. Then she tore it out and wrote it again with better handwriting because the first version had looked like a plea.

She tucked the notebook in the drawer by the cooker where the lighter and old batteries lived. She shut the drawer firmly, as if to trap sense.

In the afternoon she put the baby in the pram and walked to the corner shop for bread and milk and the dignity of leaving the house. The pavement smelt of rain and tomorrow. The wind pushed at her in polite, chilly hands. A neighbour with purposeful hair said, "She's grown," and meant the baby and meant the days.

At the zebra crossing a schoolgirl with blue nail varnish hummed *Ring a Roses* under her breath, the correct, ordinary way. Clara felt her throat narrow and then open again. She stepped off the kerb like a person learning stairs.

Outside the chemist the window display showed thermometers and vitamins arranged to look like a helpful robot. Clara looked past her own reflection and saw the baby inside the pram's rain cover, eyes open, alert, solemn. For one passing second a second face seemed to hover beside the small one — a trick of glass, a smear of the world — and then the angle shifted and there was only herself, thin and too serious, and the baby, who blinked as if to say *you're being stupid in an interesting way.*

On the way home, a gust lifted the corner of the pram blanket. Clara smoothed it down and found, in the fine condensation on the plastic cover, a print shaped like four small fingers and a thumb. Children leave marks; physics is generous with patterns; her hand might have done it earlier.

She washed it off with a tissue anyway, then wiped the tissue on her jeans, and told herself she was not doing that because she was frightened.

***

Five o'clock arrived and with it the witching hour, which is folklore and therefore true. The baby decided to detest the world. Clara walked, swayed, patted, sang, offered milk, offered patience, offered judgement, and the cry cut through all of it like kitchen string.

Mark hovered, the way men hover when they are both eager and wary. "What can I do?"

"Stop asking me that," she said, softer than it looked.

He took the baby, achieved thirty seconds of negotiated peace, and handed her back as if her heat scalded. "She doesn't want me."

"She wants everything."

The monitor on the sideboard breathed its small red breath. In, out. It had no right to be smug.

Clara's spine began to buzz with useless panic. She tried the boat song. The first line caught. The second line steadied. The baby's cry shivered into a protest and then into the irritable silence that means a child has decided to forgive you later.

Mark exhaled, hard, like a person after a difficult exam. "See? You've got the touch."

"It wasn't me," she said without meaning to. He looked at her and the look was a decision not to argue, which was worse.

The mobile above the cot turned a fraction, though the window was shut and the radiator was off. Paper stars shifted themselves into a different mood. "Draft," Mark said, with a conviction that had nothing to do with air.

"Obviously," Clara said, and the word tasted like metal.

On the kitchen window a faint handprint bloomed out of the steam and then faded. She could make physics for it if she wanted to. She did not want to.

She rocked the baby and counted her own breaths and felt wildly, briefly certain of two things at once: that her sister had come to stand behind her, and that her mind could build a cathedral out of fear.

They ate late, both of them pretending the pasta had not coagulated into regret. Mark washed up like a man dealing with facts. Clara wiped the table and then wiped the bit she had already wiped. The baby slept with the fierce abandon of the freshly exhausted.

"I'm proud of you for seeing the GP," Mark said, drying his hands. "It's a step."

"It's a step," she echoed, and wanted to ask *towards what?*

He came to stand behind her and wrapped his arms around her and rested his chin on her head. The weight and warmth of him made her eyes sting. She closed them and said, because she needed him to be real, "Tell me something only you would say."

He laughed, uncertain. "What, like a password?"

"Like a person."

He thought a second. "You chew the left side of your lip when you read and pretend you don't, and it's how I can tell you're concentrating."

She smiled despite herself. "That's true."

"You make Marmite toast for breakfast when you think a day's going to be hard."

"Also, true."

"You married me because I'm boring."

She turned in his arms and kissed the soft place under his jaw, the one she knew would make him huff a laugh. "I married you because you're steady," she said. "They are not the same."

He nodded solemnly, as if given a mark to aim for. "Steady," he repeated.

Above them, the heating clicked like a code. In the nursery the mobile forgot to be still.

***

Near midnight, Clara stood in the bathroom with the light off and watched the landing through the open door. Night had shaved the house to its essentials. The banister made its long dark line. The carpet held the day's footmarks the way sand records what it forgives.

She should sleep. She didn't. She went to the nursery instead, where the night-light did its little moon and the room smelt of warm cotton and the sweet milky breath of someone who trusted the universe without qualification.

She put two fingers on her daughter's chest and stole the metronome. Rise, fall. She unclenched. The rabbit sat at attention. The window catch sat down and correct, both parts engaged, two clicks. She told herself not to check it. She checked it. It held like a polite hand.

The monitor on the dresser breathed red. A small crackle. Clara waited without wanting to be seen by herself wanting.

"Clara," said the voice. Close and pleased. "Don't let him silence you."

"Who?" she whispered, ridiculous, as if the question had room for options.

A soft hum, almost a laugh. "You know."

She glanced back at the door, the crack of light from the landing, the corner that made shape out of shadow. For a second she had the disobedient impression of a girl her size leaning there, arms folded, enjoying herself. She blinked and the corner returned to its job.

"What do you want?" she asked, and it came out steadier than she felt.

"To be remembered," said the voice, and there was, inside it, a cruel tenderness. "To keep her safe."

"From whom?"

"From the leaflet people," the voice said lightly, which would have been funny if it hadn't made Clara's teeth ache.

The baby made a small feeding noise and settled again. Clara rested a hand over the little heart. Inside her own chest something gave way, not a break, but the loosening of a knot tied wrong.

"I am remembering you," she said, and the saying of it felt like stepping onto a bridge she hadn't tested. "I always have."

The voice did not say thank you. It said, with affectionate impatience, "Write it down."

She smiled, stupidly. "All right."

The red LED dipped and climbed as if satisfied. The room held its breath until the house had finished thinking.

***

Back in the kitchen she took the notebook from the drawer and wrote: *23:58 — nursery. Voice (monitor): "Don't let him silence you... You know... From the leaflet people... To be remembered... To keep her safe... Write it down." Window catch both parts engaged (checked). Mobile moved (no draught).* She paused, added, *Baby soothed with left-right rock earlier; smile in sleep.* Then she underlined *left-right* and drew a small boat without meaning to.

She stood at the sink and let the cold tap run until it decided to be cold properly. In the black line of the window she saw herself reflected, pale and slimmer than her life, and for half a breath a second face leaned in, same bones, same mouth, eyes set half a degree wider. She didn't startle. She lifted a hand. The other hand lifted. She didn't wave. Neither did the other.

A drop ran down the glass between their palms like a clock.

Behind her, Mark said, "Can't sleep?"

"Not yet."

He came to stand beside her and looked at their two faces in the window and didn't mention the other. He put a hand in the small of her back and she leaned into it like a person who had done something brave and needed a receipt.

"Come to bed," he said.

"In a minute."

He nodded. He left. The house accepted their arrangement.

In the glass the second face had gone, or had stepped further in so the reflection read as one.

Clara laughed quietly, because the other choice was to cry, and turned off the tap.

***

She dreamed a corridor that smelt of steam and soap. The caravan's window blistered with heat. Two girls knotted rope into a round-the-world that could be undone by anyone who knew the trick. When she woke the tune of the boat was in her mouth like a lozenge, bitter and sweet.

The clock showed 03:06. The hush had that depth only found in the slabs of a night. She lay very still and let her breathing become the room's. When the whisper came it arrived not through the monitor but through the plaster, as if the house had learnt to speak.

"Clara."

She sat up, quietly, so the bed wouldn't tell on her. She carried the monitor to the doorway like a lamp. The landing had put its dark on. The nursery door stood ajar, the night-light a pale coin.

In the cot the baby had turned her head towards the gap, an animal's instinct for where the world begins. Clara crossed the carpet and stood where she had stood a hundred times and would a thousand more. She put her palm to the little chest. She rocked once, left-right, because language had become weather.

"Good girl," breathed the voice, affectionate, possessive.

"Don't," Clara whispered back. "Don't talk to me like I'm seven."

"Then don't be seven," said the voice, and made a smiling shape in the air.

Clara swallowed a laugh that wasn't a laugh. "Tell me something only I would know."

A pause long enough to be vulgar. Then: "Second drawer down in Mum's dresser, right-hand side. The tall blue jug. She thought Dad never found it. He did."

Clara shut her eyes. She saw the jug, chipped at the lip, biscuits that tasted of air and sugar, her mother's hand moving in the cupboard like a magician unwilling to learn a new trick. She opened her eyes and felt the world lay a little flatter under her feet.

"Why now?" she asked.

"Because now you can hear me," said the voice, as if that were obvious.

"And if I stop listening?"

"You won't," it said, with intolerable certainty. "You've always been the better listener."

Clara turned and looked towards the landing, where the night gathered itself. She said, because the words needed a body, "If you hurt her—"

The voice cut in, sharper. "I will keep her."

She felt all the parts of her move at once: mother, sister, woman, child. "From who?"

"From everyone who calls kindness a plan," said the voice, and left the sentence on the table between them.

The baby sighed and smiled in sleep at nothing she could see. The monitor red-lit its calm. The mobile didn't move. The window catch kept its promise.

Clara stood there, drawing breath in a way that belonged to someone wiser. "All right," she said. "We'll do it my way."

"Which is?"

"I write it down," she said. "I lock the window. I watch. I don't tell lies to myself, even polite ones. And I sing the boat if I want to."

A small, pleased noise. "At last," said the voice, and for a second she felt the old ache of being praised by the only person who had ever known precisely which praise would crack her open.

"Go," she said, and surprised herself by not saying please.

The air thinned. The room belonged to the baby again. The red light kept time like a heart that never got bored.

Clara bent and kissed her daughter's warm head and felt her chest hurt with love the way a muscle hurts when it is changing shape. She went back to the kitchen, wrote the time and the words, then drew a line under them like a door.

When she looked up, her face in the glass looked like someone who had been told a secret and was deciding what to do with it.

Morning came with a pale stripe of sun and the sound of a pigeon insisting on itself. Mark padded in with two mugs, hair pointing in more directions than a map, and tried to read her without making her feel read.

"You look—" he began, chose a better word, "—here."

"I'm here," she said, and meant it differently than yesterday.

"What shall we do today?"

"Nothing enormous. I might put the box back in the loft." She watched his face for the flinch. When it didn't come she added, "And I'll phone the perinatal lot and chase the appointment. And I'll make a list."

"Of?"

"Evidence," she said, lightly, so he could pretend it was a joke if he wanted to. "Things as they are."

He nodded, relief and worry mixing like two colours that didn't belong in the same paint. "Good."

He put the mugs down and kissed her, and for a moment the kitchen was just a kitchen and not the mouth of a story, and she let it.

The baby woke with a yawp that held complaint and optimism in equal parts. Clara lifted her, breathing in the warm, heartening smell of blanket and sleep and tiny scalp, and thought: *I am not alone in two opposite directions at once.*

The monitor on the table was quiet and pious, the red LED dark. She did not switch it on immediately. She let silence be the absence of noise and not the presence of fear.

In the drawer, the notebook waited like a small, obedient machine. When she opened it later, she would write: *Morning: no voice. House calm. Baby calm. Mark kind. (Me: here.)*

She smiled, once, then twice, as if testing a new muscle, and decided that, for now, this counted as a win.

Chapter Four
Old Secrets

Clara woke before the light had decided what to be. For a moment she lay with her eyes closed and let her body take attendance: hands, feet, breath, ache. The house answered back with its small, loyal noises — the boiler thinking about its day, the pipes gossiping gently, the fridge holding its one note like a choirboy who took things seriously. She reached for the notebook on the bedside table and wrote the date and then, beneath it, *Woke calm. No voice. Dream (caravan) faint, not frightening.*

Mark turned over. "You're up?"

"Just writing," she whispered.

"Good," he said, not quite awake. "Turn fog into furniture."

She smiled despite herself. He had listened enough to quote, which felt like a small weekday miracle.

On the landing, the baby gave the mild, early sigh of someone who was not yet angry with the world. Clara went to her and found her sprawled like someone arrested mid-celebration. Two fingers were tucked neatly in her mouth, as if she'd solved something while everyone else was looking away.

"Morning," Clara said. The word came out ordinary. She laid a hand on the little chest and borrowed the metronome. Rise, fall. She felt the soft thud of her own heart calming as if it had been offered a chair.

Downstairs, the kettle's tremor began. Mark in the kitchen, being steady. The room smelt of warm cotton and the sweet animal breath of sleep. On the dresser, the monitor sat dark; she'd left it off last night on purpose and the night had not punished her for it.

"Thank you," she whispered to no one in particular, and at once felt foolish and fond.

***

By nine, the morning had passed its useful tests: feed, change, sterilise, wash up, keep hope and temper under control. Mark brought her tea and kissed the top of her head as if she were a document he was fond of.

"Dr Vale's office called," he said, setting the mug down at the edge of her notebook as if the two objects respected each other. "They left a voicemail."

Clara's stomach turned over. "Already?"

He nodded. "Cancellation. Monday, eleven."

"That's fast."

"It's good."

She couldn't tell which of them he was trying to convince. "All right."

"I'll come with you, wait outside. Or go in, if you want."

"I'll see nearer the time," she said. She meant: I want you there and I don't, and both wants frighten me.

He touched the notebook with a finger. "What's the inventory say?"

"Calm. House obedient." She added, because she had decided to get better at true statements that made room for doubt, "I feel watched, a little. Not in a bad way."

He absorbed that, then decided to call it a win. "We should go out. Get daylight on us. Walk to the green? Or baby group? You mentioned that church hall in the health visitor's pack."

The idea of other mothers made Clara's throat do something small and unhelpful; the idea of staying in all day felt worse. "Okay," she said. "Church hall."

He grinned at her like a man who had solved something useful with nothing but legs and weather. "Church hall it is."

***

The hall smelt of polish and decades. A noticeboard near the door offered classes for toddlers and Pilates for people who said they preferred gentle exercise but looked as if they would compete to the death. Someone had made a poster in thick felt-tip that read *Stay & Play*; someone else had drawn balloons on it that looked like beans with string.

The room had been arranged to permit chaos. Mats in primary colours made islands across the floor. A low table held cups with names scrawled in marker — RUBY, SIOBHÁN, LOUIS — and a plate of biscuits that had soft corners. Babies lay on their backs and stared up at mobiles that weren't theirs as if checking whether other people's stars were better. Mothers and a few fathers sat around the edges performing composure.

Clara took the spot nearest the radiator because heat felt like a good argument for being alive. The baby, deposited on a mat, kicked thoughtfully at the air and then, pleased by her own legs, did it again. A woman with dark hair in a plait came to sit next to Clara with the ease of people who have decided to be kind on purpose.

"I'm Priya," she said. "This is Jonah. He is seven months old and disgruntled by gravity."

Clara laughed. "Clara. Six weeks." She gestured at the lemon sleep suit. "Occasionally benevolent."

Priya tilted her head. "New new. You've got that look."

"What look?"

"The one where you haven't decided yet whether the baby was a good idea." She said it warmly, making room for jokes.

"Is it terrible that I haven't?" Clara asked, and was surprised to hear herself be funny. "I think it was a brilliant idea that someone else had and then handed me the receipt."

Priya's laugh joined hers in the air. "It gets easier. Not easy-easy. But easier-easier."

A health visitor in a cardigan stood and did the singsong welcome about tea in the kitchen, loo down the corridor, breastfeeding counselor in the corner (Jade, with a badge), don't worry if anyone cries, babies cry, so do we, it's not a competition but if it were I'd win. People smiled because this was reassuring even if true.

Clara watched the other mothers mimic, in miniature, a village: swapping wipes and sympathy, lifting each other's babies with permission and expertise, comparing rashes and sleep patterns and the metaphysics of swaddles. For a minute she felt herself drop into it, as if a seat had been saved for her in a room she hadn't known about.

Then the radiator gave a delicate throat-clearing noise and, beneath it, a thin line of sound slid along the wall like a string pulled through cloth.

Clara.

She sat very still. The voice was soft enough that it could be forgiven for being a trick of air. The radiator, innocent, breathed heat. Priya was telling Jonah not to eat the corner of the mat in a tone that implied he had done this before and would again. In the far corner someone began to sing the weather song with the wrong melody; everyone else joined in and made it right by sheer numbers.

Clara looked down. The baby had stopped kicking and was gazing, quite firmly, to the left — not at the mobile above the mat, not at Jonah's intense face, but at the empty patch between the radiator and the noticeboard. Her mouth twitched into a smile shaped like recognition.

Left-right, breathed the sound. Very faint. Pleased, as if at a private joke.

Clara willed her body not to move. She rocked the baby once, left-right, in the smallest motion, as if she were part of the air. The baby emitted a contented hum, not a laugh exactly, but the rehearsal for one.

"Nice," Priya said approvingly, unaware that she had spoken into a scene. "You've got hands. Some people don't, you know."

Clara exhaled. "I'm learning."

"Come to the tea table," Priya said later, when everyone stood up together like a murmuration. "You look as if tea has to prove itself to you."

The kitchen hatch was manned by a woman with sharp cheekbones and a T-shirt that read *Twin Mums Club*. She poured with both hands. "Milk? Sugar?"

"Milk," Clara said. "No sugar. Thank you."

"Is she your first?" the woman asked.

"Yes," Clara said, and then, uninvited, "I was supposed to be two."

The woman's face changed shape. "Oh, love."

"It was a long time ago," Clara said, in the tone people use for things they have never let away. "What's Twin Mums Club like?"

"Chaotic," the woman said, and smiled. "Loud. We've got a separate hour on Thursdays. Nappies by the bale. Eyes in the back of heads."

Clara's chest pinched. She took the tea and went back to the mat before the conversation could be kind enough to hurt.

On the noticeboard, above the poster with the beans that wanted to be balloons, someone had pinned a photograph of a summer fair in front of a caravan: bunting, a trestle table bearing jam jars and hope. Clara looked at it and, for a second, the picture moved — the bunting lifted, the caravan door opened a crack, a child poked her head out and made a face like shared mischief. Then the paper went back to being paper. She laughed under her breath because no one else had seen.

The radiator ticked companionably. The voice, if it had been a voice, kept its counsel. For the rest of the hour, Clara practised being a person in a room.

***

She walked home in a bright, mean wind that made her eyes water. Priya had given her a number, written on the back of a receipt for bananas, and had said, "Text me at three in the morning or at three in the afternoon; they're the same."

Clara tucked the receipt into the notebook and felt, briefly, as if she had taken custody of something fragile and useful.

The house smelled like its own idea of clean. Mark had tidied with love and a slight sense of performance; the cushions sat to attention, the mugs were upside down on the rack, a tea towel had been folded into the shape of a suggestion. He came out from the study and kissed Clara as if he had passed an exam he'd been sure to fail.

"How was it?"

"Odd," she said, and then, because odd could mean anything, "Good. People were... kind. My favourite."

"And the small person?"

"Approved of gravity for a bit. Then held a referendum."

He smiled, the spread of it making him briefly handsome in a way that startled her back into the present. "Mum's dropping something round," he added, almost casually. "Said she was passing anyway."

Clara's shoulders lifted a fraction in a movement that wanted to be a shrug and wasn't. "Martha."

"She means well."

"She means to be right."

"Same thing in that family," Mark said, and then winced, because the joke had landed on a sore place.

Clara smoothed the muslin on her shoulder. "All right."

He reached out and touched the notebook where it peeped from her bag. "Write the good bits," he said. "The brain's a terrible archivist."

"I am improving records management," she said. The line sounded like someone else's, and steadied her.

Martha arrived with a casserole in a Pyrex dish that had survived at least three wars in the cupboard. She let herself in and called, "Coo-ee," in a voice that had managed two daughters and their father and several hard winters.

Clara took the dish and put it on the counter and thanked her without saying *this will taste like childhood and I am not ready to eat childhood with a fork.*

Martha kissed the baby with the gusto of people who find babies reliable. "You look tired," she told Clara, because information wants to be shared.

"I am," Clara said, because denial today felt dishonest and expensive.

Martha looked around the kitchen and took in the tidiness like a general doing a sweep. "You're keeping up," she said, which was praise in that language.

"Mark's helping."

"He's a good boy." She meant *better than you expected*. She meant *I am keeping an eye*. She meant *I like him* and, under that, *he is not the point*.

"Tea?" Clara asked.

"Please."

They sat at the table with the baby in the bouncer between them, the three of them arranged like actors in a scene that wanted to behave. Martha placed a hand on the baby's foot and the foot curled obligingly, as if they shared a private code.

Clara decided to say one true thing. "I found the bracelets."

Martha's mouth tightened the way a person's mouth tightens when they have been hit by a memory and don't want the other person to see the bruise. "Oh," she said. "I was wondering. They were in the loft all those years."

"I know." Clara reached for steadiness and got enough to hold. "I put them back."

"Good," Martha said, and put a sip of tea in her mouth to give the word somewhere to go.

Clara could have left it. Instead she asked, with tired politeness, "What was it like?"

Martha blinked slowly, as if she had to accommodate a light. "What was what like?"

"The hospital. The day. The... not bringing her home."

Martha looked past Clara at the window, where the garden was rehearsing a grey. "Your father drove too quickly," she said at last. "The midwife had a fringe cut too short. I remember thinking that at a time like that you shouldn't have to think about hair. I remember the smell of the hand gel. I remember thinking *this is not the order I learnt*." She gave a small, practical laugh. "They told me you were fine. You were not fine, you were perfect, which is different and worse. You were awake and cross and hungry. I liked that about you immediately."

"And Ellie?"

Martha's eyes flinched in a very small way. "A minute," she said. "Two. I don't know. They said the word *viable* and I thought, *That's a word for seeds.* They wrapped her, and then they didn't." She made the gesture of passing something very light and very heavy from one hand to another and seemed surprised to see her hands empty. "We named her because names are important. That's what you do for the dead. You give them a place to sit."

"She was called Eleanor," Clara said softly, even though she knew, because she needed to say it like lighting a candle with a long match.

Martha nodded. "We chose it for your grandmother. We put 'Eleanor' in the paper and people sent cards and then we stopped talking about it." She looked at Clara with a frankness that could be mistaken for cruelty. "Because otherwise you don't go to work on Monday. And you have to go to work on Monday."

Silence arrived and set its bag down. The fridge hummed. The baby breathed in the bright, efficient way of the contented newly fed.

Clara said, in a voice that had been practising in her for thirty years, "I hear her."

The room didn't change. Martha's face did not perform the expression it used to perform when Clara came home with a scraped knee or an unreasonable story. She put her hand on the table, flat, and said, "Of course you do."

Clara's throat burned. "Do you?"

"Not in the way you mean." Martha's mouth moved as if choosing. "I feel the shape she left. That's different. Shapes can be kind."

Clara stared at the Pyrex dish because Pyrex did not think about metaphysics. "She says things," she said. "Things only we would know."

Martha took a breath in through her nose, a breath like a count. "Like what?"

"The biscuits," Clara said. "In the tall blue jug."

Martha closed her eyes and let out air she had been keeping. "Your father thought he was clever with that jug." When she opened her eyes again they were bright in the way that makes people say *don't cry* and mean *please don't make me cry*. "It was a good hiding place. Until it wasn't."

Clara risked another step. "Did she... ever... did you ever hear...?"

"No," Martha said, kindly and without judgement. "But I'm not you."

"Meaning?"

"Meaning you have always listened harder than the rest of us." She smiled, crooked. "You used to put your ear to radiators and announce whether the house was ill."

Clara laughed, startled by the accurate foolishness of the picture. "Did I?"

"You did. You were a trial and a comfort." Martha leant forward and took Clara's hand, the baby's foot caught between their wrists. "If you are hearing something, write it down. Don't let it eat the rest of the day. And don't let anyone tell you leaflets are more real than you are."

Clara swallowed. "I thought you'd tell me to pull myself together."

"I am telling you to pull together what needs pulling." Martha lifted the baby's foot and kissed the sole, which made the baby produce a noise of theatrical outrage. "And to eat the casserole. It's chicken and nonsense."

The monitor on the sideboard, which had been quiet as a sermon, gave a small, sharp crackle. All three of them looked. The red LED, dark, pulsed once — as if in the act of remembering it had a role to play — and went out again.

Martha made her mouth neutral. "Interference," she said, and then raised an eyebrow, as if to offer translation.

Clara smiled with her lips because the rest of her was busy. "Leaflets," she said.

They both laughed, and something unclenched.

***

After Martha had gone, leaving kisses and instruction and the kind of silence that proves itself useful, Clara took the notebook from the drawer and wrote: *Martha visit. Talked about hospital (fringe, word 'viable', named E). Jug story confirmed. Advice: write it down; don't let it eat the day; leaflets ≠ more real.* She underlined *leaflets* once and drew a small blue jug in the margin like a child showing off.

Mark came in and read her face and kissed it. "How was she?"

"Better than me," Clara said, and didn't mind that it was true. "She was kind."

"She usually is to the baby," he said, and dodged a tea towel aimed without conviction.

In the afternoon, they walked to the chemist and bought paracetamol and the kind of plasters that promise cartoon distraction for tiny wounds. They stopped by the green and looked at the duck pond, which had pulled a respectable grey over itself to go with the sky. The baby grunted at a pigeon with interest. Clara texted Priya a photograph of nothing much. Priya texted back a sticker of a woman in a cape that said *You did a hard thing.*

On the path home, the pram wheels made that small rrr-rrr, and for a few minutes Clara moved in step with it, body remembering a rhythm that made sense when nothing else did.

At the house, the key stuck as it sometimes did. She wiggled and pushed and laughed at herself. When the door gave, a draft ran up her sleeves as if scoldingly. The hallway smelt of the morning's casserole as if supper had a memory.

She lifted the pram over the threshold and something snagged. She looked down and saw, impressed very lightly in the thin dust that gathers in hallways despite pride, the small suggestion of a footprint. Not a shoe. Not a sock. Not the baby's. The size of Clara's foot, almost exactly — the kind of print you'd make if you had walked through talc and then forgotten, except she had not walked through talc.

She bent and put two fingertips to it and the mark smudged obediently into the idea of dirt. She could make physics for this if she needed to. She might need to. She didn't, for now.

"Everything all right?" Mark asked from the kitchen.

"Yes," she said, and placed the notebook, before she forgot, on the hall table. *Hall dust — print? Smudged,* she wrote, then drew a line underneath to keep it from becoming a larger thought.

Witching hour arrived like a practised joke. The baby, who had been benevolent all day, decided to take offence at the air. They deployed all the tools in the right order. Mark's arms proved briefly acceptable. The boat song earned a stay of execution. The monitor, switched on against Clara's principles, breathed a delicate red in. out. in. out. and behaved itself out loud, which felt like a new trick.

"Bath?" Mark suggested, with the expression of a man suggesting a treaty.

"Bath," Clara agreed, and the word gave her a little jolt of fear she put aside like laundry.

She ran the water, hand under the tap, the way a person makes a promise. Steam wrote on the mirror and then changed its mind. She checked the temperature with her wrist because wrists were cleverer than fingers. She poured in the tiniest measure of lavender wash, which Martha had once called posh nonsense and then bought in bulk.

The baby squawked at the indignity of undressing and then, when lowered in, made the 'oh' face of someone who is not minded to approve but can be convinced. The small body became suddenly longer, the limbs stylised and frog-like. Clara poured water over the little chest with the latticed plastic cup and felt, in her own skin, the echo of impossible weight: how quickly it takes a bath to be too much; how near the line is in the best of rooms.

"Left-right," the voice breathed, so close it might have been inside her ear. Pleased. "Not front-back."

Clara rocked the water gently. The baby's expression transitioned into the kind of calm that made the world liveable.

"Good girl," said the voice. Not to the baby.

"Stop it," Clara said under her breath. "Stop talking to me like I'm a prize."

Mark looked up. "Sorry?"

"Nothing."

"Did you hear—?"

"No," she said too quickly, and then, like someone apologising to an empty room, "Yes. It's not... hostile."

Mark's mouth tightened. "It doesn't have to be hostile to be not real."

"I know."

He took the baby out and wrapped her in a towel shaped like a rabbit and she made the outraged squeaks of someone who had been removed from a good idea. Clara watched the drain take the bath water down like a slow throat, and for a second the swirl faltered — not the way water does when it meets hair, but the way a person falters when they think they've heard their name. Then the last of it went with a small, proper gurgle. She laughed at herself, and heard the laugh echo and be returned by someone with her mouth.

"Leaflets," she said, to steady the room. "Leaflet people would not approve of me."

"The leaflet people can queue," Mark said, and they both laughed, and the sound made a sort of roof.

***

They ate Martha's casserole at the table, making appreciative noises to send down the line. The rain remembered them and tapped the window with fingers that wanted attention. The mobile in the nursery version of the world was still. The window catch kept its promise.

At eleven, tiredness broke over Clara in a way she could trust. She left the monitor on because superstition had found that compromise. In bed, she took the notebook and wrote: *Bath — voice ('left-right, not front-back; good girl'). Water fine. Drain odd (halluc.?); laugh (echo?)* She closed the book and put her palm flat on it as if to seal something in or out.

"Monday," Mark murmured into the dark. "Eleven."

"I know."

"We'll go."

"We'll go."

"Thank you."

"For what?"

"For keeping the day moving," he said. "For letting me help without telling me how much help I am."

She smiled into the dark. "You're very help."

"That sounds like sarcasm."

"It's grammar," she said, and heard him smile against the pillow.

The house lowered itself into night. The red LED breathed. Clara lay on her side and listened the way a person listens when listening has become a vocation.

When the voice came, it wasn't through the monitor. It was the soft scrape of breath against plaster again, the way a wall learns a song and wants to be praised. "Don't go," it said, almost purring.

"To where?" Clara asked, very quietly.

"To the doctor woman." A small, childish disdain for the word *doctor* made the air bend.

Clara's throat was dry. She swallowed with care. "We're going."

"They'll take her."

"No," Clara said, steady because she had decided to be. "They won't."

"They'll say kindness," the voice whispered, a little sing-song. "They'll say safety."

"We say safety," Clara said. "You and me. The same thing."

A pause, like someone testing the weather. Then: "Keep the window locked."

"I do."

"And sing the boat."

"If I want," she said. "Not if you want."

A delighted, nearly wicked sound. "Bossy."

"Grown," Clara said.

Silence. Then, as if conceding in a game: "Write this down."

Clara smiled. "I will."

The red light kept time. In the nursery the mobile stirred the smallest amount, which could have been heat rising from a radiator that was not on. The baby sighed and rearranged her face into a more comfortable version of itself.

Clara lay on her side and felt a line inside her, long and taut and strong, connecting three points in the dark: the baby, her, the idea of a sister standing with her back against the door like someone keeping watch. It didn't feel like madness. It felt like grief depriving itself of drama and becoming a job.

She slept in increments and woke in the kind way that lets you be awake without punishing you for having been asleep.

Morning. The sky had washed itself and come up clean. Mark read out the news without reading it. The baby gurgled at the spoon like someone telling a joke. The house smelled of toast, which is one of the few smells that reliably insists on hope.

Clara opened the notebook and wrote: *Night — voice: 'don't go' (doctor woman); warnings; boundary set. Kept window locked; boat on my terms. Felt watched in the protective way.* She closed it and, without thinking, put it on top of the Pyrex dish lid as if to borrow weight.

Her phone buzzed with a number she didn't know. She answered.

"Clara Morgan?" The voice was clear, low, precise. "It's Dr Harriet Vale."

Clara's body reacted as if the phone had been changed to metal. "Hello."

"I just wanted to confirm Monday at eleven. And to ask — very briefly, I promise — if there's anything you'd like me to have in mind before we meet."

Clara looked at the baby, at Mark, at the monitor breathing its polite red, at the garden considering itself beyond the glass. She thought of the caravan. The jug. The jug in a voice. Martha's hands transferring a weight that wasn't there. Priya's receipt with a number. The radiator throat-clearing. The word *leaflets* trying to become a language. And she heard, as if spoken into the hollow behind her ear, the soft, satisfied whisper: *Don't.*

"Yes," Clara said, and her own voice surprised her with its clarity. "I'm hearing my twin."

A pause. Not a startled one. A space-making one. "Thank you," Dr Vale said. "We'll begin there."

After she rang off, Mark raised his eyebrows in a question.

"I told her," Clara said.

"And?"

"And she didn't flinch."

"Good," he said, and meant it, and looked down at the baby and made a face that had made schools of babies laugh before and would again. This one considered it, then condescended to a smile. "It's going to be okay."

"I know," Clara said, and felt, in the space just beneath her breastbone, the small jump of something like agreement.

On the dresser, the monitor was quiet. On the windowsill, in the steam from the kettle, the faintest imprint appeared — five small petal-shapes in a semicircle, as if a hand half-resolved had pressed from the other side. Clara lifted her palm and set it against the glass, over the mark, and the cold came through and sharpened her. When she removed her hand, the mark remained exactly the same, which meant it had been there before and meant nothing else.

She laughed once. She made tea. She cut toast on the diagonal because mornings deserved at least one good decision.

The day arranged itself around them, and the house, pleased with its part, kept their secrets for now.

Chapter Five
What We Lock

Clara woke to the sound of rain arranging itself into plans. It tapped the windows in tidy rows, then changed its mind and skittered sideways as if counting again. For a moment she lay still and let the house name itself around her: boiler's low hum, pipes conferring, a far car on wet tarmac making the long whisper of someone reluctant to leave.

She reached for the notebook on the bedside table and wrote, without sitting up: *Woke: steady. Dream (caravan) off to one side. No voice.* She underlined *steady* and found that the act of underlining made the word more true.

Beside her, Mark opened one eye like a man attempting diplomacy with morning. "Status report?"

"Green," she said. "So far."

He smiled into the pillow. "We'll take green."

On the landing, the baby gave an exploratory squeak, then a contented sigh as if deciding against anger for the moment. Clara went to her, palms already remembering the small ritual of lifting, the particular angle that spared everyone's ribs. The nursery smelt of night-light heat and clean cotton, the sort of safe odour you could hold up to the light and find nothing wrong with.

The window catch sat down and correct. Two clicks. She didn't check it. She checked it.

"Hello, tyrant," she said softly, and the baby's eyes opened wide on nothing in particular, as if the world had introduced itself again and been found acceptable.

On the dresser the monitor sat dark. No red breath. She'd switched it off before bed and the silence had done nothing dramatic in the night. That felt like a win, which was pathetic and, today, enough.

***

By nine, rain had turned purposeful. The gutters ran like small creeks. Mark stood at the hob with a frying pan and the solemn air of a man conducting eggs. He had a tea towel over one shoulder and looked so much like someone's good idea of a husband that Clara felt, briefly, grateful to whoever had written the scene.

"Supermarket?" he asked, turning slices of bacon that would make Martha shake her head in performative disapproval. "We're out of kitchen roll and hope."

Clara laughed. "Church later?"

"We can do both," he said, meaning the shop and not actual church. "I'll drive."

"Walking's fine."

"It's chucking it down."

She looked out at the garden where the fence shone like varnish. "Then we'll get wet," she said, and felt the sentence land as a kind of principle.

They walked under one umbrella that behaved like a suggestion. The pram's rain cover misted, then beaded, then misted again. The pavements reflected everything, including things that weren't there, which made Clara look twice and then laugh at herself under her breath.

They reached the supermarket with the feeling of people entering a different country where apples are identical and music plays itself inoffensively. Mark took a trolley. Clara steered the pram. They moved through aisles that arranged themselves into the sort of reassurance you can put in a cupboard.

In baby supplies, she hesitated by the dummies. Colours and promises. She didn't intend to buy one; she had decided against them. Her hand lifted anyway. Blue. Red. Yellow. The packet with the blue one looked like something from a caravan holiday in an old photograph. She shook her head at herself and reached for the yellow.

Choose the blue, breathed a thought behind her ear, so light it could have been the air remembering.

She put the yellow back, took the blue, then made herself replace it with nothing at all because obedience deserved to be rationed.

"Everything okay?" Mark asked, the kind of casual that has to be practised.

"Fine," she said, and turned the pram so the baby could look at a pyramid of nappies as if it were art.

At the tills, an elderly man in a cap leaned down and said, "She's a beauty," in a voice that held no dark. Clara wished, briefly, that all voices could be trained to that tone.

Outside, the rain paused to watch them and then resumed with renewed purpose. On the walk home a little boy in a dinosaur coat pointed at the pram and announced, to no one in particular, "Your baby's got a friend." His mother shushed him without looking up from her phone. He gave Clara an earnest, conspiratorial nod as if to say *I can see things grown-ups forget.*

"Can you?" Clara said, before she could stop herself.

"Two," the boy said, pleased with counting. Then he stamped in a puddle and the world returned to its normal facts.

They dried pram wheels on the mat and hung the umbrella to sulk in the hall. Mark put shopping away with a defence lawyer's attention to labels facing outward. Clara boiled the kettle and watched the steam write on the window and then erase itself. She felt, briefly and without good reason, watched in the kind way that doesn't demand you prove it.

"Text from Priya," she said, glancing at her phone. "Baby group on Thursday is 'sensory'. Apparently there will be scarves."

"Scarf-based salvation," Mark said gravely. "At last."

She smiled. "She's good. She said I can text at three a.m. and three p.m. because they're the same."

"Three p.m. is marginally less cruel," he said, and touched the notebook where it lay open on the table, as if blessing it.

Clara wrote: *Supermarket. Rain biblical. Boy said 'your baby's got a friend' (dino coat). Chose nothing. Felt watched (benign).*

She closed the notebook. The small satisfaction of the click as the elastic slid round it felt like a promise kept.

***

In the afternoon the house softened. Rain reduced itself to background. The baby slept in the cot with one hand open and one hand in a tiny fist, hedging her bets. Mark answered emails with the intense quiet of a man performing competence for himself. Clara tidied a drawer that did not need tidying and found, at the back, an elastic band turned brittle with age and a single safety pin that had become philosophy.

The monitor was on the dresser again, switched off, behaving itself. She stood in the doorway of the nursery and listened to the kind of silence that includes breath. She leaned on the doorframe and let the sight of her daughter sleeping make a space inside her bigger.

On impulse she took her phone out and opened the voice recorder. She didn't press record. She put it back in her pocket. She felt silly and then cowardly and then, briefly, wise. Then, because humans are inconsistent, she took the phone out again and pressed the red circle, then set the phone face-down on the changing table so the microphone pointed at the patient machine and the more patient child.

She waited. She had time to feel ridiculous. She nearly picked up the phone and then—

A sound threaded through the air like cotton pulled gently off a spool. Two breaths. Not loud. Not dramatic. One quick and small and even. One a fraction slower with the upward curl the end of a word gives breath. She had the sudden certainty she could tell them apart in the dark with her hands: her daughter, and something that had learnt to breathe by watching.

She stood very still and felt, in her own throat, a third breath try to match them and fail.

The baby's mouth twitched into the rehearsal of a smile. From the monitor—still off—came a filament-thin hiss, like the sound of some-one deciding whether to speak.

Clara waited a full minute, then another. The two breaths kept exact time with each other like dancers indulging a joke.

She picked up the phone with fingers she didn't fully command. She stopped the recording. She put one headphone in a single ear like a thief and played it back.

Static. Air. The small tick of the radiator deciding to remember heat. But no second breath, no strange mimicry, nothing she could point to and say *you see.*

She laughed, once, very softly, because laughter was cheaper than crying and kept better.

She wrote: *Recorder — nothing captured. In room: two breaths (distinct). Monitor OFF.* She underlined *off* hard enough that the page shivered.

She stood a second longer, as if the room might apologise. Then she kissed the baby's forehead and left the door ajar a finger's width like a superstition she forgave herself for.

Mark found her in the kitchen rearranging tins as if alphabet could hold back a flood.

"Shall we talk about tomorrow?" he asked, careful.

"We can," she said, pretending she didn't know he meant Monday when Monday was already a weather system moving in across the chart. "I'm going. I told her on the phone."

"I know." He took a breath and let it out as if it had been doing something else in his chest. "I'm proud of you."

"Don't be yet," she said. "It might be a disaster."

"Then I'll be proud of you afterwards."

She smiled, then, because he had chosen a form of kindness she could pick up without dropping other things. "All right."

He leant against the counter and watched her line up the tins. "Do you want me to come in with you?"

"No." She saw his face do the little flinch. "I mean— not at first. I might ask you to at some point. People are easier to believe if someone else says they're real."

"You're real."

"I am," she agreed, and the agreement felt like a small flag raised on a damp day. "Also: I heard two breaths."

"In the nursery?"

"Yes."

"The recorder...?"

"Nothing." She put the tin of plum tomatoes exactly where it had been before. "It's very well-behaved."

He rubbed the bridge of his nose with a thumb and forefinger, an old habit that made her want to kiss the place between his eyes. "There are reasons for that."

"I know."

A small silence pooled between them, warm rather than cold. He bridged it. "Whatever it is, we'll deal with it. If it's grief, we'll be kind and practical. If it's physics, we'll fix it. If it's—" He stopped.

"If it's the other thing," Clara supplied, like a woman cuing the line the play pretends doesn't exist.

He nodded. "If it's that, we'll make rules."

"We have rules," she said. "Window locked. Boat on my terms. Writing it down."

He smiled, brief and crooked. "You and your rules."

"They keep me from drowning," she said, and only after she'd said it did she realise she'd chosen the exact right word.

Martha texted to say she'd found a small jumper she'd knitted years ago and did Clara want it or shall she donate it. A small blue jumper with a row of buttons shaped like clouds. Clara stared at the photo and felt her throat hurt in the way that means you have been given a kindness you didn't ask for.

***

Yes please, she typed. *Thank you.* She added a heart and then deleted it and then put it back because adulthood sometimes meant leaving things in even when you were embarrassed by them.

Priya texted a picture of Jonah trying to wear a mixing bowl as a hat. *He insists it's couture,* the caption said. *You all right?*

I'm here, Clara wrote, and meant it exactly.

When she looked up from the screen, the shoebox sat on the end of the kitchen table.

She had left it in the hall cupboard, behind the stack of board games that held more Instructions than Joy. She had put it there after Chapter Four without ceremony. She had not fetched it out. She had not asked anyone to.

She didn't go to it at once. She stood and waited for her heart to relax its grip, then walked round the table in case it turned out, at the right angle, to be something reasonable.

It remained the shoebox: faded teddy on the lid, the subtle dent on one corner from being hurried once down a ladder. She touched the cardboard lightly with the backs of her fingers as if it were sleeping.

"Mark?" she called, lightly.

He appeared with the phone in his hand and a readiness in his face he might have been born with. "Yes?"

She nodded at the box. "Did you move that?"

He looked at it, then at her. "No."

"You didn't go in the hall cupboard for anything?"

"No."

The baby made a small contented squeak in the monitor's absence, as if to keep the soundscape honest.

"Right," Clara said. She opened the box.

Inside lay the two hospital bracelets, exactly as before. CLARA MORGAN. ELEANOR MORGAN. The card with the lamb. The tiny socks that made past tense of a life every time you looked at them.

Under the card, something else. A folded piece of lined paper, creased into quarters as if it had been put away by a careful child. She glanced at Mark. He raised his eyebrows in a way that meant *proceed carefully*.

She unfolded it.

It was not handwriting. It was a rubbing— graphite clouded thick, the imprint of stamped letters cosseted out of the paper like fossils. A hospital stamp seal. Date. Name. The lamb logo reversed but legible. She could have made such a rubbing herself by pressing paper over a textured surface and shading with a pencil. She had not. The paper smelt of dust and old pencil ends.

"What is it?" Mark asked.

"A rubbing," Clara said, and her voice sounded as if the words were travelling through weather. "From the card. Or something like it."

"Did you—?"

"No."

They stood over the table like people at an altar they hadn't meant to attend.

He touched the edge of the paper with one fingertip as if tasting heat. "Maybe Martha—"

"No," Clara said gently. "She'd have told me. She doesn't do theatre."

They looked at each other. The room held its breath. The rain returned to the windows as if remembering them.

Clara folded the rubbing back into quarters and put it under the card and closed the lid and put both hands on top of the box and pressed, a little, as if pressure could keep history from doing anything unlicensed.

"Okay," she said, to the air. "Thank you. That's very clever. Please don't move things where the baby sleeps."

Silence. Then, very faintly, like a trace left by speech rather than speech itself: *Understood.*

Mark blinked. "Did—"

"I think I heard," she said.

He swallowed. "All right."

"We write it down," she said, almost cheerful with the clarity of a rule. "We don't argue with physics in front of the baby."

He laughed once, despite himself. "New leaflet."

"Mine's better," she said.

She wrote: *Shoebox on table (moved). Rubbing (card) inside — not mine. Heard 'Understood' (faint). Rule: no moving things in nursery.* Then, because it felt wise, she wrote the rule again, larger, and underlined it twice.

***

Evening found them reading the same page for half an hour and not confessing it. The baby discovered her tongue, which kept her occupied and the adults entertained in a way that would appal future versions of themselves. The house breathed like an animal at peace.

At nine, the power went.

It didn't crash — it slipped away. The lamps became opinions. The hum quietened like a conversation that had remembered itself. The boiler sighed and decided to wait. For a second they all sat very still, as if etiquette demanded it.

"Fuse?" Mark said.

"Probably. The street looks—" Clara peered through the gap in the curtain. "—lit enough. Ours, then."

"Candles?"

"In the drawer with nonsense."

He fetched candles that had survived previous crises on the grounds of being pretty rather than useful. They found matches. Fire made its very old argument. The house put its old face on.

In the nursery, the night-light had given up its small moon. The baby grumbled. Clara went up with a candle like a woman in a painting and found the room as ordinary as rooms ever are by candlelight: the shadows a little too interested in themselves, the rabbit an artefact from a culture that believed in ears.

She checked the window out of habit and because habit has imagination. Two clicks. She didn't touch the catch. She touched the glass with the back of her fingers and felt the night through it, a steadiness she borrowed.

She hummed the boat in the key of *no fuss*. The baby slept in the middle of it. Clara felt the small swelling of pride that comes from getting away with your own superstition.

Behind her, a floorboard in the landing made the sound it had been making all her life. She smiled without turning. "Very funny."

No sound came back. No voice. Just the candle's thread of flame making clean work of oxygen.

When she turned, the candle flame leaned sharply as if something had walked past it without a body. She held it still in the air and watched it recover. The room smelled, faintly, of blown-out matches.

"Windows and rules," she said, ALMOST to the dark. "No moving things in here."

A soft, well-bred silence. Then— the mobile shifted. Not much. Not the grand theatrical turn of cinema. Just enough to re-arrange the paper stars so the smallest one faced the cot, as if keeping watch were a thing that required a face.

"Fine," she said, surprising herself by smiling. "That's allowed."

She put the candle down on the dresser and took a step towards the door and then stopped, because her foot had told her something before her head had agreed.

Under the cot, something lay at the skirting board. Small. Pale. Waiting like the punchline of a joke you didn't want told.

She knelt, the way prayer would have her do it, and reached into the clean dust. Her fingers closed on elastic.

She drew out the ELEANOR MORGAN bracelet.

She had put it in the box not ten minutes ago. The box was on the kitchen table under both her hands and Mark's gaze and the weight of two words underlined twice. The bracelet lay cold against her palm as if to prove metal had temperature.

She stood slowly, holding it the way you hold a small, difficult truth. The candle flame was perfect. The room was perfect. The baby's breath was perfect. The part of her that had been waiting for proof sat back in its chair and didn't gloat.

"No moving things in here," she said, not loudly. "We agreed."

Nothing. Then, the tiniest adjustment in the air, like a child shifting weight on a chair they weren't supposed to be in.

"I am taking this back to the box," Clara said, keeping her voice polite. "It belongs there. That is the rule."

She left the room with the bracelet in her hand and the candle in the other and felt nothing behind her and everything.

Mark stood in the kitchen with another candle lit and two cups placed beside it, as if tea had rights. His face did the careful blankness of someone trying not to be the wrong kind of brave.

"What's that?"

She showed him. He stared. He looked at the box. He looked back at her. Something moved across his face that could have been fear or could have been a calculation about what love should do next.

"I didn't," she said, and the old teenage insistence in the sentence made them both almost laugh. "I didn't."

"I know," he said, quickly, banking trust before either of them could spend it.

She opened the box and set the bracelet where it had been. The rubbing lay beneath, quiet and companionable in its folded quarters. She put the lid on the box and rested her hand there. "Rule," she said to the air. "No moving things in the nursery."

A pause. Then a small impression along the top of the box, the mildest pressure under her palm, as if someone had pressed a flat hand in agreement. She swallowed. She wanted to cry and didn't. She wanted to cheer and didn't. She wanted to sleep and couldn't.

Mark poured tea as if the act could close a scene. "Fuse box," he said, and the relief of practical talk was so large she could have touched it.

"In the understairs," she said.

He disappeared with a torch that made the hallway look like a cave mouth. She stood alone with the shoebox and the candle and the deep, particular quiet blackouts bring, and felt, very clearly, the sensation of not being alone.

"Thank you," she said, not sure which direction to send it. "For the... proof. And for giving it back when I asked."

Don't go to the doctor woman, breathed a voice so close she could have mistaken it for her own thought if she hadn't been expecting it.

Clara set her jaw. "I am going."

They take things. They say kindness. They call it safety, the voice sing-songed, as if the words were steps in a game.

"We will make safety," Clara said. "You and me. We are very good at rules."

A pause, long enough to make her feel she had perhaps been reckless. Then: *Bossy,* fond and exasperated all at once.

"Grown," she said.

The power came back with a quiet cough. The house returned to its modern face. The candle flame looked embarrassed to still be lit. The fridge sang its note. From the understairs Mark shouted, "Victory."

Clara blew the candle out. The smoke made its Bible smell. She wrote, because she needed the furniture: *Power out (20:54–21:07). Candle in nursery. Mobile moved (allowed). Found Eleanor bracelet under cot (rule broken). Took back to box. Pressure on lid ('agreement'). Voice: 'Don't go to the doctor woman... safety/kindness.' Me: going. New rule reinforced.* She added, *Two breaths earlier not captured* and drew a line under all of it like a boundary.

They went to bed with the monitor on and the volume sensible. Mark fell asleep holding her hand, a kindness he performed without ever making it look like one. Clara watched the red LED breathe its pious in and out and let herself be bored by safety.

In the distance, someone's car alarm objected briefly to the universe and then reconciled. Rain reduced itself to lace. The baby slept as if hired to model the concept.

"Tomorrow," she whispered, to the ceiling, to the shoebox, to the place under the bed where nothing was allowed to live now. "We go and we tell the truth and we keep the rules."

The house made a small, agreeable noise.

She closed her eyes. Sleep came like a train at the right platform. Inside it, a corridor smelt of steam and old plaster. Somewhere, in another carriage, a child hummed a boat that was too small for the sea. The hum wasn't a warning. It was a route.

When she woke near dawn, the window had a pale edge to it like a good decision arriving early. The monitor was quiet. The shoebox was in its lawful place. The bracelet — both bracelets — stayed where they belonged. And in the thin fog on the inside of the glass, where her breath had made a cloud she hadn't noticed, the faintest shape could be seen if you knew what you were looking for: five small petals in a semicircle, and the memory of a palm.

She laid her own hand over it and felt the cold translate into something she could carry.

"Monday," she said softly, and the room, which had learnt the word *rule*, didn't argue.

Chapter Six

Doctor Woman

Clara woke before the light had decided itself. For a few seconds she floated on the flat of the morning, neither in nor out of the day. Then the house made its little roll call — the boiler clearing its throat, the fridge holding its note, distant tyres writing commas on wet tarmac — and her body remembered its order: hands, feet, breath, ache. She reached for the notebook, wrote the date, and underneath: *Woke steady. Dream present but sideways. Going to Dr Vale at 11.*

Beside her, Mark turned over and peered with one eye. "Status?"

"Green," she said. "For now."

"We'll take green." He kissed her hair and sat up with the solemnity of a man agreeing terms with Monday.

On the landing, the baby made the small early squeak that meant the world had passed inspection. The nursery smelled of warm cotton and whatever sweetness babies are issued with at birth. The window catch sat down and right: two clicks. She didn't check it. She checked it.

"Good morning, tyrant," she whispered, resting two fingers on the tiny chest to borrow the metronome. Rise, fall. Her own breath fell into step like someone joining a march late.

The monitor on the dresser was off. It had been off all night. The night had not punished them. That felt like a miracle made of small parts.

"Thank you," she murmured, and at once felt silly and allowed herself the feeling anyway.

***

By nine she had washed, dressed, and chosen a jumper that made her look more put-together than she felt. The baby wore the lemon sleep suit because it made the kitchen kinder. Mark did his appropriate fussing — bag stocked, nappies counted, muslins squared — and then stood with his hands on the back of a chair as if bracing the furniture.

"I'll wait in the café downstairs," he said. "Or in the car if she sleeps. I can be twenty seconds away at any given moment."

"I know," Clara said, and did.

He glanced at the dark monitor. "You sure you don't want it?"

"No." She put the notebook in the changing bag and then took it out and put it in her own. "Today we try quiet."

The kettle trembled itself towards the boil. Steam wrote on the window and changed its mind. In the damp patch, five small petals arranged themselves in a semicircle and then thinned. Clara put her palm over the place and felt the cold through the glass.

"Don't," breathed a thought from behind her ear, so soft that if she wanted to she could pretend she had supplied it herself. "Don't go to the doctor woman."

"We're going," she said, and found that saying it out loud made it more true.

Mark looked up. "What?"

"Nothing," she said. "Tea."

They chose to drive because the sky had decided to sulk. Rain came in tidy lines as if it had been ruled. The pram lay folded in the boot like a conspirator. The baby slept in her seat with the grudging peace of someone who does not approve of harnesses. Mark kept both hands on the wheel in a way that made Clara love and forgive him at the same time.

On the ring road the traffic moved in patient pulses. Billboards offered holidays and savings and a mattress that promised the future. A bus pulled alongside long enough for her to see a little boy in a dinosaur coat press his face to the misted window and wave as if they had met before in a different story. Clara waved back before she could help it. He flashed ten fingers at her — twice five — then vanished behind the condensation as if swallowed by a cloud.

"It's still raining," Mark said, for the sake of conversation.

"It is," Clara said.

They parked in the obstinate car park behind the modern block where everything smelt faintly of new paint and oranges. The lift tried to be cheerful. The button lit up meekly beneath her thumb. The doors opened on a corridor in compassionate colours, information pinned neatly to cork.

"I'll text when I'm settled," Mark said. He kissed the baby, who tolerated it. He kissed Clara and didn't ask her to be brave. "I'm just downstairs."

"I know."

He took the pram and went. Clara watched them pass through the doors and felt, very briefly and very sharply, like a rope had stretched between her and the baby and someone had plucked it to check the tuning. She put her hand flat on her chest until the feeling let go.

***

Reception had a bowl of pens on strings and a plant that had been told to believe in itself. The woman behind the desk was brisk and managed to be kind without touching it.

"Morning," she said. "You must be Clara. Dr Vale will be with you at eleven. Would you like water?"

"Yes," Clara said, and was surprised by the truth of it.

The waiting area was a compromise between tidy and lived-in. Two other women sat, each with a buggy; a father scrolled his phone, thumb moving at a practiced speed; the noticeboard offered numbers that began with 0800 and words like *Crisis* and *Support* and *Call Anytime*. Someone had knitted a tiny blanket for the arm of a chair, the kind of small generosity that makes rooms braver.

Clara checked the time — still five minutes — and opened her notebook not to read it but to see her own handwriting. She ran a finger under the line she'd written that morning. *Going to Dr Vale at 11.* The neatness of the sentence made room in her head.

The door opened softly and a woman said, "Clara?" in a voice that fell somewhere between accurate and kind.

Dr Harriet Vale stood in the doorway with a clipboard and a mug. She was late thirties, maybe early forties, hair pinned in a manner that looked accidental and wasn't, a ring with a flat green stone, flat shoes chosen by a person who liked to arrive places. Her face put people at ease without promising to do more than it could.

"Hi," Clara said, standing. Her own voice sounded like a person at the top of a hill pretending not to have climbed. "Hello."

"Come through," said Dr Vale. "Tea?"

"I've had two," Clara said. "I'll drown."

"A glass of water, then." She passed it to Clara without fuss and led her into a room that smelt of books and lemon wipes.

It was not a trick room. Two chairs that matched only in intention. A low table with a box of tissues that understood its job. A bookshelf that ranged from baby-brain pamphlets to thick volumes with precise titles. On the windowsill a plant that had clearly survived previous winters. On the desk, a small white machine muttering its white noise, probably for babies sometimes. On the wall, a clock that ticked without drawing attention to itself.

"Sit where you like," said Dr Vale, taking the other chair. "Would you prefer the door ajar or closed?"

"Closed," Clara said, and put her back to it.

"Good." A small, approving nod. She set the clipboard on her knee but didn't pick up a pen yet. "You said on the phone that you're hearing your twin."

"Yes." Saying it in this room made it real and less dramatic both at once. "She's called Ellie. We were supposed to be two. I came home. She didn't."

"Thank you," said Dr Vale. "How shall we talk about her? As a voice? A presence? A memory? Your call."

"Voice," Clara said. "And… presence. And also a trick of exhaustions and grief. All three at once. I'm trying to hold two realities without letting either eat me."

"That's already good work." A small smile flickered and steadied. "Let me start with a quick safety check, then we can go at your pace. Are you sleeping at all?"

"Enough to function. Barely but lately better."

"Appetite?"

"Yes. Toast." She managed a smile. "Diagonal."

"Thoughts of harming yourself or the baby?"

"No." It came out fierce. "No."

"Good." The pen made its first mark, not quickly, not as if capturing her rather than details. "Any command voices — the voice telling you to do things you don't want to?"

"It told me not to come here," Clara said. "And to keep the window locked. And to sing a lullaby. It hasn't told me to... you know."

"If it does," said Harriet evenly, "we have a plan. We'll come back to that. For now, take me through the last few days in your words. I'm listening."

So Clara told her. She told her about the caravan and the boat song and the biscuits in the blue jug. She told her about the shoebox and the bracelets, about the tall blue jug and the word *viable* and the fringe cut too short. She told her about *left-right,* not front–back; about the night of the power cut; about the pressure on the shoebox lid like an agreement pressed back through time. She told her about the rubbing — the graphite ghost of a stamp — and about the bracelet under the cot, rule broken, then honoured when she asked. She told her about two breaths inside one room and the recorder that kept its respectable silence. She told her about the boy in the dinosaur coat who counted to two without being asked.

Harriet did not flinch at any of it. She asked for times. She asked what the room had smelt like when the candle bent. She asked what word Ellie used instead of *roses.* She didn't say *woses* for her; she let Clara say it and then nodded as if someone had placed a piece where it belonged.

"And the rules," Harriet said. "You've made some."

"Yes." Clara was ashamed and proud of them. "Window locked — two clicks. Write it down. Boat on my terms. No moving things in the nursery. That one... we had to negotiate."

"Excellent." Harriet's mouth did a small, precise smile. "Rules are an adult's form of magic. They keep fear busy while we do other work."

"Mark says they stop me drowning."

"Mark sounds useful."

"He is."

Harriet turned a page on the clipboard. The clock ticked once as if to clear its throat. "I'm going to say the obvious sentence and we'll keep both truths on the table. One: bereavement, exhaustion and hormones can produce voices, smells, vivid memories that feel external. Two: something can feel outside of you and be important even if it's coming from inside of you. Three: even if we were to assume you're being haunted by your sister, boundaries and care plans still apply. It is not either/or for me. It's *and*."

Clara's throat had been tight since the lift; it loosened as if Harriet had unpicked a knot without making a show of it. "Thank you."

Harriet nodded like someone stamping a modest document. "Let's build three things. First — safety. Second — sleep. Third — meaning. Safety is boring and therefore wonderful. Sleep is medicine. Meaning keeps you from making leaflets your gods."

Clara laughed, surprised and relieved. "Leaflet people," she said.

"Quite." Harriet's pen made another note. "Safety. Do not co-sleep when your brain is at two hours. Leave the room if you ever feel angry beyond reason. Put the baby down even if she cries — thirty seconds for cold water on your wrists. If you ever have a thought you don't like, text Mark one word: *RED*. He'll come. If you ever hear a command you do not want to obey — tell Mark, tell me, and if it frightens you call the crisis number. I am not the police. I am the floor."

Clara nodded, relief rising like a tide that had been waiting. "I can do floor."

"Sleep," Harriet went on. "Two nights this week Mark will do the first five hours. You will wear earplugs and an eye mask and pretend you're on a ferry. If you wake, you will let the ferry be the ferry. If you can't, you'll get up and read dull things on paper in another room and not reach for the phone until the ferry is sailing again."

"Okay."

"Meaning," Harriet said. "Write two columns. Evidence on one side. Interpretations on the other. Not to argue with yourself — to watch your mind. Under that, a smaller column: *Rules/Agreements*. Keep the ones that help. Add *No moving things in nursery* to the list we both hold. If Ellie is real, she gets to keep rules. If Ellie is you, you get to give yourself rules through her. Both ways work."

Clara had to close her eyes for a second. "I thought you might tell me to grow up."

"I am," Harriet said, amused. "This is how adults play."

They both smiled then, as if discovering they had the same joke.

A draft moved nothing. The blind at the window stayed proper. On Harriet's desk, a small paperweight shaped like a boat glinted and thought better of winking. Clara noticed it and made herself not read it as a sign.

"Questions," Harriet said.

"Is this... postpartum psychosis?" The word felt too large for her mouth.

"No," Harriet said, careful and clean. "You are grounded. You're sleeping some. You know what's real-ish and what's maybe-real. You're not paranoid. You're not disorganised in your thinking. You have insight. We're not in that house. If we were, I would say so and we would go together to a different clinic with more keys."

Clara exhaled like someone who had been under longer than they thought. "Thank you."

"Medication may help with sleep and anxiety," Harriet added, "but I'm not in a hurry if you aren't. I lean non-sedating: a beta blocker for the hammering heart before bed; a low-dose SSRI if the floor keeps sinking. We can decide next week after the ferry experiment."

"All right."

"Another question?"

"If Ellie tells me she's keeping the baby safe... and tells me not to come here... whose side am I on?"

"Yours," Harriet said, without a blink. "And the baby's. Which is the same side." She let the words sit. "You can tell Ellie that I'm not the enemy. If she's you: you're not the enemy either. If she's not: she doesn't get to decide you don't get help."

Clara swallowed, throat prickling. "She called me bossy."

"Good," Harriet said. "Be bossy."

They both looked at the clock as if it had spoken. The minute hand, dutiful, advanced itself.

"Tell me the most frightening moment this week," Harriet said gently. "The one you can't quite let sit."

Clara told her about the bracelet under the cot. Saying it made her want to take a breath from someone else's lungs. Harriet listened and didn't look away. When Clara reached the part with the pressure on the shoebox lid like a small flat hand pressing *Understood*, Harriet's eyes softened in a way that did not pity.

"I believe you were frightened," Harriet said. "I believe it was real for you. I believe it might be real beyond you. My job, either way, is the same. We make a list. We add a rule. We make a plan."

"What's the plan for bracelets under cots?"

"Bring them into the kitchen," Harriet said promptly. "Put them in the box. Say out loud the rule. Write the time down. Text Mark *BLUE* so he knows it's a rule event, not a red one. Make tea. You'll be in your kitchen doing an adult thing. *Leaflet people can queue.*" She wrote the words on her pad and underlined them, then tore the page neatly and passed it to Clara like a silly prescription. "Stick that on your fridge."

Clara found herself laughing in the way that has crying right behind it. "Thank you," she said, and took the paper like a ticket to somewhere that didn't exist yet.

"Before you go," Harriet said, and her voice shifted, softer, "I want to ask if you would like me to meet you where you are for thirty seconds. We can talk to Ellie together. If that feels mad, say no. If it feels like play, we can try."

Clara looked at the flat green ring and the steady hands. She thought of bathrooms by candlelight and a little paper star turning its face. She thought of the boat, the *left–right*. She managed a nod.

"Okay."

Harriet placed both feet flat on the floor and, very matter-of-fact, spoke to the air a foot to Clara's left. "Ellie," she said. "I'm Harriet. I'm looking after Clara. I'm not here to take anything away. I am the floor. She is the rules. You are the reason. We're on the same side."

The white-noise machine kept its mutter. The clock ticked with discretion. On the windowsill the plant bravely continued its plan for photosynthesis. For a second, nothing. Then — a change Clara would not have noticed a month ago — the room cooled half a degree, as if someone had opened the door to the hallway and then shut it again because, actually, better inside.

Clara's skin flickered. She kept her eyes on Harriet's face the way a person holds onto a rail on a train.

"Thank you," said Harriet into the small, altered air. "If you want to keep the baby safe, you can help by obeying the rules. Including this one: no moving things in the nursery. And this: the boat is sung when Clara chooses. And this: doctors are allowed."

Something eased very slightly, like a knot consenting to be a bow.

Clara felt the back of her neck prickle and then settle. She hadn't realised she'd been gripping her own wrists; she loosened her hands.

"Good," said Harriet, as if to a room that had completed a task. "That's enough for today. Back to the dull magic." She smiled, and the room rearranged itself into chairs and a table and a woman with a pen. "Same time next Monday?"

"Yes," Clara said. Her voice sounded like hers. "Please."

***

In the café, Mark had a paper cup and the look of a man practising serenity. The baby had that dopey, milk-drunk face that made the rest of the world amateur.

"How was she?" Clara asked.

"She thinks I'm a reasonable citizen," he said. "I have earned a place in her republic."

Clara laughed and felt the laugh belong to her. "Harriet is... proper."

"And?"

"She didn't flinch." Clara held up the scrap of paper with *Leaflet people can queue.* "Prescribed."

He read it and grinned. "My favourite doctor."

"She wants two ferry nights," Clara said. "You, first five hours, twice this week."

"I can do ferry."

"And colour codes. RED means I need you. BLUE means the rules are being enforced. No rescues needed; just... witness."

Mark nodded as if given a plan he could put into a spreadsheet. "Done."

They sat on plastic chairs and watched other lives pass the windows with their own weather. A toddler refused to accept the existence of socks. A woman in a suit told a story on her phone with her hands. The rain took a breath.

"Did you tell her the thing about the bracelet?" Mark asked quietly.

"I did."

"And?"

"We wrote a rule. And she told Ellie she's allowed to like doctors."

"Good," Mark said, and did not laugh. "Can I buy you a biscuit like a reward?"

"You can buy yourself a biscuit as a reward for not texting me every seven minutes."

He put his hand over his heart. "I only texted every eight."

They shared a look that belonged to them and the room became, for a minute, just a café where two people with a baby were being ordinary, and in that minute the day gentled.

***

Home smelt of them and of Martha's casserole reheated for lunch and of the rain that had followed them in on sleeves. Clara climbed the stairs and looked in at the nursery the way you glance into a church you don't go to. The rabbit stared like a witness with no agenda. The mobile hung obedient. The window catch clicked agreeably under her fingers. Two clicks. She didn't check it again. She went downstairs with the sense that a room had nodded at her and returned to its work.

In the kitchen she stuck Harriet's scrap on the fridge with a magnet shaped like a strawberry. It looked ridiculous and necessary. She wrote in her notebook: *Harriet. Safety/Sleep/Meaning. Ferry nights x2 (Mark first 5 hrs). RED for help; BLUE for rule. Talked to Ellie in session (room cooled, slight). Rules affirmed: no moving things in nursery; boat on my terms; doctors allowed. Leaflet people can queue.* Then, almost shyly: *I felt like me in the café.*

Her phone buzzed. Priya: *How did it go?* Jonah wore a saucepan as a helmet in the photo and did not care what anyone thought.

She's good, Clara wrote back. *She says rules are adult magic. Will text you at 3 a.m. purely for the vibe.*

Priya responded with a sticker of a witch in sensible shoes. *Adult magic = receipts + snacks.*

Clara smiled, and in the act of smiling she caught, at the edge of the window, a handprint blooming in the steam from the kettle: five petals, semicircle. She didn't rush to it. She let it stay. She lifted her palm and put it over the mark and felt the cool and then the warming, the way touch returns to itself.

"Doctors allowed," she said to the glass.

The mark thinned like breath forgotten.

They made an afternoon with small ingredients. Mark took the baby out to post a letter and came back with a loaf that claimed to be artisan and tasted like bread. Clara folded laundry and discovered she felt less like drowning if someone had put the socks in pairs. She took a ferry nap, properly, with earplugs and an eye mask that made her look like a robber from a story. She woke two hours later feeling briefly mean and then okay.

At five, the witching hour arrived to remind them that rules are suggestions to babies. They walked and rocked and made bargains with gravity. The monitor stayed off and the world did not end. The baby eventually chose to forgive everyone.

They ate on the sofa because chairs felt like ambition. At nine, Mark turned the TV to something with people renovating houses they should have left alone. Clara went to the sink and stood at the back door and watched the garden try on darkness. Somewhere, a fox rearranged a bin and muttered about it.

"You were good today," she said aloud, unsure whether she meant herself, the house, or the air. "Thank you."

"Bossy," came, very faintly, in a tone of fond complaint.

"Grown," she said, pleased to find the word had kept its shape.

Before bed she went to the nursery and did the census: catch, stars, rabbit, breath. The room gave nothing away. She did not wait for it to. She put two fingers on the tiny chest, stole the metronome, and returned it.

On the dresser the dark monitor was a calm unblinking face. She had the sudden urge to turn it on and then felt her hand stop on its own, as if someone had touched her wrist, not to restrain but to remind.

"Doctors are allowed," she said into the lamp-lit room. "So are rules."

She waited. A small movement of the paper stars — not a turn, just a settling, like a child agreeing to listen.

"Good," she said, and switched the lamp off, and left the door ajar the width of a word she wasn't going to say.

They lay in the dark, ferry nights laminated inside the promise of the week. The red LED in the corner — the one that meant the smoke alarm was dutiful behind its plastic — did its own faint breath. Mark exhaled in sleep a thing like a question, then found the answer.

Clara opened her notebook and wrote, by phone light: *Night — quiet. Rules obeyed. Felt watched in the protective way. Me: bossy + grown.* She closed it and slipped it under the bed because the sober part of her liked the idea that thoughts slept on a cooler floor.

When the whisper came, it came through the plaster in that way the house had learnt. It did not scold. It did not warn. It sounded like someone who had come to the edge of a bed and was considering whether to sit.

"Clara."

"I'm here," she said, and realised the sentence held more comfort than defiance now.

A small, amused sound, like a shared joke at someone else's expense. "Clever girl."

"Not a girl," she said, smiling in the dark. "Grown."

A pause. Then: "Keep her safe."

"Yes," Clara said, and meant it like she'd signed for a package. "With me."

"Left-right," the voice breathed, but not as an instruction — as a blessing.

Clara pictured the boat and refused to sing because she could and because she might tomorrow and because rules worked best when they were also gifts. She put her hand flat on her own chest and felt her heart do its honest work. The house adjusted itself with a little sigh, approving of the arrangements.

"Goodnight," she said.

The room did not answer in words. It stayed itself. On the window, where there had been a hand, dew made its faint script. The catch kept its two-part promise. In the cot, breath and breath and breath, the small, perfect punctuation of a world that, for the moment, had agreed to be kind.

Chapter Seven

Ferry Night

Clara woke to a Tuesday that had ironed itself flat. The sky did that white where it isn't a colour so much as a decision. For a minute she lay without moving and let the room take attendance: clock's modest tick, boiler's low hum, the frilled hush of tyres a street away. She reached for the notebook and wrote, neat as a list on a hospital whiteboard: *Woke steady. Dream—caravan, edges soft. Rules: window (two clicks); boat on my terms; doctors allowed; no moving things in nursery. Ferry night tonight (M 1st shift).*

Beside her, Mark blinked at the ceiling like a man negotiating a treaty with the day. "Status?"

"Green," she said. "So far."

"We'll take green." He kissed the top of her head. "I'll do the first five tonight. Ferry that woman across."

Clara smiled into the pillow. "You'll be promoted to captain if you behave."

From the nursery came the interrogative squeak of a citizen reconsidering her place in the republic. The room still smelt faintly of lemon wipes and the sweetness babies manufacture as proof of policy. The window catch sat down and right: two clicks. She didn't touch it. She touched it.

"Good morning, tyrant," she said, laying two fingers on the tiny chest to borrow breath. Rise, fall. She returned the metronome gently, like a borrowed book.

On the dresser, the monitor sat dark. It had been off all night and the world had not punished anyone. That felt like a small miracle that didn't mind being called small.

"Thank you," she whispered to no one in particular and, for once, didn't immediately tell herself off.

They made the morning out of ordinary parts. Nappy, bottle, steriliser; a load on; mugs rinsed; the kind of banter couples do when they've discovered it's useful to pretend normal is a skill.

"I'll call the health visitor," Mark said, half-turned to the sink. "Just to update. Jade? Or is that the breastfeeding one?"

"She's both," Clara said. "A Swiss Army Jade."

"Tell her ferry nights are in operation."

"Tell her I have a captain's hat."

Mark made an approving noise. "I'll pick up earplugs from the chemist anyway. The ones you said don't feel like you've lied to your ears."

Clara touched the notebook with the back of her hand. "Put *BLUE* on the fridge in thick pen for rule events. We promised Harriet."

Mark wrote *BLUE = rules* on a sticky note shaped like a star and stuck it beside *Leaflet people can queue.* The fridge looked like a child's homework. It felt like a plan.

Late morning, Jade arrived with a tote bag that announced she liked a charity and a cardigan that made rooms behave. She washed her hands as if to set a tone. The baby stared at her with polite suspicion and then smiled, because that was currently her policy.

"How are we?" Jade asked, the *we* pitched so it could include or not include anyone in the room, depending on their mood.

"Fair," Clara said. "Rules written down."

"Love a rule." Jade watched the latch, counted the swallows, recorded the head circumference with the efficiency of someone who has done this more times than seasons. "Any concerns?"

"Sleep," Mark said. "We're trying ferry nights. I'm on first shift."

"Good. Sleep is medicine. Partners are ferries." Jade smiled at the baby with the serious joy only professionals manage. "How are you in your head, Clara?"

"Less underwater," Clara said, because that was true enough to pass. "I'm seeing the perinatal psychiatrist."

"Excellent. Do you feel safe?"

"Yes."

Jade's eyes softened at the speed of that answer. "If you ever don't," she said, as if dropping a key in Clara's pocket, "I'm on the phone. Out of hours there's a crisis number on the card. No leaflets will be harmed in the making of your call."

Clara laughed, startled by the rightness of the joke. "Everyone's got the memo."

Jade weighed the baby and made the happy noise adults make when numbers behave. "She's thrived since last week. Look at you, growing like a rumour." She adjusted the cardigan and glanced around the nursery without judging it. "This is a good room."

Clara saw it a new way through Jade's eyes: cot, rabbit, paper stars, the neatness that had started as defence and become habit. The window catch sat in its smug correctness. The shoebox was not in here. Rules were doing their small work.

Jade said the usual things kindly: tummy time, safe sleep, a reminder about room temperature that assumed everyone owned a thermometer that didn't get lost behind the bread bin. She kissed the baby's brow in a fashion that made even cynics forgive her and wrote the next visit in her diary.

At the door, she squeezed Clara's hand once. "You're doing much better than you tell yourself," she said. "Tell yourself that."

After she left, the house let out breath through its ribs. Mark raised both eyebrows at Clara like a man proud of his ferry enlistment. "She's good."

"She made a joke about leaflets," Clara said, and felt a little less alone in the world.

***

After lunch, the day lost definition around the edges. Rain gave up the performance and left air that smelt of wet wood and bus stops. The baby slept with open, complicated hands as if translating dreams. Mark went to his laptop and did the work of a person who needed his own list to keep from flying off.

Clara opened a fresh page and drew two columns as Harriet had instructed. *EVIDENCE* on the left in capitals and childish pride. *INTER-PRETATIONS* on the right, smaller, calm. Underneath, in a neat third, *RULES/AGREEMENTS*.

She filled in Monday's things, then today: *Jade—kind; safe; numbers good.* She enjoyed giving blue ticks to the rules. She wrote *Ferry nights x2 this week* and underlined *tonight* the way a child underlines a trip.

Half an hour later she added, in the left-hand column, because honesty had begun to be a practice: *Felt watched (benign)*. In the right-hand, *habit, not threat.* Under rules, she wrote: *No moving things in nursery (repeat)*. Writing the same rule twice soothed her in the way hymns must soothe believers.

She put the notebook down and went to the sink. In the steam on the window five small petals arranged themselves and faded. She did not rush to cover them with her palm. She watched them go, as you watch wildlife and try not to be greedy.

"Doctors allowed," she said, not because the glass needed telling but because ears learn by hearing.

The house stayed itself.

At four, Priya texted a photo of Jonah in a scarf that had been designed by a committee with no taste. *Sensory Thursday: prepare to be dazzled by chiffon.*

Clara replied with a picture of the sticky-noted fridge. *Adult magic.*

Priya sent back a heart and then: *You okay?*

Ferry tonight. Will text at 3 a.m. for the vibe.

Send biscuit emojis instead, Priya wrote. *Fewer arrests.*

Clara put the phone down and, because you can't control the moment things arrive, smelt apples. Thin, clean, fresh-cut, the precise smell of the caravan step in a summer that didn't decide to be rain until three. The air didn't change temperature. Nothing in the room moved. She closed her eyes and let the scent pass through her like someone's memory brushing her shoulder on a crowded pavement.

When she looked, the rabbit sat as it always sat. The paper stars were still. In the hall, a floorboard made its familiar complaint and then thought better of developing a personality.

"Thank you," she said, because gratitude, too, was a rule that seemed to help, and went to put the kettle on with hands that had learnt not to shake in order to be believed.

*****

They organised the evening as if planning a silly expedition. Mark set the alarm for midnight to wake him at the end of his shift in case kindness became sleep. He laid out bottles in a neat row as if they were men called up. He checked the smoke alarm and the monitor's battery for the theatre of it, then left the monitor off because the theatre was enough. He placed earplugs and an eye mask on Clara's pillow with a flourish and bowed as if presenting a crown.

"Should I do a speech before boarding?" he asked.

"Please confine speeches to the aft deck," she said, and loved him more than she could fit in a sentence.

At eight, the baby ran the usual referendum on gravity and noise. At nine, she forgave everyone. At ten, Clara went upstairs and arranged herself with the alien dignity earplugs and an eye mask bestow. She lay on her side and thought about ferry decks and white lines and the serious men who tie ropes. She thought about Harriet's flat green ring and her steady hands. She thought, with a small rush of something that wasn't quite fear, of the corridor in the dream and the gentle scrape of voice against plaster.

She woke to a different dark entirely.

The house had gone to ground. Earplugs had taken the small sounds away and left the felt of the night. She sat up, mask pushed to her forehead, and listened with other senses: skin, throat, the small bones inside ears trying to earn their keep.

It was half one. Downstairs, a light made the kind of not-quite-shine that meant Mark was awake and being good. The baby exhaled a small sigh that crossed floors like a letter posted to the right address.

Clara lay back down and tried to think about ferry decks again. Sleep took her by the hem and tugged.

When she woke the second time, the dark had an opinion.

She sat up. Earplugs softened the edges. The room was the same shape it had been, which is sometimes how rooms trick you.

Then she heard it, through foam and bone and sense: water.

Not the house's old gossip of pipes. Not rain. A steady line into a pool, polite and sure and going somewhere it had been asked to go. The sound had purpose. It had that private, confident tone taps have when nobody is watching them and they can play at being rivers.

She stood, the room lurching once in the way rooms do when you make them get up with you. She pulled the eye mask to her neck like a very serious necklace and padded to the landing. Earplugs made her off-balance; she took them out and the world sharpened with a tiny sting.

Water, definitely. Bath-level water. The one in the family bathroom they didn't use for the baby. Cold tap. Plug in. She would swear the sound of plug in was in the water itself, a gentle dome note.

Clara moved quickly, quietly, and with that ridiculous thoughtfulness people use around sleeping babies even when the problem is clearly pipes. The bathroom was a dark square of porcelain and decent tile. The tap ran. The plug was in. The water was three fingers from the overflow and practicing pretending not to be.

She turned the tap off. The sound did that embarrassing thing of stopping. In the quiet afterwards her heart made up noise enough.

"Mark?" she called, level, not loud.

A sound from the stairs: his tread, careful. "All right?"

"Did you—"

"No." He stood in the doorway, hair at war, eyes already looking for physical causes he could fix. "I didn't run a bath."

They stood and looked at the water as if it might explain itself.

"I don't sleepwalk," Clara said, because she had tried on all the available female-guilt options and preferred not to wear this one.

"I know," he said, immediately, which was the right thing to say.

She crouched and put her fingers to the water. Cold. The chill climbed her skin like a sentence. She looked down at the bath mat.

In the pile— where damp changes the ordinary into information— a small, careful half-print something like a child might make if they had stood on the edge and looked in. Just the ball of a foot, a crescent of heel, no toes. The size of Clara's own foot when she was seven, perhaps. The size of a truth that didn't want to be rude.

She didn't touch it. She wanted to. She didn't.

"Rule," she said into the bathroom's even air, because that was the agreement. "No moving things in the nursery. No water left running. No running baths."

Silence, then the mildest impression of cool on the back of her neck, not unfriendly. She could have called it a draught if she needed to.

"BLUE?" Mark asked, low, translating the world into colours because it helped.

"BLUE," she said. "Not RED. Not danger, just rules."

He nodded and went downstairs without questions—the trust of a man who had decided to join a religion where the hymns were lists. She heard the click and whirr of the boiler, the flick of his phone screen, the quiet business of making the kitchen behave as the place where adult things are done.

Clara stayed where she was a minute more. The bath water cooled itself into politeness. She lifted the plug and let the rush down the pipe be loud. She watched the small cyclones. When the water was low enough to stop pretending to be a lake she wiped the rim with the towel and, without being sentimental about it, the place where the half-print had been. The pile lay flat again, as if advised.

"Thank you," she said, and didn't know where to send it.

Back in the bedroom, she wrote, by phone light: *01:42 — bath running (cold). Plug in. Water 3 fingers from overflow. Print on mat (small, half). Rule stated: no water; no moving things in nursery. Mark BLUE.* It steadied her the way putting labels on boxes steadies people who fear losing their things.

She lay down and sleep found her much quicker than it had any right to.

***

She woke to tea at the bed's edge and Mark doing that face that said he was proud and trying not to look as if he thought she'd done something dangerous when she hadn't.

"Ferry completed," he said. "Minor river incident at one-forty-two. Engineer dispatched. No casualties."

"You're ridiculous," she said, and could have cried at the relief of it, so she took the mug instead.

"How do you want to log bathgate?" he asked, sitting on the edge of the bed as if waiting to be sworn in.

"In *Evidence*: water, print, my eyes." She sipped. "In *Interpretations*: grief loves symbols. Houses like to be interesting. Also: taps fail. Also: Ellie wants to keep her safe and thinks this is a good way to get me to owe her."

Mark's mouth did a brief smile that made him handsome and kind. "You think owing is the point."

"I think owing is the language siblings speak in." She shrugged a shoulder into the pillow. "I don't mind owing as long as we have rules."

He kissed her forehead. "We have rules."

"Leaflet people can queue."

He saluted the fridge from upstairs with his mind and went to change the baby, who had decided to praise the morning with a businesslike grumble.

***

By ten they were all in proper clothes and the house had consented to be ordinary. The sky tried for blue. The washing machine made a voluntary sound like work. Clara put the bath towel in the basket with a small ceremonial pat, as if closing a case. She checked the nursery catch: two clicks. The rabbit: guard on. The paper stars: still. She spoke once to the room **for the record**: "Doctors allowed. Rules allowed. Water: not allowed."

The room, being a good room, combined not answering with agreeing.

She took the notebook downstairs and drew two balanced columns. On the left, under *EVIDENCE*, she listed with a tidy hand: *01:42 cold tap running (bathroom); plug in; water line; print (half) on mat; Mark witness to tap being on, not to print. No monitor involvement.* On the right, under *INTERPRETATIONS*: *Harmless but boundary test; guardian not menace; possible human error (tap) + pattern-finding (print). Keep rule; do not dramatise; do not recruit leaflet people.*

Under *RULES/AGREEMENTS*, she added: *No water. No moving things in nursery. If boundary tested: BLUE + tea.*

She closed the book and felt it heavy and friendly in her hands.

"Tea?" Mark called.

"Adult magic," she said, and took the mug and the biscuit he had decided she deserved as if he had been deputised by Harriet.

In the afternoon, because staying inside meant you sometimes started to believe you were the room you were in, they walked to the green. The pram rolled with that small rrr-rrr as if purring. The sky put on coin-thin sunshine that couldn't be trusted but could be liked. The pond had a gloss on it ducks admired. The baby stared at trees with the concentrated gravity of a tiny astronomer.

Priya texted to say scarves would be available in ludicrous colours, and Clara replied with a photo of the pond that made it look like a better place than it was. *What's your rule of the day?* Priya asked.

No water, Clara wrote.

A classic, Priya replied. *My rule is never trust a sippy cup.*

They returned to find a parcel in the porch: Martha's blue jumper with the cloud buttons, folded into a shape that said *I am pretending not to want to make you cry.* Clara pressed it to her face, smelt clean wool and a hint of cupboard, then put it in the drawer with an adult movement that tried not to wake anything.

When she shut the drawer the house made that small sound houses make when they adjust to new weight and old thought. She told it, out loud because Harriet had given her permission to narrate reality, "We are all right."

The house, pleasant, didn't argue.

At five the witching hour came, because folklore keeps its own appointments. The baby, who had been a statesman all day, discovered injustice. They did the dance. Mark's arms did thirty seconds of good work; Clara's voice did the boat in a whisper without the tune, which seemed to satisfy the gods of compromise.

The monitor stayed off. The window stayed locked. The rules did their small, important, boring magic.

When the baby slept, Mark said, "Shall we tell Harriet the water thing?"

"Yes," Clara said. "I'll email her with the words *not an emergency* in the subject so she doesn't ring the police."

"New rule: titles that don't terrify psychiatrists."

"Done."

She wrote the email in the tidy, calm tone adults use when they want to be taken seriously: *Bath tap left running at 01:42 (cold; plug in; water three fingers from overflow). I did not set it. Mark Blue (witness to tap, not print). Stated rule: no water; no moving things in nursery. Felt 'understood'. No fear. Ferry night otherwise successful. Two hours' sleep in one go (!). Feeling: bossy + grown.* She hovered over *send* for the stupid amount of time and then pressed it and suffered nothing because usually you suffer nothing.

Harriet replied in under an hour with a sentence that made her feel known: *BLUE received; rules working; "no water" added to shared list; ferry: excellent; if RED ever, you call.* The email carried no weight and all the weight she needed.

Clara read it twice, then read it out loud to Mark because sometimes the same words behave differently when two people hold them.

Night came with less appetite than usual. They ate on the sofa and watched a programme where people argued about house extensions and the narrator offered the driest of moral instruction. Clara found herself agreeing with a man about a lintel and felt briefly healed by the pettiness.

Upstairs, the nursery had that concentrated quiet rooms have when they're full of breath. Clara checked the catch: two clicks; no theatre. She stood for a minute, counting the breath she loved into steadier numbers. She looked at the bath mat because she was allowed to look and found— nothing— which was the right answer. She thanked the room anyway.

In bed, earplugs and mask waiting, she wrote, in a margin because the page had run out of lines: *I felt like me at the pond.* She thought that might be the kind of sentence you kept to hold against less obedient hours.

When the voice came it arrived without the old trickery. It had learnt politeness and discovered it could use it as a way to get what it wanted.

"Clara."

"I'm here," she said, not sitting up. "We are all here."

A small pleased breath that might have been someone approving a plan. "No water."

"Correct," she said. "No water."

A silence that felt like someone practicing not to argue. Then, very soft, as if it had been saved for the right time: "Left-right."

She smiled in the dark and did not sing because she could choose not to. "On my terms," she said.

A hush that didn't feel like sulking. A room that had agreed to keep its face. The small, pious green of the smoke alarm doing its blink. The honest work of the small heart in the cot. The larger work of the adult heart in the bed that had found the ferry's rhythm and meant to keep it.

Clara put her hand flat on her own chest and counted once, twice, in gratitude rather than fear, and decided that for tonight, that would do.

Chapter Eight
Sensory

Clara woke into a Wednesday that had put itself in order. The sky had decided on a pale, undecided blue; the clouds held their breath like polite guests. She lay very still and let the room do its roll call: the boiler clearing its throat, the fridge holding its one true note, a bus far off sighing like a man late for something he could not name.

She reached for the notebook and wrote: *Woke steady. Rules: window two clicks; boat on my terms; no moving things in nursery; no water. Ferry night last night: one-thirty-two bath incident; BLUE; slept after. Today: home. Tomorrow: sensory group.*

Beside her, Mark opened one eye like a man greeting a dog. "Status?"

"Green," she said. "As pledged."

He smiled and sat up with the solemnity of a person who intended to keep promises to Monday even on a Wednesday. "We'll take green."

On the landing, the baby produced a small social squeak. The nursery smelt of night-light and cotton and the warm animal sweetness that made Clara feel both heavier and lighter. The window catch sat down and correct: two clicks. She didn't check it. She checked it.

"Good morning," she said to the small republic in the cot. Two fingers on a tiny chest. Rise, fall. Her own lungs remembered their bureaucracy and complied.

On the dresser, the monitor sat dark. The night had not punished them for silence. Clara put her hand on the empty air above it as if blessing a sleeping creature and felt silly and let herself.

They made a morning out of toast and decency. Mark put a load on and folded damp towels with a care that felt like prayer. He placed an earplug packet on the mantel with satisfaction, as if the house were collecting badges.

"Tomorrow," he said, buttering with gravitas, "I shall transport you to the Church of Chiffon."

"Priya said scarves." Clara made a face. "I'm afraid of cheerful fabric."

"You'll be brave," he said. "And text me BLUE if the scarves misbehave."

She used the last of the decent jam with the stingy grace of a person who knew how desire wanted to be managed. "If a scarf ties itself," she said, aiming for light, "we move to red."

Mark nodded, then touched the star-shaped sticky note on the fridge — *BLUE = rules* — as if checking its hold. The scrap from Harriet — *Leaflet people can queue* — sat beneath, ridiculous and necessary.

Clara added today's date to the corner of the fridge in dry-wipe pen and drew a line beneath it, a boundary the room could see.

***

After the 10 a.m. feed the baby fell asleep with her mouth open, a small coin of breath moving in and out. Clara stood a second longer than she needed to and watched that tiny income and expenditure of oxygen and gratitude. The rabbit sat to attention. The mobile hung obligingly still. The window catch smirked its two clicks.

In the hall, the doorbell tried to be a visitor and succeeded. Priya stood there with Jonah on her hip in a knitted hat he had clearly argued with.

"Emergency delivery," she said. "Spare muslins. The ones that don't smell of whatever the last baby had for breakfast in 2012."

Clara grinned. "Come in. We can baptise them in tea."

They drank in the kitchen while Jonah conducted a serious affair with a wooden spoon. Priya took in the sticky notes, the leaflets magnetised into submission, the notebook open at *EVIDENCE / INTERPRETATIONS / RULES*. She didn't comment. She sipped and nodded once, as people do when they're meeting someone exactly where they've said they are.

"How's your head?" Priya asked, a question with lanes to choose.

"Less underwater," Clara said, and put a hand on the notebook without meaning to. "Doctors allowed."

"Good," Priya said. "I like allowed. It's such a reasonable word."

"Tomorrow, church hall."

"Chiffon apocalypse," Priya said gravely. "Bring snacks. Myself, I survive on custard creams and the knowledge that none of us is special."

Clara laughed, properly, and felt something inside her unclench a little more. "A doctrine I can endorse."

Jonah, having resolved his affair with the spoon, banged it once on the table and then looked deeply pleased with himself. "That's the spirit," Priya told him. "Go forth and make helpful noises."

They arranged to walk together to the church the next morning. Priya hugged her at the door in a way that made the hug feel like a decision rather than an invasion. "Text if you need me before," she said. "Or after. Or in the middle."

"Thank you," Clara said, and meant all three.

In the quiet after, the kettle trembled itself towards the boil. Through the steam on the window, five small petals arranged themselves in a semicircle and thinned. Clara didn't rush to meet them. She watched them fade the way you watch a boat become line, then dot, then absence.

"Doctors allowed," she said to the glass. "Also: friends."

The house, prudent, did not reply.

The afternoon took on that soft focus hours wear when nothing is asked of them. Mark went to his laptop and did useful things to emails. The baby slept and woke, practised frowns and then forgave them. Clara cleaned a drawer she did not need to clean and found at the back a packet of birthday candles from another life, thin and pastel and offended to be discovered. She put them in the bin and then changed her mind and put them in the cupboard where odds learn patience. It felt like a compromise the room endorsed.

At four, the rain remembered itself and tapped lightly. Clara wrote it down as if the weather were part of her case. *Rain (soft). House obedient.* Then, because she had promised Harriet meaning, she wrote on the right: *Ordinary days also evidence.*

She stood at the sink and looked at the garden trying on grey, at the fence remembering last night's water. The reflection in the glass showed her own face leaner than she felt, and for a second — not longer — a second face leaned in beside it, same bones, same mouth, eyes set half a degree wider, as if a sculptor had been interrupted between versions. Clara didn't startle. She lifted a hand. The other hand lifted. Neither waved. That felt right. She turned from the glass before she could force the moment to be bigger than itself.

Mark came and stood beside her and put a hand on the small of her back. "Tea?"

"It's the law," she said, and the kettle obeyed.

***

They ate early because the baby demanded to be consulted on every-thing. At seven, the witching hour arrived with folklore's punctuality. The baby protested the air, then agreed to tolerate it, then researched a reason to forgive everyone, then, having found none, fell asleep. Mark looked unfairly handsome leaning over the cot, the kind of domestic tableau that makes cynics say *ugh* and secretly copy it.

At nine, they watched television in which strangers knocked down internal walls and discovered load-bearing surprises. Clara found her-self invested in lintels again. It felt like someone giving her another brain to borrow for an hour. When the programme ended, she found she could remember the plot and, behind it, her own.

She went upstairs. In the bathroom she looked at the bath mat; it looked back as rugs look back; nothing there, the right answer. She thanked it anyway, because gratitude had taken up residency.

In the nursery she did her census: catch, stars, rabbit, breath. Every-thing consented to be itself. She put two fingers on the small chest and borrowed the metronome. She whispered, for the record, "No water. No moving things in here. Doctors allowed."

The room agreed by not arguing.

She slept properly. This was itself a kind of haunt.

***

Morning put Thursday on its face like a fresh sheet. The sky looked like it wanted to be helpful. Clara wrote: *Woke steady. Sensory group — church hall — 10:30 with Priya. Rules first; witness later.* She liked the thought of witness. Writing *witness* made her feel less mad and more church.

Mark did the packing as if preparing a small expedition to a known coast. Nappies, wipes, spare vest, spare spare vest, muslin, snack for adult, snack for adult who denies needing snacks, notebook. The baby wore the lemon sleep suit because it improved the public mood.

"You'll be fine," he said, and didn't add *if anything weird happens* because they had agreed not to invoke weirdness before coffee.

"Scarves," Clara said, and attempted a face.

"You've confronted worse fabric."

He kissed her temple with the lightness of a person who knew how much heaviness weighed. "BLUE if rules; RED if rescue. I will be twenty seconds away in spirit if not in geography."

"You'll be twenty seconds away in the wilfully bad café," she said.

He looked wounded. "Their almond croissant is adequate."

"High praise."

They left the house. The air smelt like something promising to rain later but willing to leave them alone for now. On the pavement outside, chalk arrows from last week's street playday still pointed nowhere in children's colours. Clara stepped over an indecisive hopscotch and felt seven for a heartbeat and then thirty-two again.

Priya waved at the corner in a coat that refused to take the weather too seriously. Jonah wore a hat shaped like a fox and looked like a small crime. "Sensory salvation," Priya announced. "Chiffon and bubbles and the general public."

They walked together, pram wheels making that rrr–rrr that soothed everyone involved. Priya talked about budgets at work and how some-one had attempted to cheer the office with a cactus and how the cactus had undertaken violence. Clara found she could answer in sentences with beginning, middle, and end, not just the urgent little fragments newborn life produces. The church hall appeared with sober brick and a noticeboard that tried to be legible from the pavement.

"Ready?" Priya asked.

"No," Clara said. "Yes."

The hall smelt of country fairs and polish and a hint of nappies. The radiator under the bay window wore its paint like a good suit. A table at the back was heaped with scarves — pinks, greens, yellows that had survived previous winters; a cardboard box of maracas waited with the patience of instruments that believed in their work. On a low shelf, a tub of bubbles sat like an idea.

The health visitor — not Jade, another one with a lanyard and the expression of a person who knew how to find a plaster at speed — led the circle time with a voice that could have booked trains. Parents arranged themselves in degrees of composure. Babies lay on mats and sucked their own fists and regarded heaven.

Clara took the spot near the radiator again because heat made a case. Priya sat to her right with Jonah, who immediately tried to eat a scarf as if it had personally offended his lineage.

"Welcome!" said the woman. "We're going to do some gentle sensory play today — lights down for bubbles, some music, lots of colour. Don't worry if anyone cries — we'll out-sing them."

Clara smiled, the kind you do for other people's benefit and then realise is also for you. The bubble machine, when plugged in, made a satisfied small sound. Bubbles drifted out in a slow, undecided parade. Babies batted; parents made cooing noises they would deny in court. The lights lowered fractionally and became generous.

A scarf crossed Clara's lap, uninvited, light as thought. She looked up for its owner and found no one reaching. The fabric lay there a second — green — as if saying *allow me*. She laughed, an actual laugh, and held it up. Priya made a small approving noise. "Go on. She'll love the texture."

Clara let the scarf ghost over the baby's cheek. The baby's mouth formed an O of philosophical concern, then a smile that arrived one-sided and generous. Clara touched the scarf to her own face and felt the tickle of thread and static and something like memory going the other way.

She lowered it again; it moved in her hand. Not wind — the hall was still; not gravity — the movement had reception in it, not fall. The scarf bunched itself, the two corners drawing together in a neat, small knot. Not a clumsy twist. A reef knot: right over left, left over right. Her hands knew it before she did. The very knot she had tied between bunks in a caravan when she was small enough to live in a cupboard and call it an adventure.

Left-right, breathed a voice, not through the hall, not through the monitor that was asleep at home, but through the thin place under her ear where the caravan wall had once rubbed.

Clara went very still. Priya's chatter continued like a radio in another room. Jonah attempted to eat a maraca. The circle sang *The Wheels on the Bus* with the moral fervour of people who did not accept that buses may have no place in a baby's day. The health visitor bopped bubbles with a controlled violence that implied training.

Clara looked at the knot in her hand. The reef knot sat there, prim, correct, definitely not a bow. Slowly, so as not to alarm anyone who had decided not to believe in unusual things today, she rested her fingers upon it. The fabric warmed under her touch, as fabric does when held. That was all. That was enough.

She untied it. The knot gave easily, no sulk. She shook the scarf out, spread it, and let it fall over the baby in a half–peek-a-boo the child found intellectually acceptable. The hall did not collapse. The radiator maintained its decent heat. Someone's toddler across the room said, very distinctly, "Woses," during *Ring a Roses,* and his mother failed to correct him because she was out of hands.

Clara exhaled in a way that did not entertain an audience. She let herself smile at the toddler. He saw her and grinned, delighted to be joined in the wrongness.

When the scarf cleared, the baby gazed left, past Clara, to the strip of wall between radiator and noticeboard. The exact place she had looked in Chapter Four. Her eyes narrowed in that way babies have when doing immediate algebra. Her mouth twitched as if about to rehearse laughter. Then she returned to the practical matter of a fist.

"Tea," Priya murmured after the closing song, because this was how you exit rooms, with warm liquids. "You okay?"

"I'm okay," Clara said, and to her surprise it was true. The knot lay in her hand memory like a cool coin you could spend or keep. "Bubble theology nearly defeated me."

"The bubble machine is a test," Priya said. "We must not idolise it; we must use it judiciously."

They went to the hatch and accepted weak tea as sacrament. The volunteer in a *Twin Mums Club* T-shirt smiled politely at everyone's babies and added biscuits like either apology or celebration. The room brightened itself back to ordinary.

On the noticeboard, beside the felt-tip balloons that wanted to be beans, someone had pinned a photograph of the summer fair again. Clara looked at the caravan in the background, the door a dark rectangle like a missing tooth. A rope hung from a post, knotted at plausible intervals. In the photo, the knot at the bottom had the precise, crisp look of a reef. She felt the small madness of wanting to press a finger to the gloss to feel the bump of the pencil line. Of course there would be no bump. She laughed under her breath at herself, the kind, private laugh that had practised not humiliating her.

"You're doing the face," Priya said gently.

"I'm doing the face," Clara admitted.

"Is it an okay face?"

"It's a *this is a lot but I am grown and bossy and have biscuits* face," Clara said.

"Excellent," Priya said, and stole her a second custard cream as if the universe required bribery to remain on its better behaviour.

***

On the way home, the day held. The sky increased its blue half a tone. The pram wheels purr–purr–purred. A bus went by and a boy in a dinosaur coat pressed his face to the window and waved as if continuing a conversation from another day. Ten fingers; this time, three, then two, then one, as if under instructions unknown to his mother, who checked her phone and frowned at the news.

"Friend of yours?" Priya said.

"Apparently."

They parted at the corner with the easy promise of future tea. Clara pushed the pram down her street and felt the quiet of houses during the working day — curtains at half-mast, bins waiting like bored companions, a cat convinced of its mysterious purpose.

At the front step she paused. The door, obedient, was closed. She unlocked it, pushed in, set the pram brake with her foot, lifted the baby out with the practised, reverent movement of anyone lifting the world. She could smell apples. She didn't mention it to herself out loud.

In the hall, something small and hard nudged the wheel of the pram. She looked down. A knot lay on the mat: a small, tidy reef tied in a strip of green fabric very like the scarf, but narrower, as if someone had torn a piece from a larger flag. She didn't touch it. She stared at it with the specific lack of expression you do when the present has arrived disguised as proof and you're not ready to be its witness.

"No moving things in the nursery," she said, voice even. "No water. Doctors allowed. If you want to leave something, you may leave it on the hall mat. That is the rule. This is the mat."

The air very nearly cooled. Or she let herself think it did. It was the kind of half-degree Harriet would have called *real-ish*, which is the only temperature some truths get.

She picked up the knot. It weighed what fabric weighs. She placed it on the little table in the hall where keys meant to be important sat waiting for promotion. She wrote in the notebook: *Hall: green strip with reef knot placed on mat. Baby group this morning: scarf tied itself (reef). Toddler said "woses" during song (coincidence?); caravan photo with rope in hall.* She wrote *BLUE* in the margin and underlined it, then crossed it out because it wasn't a boundary broken but a boundary tested. *GREY,* she wrote, and smiled despite herself. She put the strip in a drawer and shut the drawer and felt as if she had shouted quietly.

She texted Priya a picture of the knot with no context. Priya replied: *Who do I fight?* Then: *Come round. Or I come round. Or we both don't. I like all three.*

I'm okay, Clara wrote. *Grown. Bossy. Tea required.*
Tea is en route in spirit, Priya wrote. *In matter later.*

***

The day performed decency. Mark came home with strawberries that had to travel too far to be truly sweet and therefore required grace. He listened to the story of the scarf, the knot, the boy in the bus, the photograph rumour. He did not rush to fix or frame it, which was adult of him. He put his hand on the small of her back and said, "BLUE?" and Clara said, "GREY," and he accepted her invention without making her justify it.

They ate pasta that had aspirations above its class and applauded the baby for a burp of unusual musicality. After, Mark ran the bath in the baby's tray and narrated the procedure in his amiable manual voice: warm water, two fingers depth, towel warmed on radiator, boat not mandatory. The baby waved her legs in the way of a person who intended to be a swimmer or a magistrate — possibly both.

Clara stood in the doorway and felt fine. This was worth writing down between the strange. She went to the bathroom and looked at the mat; it told her nothing, responsibly. She looked at the plug: out. She looked at her face in the mirror and thought: mine.

Downstairs, her phone buzzed. HARU (PERINATAL) — the clinic address as a contact — had sent an appointment reminder. Monday, eleven. *We will meet you on the ferry.* The line felt like a person with her sense of humour had got hold of the text template. Clara wrote *Thank you* back and imagined the administrator who would understand what that meant.

At nine, when the room with the television had done its work as a temporary spell, Mark took the first shift again, because the ferry had found a rhythm in them. "Go," he said, shooing her to bed with the kind of authority that understood its limits.

Clara lay down with earplugs and the eye mask as if boarding. She wrote one line by phone light: *I held the scarf without becoming a lunatic.* She smiled at herself for the cruelty of the past tense and slept.

She woke to the feeling of being watched in the protective way — the sensation of having a coat placed over your shoulders by a person who approves of coats. She kept still and let the house declare itself: Mark's soft tread somewhere, the baby's breath a tidy metronome, the fridge singing its one line, the wind reminding the window of branches.

"Clara," the voice said, not through the house, not through the monitor that stayed respectfully asleep, but through the sensible place under her left ear where names arrive when they intend to be written down.

"I'm here," she said quietly, and stayed lying down, because standing made everything silly.

A pleased hum. Young. Familiar. Not kind, exactly; affectionate the way sisters are when they know they can be. "Good girl."

"Not a girl," she said, and felt the smile arrive by itself. "Grown."

A pause, the length of a little shrug. "Left-right."

"On my terms."

Silence, but not sulking. The sense of someone putting down something heavy and deciding to leave it for now. The faintest movement of air near her ankle, which her sensible mind called draft and her reckless one wanted to call attention.

"Doctors allowed," she said into the dark, stating the article of faith they had agreed.

A breath like a laugh, once. Then a soft, reluctant, "Bossy."

"Grown," she repeated, and the repetition did the work.

She fell asleep before the house had finished deciding what to think of her.

***

Morning — Friday now — unpacked itself gently. The baby woke with a singer's yawn. The sky admitted grey and promised quite reasonably to be rain later. Clara reached for the notebook and wrote: *Sensory achieved. Reef knot (hall & scarf). Toddler "woses". Boy on bus. Priya — witness. Rules held. Me: bossy + grown. Doctors allowed.* She underlined *witness* because the word seemed to like it there.

Mark brought tea and looked at her face like a man reading a forecast he had invested in. "Status?"

"Green," she said, then added, because she liked accuracy now, "with grey bits behaving."

He lifted his mug in a solemn toast. "To behaving grey."

She laughed, and a small, inconvenient gratitude rose and made her eyes prickle. She let it, because adults cry also, and then make lists afterwards.

"Today," she said, "I want ordinary. Laundry. Maybe the bin. Adult magic in the kitchen."

"Adult magic is scheduled," he said. "I have mending."

She went to the nursery and found the room exactly as it had promised to be: catch set, stars waiting, rabbit on watch, breath making faith easy. On the dresser the monitor sat with its pretty useless face, out of work and not sulking. She placed two fingers on the tiny chest, borrowed the metronome, and returned it with interest.

"Morning," she said to the world. "No water. No moving things in here. Doctors allowed. Witness permitted."

The room, pleased with its part, kept her secrets the way good rooms do — by not keeping all of them.

In the afternoon, Priya sent a voice note of Jonah shrieking at his own reflection and then demanded proof of Clara's toast. Clara sent a picture of the diagonal cut and received a sticker of a medal. Martha texted a heart and a cloud and *jumper fits?* Clara sent back a photograph of those small cloud buttons content in a drawer, because she was not ready to see them on a body yet, and Martha replied *right* and nothing else, which was perfect.

When she opened the hall drawer for a pen, the green strip with the reef knot waited where she had left it. She stared at it a moment, then lifted it and untied the knot and tied it again, her fingers remembering summer. She tied it wrong, deliberately, into a granny knot, and laughed because you had to amuse yourself in this life. She put the strip back and shut the drawer with a firmness that felt like grammar.

At five the witching hour tested them and found them reasonable. At seven, the casserole on the hob smelled like a childhood that could be eaten safely. At nine, the programme about the house extensions taught her new jargon and made her unreasonably angry with a man who had decided to remove a wall without asking a lintel's permission.

At ten, she checked the bath plug. Out. The mat: undisturbed. The window catch: two clicks. The rules: intact. The voice did not come through plaster or machine. The night, at least at this hour, belonged to the honest business of sleep.

She stood at the back door and looked at the garden. A fox went by like a thought with its own errands. She placed her palm against the cool glass and said, because she liked how it felt in her mouth, "Witness." She waited. Nothing wrote itself in condensation. It was a relief.

In bed, she wrote: *No incident. Ferry tomorrow (second night). Rules holding. Me: here.* She closed the notebook and slid it under the bed as if thoughts liked the cooler floor.

The red blink of the smoke alarm did its pious small light. The house settled its bones. The baby's breath inserted its ellipses into the paragraph of the night. Clara turned on to her side and let the room be a room and not a sign. She felt watched in the protective way and did not mind. She let it help.

When sleep came, she did not inspect it for wires. She boarded the ferry and left the platform without argument. The last thing she heard — or thought, or both — was a voice that had started to accept low lit boundaries.

"Left-right," it said, as if wishing luck.

"On my terms," she answered, already almost dreaming, and the boat, for once, did not feel too small.

Chapter Nine

Knots

C lara woke into a Saturday that had chosen steadiness. The sky was the colour of washing-up water when you've already done the plates; a soft, serviceable grey. She stayed still and let the room speak: the small tick of the clock, the boiler's low hum, the weary optimism of distant tyres on a damp road. She took up her notebook and wrote: *Woke steady. Rules: window (two clicks); boat on my terms; no moving things in nursery; no water; doctors allowed; witness permitted. Ferry night two tonight (M first shift).*

Mark surfaced beside her with one eye, an expression like a man negotiating fair terms with the day. "Status?"

"Green," she said. "With well-behaved grey."

"We'll take green." He kissed the top of her head. "Captain reporting for duty this evening."

On the landing the baby issued an inquisitive squeak. The nursery smelt of warm cotton and the small sweet animal of sleep. The window catch sat down and correct: two clicks. She didn't check it. She checked it.

"Good morning," she said, laying two fingers on the tiny chest and borrowing the metronome. Rise, fall. Her own breath fell into step like someone joining late and pretending they hadn't.

On the dresser the monitor sat dark and blameless. The night had not punished silence. She placed her palm a breath above it, ridiculous and fond.

***

They made the morning out of toast and reason. Mark put a load on with the purposeful solemnity of a man entering a small contract with a washing machine. He folded yesterday's towels with such devotion they forgave him for everything. He stuck the *BLUE = rules* star back down where it had begun to peel, then tapped *Leaflet people can queue* like a man saluting a flag.

"Do you fancy the market?" he asked. "If we get out before the real people do."

"Let's be counterfeit people," she said. "I'll wear the coat that makes me look like I've made decisions."

The pavement had dried to a dull honesty. They pushed the pram under a sky holding back rain like a polite cough. The market did what markets do: smelt of onions and comfort and hot things pretending to be lunches. A woman sold bread that was more suggestion than loaf. A man with a scarf he'd chosen on purpose offered winter apples with scars and good manners.

"Do you smell—" Mark began, then stopped, embarrassed by noticing.

"Apples," Clara said. She smiled. "Yes."

He looked relieved to have his nose backed up. "They're everywhere. I should have guessed."

"Local ghosts," she said lightly. "Support independent greengrocers."

He bought a bag purely to have bought it. The stall-holder pressed in a small knobbly extra with conspiratorial kindness. "For the little one," he said, as if the baby ate apples on weekends and wrote the reviews on Monday.

They turned down the lane that cut behind the hall. A bus grumbled past. Pressed to the window was the boy in the dinosaur coat; he had become a recurring character. He saw them, brightened, pressed both hands to the glass in an ecstatic smear and then flashed fingers at her: three, then two, then one, then a proud zero, as if finishing a countdown only he could hear.

"Friend," Mark said, amused.

"An accomplice," Clara said.

The church noticeboard still held the photo of the summer fair. Rope hung from the post; her eyes sought it without permission. She didn't go closer. She didn't need to.

Back home, the house did the decent thing of being ordinary. The baby held a conference with her own tongue and came away impressed. Mark emailed as if it were a solvable puzzle. Clara washed mugs and drew two columns on a fresh page because meaning had to be earned. *EVIDENCE* on the left, *INTERPRETATIONS* on the right. She wrote: *Market: apple smell (shared). Dinosaur boy (countdown). Mood steady.* Opposite, she wrote: *Benign witness. Ordinary day = evidence too.*

She added to *RULES/AGREEMENTS*: *Friends allowed.* She underlined *allowed.* It pleased her to make permissions as well as prohibitions.

Around midday, Martha texted a photo of a pan of stew with the caption *Boring but useful.* Then: *Fancy seeing a boring useful person this afternoon?* There was a heart and, beneath it, a cloud — her own language for the blue jumper.

Clara looked towards Mark. "Martha?"

"Let's," he said. "We'll bring market apples and adult conversation."

***

Martha's house had the smell of an old place that has kept its promises to more than one generation. She opened the door with her hair done like a plan and kissed the baby with the firm accuracy grandmothers have. "Come in," she said, as if into a club. "I've warmed the good room."

The "good room" had in it a low table and a pile of coasters and the kind of radio that knows its job. There was no blue jug; there never would be again. The absence had acquired a tact.

Clara put the apples on the sideboard. "For you."

"Lovely," Martha said, and because subtext was a language both of them spoke, added, "We'll stew them. Nothing dramatic." She took the baby and did the walk people do when their arms are happy. "You look better."

"I slept," Clara said. "We're on ferry nights. Harriet approves."

"Good woman." Martha touched the baby's toes and then, in the direction of both of them, "Good women."

They ate stew with bread that had delusions of grandeur, and the baby supervised from the bouncer with an air of benevolent regulation. Mark and Martha tried not to compare recipes and failed politely.

After, Martha fetched a small box from a shelf. It was sensible, wooden, and entirely unromantic. "Photos," she said. "I thought you might want to borrow some. Caravan summer. Your father took too many."

Clara held the lid as if it might change its mind. "Thank you."

They looked through together. A field that couldn't decide between Cornwall and Heaven. The caravan: cream sides, green stripe, door open just enough to see the dark within. Her mother on the step, peeling apples with concentration. Herself, gap-toothed, hair plaited badly, making a face as if being seven meant having enemies. Rope between bunk and bunks — a ridiculous rig designed by imagination and uninspected by health and safety. Knots at intervals. Not bows. Knots with intent.

"Dad showed us," Clara said, her voice doing that quiet thing it did when a memory sat on it. "Right over left, left over right. Reef. He said reef was fast and honest. I liked bowlines but he said those were for men who wanted to look clever."

Martha laughed, genuine. "He would. He liked an honest knot."

Clara traced a fingertip over the rope in the photograph knowing she would feel only gloss. "Do you remember the song?"

"I remember *you* singing," Martha said. "I remember thinking the boat was too small and deciding to forgive the lyrics."

The clock on the mantle gave itself away. The radio, which had been doing a voice about weather, marched into the news as if to prove it could. The baby made the small grunting notification that meant a change of management would be required shortly.

Clara slid a few photos aside and paused. There, at the edge of one frame, looking out of the caravan's window — a child's face in reflection more than presence, the way glass keeps copies — two heads almost aligned, one a fraction behind, same bones, same mouth, eyes set half a degree wider. Not proof; not theatre. A familiar trick of gloss and angle and longing. She smiled, privately, because longing done honestly didn't deserve to be punished.

Martha watched her watch. "What?" she asked, neutral.

"Nothing," Clara said. Then, more honest: "Everything."

Martha nodded as if given the answer on a page. "I meant to ask," she said carefully, "how is *she*?"

Clara looked up. "Present," she said. "Obedient—to the rules. Mostly."

"Mostly is human," Martha said. She did not ask for particulars. She did not ask for proof. She did not say the words *grief* or *hormones* or *phase*. She sat with her hands folded like a person who had decided to be furniture a while so you could lean.

Clara found, to her surprise, that she could be grateful without having to perform gratitude to be believed. She put the photos back and lifted the box as if taking custody of a sensible dog. "We'll borrow these," she said. "We'll return them in good order."

"Take them," Martha said. "Keep them if you like. I've got them in my head."

On the way out, in the hall, the baby sneezed in the precise way babies sneeze when being filmed; nobody was filming. Martha laughed. Then she sniffed. "Do you smell...?"

"Apples," Clara and Mark said together, too quickly, and then all three of them laughed, and the house, which had its own opinions, allowed it.

***

Back home, grey tried to be light and nearly achieved it. Mark put the kettle on, because that is how you set down boxes without making a fuss. Clara carried the photo box to the table like a reliquary and then told herself off for being dramatic.

She opened the drawer for a pen. The green strip lay where she had left it. The knot she had tied wrong smiled a little idiot grin back at her.

She untied it and tied a reef with firm hands, right over left, left over right. She told the air, mildly, "Knots on the hall mat only." She added it to *RULES/AGREEMENTS* in capital letters: *KNOTS ON HALL MAT ONLY*. She drew a small star.

Mark appeared with two mugs. "Amendments?"

"Codicil," she said, and read the rule aloud, and he nodded as if to say *passed*.

They ate apples cut into quarters with the solemn happiness apples deserve. The baby watched and drooled an opinion.

Evening put itself together without demanding applause. The witching hour arrived on cue and behaved itself with dignity. The baby forgave everyone. The oven made noises that sounded like food being useful. They watched a programme in which a man insisted a wall was not load-bearing and was confronted by physics. Clara felt soothed by the arrogance of strangers.

At ten, Mark gathered ferry equipment with ceremony: earplugs presented, eye mask aligned, water glass topped, phone on silent except for the one number that would not be. He kissed her, brief and practical.

"I've got first five," he said. "BLUE for rules, RED for rescue."

"Friends allowed," she said, because she liked saying it, and he grinned and saluted the fridge notes.

Clara lay down, did the eye mask, did the earplugs, boarded her imaginary white-lined ferry with practised grace. She slept quickly and without interrogation.

She woke at one-thirty-two to the feeling of a room that wanted her attention in the kind way.

She slid the mask up, removed the earplugs. The world returned, soft-edged. Downstairs there was the not-quite-silver of a lamp on low; Mark had found the exact wattage for gentleness. The house was a creature breathing. She sat up and listened and made the useful internal question: *Is it rules or rescue?*

No water. No voice. No sudden cold.

She stood anyway, because sometimes you got up to show fear you weren't at its mercy. On the landing a small draught that had lived there longer than any of them met her shins and made a case for old houses. She looked in at the nursery because *look in at the nursery* had become its own phrase. The window catch sat two-click smug. The rabbit stood its watch. The paper stars hung up their opinions. The baby breathed with confident punctuation.

On the landing, the new stair gate that Mark had finally installed yesterday — after three weeks of sighing at the idea of it — stood shut and tidy. Across the top rung, binding the latch to the banister, a neat length of green fabric knotted into something a person who knew names would call a bowline. Safe, quick-release if you understood it; if you didn't, it would hold better than you deserved.

Clara did not startle. She stood and looked at the knot like a person looking at a sentence they had forgotten they could read. She put a fingertip under the loop, felt the clean logic of it. *The rabbit comes out of the hole, runs round the tree, goes back down the hole.* She heard her father say it and, in the same space, heard a girl laugh.

"Knots on the hall mat only," she said, clearly, not cross.

Silence. Then — because the house had learnt to humour — a small cooling of air on her wrist, not unfriendly. She read it as *understood* because that made her kinder.

She undid the bowline in one clean pull and put the strip in her dressing-gown pocket. She opened the gate and closed it again. She stood there longer than anyone would call reasonable and borrowed the metronome from the other room the way you can borrow courage.

Downstairs, Mark looked up from the book he didn't like but was reading as a sacrifice to sleep's gods. "Everything...?"

"BLUE-ish," she said. She took the green strip from her pocket and laid it on the hall table, and watched her own hand be steady. "Boundary test. Elegant knot. Stair gate."

He didn't swear, which she loved him for. He put the book down with the kind of care you use for live things. "Bowline?"

"Bowline," she said, and it broke something in both of them in a way that let something else in.

"Rule," he said, gently but with a touched steel. "Knots on the hall mat only."

"Added," she said. "No ties on gates or things with hinges. No ties where a person could be caught."

He nodded. "No ties on the pram, either."

"Thank you," she said. She put the strip on the hall mat with deliberate ceremony. "Here," she told the air. "Allowed here, if you must."

The air stayed air. The house behaved like furniture. They both stood there feeling a small, mutual ache for how ridiculous brave looked.

Mark lifted his phone and typed *BLUE* to himself and then to Clara because the act of sending made the colour more real. "Documented," he said.

She smiled, small and tired and grateful. "I'm going back to the ferry."

"Captain's orders," he said, and kissed her, and she went.

She slept. This was already more than she had promised herself in June.

***

Morning left a pale slice of light on the curtain, as if day had written to say *I will be late but I am coming.* Mark brought tea and looked at her the way people look at weather forecasts that will decide their mood.

"Status?" he asked.

"Green," she said, surprised and pleased to find it true. "BLUE last night, but steady."

"Noted." He sat on the edge of the bed. "About the knot—"

"Mat only," she said. "We were clear."

He smiled. "We were."

On the landing, the baby provided the daily brief: a squeak, a sigh, the throat-clearing of someone who has plans for the morning. The nursery had that specific good-room feeling that rooms have when they've kept their half of the bargain. Catch: two clicks. Rabbit: guard. Stars: still. Breath: innocent.

Clara put two fingers on the small chest and borrowed the metronome. "Morning," she said, to the baby, the house, the version of herself who had been taught to keep rules and found they kept her back. "No moving things in here. No water. Knots on the hall mat only. Doctors allowed. Friends allowed. Witness permitted."

She went downstairs and opened her notebook and wrote in the left-hand column under *EVIDENCE*: *Stair gate tied (bowline) 01:32. Undid. Strip placed on mat. Mark witness after the fact. Nursery untouched.* On the right, under *INTERPRETATIONS*: *Safety impulse + boundary push. Not menace; control. Continue rules.* Under *RULES*, she added: *No ties on gates/pram/hinges; knots allowed: hall mat only.* She drew a neat box around it because neat boxes are adult magic.

Her phone buzzed. Priya: *Survived night?*

Yes, Clara typed. *A bowline had opinions. I had bigger opinions.*

You are my favourite boat, Priya replied. *Tea later?*

Tea always, Clara wrote, and felt the muscle of her mouth learn a new, less frightened shape.

She set the green strip on the mat, tidy, deliberate, a place set for a guest who had been told where to sit. She breathed in and smelt, faintly, clean apple and the dust that makes houses honest.

When Mark came in from taking the recycling out (adult magic of the cold kind), he paused and sniffed. "Apples," he said, puzzled, pleased.

"We're very fashionable," she said.

He put a hand at the small of her back and left it there the proper amount of time. "Monday," he said softly. "We tell Harriet about the bowline."

"We will," she said. "She will write *no knots except on hall mat* and underline it, and then prescribe biscuits."

He laughed. "Excellent medicine."

Clara looked down at the strip on the mat and decided that, for today at least, she did not need more proof than a knot tied neatly where the rules allowed it. She picked up an apple from the market bag, cut it in quarters with the knife that had learnt to be patient, and ate a slice. It tasted of childhood and now, which is what she had been aiming for all along.

In the cool steam on the kitchen window five petal-shapes arranged themselves, then thinned back into nothing. She lifted her palm and didn't lay it there. She let the glass keep its own memory for once.

"Ferry night two: completed," she wrote at the bottom of the page, and underlined *completed* because completion itself felt like a kind of prayer.

The day set about being ordinary with an eagerness that made her forgive it. Upstairs, her daughter practised smiling in her sleep. Somewhere in the walls a pipe cleared its throat and chose not to develop a personality. On the hall mat, a knot behaved.

Clara went to make tea, bossy and grown, and the house — relieved and complicit — kept her secrets, which is to say it allowed her to share them on her own terms.

Chapter Ten
Witness

Clara woke into a Sunday that had ironed itself sensible. The light through the curtains was the grey of a shirt that had done its best. She stayed very still and let the house say its name — boiler's low hum, fridge's one note, tyres on damp tarmac making commas. She took the notebook, wrote: *Woke steady. Rules: window (two clicks); boat on my terms; no moving things in nursery; no water; knots on hall mat only; doctors allowed; friends allowed; witness permitted. Today: quiet + ordinary. Tomorrow: Harriet 11. Aim: arrive with floor under feet.*

Mark opened one eye like a man greeting a shy animal. "Status?"

"Green," she said. "Grey behaving."

"We'll take green." He kissed her hair and got up with the politeness of a man asking the morning for a dance.

On the landing, the baby made the social squeak of a citizen filing an early report. The nursery smelt of warm cotton and that newly minted sweetness babies issue as proof of policy. The window catch sat down and proper: two clicks. She didn't check it. She checked it.

"Morning," she whispered, laying two fingers on the tiny chest to borrow the metronome. Rise, fall. Her own lungs remembered their paperwork and complied. The rabbit stood its silly watch. The paper stars were obedient. On the dresser, the monitor sat dark and pious, off as doctrine. The night had not punished anyone for silence.

"Thank you," she told no one, and let herself mean it.

***

They made breakfast out of toast and decency. Mark folded a tea towel with the reverence of a person negotiating with laundry. He aligned the mugs in an approving row and straightened the *BLUE = rules* star-shaped note as if you could square a colour. Beneath it, Harriet's scrap — *Leaflet people can queue* — had become ridiculous and necessary, a sort of house blessing.

"Car boot at the school?" Mark said, buttering with gravitas. "We can buy tat we don't need and see actual humans."

Clara smiled. "I'll wear the coat that makes me look like I've got a pension."

"The baby can wear the lemon. Public morale depends on it."

They packed the bag as if preparing for a modest expedition. Nappies, wipes, muslin, spare vest, snacks for adults who denied needing snacks. She added the notebook because truth liked a pocket. The sky outside had pulled its grey up neat. The pavement smelt of last night's rain remembering itself.

On the corner, chalk arrows from last weekend's street play still pointed towards nowhere. A cat looked at them and chose to disagree. The pram wheels made their rrr-rrr like a creature purring.

At the school gate the PTA had arranged tables into a doctrine of bargains. An elderly man in a wax jacket rotated a crate of ropes and bungee cords and produced, with showman's delight, a board with knots tied in fat off-white line. *REEF, BOWLINE, CLOVE HITCH*, written underneath in biro that had soldiered through damp.

"Choice knots!" he announced to no one in particular and to them. "Honest knots."

Mark, helpless, drifted closer as if pulled by a tide of childhood Scouts. Clara stood and did not touch the board. Her hands knew every shape anyway, the way muscle does.

"Favourite?" the man asked her.

"Reef," she said, and couldn't help herself. "Fast and honest."

"Smart girl," he said, and her mouth moved before her dignity could.

"Grown," she corrected, softly. The man didn't hear. Someone's baby cried. The man demonstrated a bowline, the rabbit visiting its hole as if by right. Mark bought a short length of braided rope because it felt, faintly, like control.

They came away with a book about hedgerow birds, a wooden rattle that had once been painted with good intentions, and a punnet of strawberries that would require charity. "Adults allowed," Clara wrote in her head, and was pleased with the permission.

On the walk home a bus went by and, as if Sunday had decided to keep its cast, the boy in the dinosaur coat pressed his face to the glass, spotted them, and performed an elaborate series with his fingers: one, two, three, two, one, zero. He mouthed something that could have been "Ready." The condensation stole it as soon as he made it.

"Your accomplice," Mark said.

"He's doing a countdown," Clara said, and raised her eyebrows at the universe for being theatrical.

Back home, the house behaved. The baby practised vowels as if teaching them manners. Mark answered an email about something that mattered to someone with a careful kindness he would never call kindness. Clara tidied a drawer that didn't need it and found, at the back, a pencil with no rubber that made her want school. She wrote two columns like prayer. EVIDENCE: car boot; knot board; dinosaur boy (countdown); mood steady. INTERPRETATIONS: ordinary day is still a day; witness is not always a person; superstition wants a job.

RULES/AGREEMENTS: as before. She drew a small box round *witness permitted* because boxes make thoughts stand in line.

Around noon Martha texted a photograph of a cake that looked bored and therefore reliable. *Come for tea?* there was a cloud and a heart and nothing more, which was code for *no drama*.

They went, because refusing cake on a Sunday is grounded in poor theology.

***

Martha's sitting room had remembered the shape of winter and decided to keep it. She placed the baby on a blanket knitted in a colour that had been fashionable a decade ago and looked very pleased with its survival. The radio managed a poem about the sea and then a gentle lecture about fog.

"You look softer," Martha said, pouring tea with a steadiness that made the cups feel safe. "Not fewer edges. Cleverer edges."

"Harriet is a good carpenter," Clara said.

"Always helps when the doctor builds furniture." Martha sliced cake with the precision of someone who would be gauged if she weren't careful. "How's the house?"

"Obedient," Clara said. "Mostly."

"That's all any of us can claim." Martha put a saucer in front of Clara as if granting a licence. "And how is *she?*"

Clara looked at the baby before she answered, as if remembering contracts. "Present," she said. "Rules observed. We negotiated knots."

Martha's mouth warmed. "Women negotiating with the dead," she said lightly. "A British pastime."

They ate cake with the calm concentration that makes cake worth eating. The baby yawned with the seriousness of a tiny opera singer. Mark went to put the kettle on again because kettle-on made confused men feel they were useful.

When he'd gone, Martha said, without ceremony, "I thought about the hospital last night." She didn't look at Clara when she said it. "The word *viable* is worse in the mouth than on paper."

Clara nodded. "I wrote *viable* in the book. Writing turns fog into furniture."

Martha smiled at the phrase, the kind of smile that admits a small defeat to pleasure. "Good." She reached for her own cup and then paused. "Do you smell...?"

"Apples," Clara said, too quick, and they both laughed because the joke had begun to have muscles.

"She is not a smell," Martha said, not unkindly.

"No. She is herself. And also a smell when it's tidy." Clara heard her voice turn careful. "She— left a knot yesterday. On the mat. We have rules."

Martha took this in the way you take a folded napkin and lay it, correct, on your lap. "Good," she said. "Rules and cake."

When they left, Martha stood in the doorway and kissed them all, and when the door closed Clara said to the air of the front step, "Doctors allowed. Grandmothers allowed. Knots on the mat only." There was the faintest suggestion of cool against her wrist. She smiled because she disliked being pandered to, even by grief.

The afternoon declined to be remarkable. This in itself felt like kindness. Mark read a chapter of the hedgerow birds aloud to the baby in a voice that made every wren sound like an intelligent aunt. The baby frowned at the pictures as if she would take a meeting with the robin later and discuss his red. Clara put a wash on and felt absurdly proud of pegging things straight. She wrote: *Ordinary: proof of floor.* She underlined *floor* and the underlining made the word heavier in a useful way.

At four-thirty the doorbell rang twice in that *I'm a neighbour, not a salesman* rhythm. A woman stood there in leggings, ponytail, the kind of sweatshirt you grab when you are cross. She held a baby monitor base unit and the expression of someone who has chosen to be reasonable.

"Sorry," she said. "I'm Lynn. Next door but one. We haven't met properly—we moved in June. Are you... have you got your monitor on at the moment?"

"No," Clara said, immediately aware of the doctrinal naughtiness of turning it on. "We don't have it on much. Why?"

Lynn shifted the unit in her hands as if it were evidence she didn't want to weaponise. "This is going to sound odd. We keep getting—well, we get singing. Through ours. Not radio. A lullaby? Same one? The last few nights. And today at nap time. It's... someone did *left-right* for ages. It calmed him right down." She gave a small helpless laugh. "My partner says interference, taxi radios, but— we don't live near taxis."

Clara felt the smile arrive and behave. "We don't," she agreed.

"I thought perhaps your frequency—" Lynn held out the unit, not as accusation, as if asking it to identify itself. "Do you mind if we...? Just to see if they're friends."

"Of course," Clara said, and felt Mark appear at her shoulder in that quiet way as if conjured. He shook Lynn's hand, put his good face on.

In the kitchen, Lynn set her base on the table beside the dark, obedient rectangle of theirs. Two small plastic altars. Everyone looked as if expecting a rabbit to appear. Nothing did.

"I'm not mad," Lynn said, gently defiant. "I know what I heard."

"I believe you," Clara said, before she could think better of it. The relief that washed over the other woman was indecently moving. "We hear it, sometimes. *Left-right.* The boat. It isn't... it isn't a danger."

"Good," Lynn said. She let out a breath like a bag hung back on a hook. "I thought— I thought I was being ridiculous."

"You're being alive," Clara said. "We're seeing someone. She's sensible. She says we can have rules. We're... finding we can."

Lynn laughed, a proper unembarrassed laugh. "Rules for...?"

"For grief," Clara said. And then, because the truth reached a hand for her and she wanted to take it, "For my twin."

Lynn's face did something complicated and kind. "Right," she said. "That feels true when you say it."

They stood beside the harmless machines until standing became its own performance. Lynn picked up her unit as if it had weight and not weight. "If you ever get— if you hear *left-right* in the afternoon, it's probably me," she said, and made a face. "I don't know if that helps."

"It does," Clara said, and meant it in a way that surprised her.

After she'd gone, Mark let out a breath that was half a laugh and half a weather report. "External witness," he said. "Not invited."

"Witness permitted," Clara said, and wrote it in the book before the thought could get shy.

***

Tea. Biscuits. Bath in the baby's tray narrated with the usual gravitas. "Water is allowed in trays," Mark intoned. "No freelancing in grown-up baths."

"No water," Clara told the ceiling, and trusted the ceiling to pass it on. The ceiling, well brought up, did not answer back.

After, the baby forgave everyone and went to sleep with the satisfaction of a person who has won an argument about milk. They ate on the sofa and watched a programme where a woman discovered her foundations were untrustworthy and did not cry on camera. Clara felt for the lintel again and forgave herself for the pettiness of wanting a beam to hold.

At nine, she went upstairs to look at the nursery because looking had become devotion. Catch: two clicks. Rabbit: doing his tour. Stars: well-behaved. Breath: tidy. She put two fingers on the tiny chest and took the metronome like a library book. "No moving things in here," she said to the room as you say grace when no one is watching. She shut the door the width of a word and went down with the quiet satisfaction of a person who has obeyed herself.

They decided, in a fit of bravery sanctioned by Harriet, not to do a ferry night. "Two nights on, one off," Mark said. "I believe in rotas." He tidied the bottles anyway because tidying is a prayer men perform when unsure.

They were both almost asleep when the voice came, and the shape of the coming was the difference.

It didn't curl out of plaster. It didn't find the thin place under Clara's ear alone. It came through the sensible air of the corridor, the same way soup smells and arguments do, and it was pitched low because the baby slept.

"Clara."

Clara sat up. Beside her, Mark did too, at exactly the same speed, as if called to a meeting where his name had been on the agenda.

He looked at her, eyes dark in the half-light. She didn't say *did you*— because she didn't have to.

"I heard," he said, very quietly. "That was— that was a person."

The voice, if it cared about definitions, didn't show it. It hovered at the edge of the door the way a teenager does when being clever about not entering a room they've been told not to enter.

"Clara," it said again, and — almost a sigh — "Mark."

The sound of his name out of that air made something inside him both reach and brace. He stood, not foolishly brave, just the brave of a man whose job had been to carry heavy things up stairs and say the right words in the hallway. He didn't go closer. He waited at the foot of the bed and lifted his chin the way you do to unthreaten dogs.

"Doctors are allowed," Clara said into the dark, into the space that had learned them both. "Rules are allowed. No water. No moving things in the nursery. Knots: hall mat only."

A pause — not sulky, thinking. Then, with affectionate impatience: "Bossy."

"Grown," she said, and was surprised by the steadiness of her own voice.

Mark swallowed. "We're not enemies," he said, to the edge of the door, to the person who had used his name as if it were a thing she could pick up and put down. "We're on the same side."

A tiny, amused breath that Clara recognised so well she could have drawn it. "Keep her safe," the voice said. It didn't specify which *her*. That felt like a kindness and an insult.

"Yes," Clara said. "With me."

"And me," Mark said.

The room altered by half a degree, the way rooms do when someone leaves without making a fuss. The corner resumed being a corner. The door regained its ordinary edge.

Mark put a hand on the bedpost like a man negotiating with wood. He sat down slowly. He looked at Clara. He laughed once, quietly, and then, because the alternative was a kind of crying neither of them had time for, he said, "Right."

"Right," she said back.

"Is it BLUE," he asked after a second, soldiering on with their language because language was a thin bridge that usually held, "or is it something else?"

"Neither," Clara said, and found herself smiling. "It's *witness*. You heard her."

He nodded, the motion neat, concise, grateful. "I did."

They lay down again in the dark of the room that had become, despite itself, a place that knew how to listen. Mark's hand found hers and didn't make a point of it. The house adjusted its bones politely.

Clara put her mouth near his ear and said, so quietly it was almost a thought, "Thank you."

"For what?" he murmured.

"For hearing," she said. "For being on the same side."

He squeezed her hand. "Always."

She reached under the bed for the notebook because discipline is romance. She wrote, by phone light: *22:58 — voice in corridor. Said my name; said 'Mark'. Both heard. Rule restated: doctors allowed; no water; no moving things in nursery; knots: mat only. Voice: 'bossy'; 'keep her safe'. Us: yes. Me: not alone.* She put three ticks next to *witness permitted*. She drew a small boat and didn't feel ridiculous.

She slid the notebook back and let sleep climb up the bed and sit on her chest the way cats do when they've forgiven you. The last thing she heard — or felt — was the lightest exhale from the doorway, as if someone had put a coat over both of them and approved of the colour.

Morning breached the curtain politely. The baby stretched like someone remembering dance. The window was a thin, honest cold under her palm. The catch clicked its two-part promise. The rabbit kept its stupid faith. The paper stars were only paper and decoration and the sort of magic that is allowed on Sundays.

Clara stood in the doorway of the nursery and spoke the rules as if reading from a book. "No moving things in here. No water. Knots on the hall mat only. Doctors allowed. Friends allowed. Witness permitted."

From the hall came Mark's voice, ordinary, cheerful, domestic. "Toast?"

"Diagonal," she called back.

She lifted the baby and smelt the warm biscuit of her scalp and knew, as much as anyone gets to know anything, that tomorrow she could take this into the room with Harriet and they would start where you start when you're building a floor— with the least romantic tools, with names, with *witness*, with rules.

On the kitchen window five small petals arranged themselves in the steam, then thinned at their own pace. Clara didn't race them. She put her hand there a second late and accepted the cold.

"On my terms," she said, which had become prayer and joke and boundary in one.

The house, content with its part, kept her secrets correctly: by letting them be told when she chose.

Chapter Eleven

Second Floor

Clara woke into a Monday that had the decency to be grey. The light behind the curtains was the colour of sensible paper; it didn't promise anything it couldn't keep. She lay still and let the house enumerate itself — boiler's low hum; the fridge holding its one true note; a van on wet tarmac writing commas on the morning.

She took the notebook and wrote: *Woke steady. Harriet 11. Rules unchanged: window (two clicks); boat on my terms; no moving things in nursery; no water; knots on hall mat only; doctors allowed; friends allowed; witness permitted.* She underlined *witness* and the underlining made the word behave.

Mark turned over and blinked like a man negotiating with weather. "Status?"

"Green," she said. "Grey cooperating."

"We'll take cooperating." He kissed the top of her head. "I'll be downstairs. Coffee and a sermon for the mugs."

From the nursery came the small, interrogative squeak of a citizen who had slept honestly and felt good about it. The room smelt of warm cotton and the faint sweetness new babies smuggle home. The window catch sat down and proper: two clicks. She didn't check it. She checked it.

"Good morning," she said to the baby. Two fingers on a small chest; rise, fall. She returned the metronome to its owner like a decent library user.

On the dresser the monitor sat dark and well-behaved. She touched the air above it with her palm. "Good," she told the room. "Thank you."

***

By ten, the baby had eaten her opinion of milk, Mark had packed an overnight bag for the possibility of nothing, and Clara had chosen the jumper that made her look like she could write down earthquakes without trembling. They drove the sensible route; the sky had shaved but not washed. The pram lay in the boot like a folded argument. Mark kept both hands on the wheel as if the car needed reassurance.

"Do we tell Harriet about the corridor?" he asked, not to decide, just to align.

"Yes," Clara said. "And Lynn." She looked out at the ring road in its queue of obedience. "Especially Lynn."

He nodded. A bus huffed past; for once the boy in the dinosaur coat didn't wave. A different child pressed hands to glass and made a face like being alive. Clara waved anyway, to practice.

The clinic smelt of oranges and lemon wipes and a certain bookish calm. Reception did the ritual with the bowl of pens and the plant trying its best. The clock moved without showing off. At three minutes to, the door opened with a meaningful softness and Dr Harriet Vale said, "Clara?" as if summoning a room.

"Hello," Clara said, and heard herself sound like someone who had slept.

"Come through," Harriet said. "I've reset the ferry."

The office had the same courteous furniture: two chairs that matched only in intention, tissues that knew their job, the white-noise machine muttering its proper nonsense. On the desk, a paperweight shaped like a boat refused to wink.

"Door?" Harriet asked.

"Closed."

They sat. Harriet rested the clipboard on her knee but didn't lift the pen yet. "What changed since Monday?"

"Witness," Clara said. "Plural."

Harriet's face did that small, approving neutrality. "Tell me."

"The corridor. Last night." Clara felt her throat consider being unhelpful and decided not to indulge it. "The voice said my name. Then said Mark's. We both heard. He said 'we're on the same side' and — this is absurd, but true — it agreed with a sort of amused breath. It asked us to keep 'her' safe and didn't specify which 'her' which felt like a kindness and an insult. Mark heard it. He didn't flinch."

Harriet's eyes warmed without performing sympathy. "Good. And the neighbour?"

"Lynn." Clara's hands were calm in her lap, which felt like borrowed sophistication. "She came with her base unit. She's heard *left–right* through her monitor the last few days. It soothes her son. She thought taxis. We informed her of our local taxi shortage. We… didn't try to convince her of anything. She believed herself. That was new."

Harriet lifted the pen then and wrote something fast and private. "External witness," she said. "Not solicited. That matters."

Clara exhaled. "I didn't think you'd say that."

"I am the floor," Harriet said, gently crisp. "Not the leaflet police. Two witnesses who don't share a delusion strain a leaflet."

Clara laughed, surprised by the relief and by the image of an officious pamphlet being stretched. "Good."

"Sleep?" Harriet asked, businesslike again.

"Ferry working. One BLUE in the week. Water in the big bath. Plug in. Three fingers from overflow. I stated 'no water'; it stopped. Print on the mat — half of one — I chose to erase it. Another night, a bowline on the stair gate. I made a codicil: knots only on the hall mat. That... worked."

Harriet's mouth flickered; a smile that didn't risk the subject. "You're running a very civil parish council," she said. "I approve." She tapped the pen once, a metronome. "I'd like to add a rule."

"Please."

"No requests to you as commands," Harriet said. "If the voice asks you to do something for her safety that risks yours or the baby's, you do not comply. You reply: 'I have heard you. I will consider it with my rules.' The wording matters. It honours the witness without ceding control."

Clara repeated it until the rhythm sat in her mouth. "I have heard you. I will consider it with my rules."

"Good." Harriet made a note under a column Clara imagined was titled MEANING. "Now. Lynn's unit. Would you be willing to do a controlled test? Borrow hers for a morning; leave your monitor off; write down precisely what is heard, by whom, and when. No recordings tonight. We start boring."

"Boring saves lives," Clara said.

"It does," Harriet said, and then, with a glint of humour, "and marriages."

They both smiled.

"Anything else make your stomach drop?" Harriet asked, the kind of invitation that makes the truth easier to wear.

"The knot at the church hall," Clara said. "A scarf tied itself. It was a reef; it untied easily when I asked. That felt like a conversation."

"Consent," Harriet said, approving. "We like consent."

They sat in the good, practical silence people make when they're trying to live in the world and in a stranger one at once. Harriet shifted papers into a tidy pile.

"I'm going to ask something slightly annoying," she said. "Would Mark join us for the last ten minutes?"

"Yes," Clara said immediately, and then felt the echo of *always* in the bones of the word.

***

Mark came in with the careful face he put on for other people's rooms. He watched the chairs for a second, made the decision to take the one on the angle (not the power seat), and smiled in that tilting way that had made Clara agree to a second date.

"Hello, Mark," Harriet said. "I hear you've been promoted to witness."

He laughed once, short, and nodded. "I heard a voice say my name," he said, sparing them both the preamble. "It wasn't in my head. And I don't think it was in hers."

"Thank you," Harriet said. "How do you feel?"

"Oddly... calmed?" He frowned at the confession. "It's easier to be on the same side of a thing that's real, whatever it is."

Harriet looked between them, weighing the room like a good carpenter checks where the weight falls. "Here's my proposal," she said. "You continue the ferry twice a week. You keep BLUE/RED. You add today's rule — 'requests are not commands'. You perform one controlled monitor test with Lynn's unit. If anything commands you, Clara, you text RED and you do nothing until you're not alone. You both document like civil servants. Everyone laughs at themselves once a day on purpose."

Mark nodded, mouth crooked. "We can laugh on rota."

"Excellent," Harriet said. "Last thing. I want you to add one permission to your fridge." She looked at Clara. "What's the permission you won't grant yourself?"

Clara knew and hated that she knew. "To enjoy the baby without looking over her shoulder," she said. The truth pricked; it was supposed to. "To stop checking the catch and check the baby."

"Write it," Harriet said. "Stick it above *Leaflet people can queue* so it has seniority."

Clara swallowed, nodded. "Yes."

Harriet stood in the way that lets other people stand first. "Same time next Monday. Bring me boring notes and one good joke. If a wall falls down, we'll mend it. If nothing falls down, we'll eat biscuits."

Mark grinned. "Yes, doctor."

"I'm not the police," Harriet said, tolerant. "I'm the floor."

The café downstairs did almond croissants that wanted forgiveness. They sat with paper cups and croissant flakes like confetti on offences already pardoned.

"Second floor," Mark said, irreverent. "How do we feel?"

"Grown," Clara said. "Bossy. Permitted to be happy for thirty seconds in a row."

"Ambitious," he said. "Let's try for forty five."

Her phone buzzed. *Lynn: Are you back? If you want the base unit for the boring test, I'm in all day.*
Yes please, Clara wrote. *Boring is our house style.*

Lynn sent a thumbs-up and a picture of her baby doing a face that suggested suspicious excellence. Mark looked and laughed. "He knows secrets."

"They all do," Clara said. "Some of them keep them."

***

Lynn's house smelt of the same oranges (the brand new-builds issue) and the lived-in of laundry drying on radiators. She handed over the base unit as if it were a borrowing of salt. "If it does the thing, text me. If it doesn't, text me."

"We'll text you either way," Clara said. "We're becoming tedious."

"Tedious is civilised," Lynn said, and then, lower: "When it does the *left–right*, he goes quiet. If that's... if that's your Ellie, tell her thank you from me, please. But not in a way that gives her ideas."

Clara smiled like a woman showing a passport. "I'll pass it on judiciously."

On the pavement outside, the sky decided to try blue. A bus pulled up at the stop opposite; there, at the window — the boy in the dinosaur coat again, the returning chorus. He saw Clara and performed the fingers: one, two, three; two; one; zero. Then, solemnly, closed his hand into a fist and pressed it to the glass as if sealing a pact. His mother looked up in time to see nothing unusual and smiled apologetically at the world.

"Witness," Mark said.

"Permitted," Clara said, and felt the word choose its chair in her mind.

At home, she put Lynn's unit on the hall table where keys queued for promotion. She kept their own monitor off as doctrine. She wrote *TEST RUN (Lynn's base; ours OFF)* at the top of a clean page and divided the sheet into three columns: *Time, Heard by whom, Content*. She drew the lines neatly. Neat lines make good shelters.

The baby slept the incorruptible sleep of a citizen who had met their quota. Mark worked at the kitchen table with his laptop at the angle that meant he was listening out. The house lowered itself into an afternoon posture.

At 14:12 Lynn's base made a tiny, courtly throat-clearing. The red bar lifted two notches and held.

Clara stood where she was. Mark looked up but didn't speak.

A breath, quick and small; the baby's. A second breath, older; Clara's own matched it, unhelpfully. Then — soft as you touch the surface of water with a hand — words formed.

"Left–right," the voice said, not through the walls, not in her head only, but in the polite plastic of Lynn's borrowed machine, tuned to a channel that didn't exist. "Left–right."

Clara's hand shook and didn't spill. She wrote 14:12 — heard by both — "left–right" (clear, twice). Mark nodded, as if to say *yes, accurate*, and did not look at the ceiling the way frightened men look to find a god.

The machine hushed. The red bar fell. The afternoon resumed its day job.

Clara waited. The waiting did not puncture her.

At 14:19 the unit lifted again, as if remembering a promise.

"Good girl," the voice said, with affectionate impatience. "Grown."

Clara shut her eyes. She opened them. She wrote 14:19 — both — "good girl... grown" (fond). She added, under Interpretations, *consent acknowledged; rule language reflected back.*

The unit went still. No music. No theatrics. It was, if anything, boring. The right kind.

She sent a text to Lynn: *Two short phrases. Clear. Ours remains off.*
Lynn: *Thank you. Tea later if you need a debrief?*
Clara: *Yes. After nap o'clock.*

Mark poured tea as if officiating. "Requests are not commands," he said, like a vow.

"I have heard you," Clara said to the quiet machine, "and I will consider it with my rules."

Nothing. Which, today, meant everything.

***

At six, after the witching hour had made its ceremonial demands and accepted their terms, Priya came in like weather people bring themselves. She kissed the baby as if awarding a medal, stole a biscuit, looked at the borrowed base unit with healthy irreverence, and said, "Well?"

"Boring success," Clara said. "Documented."

Priya pointed at the fridge. "New permission?"

Clara uncapped the marker and wrote, above *Leaflet people can queue*, in letters that couldn't wriggle out of their duty: ALLOWED: ENJOY THE BABY WITHOUT CHECKING THE WINDOW. She stepped back and let the sentence be larger than she was.

Priya saluted it with the biscuit. "Adult magic," she said. "Promotion granted."

They ate pointless cake, which performed its point immediately; they laughed at a man on television who underestimated a lintel and was schooled by physics; Mark invented a game called *BLUE or Biscuits* that made Priya snort tea.

At nine, Clara stood in the nursery doorway and took the census. Catch: two clicks. Rabbit: guard. Stars: at ease. Breath: immaculate. She put two fingers on the tiny chest, borrowed the metronome, returned it with interest.

On the hall table, Lynn's base sat like a sensible ally. It made no comment.

Clara went to bed without interrogating the dark. She lay on her side. Mark found her hand. The house made the small, approving sounds of a dwelling that had accepted the new signage.

"Tomorrow," she said into the near silence, "we begin Act Two."

"Not until you've eaten breakfast," Mark said, and the normality of it unstitched something tight in her. She laughed, quietly, and let sleep come without searching it for wires.

In the kitchen, the window steamed and un-steamed at its own pace. No handprint formed. That, tonight, was the proof that mattered.

Chapter Twelve
The Photo That Moves

Clara woke into a Tuesday the colour of unambitious paper. The light behind the curtains was steady; it didn't promise and it didn't threaten. She lay still and let the house list its facts: the boiler's low hum, the fridge's single note, a bin lorry somewhere finishing an argument with rain.

She reached for the notebook and wrote: *Woke steady. Rules: window (two clicks); boat on my terms; no moving things in nursery; no water; knots on hall mat only; doctors allowed; friends allowed; witness permitted; requests not commands; ALLOWED: enjoy the baby without checking the window.* She underlined *allowed* once and made herself believe it.

Beside her, Mark opened one eye with diplomatic caution. "Status?"

"Green," she said. "Grey obedient."

"We'll take obedient." He kissed her hair. "What's our nonsense today?"

"Boring test part two," Clara said. "Lynn's bringing cake to apologise for lending us her base unit. Priya said she'd humiliate chiffon again by turning up with biscuits. We'll scan the caravan photos for Martha. If we're very lucky, nothing will happen."

"An ambitious plan." He stretched with the seriousness of a man negotiating with twinges. "I'll make the kitchen behave."

On the landing, the baby produced her early squeak like a low-stakes question. The nursery smelt of warm cotton and newness. The window catch sat down and proper: two clicks. She didn't check it. She touched it, gently, and then forgave herself for touching.

"Good morning," she said, laying two fingers on the tiny chest. Rise, fall. She borrowed the metronome and returned it, the way you return a library book because you are trying to be the sort of person who returns things on time.

On the dresser the monitor sat dark, pious, and unemployed. She rested her palm above it and felt silly and kept doing silly because silly seemed to work.

***

By ten-fifteen the kitchen had arranged itself into competence. The table was wiped the way a blackboard is wiped to invite better maths; the good daylight fell across the wood like an honest inspector. Mark had made stacks: the sensible photo box borrowed from Martha; a neat towel so the glossy prints wouldn't skate; three phones fully charged; a notepad beside Clara's notebook because some redundancies felt like prayer.

"You're doing a ceremony," Priya said from the doorway, her coat throwing off rain without quite minding it. Jonah wore a hat with ears and a look of generalised approval. Priya put a packet of custard creams on the table as if awarding a medal. "I brought biscuits and a willingness to be bored out of my head."

"Bless you," Clara said. "We are huge fans of boredom."

Lynn arrived five minutes later with a Tupperware box of cake in a flavour that sounded like a boast and smelt like a kindness. She held up her phone like an object of modest worship. "I've put it on airplane mode," she said, "so nobody can accuse us of inviting the internet."

"Adult magic," Mark murmured, pleased. He took the cake and made a ceremony of plates.

"Rules?" Lynn asked, cheerful and unafraid in a way Clara had begun to rely on.

"Usual," Clara said. "No moving things in the nursery; no water; knots on the hall mat only; requests not commands. And a new one from Harriet: no altering records— written, photographed, or recorded— without permission." She hesitated. "That one's pre-emptive."

"Good," Lynn said. "Records are the gods I understand."

Priya dumped her bag under the table with the air of a woman settling in. "What exactly are we doing to poor Martha's photos?"

"Digitising," Mark said. "For her. And for us. Insurance against lofts."

"And because we like pictures of the caravan more than is rational," Clara said, and lifted the lid of the box like a librarian opening a sensibly bound past.

On top: the field that couldn't decide between Cornwall and Heaven; the caravan with its cream sides and green stripe; the step where her mother once sat peeling apples with a knife that had personal history. Underneath: the rope, strung ridiculously between bunks like a promise. Knots at intervals. Reef; reef; reef.

"Right," Mark said, picking up his phone. "No flash. Natural light. Same position each time. We'll take two of each and make sure they're boring."

"Boring saves lives," Priya said solemnly. "Also marriages."

"Also what's left of my sanity," Clara said.

They arranged the first photo on the towel, squared and exact. Mark's phone hovered, then made the courteous, apologetic sound of a shutter pretending to be old-fashioned. He showed them the screen: the caravan, the stripe, the open door, the square of shadow within.

"Again," he said, and did it. Two. He lifted the phone and laid it down and changed nothing else. "Next."

They slid the next print into place. The rope between bunks hung in an arc that had made all kinds of sense to them then and none to anyone sensible now. The knots had that tidy arrogance of properly learnt things.

"Reef," Priya said, pleased with herself. "Right over left; left over right. My father taught me in case I went to sea. We lived in Croydon."

"Useful on the 119," Lynn said.

Mark took a shot. The shutter made its sound: sorry to bother you, I'm from the past. He took another, then set the phone down, precise. "Compare?"

"Later," Clara said. "If we look at each after each we'll lose the thread. Batches. Then we'll see whether we've collected any ghosts."

"Ghosts in multiple sizes," Priya said gently. "Like tights."

They worked like people at a long table in a parish hall: quiet, companionable, occasionally swearing at reflection. Hands slid prints in and out; mugs grazed saucers; Jonah made the polite grunts of a small admiral overseeing a drill. Lynn kept up a running commentary about the uselessness of modern bread, which comforted everyone.

"Last one," Mark said, laying down the caravan at the angle Clara knew in her bones. Door half-open; the window catching the field like a rumour; the rope across the little bunk; the shadow within.

He took two shots. Everyone breathed.

"Tea," Priya decreed. "Then science."

"Biscuit," Jonah decreed. He used vowels with new ambition. Priya awarded a corner the size of a stamp and received in return a look of benediction.

They drank. They ate. The baby breathed in the nursery like a well-run engine. The house behaved.

"Shall we?" Lynn said after a minute, voice bright and level.

Mark unlocked his phone and scrolled, thumb steady. He opened the first pair. Caravan; caravan. Two squares of the past pretending to be the present by using the same light. He put them side by side. Nothing seemed wrong. He swiped. Next pair. Field; field. A woman in a summer dress carried a bowl as if the air required it. Nothing wrong. He swiped.

The rope between the bunks.

Two photos of the same rope. Knots at the same intervals. Reef; reef. In the first shot the left-hand knot sat straight and prim. In the second, the same knot had a different posture by an eighth of a turn, like a person who has been told a joke they will not laugh at but are thinking about. The tail—a short, neat tongue of rope— pointed an angle to the right in one and to the left in the other.

"Reflection?" Lynn asked.

"Could be," Mark said. "Angle. Light. Handshake."

"Or you have moved," Priya said kindly, "the distance of a thought."

They didn't perform panic. They performed method.

"Let's do it again," Clara said, keeping her voice like a white line. "Same photo. New pair. New phone. Then yours."

"Agreed," Mark said, delighted by a plan that could be spreadsheeted. He set the rope photo the same way on the towel, squared it with corners. He put his phone above it, took two shots. He picked up Priya's phone—android, different lens, different lies—and did two. He picked up Lynn's—third phone, third set of secret preferences—and did two more.

They lined all six in a grid and leant over them the way people lean over a missing cat poster.

First: reef; neat tails down; the line of the rope a small, good curve.

Second: the left-hand knot's tail lifted a fraction, as if a draft had found it. No draft. No window open. The kitchen was as obedient as kitchens get.

Third: the right-hand knot— which had been an unremarkable citizen— seemed to have been dressed by someone else. The wrap crossed a little higher. The crossing wasn't wrong. It simply wasn't *the same*.

"Zoom," Lynn said softly, and they did. Pixels declared themselves, honest and uninterested in anyone's beliefs. The fibre of the rope— fat, double-braided— was consistent. The light fell at the same angles. No shadows had learnt new tricks. The tiny fleck of dust in the gloss of the print—a white freckle near the rope— remained in the same place, the way a mole remains in a face. Only the knot— that necessary small truth— had altered its manners by degrees impossible to attribute to lens correction or hand tremor.

Priya breathed out as if she had been holding a heavy thing. "Okay," she said. "Okay. Valid excitement but not hysteria." She picked up her phone and, without theatre, took another shot. The shutter made its polite apology.

They added it to the grid. The left-hand knot now sat in the crisp exactness of a bowline.

"Don't be ridiculous," Mark said, not to Priya, not to the rope, to something in the world with opinions. He looked at the print with outrage as if the glossy rectangle might confess. In the *print itself*, the knot remained the same— a neat reef, prim and boring. Only the picture of it had chosen to remember differently.

Clara felt her skin tighten along her arms as if something had put a neat cool hand there to remind her of answers. She put one finger to the edge of the photo and held it to the light. The paper gave back nothing but paper. Her reflection obliged briefly, then retreated. Her heart did regrettable arithmetic. She made herself stop the sum.

"Different phone," Lynn said, her voice professional now, as if presenting evidence to a hostile but fair committee. "My turn again. Then yours. Then yours. Start a new row."

They did. They took turns. They lined them up. They placed the grid on the towel and squared the edges as if exactness could keep the sea out. The caravan door stayed ajar by the same credible inch. The field behind it stayed that particular summer green that is either Cornwall or Heaven. The thin line of shadow just inside the caravan stayed thin. The rope stayed rope.

The knot, between one shot and the next, changed its mind.

Reef. Bowline. Reef again, but with its tail tucked. A granny knot— sloppy, incorrect— as if someone had tied it reluctantly. Back to reef. A bowline once more, the rabbit visiting the hole, the tree very clear this time.

"Stop," Clara said, and was shocked by how ordinary the word sounded. She stepped back from the table. "This is the kind of proof that eats people if you let it. We are not letting it eat us. Rules."

"Records," Lynn said. "No altering them without permission." She pointed at the glossy rectangle. "We did not give permission."

"True," Mark said. "But the record being altered is... our record of the record."

Priya's mouth twitched into a pulled smile; the joke was too complicated to tell and too necessary to ignore. "A very modern haunting," she said. "Haunted metadata."

Clara took a breath the way Harriet had taught her— to give the breath something to do other than run away. She looked at the grid without looking *into* it, the way you look at the sea when you're not ready to swim. "We'll do one more, and then we stop for tea. If it's different, it's different. Then I email Harriet with *not an emergency* in the subject, and we seal the original in an envelope and write the time on it. And we absolutely do not bring the baby anywhere near this table while we are being daft."

"Good," Priya said. "Tea is a sacrament and sealing envelopes is adult magic."

Mark set the caravan print before them. The rope lay untroubled, ignorant. The light fell politely. He lifted his phone and, with the deliberation of a man performing a duty in front of supervising officers, took one photo. He set the phone down and did not look. He took Priya's, did the same. Lynn's. Finally, he held out his hand for Clara's. She passed it over. He took a breath like a pep talk and took the shot.

"Count of three," Priya said. "We look. We manage our faces like grown-ups."

"Three," Mark said, because everyone else had promised to be adults and he enjoys being the one who forgets to obey the rules in order to make them better.

They looked.

The caravan— the same. The stripe— the same. The door— the same, and also not. In one image it opened a crease wider. Not enough for cinema. Enough that a person who has known a door all her life could not call it the same.

Inside the dark beyond the door a square of shine appeared as if a hand had turned something in there to catch light: the face of the *tall blue jug*, reversed, the lamb logo shyly throwing itself backwards.

Clara's throat behaved like a person who had just been told a secret she both already knew and had not wished to be reminded of, not in front of friends.

"Still *not* an emergency," she said, and marvelled that the sentence arrived in English. "Tea."

They did tea as if it were a structural intervention. Cups clinked into saucers and grew up. The baby's breath moved gently in the other room. The house picked up its tools and stayed a house.

"Okay," Lynn said, practical. "Two possibilities. One: we're insane but coordinated. Two: the images are changing. Either we are not in control, or we are in charge of the rules of the being-not-in-control. We will choose the second because civilisations are built on pretending the second is true."

"Leaflet people can queue," Priya said fiercely, and ate a biscuit as if awarding herself a medal.

Clara laughed, and the laugh arrived as a proper laugh for perhaps the first time in a month in the presence of proof. "Agreed. New rule proposal: *No altering records that other people rely on.* That includes baby photos, medical notes, the fridge list, and—" she gestured at the table "—the actual past if it's printed on glossy paper."

"Seconded," Mark said. "Thirded."

"Passed," Lynn said, playing council. "We could add a permitted place— if the changing *must* occur, it occurs on the hall mat like the knots. One place, limited, supervised."

Clara looked at the mat and did not dislike the idea of telling the weird where to sit. "Permitted: the hall mat. One photograph at a time. No baby pictures. No family documents. No passports." She wrote it down with the neatness that makes rules more likely to obey themselves.

Jonah chose that moment to discover his feet and proclaim them fantastic. Priya applauded his toes. The room tilted back towards the human.

"Let's seal," Mark said quietly, and fetched an envelope as if he'd been hoping all morning to have that verb. Clara slid the caravan print in, squared its corners against the paper, and licked and pressed the flap. She wrote, in neat capitals across the join: SEALED — 11:38 — KITCHEN TABLE — WITNESSES: C.M., M.M., P.S., L.T. She dated it. She drew a small boat in the corner and did not hate herself for it.

"Protocol," Lynn said, proud as if she had invented envelopes.

Clara sat down and let her hands be empty a moment. Inside her, the old wanting rose— to go to the caravan, to stand on the step and sing the boat, to call out the name that would open everything and ruin it. She felt it, and then she obeyed Harriet's rule instead.

"I have heard you," she said, not loudly, not to startle anyone who needed not to be startled. "I will consider it with my rules."

No breath came back from the polite air; no rearrangement of temperature made itself important. The house did not say *bossy*, which made her smile because it meant she had told that word to sit, and it had sat.

"Let's look at the last four again," Priya said, brisk. "I want to hate them correctly."

They did. They scrolled left and right. The rope, the knots, the door's small manners. The blue jug a square of shine in exactly two images— one on Mark's, one on Lynn's— both taken within a minute of each other. On Priya's and Clara's, no jug. In each, the fleck of dust on the gloss stayed where dust stays. The EXIF timestamps— small, bossy— recorded what cameras record. None of the phones had flinched. None had improvised. Only the pictures had done it.

"I'm going to email Harriet," Clara said. "Subject: NOT AN EMERGENCY, WITNESS: images changed between shots." She typed with the care of a person ordering medicine. She attached three images— one reef, one bowline, one with the jug— and the photo of the sealed envelope with their names crossing the flap like a hand laid in blessing.

Harriet replied before the kettle had finished its second justification: *Received. Not emergency. Protocol: keep original sealed; print two of each image; mark times; note witnesses. Add rule you proposed re: records. Very good. Floor remains. Biscuits recommended. H.*

"God, I love her," Priya said. "She prescribes biscuits."

"She is the floor," Clara said, and felt something inside her finally stand with both feet.

***

The afternoon moved forward, incorrectly ordinary. Lynn's base unit sat on the hall table like a small, polite witness at a trial no one hoped to attend. They printed the pictures on the little home printer that insisted on sulking before working. Mark marked the backs in pencil: *11:22 — reef; 11:23 — bowline; 11:27 — jug visible.* Priya stuck Post-its to each like awards. Clara wrote the rule on the fridge, above *Leaflet people can queue*, in tidy capitals: NO ALTERING RECORDS WITHOUT PERMISSION. Beneath, in smaller letters: PERMITTED LOCATION (IF ANY): HALL MAT — ONE ITEM AT A TIME — NO BABY PHOTOS.

"Adult magic," Lynn said, standing back. "I would live in this kitchen."

"Come round and practise," Clara said. "We run services at ten and three."

They laughed, and the kind of laugh it was made Clara want to cry and didn't make her cry. She felt tired and not afraid. She felt watched in the protective way and not controlled.

At five, the witching hour tried to make a case and was negotiated with. Mark narrated the baby's bath with his manual voice like a man reading agrichemical safety instructions in a loving way. "Water is allowed only in trays," he intoned, and the baby kicked as if applauding compliance.

After, they ate pasta and agreed with a stern woman on television about lintels. Lynn went home with her base and a slip of cake; Priya went home with Jonah and a promise to mock chiffon again Thursday; the house rearranged itself around the knowledge of witnesses as if adding a chair.

"Walk?" Mark asked at nine, and meant the small walk you do in a small house from sofa to stair to nursery, counting breath and laws.

They stood in the nursery doorway like parishioners. Catch: two clicks. Rabbit: guard. Stars: hanging their quiet. Breath: perfect. Clara put two fingers on the tiny chest and stole the metronome for three beats and put it back quickly, as if keeping rhythm were a thing she now knew how to do without stealing.

She spoke the rules, not a charm, not a dare, a list read with care: "No moving things in here. No water. Knots on the hall mat only. Requests are not commands. No altering records without permission. Doctors allowed. Friends allowed. Witness permitted. Allowed: enjoy the baby without checking the window."

From the hall, the sealed envelope sat on the dresser like an object that had been made respectable by biro. On the kitchen window five petals arrived in steam, then thinned without being touched. The house made that small approving sound it had learnt, which was perhaps plumbing and perhaps gratitude.

"End of Act One?" Mark said, light, as if guessing the page number. He had already put the kettle on. He liked to put the kettle on in important moments because important moments often crave small heat.

"End of Act One," Clara said. She felt the sentence land like a weight being set down rather than dropped.

Downstairs, her phone buzzed. A message from Martha: a photograph— the caravan, taken by her father on a different day, from a different angle. In the window, by accident, a reflection of two girls the age the world had said only one of them had been. It was, of course, trick of glass and angle and longing. It was also an image of two heads.

Found another for your scanning, Martha wrote. *Don't read ghosts into it; I already did that in 1989.* There was a cloud and a heart and nothing else.

Clara laughed. She put the phone face-down and stood in the doorway of the nursery and felt something ease in her back like a knot agreeing to be a loop.

"Tomorrow," she said into the landing— to the house, to the woman in the corridor who had said Mark's name, to the girl with her voice who had tied the correct knots in the wrong places, to the mother who had once hidden biscuits in a tall blue jug, to the doctor who had declared herself the floor— "we'll start the next thing. On my terms."

A breath like a small laugh approved. It wasn't a wind. It wasn't a draft from a window that had forgotten its promise. It was the sound of a house and everyone in it consenting to a new list.

Clara went downstairs and made tea. Mark handed her a biscuit with the solemnity of a man officiating at a rite. She wrote, for the last time at the bottom of that week's page: *Act I complete: proof obtained (images change between shots). New rule added. Witness outside family. Floor holds. Me: bossy + grown. Onward.*

They drank in the quiet. The envelope held its breath with them and then, like all sensible objects, went back to being paper with glue and names. Outside, the road held the end of the day to its chest and promised to bring it back in the morning.

The house settled. The baby dreamt. The window stayed shut with its two clicks and did not need to be checked.

Clara let herself be happy, for longer than thirty seconds, without looking over anyone's shoulder. And that— more than the jug in a photograph, more than a knot deciding its own shape— felt like a change of state the world would have to accept.

Act II: The Fracture

Chapter Thirteen
Paperwork

Clara woke into a morning that looked like a form waiting for its boxes to be ticked. The light behind the curtains was tidy and undecided, the colour of old photocopy paper. She lay still and let the house do its census: boiler's civil hum, fridge's single note, tyres on damp tarmac writing punctuation on the street.

She took the notebook and wrote the date, then: *Harriet's rule added: requests ≠ commands. Records rule: no altering without permission. Allowed: enjoy the baby without checking window.* She underlined *allowed* once and made herself believe it.

Beside her, Mark rolled towards consciousness and blinked like a man negotiating a lease with the day. "Status?"

"Green," she said. "Grey cooperative."

"We'll take cooperative." He kissed her hair. "Hospital at eleven?"

"Archives," she said, and felt the word put its shoulder to the door inside her. "PALS at reception, then Records. I have the email."

On the landing the baby made the small, officious squeak of a junior official opening the office. The nursery smelt of warm cotton and the faint biscuit of sleep. The window catch sat down properly: two clicks. She didn't check it. She touched it and forgave herself for touching it.

"Morning, tyrant," she said, laying two fingers on the tiny chest and borrowing the metronome. Rise, fall. She returned the beat to its owner like a decent librarian.

On the dresser the monitor sat dark, pious and out of work. She rested her palm over the air above it as if blessing a creature that needed no blessing.

***

The kitchen behaved as kitchens do when asked politely. Mark aligned mugs like witnesses. The good pen found its cap. The star-shaped sticky note—*BLUE = rules*— clung to the fridge like a small flag. Above it, Harriet's scrap—*Leaflet people can queue*—had acquired seniority under the new permission: ALLOWED: ENJOY THE BABY WITHOUT CHECKING THE WINDOW.

Clara read the email again though she'd read it at four a.m., then at five in a different tone. *Dear Ms Morgan, Further to your Subject Access Request, the original bound maternity notes and associated loose-leaf labels are available for supervised inspection at 11:00 today in Health Records (Lower Ground). A PALS officer will meet you at Main Reception. Please bring photographic ID. Copies can be made on request. Please do not remove documents. Regards, S. Keane (Records).*

"Keane," Mark said, peering over her shoulder. "Solid name."

"Sounds like cardboard and string," Clara said, and wished gently for both.

Her phone buzzed. *Harriet: Before you go in: repeat the sentence. Requests ≠ commands. "I have heard you; I will consider it with my rules." If you feel commanded, step out; text RED. Boring over heroic. Floor holds.* Clara replied: *Understood. Bringing biscuits as a bribe to the floor.* A minute later: *Harriet: Floor accepts chocolate digestives.*

A second buzz. *Martha: Do you need me.* No punctuation; the kind of question that rests its hands flat.

We'll look and report, Clara typed. *I'll bring the box back later. No ghosts— just paper.*

After a moment, Martha sent a cloud and a heart, then: *Ask about bands.*

Clara looked at the bracelets in her head the way you look at dangerous steps in the dark. "We'll ask," she said aloud.

***

They drove under a sky that had made a good effort at neutrality. The ring road performed its patient ceremony. A bus pulled alongside and a child in a dinosaur coat pressed his face to the glass, then lifted his hands for a new series: two, then one, then a small firm fist. He tapped the glass with the fist and beamed. His mother did not look up.

"Witness permitted," Mark murmured, not taking his eyes off the road.

"Permitted," Clara said, and watched the boy vanish into mist on the inside of the window.

The hospital had the smell it had always had— of oranges and old lino and arguments done in low voices. In the atrium, a sculpture pretended to be kind. PALS sat behind a desk like a civilised rock. A woman with a badge that said *Tamara (she/her)* looked up and tried to smile on their behalf without taking their agency.

"Clara?" she said. "And Mark?"

"Yes," Clara said. She showed ID as if entering a reasonable country.

"Records know you're coming," Tamara said. "I'll walk you down. You can take notes. They'll photocopy what you need. No originals leave the room. If anything feels—" She searched for a neutral word and found one. "—upsetting, we pause. All right?"

"Thank you," Clara said. The kindness was like being offered a chair when you thought you were going to have to stand for hours.

They took the lift down. It opened on a corridor with a temperature problem. Posters about hand hygiene wore their moral certainty lightly. Down here, the hospital smelt less of oranges and more of paper; a papery damp that belonged to cupboards and basements and civility that had to be defended.

Mr S. Keane was exactly the man his email had promised: sleeves rolled, tie not in the way, glasses that had watched decades of paper behave. He shook Mark's hand and did the little nod to Clara as if acknowledging that names carry weight.

"Ms Morgan," he said. "We've pulled everything with your NHS number, plus the hard copy of the maternity case notes. Some of the labels are loose. Don't worry— that's how they were stored." He gestured to the table with the politeness of a host introducing a buffet. "We'll supervise. We'll copy what you ask."

On the table: a blue, A4-bound set of notes with elastic that had lost some of its dignity; two brown envelopes with those satisfying string-and-disc closures; a smaller plastic wallet with a label that said *ID BAND LABELS (ADMISSIONS)* in a handwriting that could have belonged to three different decades.

Clara sat with care. The chair made a sound like a person settling in to listen. Keane took a pair of cotton gloves from a drawer but didn't hand them to her. "You won't need these," he said. "Just clean hands. We like hands. Hands know what to do."

Mark placed the chocolate digestives on the table with the air of a man making a pledge to a guild. Keane's mouth softened by a measurable degree. "Good floor food," he said neutrally, and pushed the plate to the side like an altar he approved of but would not pray at.

"Shall we," Tamara said, cheerful and not cheerful, "begin with the bound notes?"

Keane opened the blue file. The elastic gave up with a sigh. Inside, a first page with lines and a faded stamp that said *Queen's Park General — Maternity*. Names in biro that looked bored and careful: *Morgan, Clara*. DOB. NHS number. Then— lower— *Para 1 (twins; one non-viable)* in a scrawl that looked like it had been written by someone wanting not to write anything at all.

"Who writes *non-viable* like that," Mark murmured, so low only Clara could hear.

"Leaflet people," she said under her breath, and felt his mouth twitch, then steady.

They turned pages. There were the blood pressures— neat numbers marching. The urine dipsticks— a small army of negatives with the odd-plus like a gossip. The labour sheet— time, dilation, more times, more centimetres. Midwife initials that looked like two letters trying not to have a personality. A line Clara didn't know whether to bless or hate: *twins expected; Twin 1 vertex; Twin 2 breech*. A column for Apgar scores, filled for one baby, left blank for the other, a blank that felt like a decision rather than an absence.

Clara's throat made the small tight rope of itself and then obeyed. "What's this?" she asked, and pointed. On the admissions page, in the box for *ID bands issued*, a number of tiny peel-off labels had once lived. Most were gone, removed and stuck to the babies themselves on the night they were born. Two remained, skew, their glue dried and brown at the edges, printed in that dot-matrix font that made old machines sound like insect choirs: *MORGAN, CLARA — 27/08 — 02:12 — ID: 103984*. Below it, another, same line: *MORGAN, ELEANOR — 27/08 — 02:12 — ID: 103985*.

"Two bands," Keane said, almost to himself, approvingly. "That's how it should be for twins. Babies get their own."

"I brought the bracelets," Clara said, as if admitting to carrying contraband from a childhood. She didn't take the shoebox out. "They're... they're elastic. With the tabs."

"Different system," Keane said, mellow. "These print-out labels get stuck to the tabs. You'd have had two little plastic ovals— ah." He lifted the plastic wallet with *ID BAND LABELS (ADMISSIONS)* written in patient capitals. Inside, a strip of labels still on its backing had been folded and unfolded many times. He slid the strip out with two fingers. Dot-matrix had done its polite work: *MORGAN, CLARA* repeated five times on perforations; beneath, *MORGAN, ELEANOR* repeated. On the *ELEANOR* line, someone— some careful, un-showy hand— had drawn a single diagonal biro stroke across the surname, then written, small, above it: *void*.

The word was not violent. It did not shout. It was the sort of neat verdict bureaucracies issue when they mean to be kind and aren't sure how.

Clara felt her stomach try the lift that drops half a floor too far. "Who... voids a newborn," she said, and then heard her mouth making a theatre of it and pulled herself back into the chair. "I mean— who writes it."

Keane rolled his glasses up and massaged the bridge of his nose the way people do when they are searching their index of acceptable words. "Usually," he said, "if a band is printed in error— name spelt wrong, wrong date— the label sheet gets marked and a new sheet printed. The voided strip should be kept. If there was an emergency and someone hit print twice... we'd still keep both. The fact it's here is— admirable."

"Is there—" Clara swallowed and forced the sentence on— "a log of the print job? A time?"

Keane nodded once, pleased by the question. "There can be." He lifted the second brown envelope. On the front: *ADMISSIONS — BAND PRINTER LOG — AUG–SEPT (ARCHIVE)*. Inside, a sheaf of thermal paper— the shiny kind that fades itself as a hobby— torn neatly at days. He placed the stack down and flicked gently to the date.

27/08 — 02:12:04 — ID Print — MORGAN, CLARA — ID 103984

27/08 — 02:12:21 — ID Print — MORGAN, ELEANOR — ID 103985

27/08 — 02:13:00 — VOID — ID 103985 — User: JS

27/08 — 02:13:14 — ID Print — MORGAN, ELEANOR — ID 103986

27/08 — 02:13:50 — VOID — ID 103986 — User: JS

"Two prints," Keane said, eyebrows that belonged to a different generation attempting not to contribute too much. "Two voids. Same user initials."

"JS," Mark said. "Who is JS?"

Keane turned a page in the bound notes with practised sympathy. On the front sheet, lower right, a list of attending staff had been written before the night went feral: *Consultant: S. Vale* (Clara blinked— Harriet? No— no. Another Vale. Her brain filed the coincidence with some relief and some private humour), *Registrar: Dr K Sandhu; Senior Midwife: J. Snow; Midwife: M. Doyle; Student: L. Herries.* He tapped the second line of midwives. "J. Snow. Likely. Senior. Good reputation. I remember the name."

"Two voids," Clara said. "Printed again and still void. And then... no third?"

"Not on this log," Keane said. "You'll notice not everything got kept in 2000-and-whenever. The fact we have this much is a minor miracle."

Clara felt the air put its hand against the back of her neck— not cold; not hot; attentive. Apples, faintly— or it was the disinfectant arguing with her nose. She kept her face like the front of a building and wrote, in her notebook: *02:12:04 103984 (C); 02:12:21 103985 (E); 02:13:00 VOID 103985; 02:13:14 103986 (E); 02:13:50 VOID 103986 — JS.* She wrote *VOID x2 (E)* and drew a small square around it.

"Shall we copy those?" Tamara asked softly, as if asking whether they could take a plant cutting.

"Please," Clara said, and did not look at Mark.

Keane stood and took the thermal strip, the labels sheet, and the admissions page with the two little labels still clinging on like well-behaved witnesses. "Back in two," he said, and left, a man carrying a tray to a kitchen.

Clara exhaled. The room breathed with her.

"Requests are not commands," she said into the polite air. "I have heard you; I will consider it with my rules."

Mark, who had not looked away from the page with *void* on it, blinked. "Is she—"

"She's behaving," Clara said. "I'm telling her how we're going to do this."

"Good," he said. He put a finger on the word *void* without touching the ink, like a man testing whether the past was still wet. "I don't like it."

"Me neither."

They looked through the rest. A discharge summary that had been signed with boredom. *Ms Morgan discharged Day 2. Baby feeding, settled. Follow-up with HV.* In the box where there might have been a second baby, someone had drawn a line, neat and unshowy. On a smaller sheet— *NNU involvement?*— a box had been ticked *No*. The word *viable* appeared once, in a paragraph made of sentences that had good intentions and bad bedside manner.

"Leaflet people wrote this," Clara said, but gentler, as if admitting even leaflets wanted to be helpful sometimes.

Keane returned with the copies— good, sharp A4s, each stamped with the small rectangular smirk that said *Copy from Original*. He laid them with ceremony. "You'll see the thermal isn't keen on being copied," he said. "We've coaxed it. I've put the labels on one page so you can see the strike-through."

Clara looked. On the photocopy the *void* line across *ELEANOR* wasn't only a line. It had the faintest suggestion of text underneath, like a rubbing that wanted to declare itself: the dot-matrix squares that made *MORGAN, ELEANOR* visible again under the biro, as if the copier's light had gone around the stroke and found the shape it had hidden.

"Is that—" Mark leaned in. "Am I seeing things?"

"It's the machine," Keane said briskly, as if not indulging magic in the Records Department were an oath. "They lift differently. Your brain is very good at finding ghosts in toner."

"Print another?" Tamara suggested, lightly, as if asking for a different pastry.

Keane fed the sheet again. The copier made its reasonable noises. Paper slid out with the satisfaction of work done. On this one, the stroke through *ELEANOR* looked faintly heavier, as if it had been going to be red and then not. Under it, the surname was— to Clara's eye, trained by a lifetime of commas— absolute. Untouched. Unvoided. The letters were crisp with the way a memory is crisp when the person telling it wants to be believed.

"Again," Mark said, and then laughed at himself and at Keane's face. "Please."

"Three's a data set," Keane allowed, just this once, and sent it through. The third sheet came out with the stroke and the name in equal competition, like two lines on a map crossing at a village neither had expected. *MORGAN, ELEANOR* readable; *void* legible; neither winning.

"Records rule," Clara said, almost to the machine. "No altering records without permission."

"We haven't altered anything," Keane said, in the voice of a man who will not have his kingdom turned into theatre. "We've made copies of what exists."

"Exactly," Clara said, and gave the air her serious face. "We're keeping them sealed."

Tamara produced an envelope without having to be asked. She had the manner of someone who had been to this play before, albeit with different props. "Write across the flap," she said. "Date, time, witnesses. We'll keep one. You take one."

Clara wrote neatly: SEALED — 11:34 — Admissions Band Log & Labels — Witnesses: C. Morgan, M. Morgan, S. Keane, T. Lowe (she had seen Tamara's surname on her badge). She drew the small boat with the same absent-minded correctness she used on the fridge.

"Do you want a cup of tea," Tamara asked, kind to the question. "You can sit for five."

"We will sit for five," Mark said, grateful to be told.

***

The canteen was two corridors and one broken clock away. Its tea was always hotter than expected, the cups heavier. They sat near a plant that had learnt diplomacy. People came and went with their sadness disguised as errands.

"What do we do with *void*," Mark said, not in outrage now, just in the tone of a man who needs, before lunch, to know how to hold a word without letting it cut him.

"We don't let it decide everything," Clara said. "We ask why it happened twice. We ask who JS was and whether void meant *error* or *decision* or *a decision someone made to spare us something*. We don't let the copier trick us into making religion of a strike-through."

He nodded. "Harriet will like that sentence."

"She will prescribe biscuits for it," Clara said.

Her phone buzzed. *Lynn: How's your paperwork haunting? I'm available to not be helpful in any way.*

Ghosts in toner, Clara wrote back. *We're okay. Will debrief later.*

Another buzz. *Harriet: Good. Copies sealed. Don't chase certainty in a basement. Bring me ambiguity and biscuits.* The calm of it altered ten muscles in Clara's back. She didn't know which ten until they let go.

"Shall we," Mark said softly, "ask your mother about JS."

"J. Snow," Clara said, thinking of midnights and lists and clean block capitals. "She'll remember a face, even if she says she won't."

They walked back through the corridor that smelt of paper and civility. In the lift, a woman held a bunch of carnations wrapped in cellophane like something sworn to try. The doors opened briefly on Neonatal, then shut again on nothing. A small voice over the speaker said something about *viable* and then corrected itself to *valuable— valuable property should not be left unattended.* Clara stood very still until the doors made the bright sound and let them out.

Back in the Records room, Keane had laid another item on the table. "This was in the loose-leaf envelope," he said, as if apologising for it. A Polaroid: the old kind, square, a white frame. Baby, minutes old— not hers, not anyone's she knew; a stock image taken in Maternity in 2001 to test the instant camera. A midwife's hand holding a wrist near the lens, the little white oval of a band with pen writing on it and a smear of blood that had made its own meanings at the time. Over the white frame, someone had written: *Check bands — both correct — MD.*

"MD," Keane said, tapping the initials. "M. Doyle. The junior that night."

"Two bands correct," Clara said, and wanted it to be a judgement that could be applied to a life. "Thank you."

"Take a copy?" Tamara asked. She made the photocopier sound like a polite animal.

They copied it. The copy came out as reasonable as a copy could be. The pen on the band read *MORGAN, CLARA*. There was no second band visible, no trick of double exposure. It was an artefact that wanted to be helpful and could only be charming.

"Enough," Clara said, and felt like someone who has eaten enough to be hospitable and intends not to be sick later. "We have enough."

Keane reassembled his kingdom. The bound notes closed with the resignation of old elastic. The labels went back into their plastic wallet. The thermal strip was tucked as if into bed. He placed their sealed envelope on the table and added, with bureaucratic kindness, two small round stickers as if to keep the flap from misbehaving.

"Thank you," Clara said, standing as if closing a service. "For not... hating us for looking."

"People come," Keane said, and surprised himself by sounding gentle. "They try to put things back with paper. We don't let them, but we let them look."

"It helps," Tamara said, practical compassion. "Even when it doesn't fix."

They left with the envelope in a plain hospital bag that had carried sicker things. The lift decided to behave itself all the way up. The atrium did its impression of a hotel for people in trouble. Outside, the air had decided on pale blue like a statement toned down for public consumption.

Clara stood on the steps a second longer than necessary and let the building take its shape in her head. "JS," she said. "J. Snow. Martha will know her name without saying she knows her."

"We'll ask gently," Mark said.

"Requests ≠ commands," Clara said, as if reminding the day.

"Leaflet people can queue," Mark said, and held the bag like a priest who had learnt when not to do theatre.

***

Martha's kitchen smelt of stew rehearsing. She listened to the facts the way you listen to a language you used to speak fluently: slower, careful, paying attention to cadence.

"J. Snow," she said, frowning thoughtfully. "Janine. Senior midwife. Good hands. Tidy mind. She was the one who liked real butter in the staff fridge and nobody minded. She kept a list of who owed her slices of toast. She had a laugh like a piece of cutlery being put down on wood." Martha paused. "She was the one who told me *viable* as if she were saying a prayer not to a god she loved. She liked you. Everyone liked you."

Clara waited for the rest and didn't hurry it.

"She thought—" Martha tapped a nail twice on the table as if to line up youth and patience— "that the second band had been printed because someone had hit the button twice. She told your father she voided it. Twice, because the machine had hiccuped. She said she would have kept it in the file because she liked... she liked to keep untidy truths." Martha looked at her daughter with a force she usually saved for knives. "That's all there is. A printer that coughed at the wrong moment. A person with good hands trying to make the world look straight."

"Thank you," Clara said. She felt a complicated love for Janine Snow, who had voided and kept, who had liked butter, who had written small neat verdicts in biro. "Thank you for remembering the cutlery."

Martha's mouth bent, the kind of smile you keep in the dark so it won't get stolen. "It is my one useful talent," she said.

Mark laid the sealed envelope on the table with a small reverence. "We'll keep this at ours," he said. "If we open it, we do it together. No solo archaeology."

"Good," Martha said. She reached out and put her hand on the flap for a second and then took it away as if rules matter.

They didn't talk about *void* again. They talked about stew and whether stew should have carrots (yes) and whether carrots should be cut coins or oblique (oblique). They talked about the boy in the dinosaur coat whose mother, surely, must also need biscuits. They talked about Priya's scarf doctrine and Lynn's base unit as if discussing municipal equipment. The ordinary words put furniture back in the room.

As they left, Martha stood in the doorway and kissed the baby with the accuracy of women who invented accuracy. "Don't take ghosts to bed," she said, matter-of-fact. "They never sleep."

"Requests are not commands," Clara said, and liked the way Martha nodded as if hearing a good rule.

At home the hall met them with its old patience. The sealed envelope sat on the console table like a small, self-contained weather system. On the mat, where rules say strangeness may sit if it must, there was nothing— which felt like compliance.

Clara propped the envelope against the wall and wrote in her notebook: *Hospital — copies sealed (band log; label sheet; admissions page). VOID x2 for ELEANOR (103985, 103986) — JS (Janine Snow). Polaroid note ("Check bands—both correct—MD"). Copier showed underlying name variably. Rule repeated: no altering records.* She added, because it was good practice: *Me: here.* She underlined *here* and found she meant it.

Lynn texted her a selfie under a hairdryer with a caption: *Administering salon therapy to my grief. Debrief later?*
Yes, Clara wrote. *Ghosts in toner but floor held.*

Harriet sent a one-line response to the photo of the sealed envelope Clara had forwarded: *Excellent. Keep one for me to view in session. Bring biscuits. Sleep tonight.*

Clara stood in the kitchen and listened to the house one more time. The window steamed a little and did not write anything she had not asked it to. The fridge sang its one song. Upstairs, the baby exhaled in pairs and commas. The envelope existed, sealed, not an altar, not a bomb. A word she had been taught as a child— *records*— had put on a coat and become a character.

"Bossy," whispered the day in a way that didn't require a voice.

"Grown," Clara said, and put the kettle on.

At nine, when the programme about lintels had once again humbled a man into sense, Clara carried the sealed envelope to the hall mat and set it there because the rule permitted one thing there at a time. She placed the green knot beside it. She put her hand on the flap and said, for the record: "No altering records without permission. If anything is going to change: ask. Hall mat only. One at a time. Not the original."

The air did not cool. Apples did not arrive. The envelope sat and kept its promise of glue and names.

Clara left it and went to the nursery. Catch: two clicks. Rabbit: guard. Stars: obedient. Breath: immaculate. She put two fingers on the tiny chest and borrowed the metronome. She returned it with interest.

"Requests are not commands," she said into the good room that had learnt to keep its face. "I have heard you. I will consider it with my rules."

A breath—fond, impatient—did not cross the floorboards. It did not have to. The rules sat like chairs; the room agreed to them by being a room and not a sign.

In bed, she wrote: *Paper proof exists; ambiguity honest. We are not chasing certainty in a basement. Floor holds. Next: ask Harriet for JS note; plan Lynn test v2; return box to Martha. Me: bossy + grown.*

She put the notebook under the bed and let thoughts find the cooler floor. Mark took her hand in the dark and didn't make a speech. The house made the small, approving sounds of a dwelling that has decided to be on your side as long as you keep your part of the bargain.

The last thing she heard before sleep was the civilised hush of paper behaving in its envelope. If it was a trick of wires or photocopiers or grief, it was a trick they could seal and carry between them. It wasn't the end of a story. It was what stories do when they decide to be true: they put their names down, in biro, and agree to be kept.

Chapter Fourteen
The Jug

Clara woke into a Wednesday that had made itself resemble a form. The light behind the curtains was the colour of old photocopy paper—tidy, undecided, prepared to be written on. She lay still and let the house take roll: boiler's civil hum, fridge's single note, the whisper of tyres finding commas on wet tarmac. She took the notebook and, neat as a clerk, wrote: *Woke steady. Rules unchanged: window (two clicks); boat on my terms; no moving things in nursery; no water; knots on hall mat only; requests ≠ commands; no altering records without permission; doctors allowed; friends allowed; witness permitted; ALLOWED: enjoy the baby without checking the window.* She underlined *allowed* and let her eyes agree.

Beside her, Mark turned, blinked like a man negotiating a truce with morning. "Status?"

"Green," she said. "Grey cooperative."

"We love cooperative grey." He kissed her hair. "Martha today?"

"Return the photo box," Clara said. "Ask gently about *JS*. And the jug." The last word arrived and sat between them like an object revealed from under a tea towel.

"You'll lead," Mark said. "I'll make tea and be furniture."

On the landing, the baby produced her administrative squeak. The nursery smelt of warm cotton and clean, new animal. The window catch sat down and correct: two clicks. She didn't check it. She touched it and forgave herself for touching it.

"Good morning," she said to the small republic in the cot. Two fingers on a tiny chest. Rise, fall. She borrowed the metronome and returned it with interest.

On the dresser, the monitor sat dark and obedient. She held her palm an inch above it and smiled at herself for the silliness of blessing plastic, and did it anyway.

***

In the kitchen, rules were visible. The star-shaped sticky note—*BLUE = rules*—clung to the fridge like a flag someone's child had cut out. Beneath, Harriet's scrap—*Leaflet people can queue*—had gained gravitas under the newer line in sober capitals: ALLOWED: ENJOY THE BABY WITHOUT CHECKING THE WINDOW. Next to them, yesterday's copies—band log, labels sheet, admission page—sat sealed in an envelope propped against the wall, biro crossing the flap like a hand placed to bless.

Clara texted Harriet: *Going to Mum's with the box. Intend to ask about the jug when tea is made and doors are shut. Will avoid commands both incoming and outgoing.*
The reply arrived quickly, as if the floor had an efficient inbox: *Excellent. Ask for stories, not verdicts. If voice intrudes, say the sentence and step out. Boring beats dramatic. Floor holds.*

She wrote the sentence once at the top of the day's page—*I have heard you; I will consider it with my rules*—not because she thought she'd forget it but because writing makes breath behave.

They packed the photo box, biscuits she would not let herself call *for courage*, and the good towel in case the gloss needed to be persuaded again. The sky outside tried a thin blue and then, sensibly, gave up.

In the car, traffic had decided to be polite. A bus idled beside them at the lights. The boy in the dinosaur coat had been replaced by a girl with hair plaited like determination. She pressed a hand to the glass and kept it there as if taking an oath. Clara pressed hers to the air and let it be enough.

"Witness permitted," Mark said, checking his mirrors as if witnesses travelled in the blind spot.

"Permitted," Clara said, and watched the girl become a blur of buses being buses.

***

Martha's house smelt of stew considering its ingredients and the particular warmth of a radiator that had earned its keep. She opened the door with her hair done like a plan. "Come in," she said, making space with the authority of a woman who remembers welcoming in bad weather.

The "good room" had arranged itself for conversation: the low table cleared; coasters chosen; the radio in that volume that indicates it will take your hint. The tall blue jug stood on the dresser as it always had—upright as a person who knows their height, enamel a good holiday sea, a white line of chip on the lip like a healed cut. It had belonged to the house before this one; it had belonged to their caravan summers; it had belonged, in a quiet way, to everyone in the family who needed a container for something that wasn't to be spilt.

Clara placed the photo box on the table and tried not to look at the jug the way you try not to look at a door in a dream. "We brought your pictures."

"Thank you," Martha said, and her hand went to the box with an absent-minded care that made the cardboard feel seen. "Tea?"

"Please," Mark said, performing furniture impeccably. He found the kettle, found the cups that could be trusted, felt the muscle memory of being useful in other people's kitchens. He did not touch the jug.

They sat, and the tea behaved. For a minute they talked about stew (carrots: oblique) and radiators (air: bled) and Priya's doctrine on chiffon. Martha poured and then sat down without fuss, the posture of a woman who intends to stay seated for as long as necessary.

"Mum," Clara said, and placed her finger lightly on the photo box lid instead of pointing at the jug. "We went to Records yesterday. We met Keane. And Tamara. There were labels. The printer log." She watched Martha's face the way you watch a lake for the moment a fish shows and is gone.

Martha's mouth did a remembered movement, a private arithmetic. "Did you find *JS*?"

"Janine Snow," Clara said. "You remembered her."

"Good hands," Martha said. "Proper tea. She said *viable* like a prayer she was trying not to resent. She put toast in a pocket when she was late and forgot she'd done it until the toast broke itself. She liked you."

"She voided the second label twice," Clara said, not accusing, not inviting defence. "The log had it."

Martha nodded once, eyes on her own hands. "The printer coughed," she said, in a voice that respected photocopiers. "Those little machines did that then. She said there'd be two anyway—Clara, Eleanor—and she wasn't going to stick a misprint on anything that touched you. She voided the wrong one. Then the right. Then she kept the strip, because she had that mind. She gave me the clean one, later, in a side room with a paper towel and the bin that smelt like lemons." Martha took a breath. "She said, 'You may want this. Not now. One day. I cannot write it on a form. But I can put it in your hand.'"

Clara pictured it—the folded strip, the corridor with righteous posters, the kindness of someone who had decided to be practical. "And you...?"

"I put it in the blue jug," Martha said, as if telling a child where the biscuits were kept.

They didn't rush into the silence. Mark stared at his cup as if waiting for it to prefer him. The radio made itself smaller. The jug stood, exactly itself.

"Why there," Clara asked, when the quiet had done its job, "and not the shoebox?"

"The jug was *in the room*," Martha said. "The shoebox was in the loft, inside someone else's mind. The jug—" she glanced at it as if it might be tempted to answer for itself, and then, wisely, didn't ask it to—"the jug had been on the caravan step, catching peel and water and sun; it had been on the floor by the cot when we put it there to look like we knew what we were doing; it had been full of milk when you were sick and full of flowers when you weren't; it had *handled* the truth before we had language for it." She laughed softly, embarrassed by the accuracy of her own metaphor. "It was tall. Which sounds silly. But I needed somewhere the world couldn't see into when it stood up to look."

"You hid biscuits there," Clara said. The sentence came with the small rush of being able to say a thing that had been said already by another mouth. "That was our secret phrase. 'Mum hid the biscuits in the tall blue jug.'"

"I did," Martha said. "Because children require bribes, and because, if anyone asked me what was *in* the jug, *biscuits* was the sentence I could say without swallowing glass." She put her hand flat on the table. "I also put the second band there, and the spare labels, and a paper with her name on it, written by me, in my worst nurse's handwriting. I didn't tell your father for a week, and then I told him badly."

"Why badly," Mark asked, blunt in the gentle way that told the truth to sit down and drink tea.

"Because he *wanted* one story," Martha said, and the sentence was very tired, and very kind. "He wanted the doctor's version, the leaflet, the discharge. *Twins; one non-viable; home with one baby.* He wanted a shape he could move through without stepping on anything sharp. I tried to tell him that another shape existed. I said, 'Her name is Eleanor.' He said, 'Don't make this harder by stacking stories.' He wasn't cruel. He was frightened. He had decided that if we took home only one, we *must only* take home one, in every way there is. I decided to disagree and to do it without breaking him."

"So you kept *untidy truths*," Clara said, aware of how the phrase belonged to Janine and to Martha and to herself now, a little inheritance she had not asked for and was relieved to receive.

"I did," Martha said. "In a jug. Like a sensible woman hiding her contradictions in the tallest thing she owned."

Clara swallowed. The jug seemed to lean forward without moving. She could smell apples, but this was a kitchen where apples were allowed, so she didn't scold herself. "You did something else," she said, not as a guess, as a sentence that had arrived with its own feet. "You used water."

Martha's face altered by a degree, the way faces alter when surprised by someone remembering their better lies. "I did," she said. "I took water from the jug—clean, boiled, cooled like you're supposed to, because I am a grandmother with standards even when I am twenty-six—and I stood at the sink and I said a very impudent version of a prayer and I put water on your head and I said *both* names. No curate. No certificate. No argument about who is allowed to stamp what. I thought, 'If the world insists on *void*, I will insist on *name.*' I did it when your father was out getting more muslins. I dried your hair with the towel we kept for luck. I made tea. I did not tell anyone. That is all."

Clara put her hand over her mouth because something wanted to come out of it that would break the moment, and she wanted the moment to hold. "Thank you," she said, when she trusted the word not to turn into something else. "For naming us."

Martha stared at her own hands as if they had written letters to each other without her. "It seemed reasonable," she said. "I have found, over the years, that *reasonable* is a very good spell."

"The jug mattered," Mark said, not as a question.

"It did," Martha said. "Not because it was magic. Because it was *present.* It had stood on the caravan step catching peel and sun when we were happy; it had sat beside the cot when we were not; it had been a place I could put things when I needed to. I moved the band to the shoebox when you were pregnant because it felt unkind to make the jug carry it still when it could carry flowers. But I left a *slip* inside anyway, folded very small—her name in my hand. You know, like you leave a fiver in the pocket of a winter coat and then pretend to be surprised in February."

Clara laughed, because laughter sometimes escorted grief down the stairs without making a scene. "And the biscuits?"

"Always biscuits," Martha said, with the gravity of a mother. "Hiding sweetness is a form of optimism."

They sat with it. The radio offered the weather a second time, as if to give it another chance. The house made a small approving sound; it could have been plumbing; it could have been something consenting.

"May I..." Clara began, and let the politeness of the request be its own rule. "May I see inside the jug?"

"You may," Martha said, at once. "You are the only person who has ever asked me in a way that didn't sound like a raid."

Clara stood. The jug felt heavier than enamel, lighter than guilt. It had the cold of proper things. She tipped it slightly and peered in. The interior was clean because Martha kept things that way; a thin white line of old water lived just below the lip where water dries and leaves its opinion. At the bottom, not biscuits now— they would have gone soft— but a very small slip of paper folded to something the size of a thumbnail.

She looked up. Martha nodded as if she'd been waiting to be asked to nod for twenty years.

Clara loosened the fold with the careful fingers you use for moths. Inside, in Martha's nurse's hand—upright, brisk, the ink softened by history—*ELEANOR MORGAN*. The *E* had a crossbar that meant business. The *R* in *MORGAN* had a leg that refused to dawdle.

She returned the slip to the jug and put the jug back in its place. "No altering records without permission," she said under her breath, because even jokes can be rules.

Martha exhaled, soft and surprised by it. "Thank you," she said, as if someone had returned a library book on time and the library had chosen to feel loved rather than merely obeyed.

"Do you smell..." Mark began, then stopped, embarrassed.

"Apples," all three of them said at once, and then laughed at themselves and at the kitchen for tolerating them.

***

The baby in the good room made a noise like a violinist tuning properly. Martha stood, gathered the small tyrant with the confidence of women who have done the carry a thousand times and never once dropped the republic, and kissed the top of her head with the accuracy of a person who has earned the right. "You will grow into your rules," she told the infant, who blinked as if prepared to meet the assignment.

Clara stared at the jug once more and felt the old wanting—the caravan step, the ropes, the song about the boat. She thought of the photograph from yesterday—the jug appearing as a square of shine in the caravan's doorway between shots—as if images had decided to remember what kitchens remember. She put her hand flat on the table to keep the room stable and spoke, not loudly, not with theatre. "If you are listening," she said to the air with civility, "I have heard you. I will consider it with my rules."

The air did not lower its temperature or raise it. It did not discover a wind. It did not whisper *bossy*. It behaved as good air does. The room, having been asked to hold a story and answer with politeness, complied.

"Will you take the jug," Martha asked, casual as a woman offering a spare tin, and entirely not casual.

Clara blinked. "Now?"

"If you like," Martha said. "Or leave it and I'll talk to it like a lunatic for another decade. I don't mind. But if you make rules for houses to keep their faces, jugs should be under those rules too."

Clara looked at Mark, whose face had become that interesting combination of affection and logistics. "We could... permit it," he said. "Hall mat. We set terms. No water in it unless invited. No moving on its own. No ovens for it to look at" —he smiled faintly; the joke helped— "and if it sulks we post it back to Martha by second-class post."

Martha stared at him with the good, grateful arrogance of mothers watching men be funny and useful at the same time. "Second class only," she said. "We do not dignify sulks."

Clara nodded. "We'll take it. On loan. Under the rules." She looked at the jug and, because she had begun to enjoy speaking to objects as if they were employees, added, "No heroics. No moving things in the nursery. No water left where it shouldn't be. No altering records. If you must change something, you ask, and you do it on the hall mat. You may, if you absolutely insist, smell like apples."

"Allowed," Martha said, dry.

They wrapped the jug in a towel as if it were a graduating student. Mark carried it with the modesty of a man holding someone else's law. Martha, in the hall, put a hand on the jug's shoulder as if sending a child on a coach and then removed it because dignity matters.

"Come back for the photo box when you need to," she said. "Bring biscuits and your clever doctor. I like the sentences she puts in your mouth."

"She'll enjoy being told that," Clara said. "She believes in biscuits as medicine."

Martha kissed them both and kissed the baby with the aim of womanhood and shut the door as if closing a good chapter.

***

They drove home in the kind of light that lets you believe in moderate hope. The jug sat on the back seat in its towel like a passenger who had bought a ticket. At a red light, a bus pulled up alongside. No dinosaur coat today; a teenager with headphones looked at the world like someone who had learnt to pick out their own frequencies. He glanced at the jug, did a small double-take, then— without knowing why— made a little knot with his fingers: right over left; left over right. He frowned, surprised by his own hands, and looked away.

"Witness permitted," Mark said, almost to himself.

"Very," Clara said, and decided not to make a religion of teenagers.

At home, the hall had done its best impression of being a stage pre-pared for a modest ceremony. The mat lay ready, upright, at ease. The sealed envelope against the wall looked like a stiff-backed aunt. The green strip—reef tied—sat behaving.

They set the jug on the hall mat. They did it without theatre and with enough reverence to satisfy the part of themselves that likes rituals because rituals tell the day where to stand.

Clara spoke the rule once, out loud, for the room and for the jug and for the version of herself who sometimes needed to be told in English, not in dread: "Permitted location for change, if it must happen: hall mat only. One item at a time. No baby pictures. No family documents. No passports. No water running. No moving things in the nursery. Re-quests are not commands." She placed two fingers lightly on the jug's enamel as if to steady something that might not want to be steady.

Mark stood, hands in his pockets, the exact posture of a man being furniture on purpose. "BLUE?"

"BLUE," she said. "Rules restated. No emergencies. The floor is not alarmed."

Her phone buzzed. *Harriet: How did the jug conversation go?*
Clara typed: *She named us with water from it. Kept the band there. Hid biscuits there to make the sentence survivable. Jug now on our hall mat under rule. Not an emergency. New boundary: "No heroics; jug is subject to rules."*
Harriet replied with a speed that made Clara imagine her handwriting:
Very good. Jug is an anchor; treat it as such. If it gathers requests, reply with the sentence. No rituals until we discuss. Floor pleased by the word "loan".
Clara smiled at *loan* sitting tidily in her own mind.

They left the jug where it was, as instructed by nobody but them-selves. The rest of the house performed decency. The washing machine attempted meaning with its drum; the kettle rehearsed; the baby sneezed like a small, accurate plucked string. Clara stood in the doorway to the nursery and did the census, because the census calms: catch—two clicks; rabbit—guard; stars—hanging their quiet; breath—immaculate. She placed two fingers on the tiny chest and borrowed the metronome and returned it properly.

On the kitchen window, five small petals arrived in steam and thinned at their own pace. She did not press her hand there. She let the glass keep its own secrets.

***

In the afternoon, Priya texted a photograph of Jonah in a hat with ears that suggested he belonged to a committee. *Salon report?*
Clara sent back: *Martha named us with jug water in 200-, hid band & biscuits in it; jug now on our mat under rules. Not an emergency. Boring tea advisable.*
Priya: *That is the right sort of madness. I have custard creams.*
Clara: *Bring them. Witness permitted at four.*

Priya arrived at exactly the right time wearing a coat that had never known a proper winter but believed in itself. She kissed the baby and saluted the jug with a biscuit. "Look at you," she said to a piece of enamel like a woman greeting a minor local official. "Subject to the council. We welcome your contribution."

"Do not make it feel important," Mark murmured.

"I can be rude to ceramics and kind to babies," Priya said. She looked at Clara and did the checking-without-fussing face that people who love you get very good at. "You okay?"

"I am," Clara said, and was satisfied to find the present tense fit. "Martha did a naming. With water from it. Alone, at the sink. She decided to tell the universe both names existed. It felt... like furniture. Like something that was there already and we've been walking around it."

Priya went to the jug and peered in as if at a tame animal's den. "Any biscuits?"

"Retired," Clara said. "It holds a piece of paper with a name in her hand. That's better than biscuits."

"Debatable," Priya said, and then swallowed the joke and did the serious thing with that same mouth. "I'm glad it's here," she said. "Under rules."

They sat at the table and drank tea and, because you must let normality do the lifting sometimes, laughed at a clip of a dog who had learnt to ring a bell for cheese. The house, pleased by the tone, kept its opinions tidy.

At four-thirty, the baby began the negotiations that led inexorably to bath-time. Mark ran the baby's tray with his manual voice: "Warm; two fingers; towel on radiator; boat optional." The jug, in the hall, stayed where it had been told to stay. The bath mat upstairs looked back at Clara in its correct way; she smiled at it anyway.

After, the witching hour arrived with its clipboard and took notes as everyone did exactly what they always do in the witching hour. There was no corridor voice. There was no cooling on her wrist that needed to be turned into a religion. There was only a small republic recovering from the trauma of having to put on a fresh vest.

Evening had the decency to be boring. They watched a programme in which people discovered that walls, even when encouraged by zealots, continued to behave as if they were load-bearing. Clara enjoyed it more than was fashionable. Priya stood at the door with the air of someone awarding medals. "Text me if the jug sulks," she said. "I'll come round and practice disdain on it."

"If it sulks we post it second-class," Mark said, solemn.

"Excellent," Priya said, and was gone like necessary weather.

They cleared the mugs and plates with the ceremony of people who understand that tidying now is a present you give to your future selves. The jug waited on the mat, upright, earning no attention. The sealed envelope stood beside it like a chaperone.

Clara stood at the kitchen sink and washed two cups that did not need washing because the feeling of making circles soothed the part of her that did not trust her own spine. She smelt apples, and allowed it, because Martha had peeled one into a bowl this morning and smells have rights.

She dried her hands, went to the hall, and stood in front of the jug the way you stand in front of family members you're practising not to be afraid of.

"I'll say it once," she said to the jug because treating the jug as a person prevented her being cruel to actual people. "No heroics. You may be present. You may suggest. You may summon apples at a strength that can be plausibly explained away. You may *not* move on your own. You may *not* request water. You may *not* alter any record. If you must show us a thing, you do it here, on the mat, and you do it in a manner that a tired adult can bear."

The jug, proud of its height, did not change shape. The air stayed obedient.

From the stairs, Mark said gently, "We are ridiculous and correct."

"We are," she said. "It's the only combination that works."

They went up, checked the nursery—catch, rabbit, stars, breath; the holy four—and went to bed with the decency of people who intended to sleep and then see what they could make happen afterwards.

Clara woke at one-thirty-nine to the kind of quiet that means the house has decided to be a good house. She resisted the old habit; she did not put on the eye mask and call it preparation; she did not take out earplugs because they were not in. She lay and listened to the sincere sounds: pipes clearing throats, wind reminding glass that trees exist. There was no voice. There was no corridor standing up and putting on a person.

She went to the landing anyway because rituals are scaffolding while you build the wall. The nursery kept its face: catch—two clicks; rabbit—guard; stars—behaving; breath—proof. The bathroom behaved. The bath mat was not a message, simply a rug.

Downstairs, the hall was ordinary in the way of stages waiting for actors. The jug stood; the sealed envelope stood; the green strip lay folded once, tidy. On the jug's lip, just inside the enamel, the tiniest smear of water had dried in a shape that looked like a cross between a loop and a line.

Clara put her finger to the smear and felt nothing because time had taken it already. She nearly scolded the room for breaking a rule, then remembered: *no water left running* is the rule; water *in* things is permitted if you organise it. You can't ban kettles. You can't ban tea. You cannot ban the memory of water.

She laughed once, quietly, like a person turning on a bedside lamp for five seconds to check the clock and then turning it off because the dark had earned its place. "Bossy," she said, fond, to the invisible bureaucracy they had created between them. "Grown," she answered herself, and went back upstairs, and slept.

***

Morning made a bright thin line at the curtain—a line that looked like it had been drawn with a decent pencil and the right ruler. The baby woke with a yawn that promoted itself to a policy. Mark brought tea in mugs with hairline cracks and the kind of grin men get when they've slept enough to allow themselves language.

"How's our lodger?" he said.

"Present and obedient," Clara said. "No heroics. A memory of a water ring. Acceptable." She wrote *Night: uneventful. Jug: stayed. Water memory: permitted* and drew a small box around *permitted* because the word had muscles.

Her phone buzzed. *Martha: How is the jug behaving?*
Like a civil servant, Clara wrote. *We gave it a desk. It has sworn to be dull.* After a moment: *Good. Bring it back if it gets above itself. I shall demote it to flower duty.* There was a cloud and a heart and nothing else.

Another buzz. *Harriet: Good morning. Floor approves of "no heroics". Add: "No requests about water at night."*
Clara wrote it on the fridge, neat, above *no water*, so it would be read together: NO WATER LEFT RUNNING; NO REQUESTS ABOUT WATER AT NIGHT. She stood back and admired the proportion of the words, the way they made space for breath.

She went to the nursery and spoke the rules to the good room that had kept its promise: "No moving things in here. No water. No requests about water at night. Knots on the hall mat only. Requests are not commands. No altering records without permission. Doctors allowed. Friends allowed. Witness permitted. Allowed: enjoy the baby without checking the window."

The room, proud, didn't argue. The baby exhaled and tilted towards the day with that complete trust that makes adults practise being worthy of it.

Clara lifted her. In the hallway, the jug stood with the dignity of a relic that has decided to try being a household object again. The sealed envelope stood beside it like a chaperone. The house made the small, approving sound that might have been a pipe, might have been a decision.

"Mum named us with water from you," Clara said, half to the jug, half to the house, half to the version of herself that had required someone to put a name into air and mean it. "That is why you mattered. Now you matter because you agreed to be ordinary. That is what grown looks like."

She went to make toast, diagonally, because diagonal toast improves mornings by a fraction. Mark stole the golden triangle and bit it with a face that pretended to be scandalised by his own theft. The baby considered fairness and decided to forgive everyone.

On the kitchen window, five small petals arrived in the steam and thinned back into air. Clara thought of the caravan, the door, the jug's shine between shots. She thought of Janine Snow voiding, and not entirely voiding. She thought of biscuits hidden so you can say *biscuits* without swallowing glass. She thought of a private naming at a sink conducted by a woman who has always believed in reasonable spells.

She wrote at the bottom of the page: *The jug: why it mattered—because it held the name in the house when the paper wouldn't. Rule added: no requests about water at night. Loan continues. Witness permitted; no heroics.* She underlined *loan* because Harriet liked the word and because loans require responsibility.

The day set about being helpful. If it wasn't, they had rules. If it was, they had biscuits. Either way, the jug stayed put, and that, for now, was what acceptance looked like: a tall blue thing on a mat, behaving.

Chapter Fifteen
The Boy on the Bus

Clara woke into a Thursday that looked like a clean page. The light behind the curtains was the colour of old fax paper making a comeback. She lay still and let the house read itself aloud: boiler's civil hum; the fridge's single note; a delivery van writing commas on damp tarmac. She took the notebook and wrote: *Woke steady. Rules unchanged: window (two clicks); boat on my terms; no moving things in nursery; no water; NO REQUESTS ABOUT WATER AT NIGHT; knots on hall mat only; requests ≠ commands; no altering records without permission; doctors allowed; friends allowed; witness permitted; ALLOWED: enjoy the baby without checking the window.* She underlined *allowed* to make the word hold still.

Mark opened one eye like a man negotiating jurisdiction with morning. "Status?"

"Green," she said. "Grey cooperative."

"We do love cooperative grey." He kissed her hair. "High street later? I can carry your adult magic while you buy wipes."

"Priya at ten," Clara said. "Lynn at eleven-ish if the salon lets her go early. I may attempt to buy a cardigan that makes me look like a person who remembers birthdays."

"Ambitious," he said solemnly. "I'll pack snacks for the attempt."

On the landing the baby made the small, bureaucratic squeak that meant a meeting was about to begin. The nursery smelt of warm cotton and the faint biscuit of sleep. The window catch sat down and correct:

two clicks. She didn't check it. She touched it and forgave herself for touching it.

"Morning," she said to the small republic. Two fingers on a tiny chest. Rise, fall. She borrowed the metronome, returned it promptly, like a woman with library manners.

On the dresser the monitor sat dark, pious, and out of work. In the hall, the jug stood on the mat where it had been told to stand, upright as a citizen who had signed the register. The sealed envelope leaned against the wall like a chaperone with standards.

***

They left the house under a sky that wasn't trying to make a point. The pavement remembered last night's rain and asked for a little care at the kerb. Priya waved from the corner in a coat that refused to take the weather seriously. Jonah wore a hat with ears and a look of general approval.

"Ready to spend four pounds on cake we'll call solidarity?" she said.

"Solidarity is expensive," Clara said. "But it comes with icing."

They meandered towards the high street at pram speed, which is the speed at which the world reveals its true shape. Newsagents displayed papers promising everything; a dog examined a bollard as if conducting forensics; a woman in a puffer coat negotiated with a toddler who had discovered the word No and intended to take it out for a spin.

At the bus stop by the church wall, a number 73 sighed to a halt. The windows were fogged with other people's breathing. A small face imprinted itself against a pane like a seal surfacing: the dinosaur coat boy, teeth bared in happiness rather than threat. He saw Clara and lit up as if a private countdown had reached zero. He slapped the glass with both hands and then, with ceremony, showed his fingers: one, two, three; two; one; zero. This time he added something else: he tapped his fist to the glass twice and then carefully looped his index finger round his thumb, as if making a tiny knot. He looked very pleased with himself.

Beside him, a woman—thirty, maybe, tired in the way that has nothing to do with pillows—lifted her head from her phone and, seeing what her son was doing, smiled at Clara through the glass with that apologetic solidarity strangers share in cities. She mouthed, *He does this*, and rolled her eyes affectionately.

Clara mouthed back, *He's brilliant*, and meant it. She lifted her hand, palm out. The boy pressed his palm to the window in perfect alignment as if the glass were some honest border that could be trusted. For half a second the condensation cleared in a neat oval around the two hands and then resumed misting. The woman clocked it, frowned at the physics, and then the bus lurched and carried them off.

"Is he going to become my favourite citizen?" Priya asked, pretending not to be charmed.

"He already is," Clara said.

***

The café on the corner pretended to be Paris and got as far as decent coffee. They took the window table because people-watching is free. Lynn arrived ten minutes later with hair that had been persuaded to behave and the expression of a person who had chosen to be cheerful and was carrying that choice like a small, lovely jug.

"Right," she said, depositing her base unit in Clara's bag like contraband. "Salon therapy successful; fringe subdued. How's your civil service of ghosts?"

"Boring," Clara said, proud. "Jug obedient. No requests about water at night. Papers sealed. Today we're investing in a cardigan."

"Heroic," Lynn said, and stole a corner of Jonah's biscuit as if the law demanded it.

Mid-coffee the boy and his mother came in, trailing the domestic weather of bus air and crisps. The boy wore his dinosaur coat open to the sternum as if daring winter to do its worst. He saw Clara and did a small double-armed wave like a signalman. The woman clocked the recognition and hesitated—London's wariness—then chose friendliness.

"Sorry," she said, approaching their table with a caution that didn't spoil the courage. "It's just—he keeps waving at you from buses and then sulking because the bus won't stop so he can say hello properly." She smiled with a proper mouth. "I'm Ruth. This is Albie."

"Albie," Clara said, delighted to learn the word that went with the small whirlwind. "I'm Clara. This is Priya and Lynn. And this tyrant is my daughter." She didn't say a name for the baby because naming in public had begun to feel like crossing a line she now knew existed.

"Albie," Priya said, offering a solemn handshake that he took gravely, "your coat is a crime and I support it."

Albie beamed. He made his little knot gesture again—finger looping round thumb—and then put both fists on his hips like a man who had tied a ship to a quay.

"Knots," Ruth said, in the tone of a mother gently apologising for her child's unusual hobby. "He's obsessed. Video after video. He ties everything. Shoelaces, napkins, my *hair* once. The lady at nursery says she's never seen hands like it. I keep finding little bits of string in his pockets like he's running a black market."

"He has a calling," Lynn said, half-serious. "We should hire him for municipal improvements."

Albie had already fished the café's paper napkin from the middle of the table, rolled it tight the way sailors do rope, and made—swift, sure, laughing with his hands—a neat reef knot. He held it up for inspection like a jeweller showing a stone.

"Right over left; left over right," Clara heard herself say, and didn't know whether the voice in her mouth belonged to her father or to that corridor or to herself finally remembering the things she had always known. "That's perfect, Albie."

"Mummy says *no knots on doors*," Albie announced to the table and quite a lot of the café. "And *no knots on people*. But napkins allowed." He looked to Ruth, checking he'd remembered the house constitution correctly.

"That's the rule," Ruth said, smiling, then to Clara, sotto voce, "He tried to tie the pram to the bannister. We are a nation of treaties."

"Treaties are adult magic," Priya said. "Would he like to tie a... teaspoon?"

Albie looked personally offended by the idea of tying cutlery. "Spoons don't *want* knots," he said, with the gravitas of a parliamentarian.

"Wise," Lynn said. "A shame so few spoons get a say."

They laughed, the kind of laugh that makes rooms feel inwardly glad.

At the next table a woman with a buggy kept half an eye on Albie's industry and smiled, indulgent; the barista behind the counter paused to watch, arms folded, mouth tilted. People like to be near competence and prefer it when it's small and cheerful.

Albie, finished with his first demonstration, set the napkin down, and picked up—oh no—the hoodie string hanging from Ruth's neckline. "Not that one," Ruth said automatically, a mother by reflex. Albie hesitated, fingers poised.

Clara felt the tug of habit—say nothing; be normal—and then re-membered Harriet saying *"witness permitted."* She also remembered requests ≠ commands. Nobody had asked anything. A small boy was about to be silly in a café.

"Albie," she said lightly, "I like your rules. Shall we tie the napkin instead of Mum?"

"Napkin," he agreed, reasonable, and dropped the hoodie string.

He took two napkins, rolled them, crossed, tucked: reef. He did the second: *left–right.* He did a third without looking. It wasn't perfor-mance—it was delight. The barista clapped once. The woman with the buggy said *clever boy* to the air with the forced casualness British people use to avoid superstition.

Ruth laughed and rolled her eyes because smiles can't do all the work. "He'll tie the world if I let him. You should have seen the bus driver's face yesterday when Albie tried to secure his seatbelt properly." She mimed a small boy diagnosing public infrastructure.

As if she had summoned it, a bus sighed outside at the stop. The café window steamed— three breaths, four— as people came in and the door misbehaved. Through the fogged glass, the shape of the 73 waited, half its passengers dedicated to the doctrine of looking out and seeing nothing much.

Albie pressed both palms to the window and wrote unselfconscious-ly with his heat: a clumsy A, then a loop like an O that became a B, then an L; he paused, discovered an E and improved it with his finger. He stood back, pleased. ABLE, he had written. The barista laughed; the woman with the buggy said, "Useful," and offered him a thumbs-up.

"Albie," Ruth corrected, affectionate, and drew the second I with her knuckle. The steam accepted the amendment graciously and then— slowly, politely— the tail of the E lifted, straightened, and— without a hand anywhere near it— tidied itself to a crisp E that matched Ruth's.

Everyone saw it. There was a soft, collective oh broken into separate little noises— "That's the heat," the barista said quickly, almost cross with physics for being insufficient; "Convection," the buggy woman offered, pleased to have a companionable explanation to hand.

Clara did nothing with her face. She felt the house under her feet without standing in it: witness permitted; no theatrics. She placed Albie back between the café and mystery. She looked at Ruth and saw it— the flicker you see in mothers when they are required to pretend they've understood something they have understood, but in the wrong language.

Ruth smiled, very sane. "Steam does that sometimes," she told her own nerves, and the café listened as if the sentence were a spell. "Come on, small sailor. Leave the window for the next genius."

"Biscuit?" Priya suggested to the table at large, the perfect diversion. She offered one to Albie the way you offer medals to small heroes. He accepted with suitable ceremony.

They settled. The fog on the glass resumed its hobby of being fog. Nothing else moved. The barista shook his head as if dislodging a draught. The woman with the buggy resumed telling her baby about spoons and their rights.

"Right," Ruth said after a minute that had the right number of seconds. "We must go or we'll miss the nursery drop-off window and the window will have words."

"Thank you for saying hello," Clara said. "I'm glad to know his name."

"Albie," Ruth repeated, as if pinning the word to the air so it wouldn't wander. "He'll wave again. He likes a ritual."

"We're in the market for rituals," Lynn said, and they all smiled, and then Ruth manoeuvred pram, bag, boy in a way that would have impressed a longshoreman, and was gone.

***

They watched the door close. People breathed. The room found its proper size.

"Public slip," Priya said softly, not as theatre, as a note in a notebook. "Tiny, deniable, witnessed by three civilians and a barista who will tell his girlfriend."

"Witness permitted," Clara said. She wrote Able / Albie — steam letter corrected itself in the left column of her head and interpretation: benign; keep rules; don't chase on the right.

Lynn leaned in, elbows on the table, hands responsible. "We need a new rule," she said, looking at Clara and then at the space that had not cooled. "Nothing that uses other people's children. If the... if she tries to show off through them, we refuse. Politely."

Clara nodded. The floor of her chest approved. "Agreed. 'No requests through children who are not ours.'"

"Add: 'No teaching other people's children,'" Priya said, with a look at Clara that managed to be kind and teasing at the same time. "Sorry, you were radiating *let me show this prodigy a bowline*."

"I was," Clara said, and let herself be teased because she had been thinking show him a bowline and Harriet would have written NO on her forehead with a biro. "Okay. No teaching. No requests. If anything happens, we label it *witness* and go home."

***

"Text Harriet?" Lynn suggested.

Clara typed: *Café. Boy = Albie. First public slip: steam letter self-corrected with strangers watching. We stayed boring. Proposal: add rules—no requests through other people's children; no teaching them; withdraw if attention gathers.* She hit send. The reply arrived with Harriet's decent speed: *Agreed on both rules. Good management. If crowded, remove yourselves. Witness ≠ performance. Floor pleased.*

Clara's shoulders let go of two degrees of something she hadn't wanted to name. "Right," she said. "We'll buy a cardigan and go home."

On the high street, the cardigan did what cardigans do: disguised tiredness as taste. They bought wipes and a small, unnecessary wooden rattle shaped like a fish because unnecessary objects sometimes stop the world slipping. Outside the chemist, the 73 sighed again. Through the window—there he was—Albie, already fogging the glass on purpose. He saw Clara and did not do the countdown this time. He held up both hands, palms outward, then mimed tying—two precise little gestures in the air—then tapped twice on the glass as if sealing a pact. He grinned and was gone, a boy being a boy on a bus in a city on a Thursday.

"Name acquired," Mark said, appearing from the hardware shop with picture hooks and the air of a man who had solved the house in five minutes. "How goes knitwear diplomacy?"

"Successful," Clara said. "We also added a rule about other people's children."

"Good," he said immediately, as if Harriet had texted it to him directly. "No recruiting the youth."

They walked home through a sky that had decided to be honest about its grey. People had their heads down and their errands upright. The house met them with the old steady patience. The jug stood on the mat with the pride of a thing that had learnt ordinary. The sealed envelope chaperoned without complaint. The green strip lay folded—reef—tidy.

Clara set the new rule in pen on the fridge beneath *witness permitted* so the words could discuss it with their neighbours: NO REQUESTS THROUGH OTHER PEOPLE'S CHILDREN. NO TEACHING THEM. WITHDRAW IF ATTENTION GATHERS. She underlined withdraw because one day she might forget and because underlining seemed to pin the day to the table.

She wrote in the notebook, neat: *Café: Albie named (Ruth mother). Public slip (steam E corrected self; barista + buggy woman saw). We stayed boring. Rule added re: other people's children. Jug: behaved. House: compliant.* She added, because the word liked being told it had a job: *Me: here.*

At four, the witching hour turned up with its clipboard and transparency. The baby forgave everyone for existing and then asked for recompense in milk and silliness. Mark ran the baby's tray with manual dignity: "Warm; two fingers; towel; boat optional." The jug in the hall made no comment. The bath mat upstairs was a bath mat and not literature. The window in the nursery sat shut with its two clicks and didn't require applause.

After, they ate on the sofa and watched a man on television learn, slowly, that beams have opinions. Clara felt soothed by the doctrine of lintels. On the kitchen window, five petals arrived in steam and thinned in their own time. She didn't touch them. She let them be petals and not messages.

At nine, she stood in the nursery doorway and did the census: catch; rabbit; stars; breath. She put two fingers on the tiny chest and borrowed the metronome and returned it with interest. She spoke the rules in that soft voice that had begun to feel like grammar: "No moving things in here. No water. No requests about water at night. Knots on the hall mat only. No requests through other people's children. No teaching them. Withdraw if attention gathers. Requests are not commands. No altering records without permission. Doctors allowed. Friends allowed. Witness permitted. Allowed: enjoy the baby without checking the window."

The room, pleased with its part, refused to turn into a sign. The baby breathed the way honest rooms like.

In bed, Clara wrote one last line by phone light because discipline is romance: *The witness has a name: Albie. The public saw and the world did not end. We set a boundary; the day obeyed.* She slid the notebook under the bed and let the thought find the cooler floor.

Downstairs, the jug stood like a thing on loan earning trust. On the mat, the green strip lay quiet. In the sealed envelope, the paper behaved. Outside, a bus took strangers home under a sky that had decided to be reasonable. A boy in a dinosaur coat counted nothing in particular and, without knowing why, made a small, tidy knot with his fingers in the air—just to keep his hands remembering—then pressed his palm to the glass, just in case.

Witness, permitted. Boundaries, in place. The house agreed, by being a house.

Chapter Sixteen

Static

C lara woke into a Friday that had ironed itself sensible. The light behind the curtains was the colour of photocopy paper that had learned restraint. She lay very still and let the house list itself: boiler's civil hum, the fridge's one note, a delivery van practising commas on damp tarmac.

She took the notebook and, neat, wrote the date, then the usual: *Woke steady. Rules unchanged: window (two clicks); boat on my terms; no moving things in nursery; no water; NO REQUESTS ABOUT WATER AT NIGHT; knots on hall mat only; requests ≠ commands; no altering records without permission; doctors allowed; friends allowed; witness permitted; NO REQUESTS THROUGH OTHER PEOPLE'S CHILDREN; NO TEACHING THEM; WITHDRAW IF ATTENTION GATHERS; ALLOWED: enjoy the baby without checking the window.* She underlined *allowed* once, because underlining persuades breath to behave.

Mark surfaced with one eye like a man greeting a shy animal. "Status?"

"Green," she said. "Grey polite."

"We'll take polite." He kissed her hair. "Calendar?"

"Jade at ten-fifteen for the weigh-in," she said. "Return Lynn's base unit at eleven if she wants it, or keep for boring test part three. Priya threatened to bring a cardigan and opinions."

"Excellent," Mark said. "I'll impersonate a person who answers emails with grace."

On the landing the baby made the bureaucratic squeak of a citizen opening the office. The nursery smelt of warm cotton and clean small animal. The window catch sat down and proper: two clicks. She didn't check it. She touched it and forgave herself for touching it.

"Morning," she said to the republic. Two fingers on a tiny chest—rise, fall. She borrowed the metronome and returned it with interest.

On the dresser the monitor sat dark and pious, unemployed by doctrine. In the hall the jug stood on the mat where it had been told to stand, tall and reasonable. Beside it, the sealed envelope kept its hand on its own mouth.

***

Jade, the health visitor, arrived with a bag that could have solved a country and a voice that made rooms stay rooms. She praised the baby's thighs as if awarding a prize and pronounced, with the authority of a modest saint, "You're doing exactly enough."

"Frame that," Priya said from the doorway, arriving with knitwear and a grin. "I brought a cardigan and an inability to mind my own business."

"Hang the cardigan on my self-doubt," Clara said. "See if it fits."

Jade weighed, nodded, annotated with the satisfaction of a person whose pen tells good news. "Anyone sleeping?" she asked, a joke and not a joke.

"Enough to keep civilisation," Mark said, coming down with two mugs and a face that could pass for calm at a distance.

"Good," Jade said. She looked at the monitor on the dresser, dark and obedient. "Still off?"

"By design," Clara said. "We're doing boring tests with Lynn's unit sometimes. Ours gets a sabbatical."

"Boring saves lives," Jade said, as if quoting a text. "And marriages. And the carpets."

By eleven, Jade had gone to save other carpets, and Priya had condemned two cardigans as structurally unsound and praised the third for looking like it knew verbs. The baby yawned in italics and went down for a nap with tidy self-respect. The house, pleased by the behaviour of its citizens, settled.

Clara's phone buzzed. *Lynn: Are you in? I've got the thing. It did... something.*

Clara texted back: *In. Door's on the chain but friendly.* She sent the small smile they'd adopted to mean *witness permitted.*

Lynn arrived with hair that had chosen a side and the expression of a woman who had decided to be sane. Her base unit—sleek, newer than Clara's dark, blunt rectangle—sat in her bag like contraband with an alibi. She held up her phone, already apologising.

"I know Harriet said no recordings that first week," she said, "and I swear I didn't set anything clever. But my camera app is one of those idiot ones—sound events auto-save when the base is paired. I forgot to switch it off after the salon. It... recorded something. While we were out."

"We were out?" Priya asked, because Priya is the friend who confirms your grammar.

"We were at the chemist buying the cardigan that will fix civilisation," Clara said, faint smile. "What time?"

Lynn checked. "13:12. I was still at the salon. Sam was at nursery. The room was empty. The base was on the dresser but the camera wasn't pointed anywhere useful. It shouldn't have recorded anything. It should have recorded *silence* and refused to call that content."

Clara's mouth went dry in a manageable way. "Well then," she said, "let's be very boring and listen once."

They sat at the kitchen table, because tables change less when you look at them. Mark placed mugs as if officiating. Lynn put her phone down between them like a neutral witness. She opened the app; it offered a list of "Events" with polite thumbnails: *sound detected; 13:12:04; 6s.* Another at *13:12:21; 9s.* A third at *13:13:00; 4s.* Underneath, three dots doing their patient dance.

"It's picked up a bus before," Lynn said. "Or Sam yelling about invertebrates. But not this."

"Once," Clara said, and made her voice adopt Harriet's decent crispness. "We listen once. We write down what we heard. We do not replay. We do not chase. We do not fall off the floor."

"Floor holds," Priya said.

Lynn tapped the first file. The speaker breathed static—not white, not harsh; the kind of soft hiss that sounds like rain on a tin roof in a film. In it, like someone touching the surface of water with a finger, a voice said, low and not in the room, "Left–right."

It wasn't a child's rabbit-breath voice. It wasn't the older breath of anyone standing at the door and performing for microphones. It was the voice Clara had begun to be able to tolerate without needing to leave her body: the girl curled inside her vowels.

The static breathed. "Left–right," again, with the affectionate impatience of a person reminding you how to be alive. Then—nothing. The file ended with the neatness of someone closing a book.

Lynn tapped the second. Static again, thinner. A soft, familiar sound like click... click. Not loud. Not metal against metal. The sound of a window catch doing its two clicks the way a promise does itself.

"Good grief," Mark said, under his breath, and folded his hands like a man meeting a bishop.

Clara's stomach tried to drop a floor and then remembered the floor had stairs now. She kept her face like English. "We weren't here at 13:12," she said, because naming is also furniture. "And the catch is closed."

"We can check in a minute," Priya said, mild. "Third file?"

Lynn tapped. Static. Then a sound Clara hated immediately for being accurate: the soft, clean plink of a plug chain tapping enamel; the little swirl of water and then a tiny ring as if water had run and been turned off. The file cut—tidy, obedient, brief.

"No," Clara said, to the air, to the jug on the mat, to the part of herself that holds vigils. "No and no. No requests about water at night, and no water at lunchtime either if it's for sport. No water."

The app put its three dots away. The list sat there, untroubled, as if they'd been discussing nothing more consequential than the price of apples.

"Once," Clara said, reminding herself, reminding the room, reminding the part of her that wanted to replay until it turned into proof. "Play each once. Done."

"We should check the catch," Mark said, as if being told the word *catch* would hear him and snap to attention. "And the bath." He stood, not hasty. They went upstairs together in a knot, a small procession of boredom with its sleeves rolled.

The nursery had done as promised. Window catch: two clicks, down and sober. Rabbit at his idiot post. Paper stars behaving. Breath: perfect. Clara laid two fingers lightly on the small chest and borrowed the metronome for three beats, then returned it, like a good librarian. "Thank you," she told no one and meant it.

In the bathroom the tub was dry. The plug sat where plugs sit when they have nothing to hide. The chain did not confess to having been toyed with by film sound. The bath mat was a mat. The sink spoke only of soap.

They went down again. The jug stood still, tall and permitted, a loan in good standing.

"Timestamp," Priya said, practical. "Witnesses. Write it," and pushed the notebook towards Clara like a sensible friend sliding a life-jacket.

Clara wrote: *13:12:04 — Lynn's base app (Sam's room empty) — static; "left–right". 13:12:21 — static; click click (window catch). 13:13:00 — static; plug chain; water sound; stops.* Under interpretations: *Benign (left–right); boundary-probe ("two clicks" and water); no compliance.* Witnesses: *C.M., M.M., L.T., P.S.* She underlined *no compliance* until the ink accepted that compliance was not on offer.

Lynn sat back. "I'm sorry," she said, unexpected, as if she'd brought a mess. "The app... it's set to do this. I genuinely forgot."

"You didn't do anything wrong," Clara said, and found she meant it. "You didn't ask it to be a tape recorder of the dead. It's software. It records babies crying and bus brakes. We're just... having a day where bits of the world want to say their names."

Priya, eyes still on the phone as if daring it to perform, said, "The first week Harriet said no recordings so we didn't cultivate ghosts. But this wasn't cultivation. This was careless software. We add a rule."

Mark nodded, pleased when language turns into wood you can nail. "No recording devices in the nursery. No auto-saves. No cloud. Listeners only, when needed."

"And if someone else's device records," Clara said, "we do what we did: we listen once, we write it down, we seal a copy. We do not make a religion out of playback."

"Leaflet people can queue," Priya said, fondly, out of habit; Ruth had said steam does that sometimes; everyone in the café had agreed to be boring in public. It had worked.

Lynn locked the screen as if shutting a door. "Do you want me to delete them?" she asked, careful.

"No altering records without permission," Clara said automatically, and then, more gently, "We'll write to Harriet; she'll tell us where to put them. For now, don't delete. Don't share. Don't replay."

"Understood," Lynn said. "I will treat my phone like a chest of drawers that no longer opens."

Clara texted Harriet: *Lynn's app auto-saved three "sound events" while house empty: 13:12 left–right; 13:12:21 two clicks; 13:13 water sounds (brief, stopped). We listened once. We're adding rule: no recording devices in nursery; no auto-saves; no cloud. Seal copies?* She put her phone face down because that is how you keep phones from being smug.

Harriet's answer arrived in the decent window a floor uses to encourage calm: *Correct. Keep files; do not replay. Export to a USB; label; seal. Do not invite more recordings. Add your rule in writing on the fridge and in your head. You did well not to chase. Floor holds.*

"Right," Clara said. "USB. Envelopes. Adult magic."

They printed the app's event list—timestamps, the absurd little thumbnail of the empty room with the corner of a cot—and wrote them up neat. They exported the three short files to a USB stick Mark found in the drawer that keeps screws and guilt. Clara labelled it with a piece of tape and wrote, LYNN MONITOR EVENTS 13:12 – 13:13 (COPY). They put it in an envelope and, without theatre, sealed it. On the flap she wrote: SEALED — 13:47 — Witnesses: C.M., M.M., L.T., P.S. She drew the small boat, because habit had become a kind of oath.

Mark fixed the new rule on the fridge beneath *witness permitted*, so the sentences could keep each other honest: NO RECORDING DEVICES

IN THE NURSERY. NO AUTO-SAVES. NO CLOUD. LISTENERS ONLY. In smaller letters beneath: IF OTHERS RECORD, LISTEN ONCE; SEAL; DO NOT REPLAY.

They stood and admired the plainness. Ordinary is a skill.

"Shall we reward ourselves with cake and denial?" Priya asked.

"We shall," Lynn said fervently, producing a box. "Salon therapy includes lemon drizzle."

They cut slices with the seriousness people reserve for sacraments. The baby slept through it—blameless, honest peace. The house arranged itself around the rule, like elbows moving to make room at a table.

***

At two, after naps had been negotiated with and won, Ruth and Albie went past the window like a proof of concept. Albie, seeing the adults gathered, did the little knot with his fingers and then, crucially, did not press his hands to the glass, because yesterday's rule had been learned on his side too—no requests through other people's children. He waved and moved on, fizzing with competence.

"Witness permitted," Mark said, not to the glass, to himself.

Clara texted Martha a photograph of the jug behaving and the new fridge rule. *We'll need a bigger fridge,* Martha wrote back. *Bring the jug for tea on Sunday if it gets above itself. I shall demote it to holding tulips.*

At four, Jade sent her boring, satisfying message: *Weight plotted. Well done on protecting sleep. No changes. Keep doing exactly enough.* Being told to keep being moderate is the sort of benediction adulthood craves.

The witching hour arrived with its clipboard and was persuaded to sign its name without making a fuss. The baby forgave everyone. Mark ran the baby's tray: "Warm; two fingers; towel; no water tricks," he added to the ceiling. The jug, in the hall, did not ask for heroics. The bath behaved.

They ate at seven, watched a programme in which someone underestimated a lintel and a woman in a hi-vis vest corrected him with grace. Clara found herself, to her own surprise, soothed.

At nine, she stood in the nursery doorway and took the census because the census is a religion of the kind that does not hurt: catch; rabbit; stars; breath. She put two fingers on the tiny chest and borrowed the metronome and returned it with interest. She spoke the rules softly to the room that had learnt to keep its face. "No moving things in here. No water. No requests about water at night. Knots on the hall mat only. No recordings in here. Requests are not commands. No altering records without permission. Doctors allowed. Friends allowed. Witness permitted. No requests through other people's children. Withdraw if attention gathers. Allowed: enjoy the baby without checking the window."

The room, pleased to be reminded of its job, refused to become a sign. She closed the door to the width of a word and went down.

***

They were both almost asleep when the static started.

Not from a phone. Not from Lynn's polite app. From their monitor on the dresser—dark, off, pious. A soft hiss breathed into the bedroom air the way drizzle arrives in a sentence. The red LED—which should not have been red because the unit should not have been on—showed one faint bar, then two.

Clara sat up. Beside her, Mark did too at exactly the same speed, like people who have practised a drill and intend to pass.

"We switched it off," he said, very quietly, as if speaking to a judge.

"We did," Clara said.

The static wasn't the shouty mess of a badly tuned radio. It was the rain-on-tin of the files they'd heard at lunchtime. The hiss that used to make nights feel like edges. The sound that had once opened a corridor in her mind.

Clara reached and put two fingers lightly on the smooth plastic—the blessing she'd taught herself not to be embarrassed by—and said, to the room and the unit and the part of herself that used to run towards proof, "Requests are not commands. I have heard you; I will consider it with my rules."

The red LED stayed at two bars and behaved like a person who has decided to stand their ground without being rude. The hiss softened. In it, like a fingertip making ripples on a bowl of water, a voice, low, amused, patient: "Bossy."

"Grown," Clara said back, steady.

Mark, not brave, not foolish, only precise, said, "We're not recording. We're not inviting. If you have anything to say, say it now, and then let us sleep. Doctors are allowed. Water is not."

Static breathed. A sound like a plug chain tapped enamel, once—a memory, not an action. Then—soft, as if through someone else's wall—left–right. Then, with an affectionate sigh, "Keep her safe."

"With us," Clara said.

The red LED sank to one bar, then none. The static faded like rain that has done its job. The room resumed its size.

Mark put a hand on the bedpost and looked at it as if checking that wood was still honest. He let out a breath that was half a laugh and half a weather report. "That," he said, "was a device performing beyond its competence."

"It was a device being haunted by a house," Clara said, and found, to her own astonishment, that she wasn't angry. "It recorded something it shouldn't at lunchtime. It tried to be a radio tonight. It's a child. We're the adults."

"Blue?" Mark asked, defaulting. "Rules intact?"

"Blue," she said. "We restated. We did not chase. We did not replay. We did not drown."

They lay down again. Sleep, encouraged like a shy cat, returned with its tail high. The house made the approving sounds of a dwelling that had decided to keep its bargain.

***

Morning made a thin pencil line on the curtain. The baby woke and issued her manifesto in tasteful coos. The jug on the mat stood like an honoured guest behaving itself. The sealed envelope sat beside it like a sensible aunt. The monitor on the dresser looked ordinary—dark, off, guiltless.

Clara made tea and, while the kettle rehearsed its single song, wrote: *Night: our unit (off) produced static; LED lifted; voice ("bossy"; "left–right"; "keep her safe"). We replied; no recording; no compliance; static ceased.* She added, under rules: *NO RECORDINGS IN THE NURSERY (FRIDGE + MIND). LISTENERS ONLY. If device misbehaves → UNPLUG, SEAL, TEXT H.

She took the marker and, beneath yesterday's rule, added in that sober, capital hand that made words keep their shape: IF A DEVICE

MISBEHAVES: UNPLUG; DO NOT ENGAGE; PLACE ON HALL MAT; SEAL IF NECESSARY; TEXT HARRIET.

Mark, reading over her shoulder, nodded in that satisfied way men get when policy is a thing you can touch. "We'll give the monitor a little holiday," he said. "Into the drawer with the feral chargers."

"Loan withdrawn," Clara said, amused by the legal note in her own voice, and lifted the unit with both hands as if it might spill. She carried it to the hall with the ceremony of someone relocating a mild offender. She set it on the mat beside the jug and the sealed envelope, and said the sentence because saying the sentence is the point. "Permitted location for change is here. No recording. No rehearsals. If you must be strange, be strange in a way a tired adult can bear."

The plastic was plastic. The air was air. The room kept its face.

Her phone buzzed. *Harriet: Saw your overnight note. Correct response. Add a practical boundary: "No networked devices in the nursery. Airplane rule after 7 p.m. Listeners are fine; eyes are off." Bring USB Monday. Floor pleased by "listen once" discipline.*

Clara wrote on the fridge under the new block: AIRPLANE RULE AFTER 7 P.M. — NURSERY IS A NETWORK-FREE ROOM. EYES OFF. LISTENERS ONLY.

She stepped back. The board looked bossy in a way she could love.

In the nursery the catch sat down with its two clicks. The rabbit, that idiot sentinel, held his post with honour. The paper stars hung their quiet. Breath was immaculate. She put two fingers on the tiny chest and borrowed the metronome and returned it. She looked at the window and then, deliberately, at the baby, because ALLOWED had to be practised or it withers.

"Witness permitted," she said to the room, to the jug, to the part of the house that had begun to learn English. "Recordings are not."

From downstairs came the smell of toast going honourably golden. Mark shouted, "Diagonal?" and she shouted back, "Obviously," and the ordinary joy of someone else cutting your breakfast into triangles put the morning back on its feet.

On the kitchen window, five petal-shapes formed in the steam and then thinned at their own pace. She didn't press a hand there. She let the glass keep its own memory. She wrote, at the bottom of the day's page, because writing is an oath, *Monitor recorded something it shouldn't. We stayed boring. New boundary: no recording devices in nursery; airplane rule after seven; misbehaving devices to the mat. Me: bossy + grown.*

The house approved with the tiny sound it makes when plumbing agrees. Somewhere down the road a bus sighed, and perhaps a boy in a dinosaur coat practised tying knots with his fingers in the air, for no one, for the pleasure of remembering how to keep things together without making them choke. Witness, permitted. Devices, grounded. The floor held.

Chapter Seventeen
Split

Clara woke into a Saturday that had taken the trouble to be reasonable. The light behind the curtains was the colour of paper that has agreed to be written on. She lay very still and let the house list itself: boiler's civil hum; the fridge's one note; far-off tyres drawing commas on damp tarmac. She took the notebook and wrote: *Woke steady. Rules unchanged: window (two clicks); boat on my terms; no moving things in nursery; no water; NO REQUESTS ABOUT WATER AT NIGHT; knots on hall mat only; requests ≠ commands; no altering records without permission; doctors allowed; friends allowed; witness permitted; NO REQUESTS THROUGH OTHER PEOPLE'S CHILDREN; NO TEACHING THEM; WITHDRAW IF ATTENTION GATHERS; NO RECORDING DEVICES IN THE NURSERY; LISTENERS ONLY; AIRPLANE RULE AFTER 7 p.m.; IF DEVICE MISBEHAVES: UNPLUG; MAT; TEXT H.* She underlined *allowed: enjoy the baby without checking the window* once and let herself believe it.

Mark surfaced with one eye like a man greeting a shy animal. "Status?"

"Green," she said. "Grey cooperative."

"We like cooperative." He kissed her hair. "What's the day pretending to be?"

"Errands," she said. "Biscuits for Martha; picture hooks for the room-that-needs-to-pretend-to-be-a-study; return Priya's scarf she swears she doesn't miss."

"Bold," he said. "I'll find the box of nails that bites and call it recon-ciliation."

On the landing the baby made the sensible squeak of a citizen open-ing the office. The nursery smelt of warm cotton and clean small an-imal. The window catch sat down and honest: two clicks. She didn't check it. She touched it and forgave herself for touching it.

"Morning," she told the republic. Two fingers to a tiny chest: rise, fall. She borrowed the metronome and returned it with interest.

On the dresser the monitor sat dark and obedient; the jug stood on the hall mat like a well-behaved lodger; the sealed envelope leant against the skirting as a chaperone with standards.

***

By mid-morning the house had put its apron on. Mark found the pic-ture hooks (after insulting three boxes of screws who had it coming), hung the hedgerow birds print straight enough to pacify a vicar, and discovered a latent passion for the spirit level. Clara played municipal clerk: jars labelled; nappies stacked; the good pens put where good pens go to watch over lists.

They met in the kitchen with mugs and a biscuit and the pleasure of having achieved tasks that would not impress a single god and were therefore the right ones for Saturday.

"We should talk about Monday," Mark said, too casual.

"Harriet," Clara said. "USB. Jug. Boring notes. The bit where we were grown during the static."

"And," he added carefully, "what we're doing next with... proof."

She didn't sigh. She placed the mug down in the centre of the coaster and used the distance to be kind. "We are not *doing* proof," she said.

"We are living in a house. Harriet said not to chase. We bring her ambiguity and biscuits."

He nodded, slow, but she could see the muscle in his jaw start its private PE lesson. "I know. I do. It's just—" He gestured at the sealed envelope in the hall with his mug, a small orbit. "We're amassing protocol like trophies and none of it is changing anything I can hold. I'm in the room and I'm still in the corridor."

"You're in the room more than you were," she said, gently. "You heard your name in the corridor. We're not making a church. We're making a floor."

"Sure," he said, and smiled the way men smile when they are trying not to be insufficient in the face of women who have learnt a second language of the house. "Sorry."

"Don't be sorry," she said. "Be bored. Bored is safe."

He laughed, properly, and for a while the day did its decent job. They ate something with eggs that couldn't raise a scandal. The baby forgave everybody for putting her in the lemon cardigan. Priya texted a photo of Jonah with flour in his hair as if he'd been ordained by a bakery and added: *We're making chaos cake; come save us from ourselves at four.* Lynn sent, *Salon closed. I own a fringe. Available for not courting proof.* Martha, with Saturday's bluntness, wrote: *Carrots oblique. Bring your faces tomorrow.*

***

The argument had the courtesy to wait until after lunch.

It didn't begin with a sin. It began with tidying. Mark set the sealed USB envelope a fraction higher up the console table so the baby, later, would not mistake it for a chewable. His hand hovered over the monitor—dark, exiled to the drawer since last night's hiss—and then he pulled the drawer shut firmly as if the gesture could be an oath.

"You're doing a face," Clara said, not unkindly, from the kitchen where she was finicking pegs into a line.

"I'm doing a face," he admitted. "I want—" He paused long enough to allow a better word to arrive and then rejected it. "—a thing. Something we can take to Saturday, not just Monday. A baseline. A... a controlled ask."

"No asks," she said, softly. "Requests are not commands."

"Not to her," he said, and the pronoun made the room tilt by half a degree. "To the house. To the... to the physics of it. We set the jug on the mat. We say: 'Show us something we can put on a page that isn't going to put anyone in water or knock anything off a wall.' We stand in the hallway like rational fools and we watch."

She turned and looked at him properly. He looked like a man asking to drive in fog because he needed to get somewhere and had convinced himself the lines would be enough. "That's a request," she said, calm. "That's *performing* with a prop we've deliberately demoted to loan. That's trying to get out in front of a thing that behaves better when we don't chase it."

"And it's asking our own house to calm down for thirty seconds," he said, still calm, which was worse. "We need to know if we're holding a handrail or a ribbon. Last night our own monitor tried to... do work. Today we choose to be in charge of what tries."

She felt the hot, low pulse of the panic that dresses as competence. "You want me to sanction an experiment. On a Saturday. With our daughter asleep." She heard Harriet's voice in her mouth: no rituals until we discuss. "We're not doing a séance in our hallway, Mark."

"I'm not asking for candles," he said, with the gentleness that used to persuade her into second drinks and now made her want to hold him still. "I'm asking for a measured set of eyes. We place the jug and the silly green rope and the sealed envelope exactly as they are. We stand here. We say nothing. For thirty seconds."

"Which is still an ask," she said. "Silence is also an ask if you put it on a stage."

"Then I'll stand here and not ask," he said, and now the gentleness had been retired in favour of a small, glinting stubbornness she recognised from the day he carried the cot upstairs without admitting it weighed more than a baby. "You don't have to be in my experiment. You can be in your kitchen. I'll be furniture. I'll be bored better than you."

She put the peg down because it was either that or snap it petty. "We're not splitting the house into your corridor and my kitchen. We're not... splitting."

"Clara," he said, and there it was—the little plea under her name. "I need one thing that isn't someone else telling me I did quite well not to panic. I need to push against the air and feel the air push back because I asked it to. I'm not trying to conjure. I'm trying to remain a person who didn't hand over all the levers to an invisible teenager with opinions about knots."

She opened her mouth to say the right sentence and instead found another one. "If you need to do something, hang another picture," she said, and immediately hated herself, because belittling is a sin of tidy people when they are tired. "I'm sorry. That was cheap."

He breathed, looked at the ceiling, and amended his plan. "I will hang another picture," he said, light. "And later, when the house is wearing slippers, I will stand for thirty seconds and not ask out loud. If anything happens, it won't be because I asked."

"That is linguistic gymnastics," she said.

"I live with you," he said, and smiled because they had both been saving that joke for a bad day. She smiled despite herself. The argument, like weather losing interest in itself, passed over, but it left a dampness.

***

At four, Priya's chaos cake required adult supervision. They walked over with the pram, the sky pretending to choose blue. Lynn joined with hair that had finally surrendered to reason. The kitchen at Priya's was the kind houses aspire to be—flour on everything; a wooden spoon that had known generations; a radio listing gently to one side like a boat that trusted its river.

"Look at you," Priya said to the baby, "arriving with the promise of inherited cake." She handed Mark a spatula and Clara a tea towel and put Lynn in charge of laughter. They ate the cake as if it were medicinal.

"Any hauntings in tins?" Priya asked.

"Only the monitor being a toddler," Mark said, carefully breezy.

"Devices," Lynn said, nodding. "They hear their names being called even when you only think them."

Priya produced a new cardigan with a flourish. "Somebody needs this because I bought it rashly and it makes me look like a tea cosy."

Clara put it on, and Priya said, "Oh for God's sake, it's yours," with fondness and despair.

They talked about lintels and leaflets and tulips for Martha's jug. They didn't talk about standing in hallways to coax the air. They walked home with the cake's sugar behaving in their blood.

Evening put on its slippers. The baby went to sleep with the tidy honour of a citizen who has completed the form correctly. They performed the census with the seriousness of people who know ritual is scaffolding, not superstition: catch (two clicks); rabbit (guard); stars (hanging their quiet); breath (immaculate). In the hall the jug stood where it had been told; the sealed envelope kept its sensible posture; the green strip lay folded—reef—behaving.

They ate on the sofa and agreed with a woman in hi-vis about beams. When the programme ended, the room took off its work face and waited to see what kind of night it was going to be.

"Ferry?" Mark said, routine turning a question into a cushion.

"On," Clara said. "I'll do first watch." She kissed him with the accuracy of teams that have made a rota more intimate than poetry and went upstairs with a book that wouldn't threaten anyone.

The house went quiet in the way of houses that have earned it.

Downstairs, Mark stood in the hallway and looked at nothing. He did not ask. He did not clear his throat. He thought of thirty seconds and then thought of Harriet and then thought of how long thirty seconds is when you've promised not to think at something. He went into the kitchen instead, opened the drawer of cables and feral chargers, and took out the monitor to place it in a different drawer—out of sight, out of ritual. He felt ridiculous and correct.

His phone was in his pocket. It was always in his pocket when he was being a father. It wasn't a recording device in the nursery. It was a father's pocket with a phone in it. Language is elastic, he told himself, and hated the taste of the sentence.

He put the phone on the counter and turned it face down. He picked up the jug.

He did it subconsciously: how you pick up a familiar weight without asking the ethics of enamel. He carried it to the sink to move it back to the mat because that was the rule: jug lives on mat. Midway he thought, it's been on the mat all day; if I rinse it, it will be cleaner at

Martha's tomorrow, and this was the moment the argument crossed the carpet and put its foot on his ankle.

No water. No requests about water at night. The rules were printed on the fridge. The fridge was in the room. He was in the room. He didn't turn the tap.

He put the jug down in the sink and— God help him— ran a finger of water to loosen a phantom ring that wasn't there. Two seconds. A premature, cowardly off. No faucet hiss. No jug filled. He dried it with a tea towel as if the towel would testify in court. He told himself he had not broken a rule because night had not properly started, it was not night-night, it was early evening with experts in hi-vis on television.

He put the jug back on the mat exactly as it had stood, a model prisoner with better hygiene. He exhaled. Nothing in the air changed shape to clap.

"Bossy," he told the house, fond, and hated himself again for liking the word.

Upstairs, the baby turned in sleep, soft as a punctuation change.

Mark stood in the hall and did not ask. He moved the green strip a centimetre so it lay more squarely. He did not ask. He placed the sealed envelope upright. He did not ask.

The bathroom tap upstairs came on.

Not a gushing theatre. A thin, polite run, the sort of flow a careful person uses to check temperature. He could hear the neat ring of the chain against enamel— the exact notation from Lynn's files— and the small thickening of water in a plugged place.

He was already on the stairs. He called, "Clara," softly, not to panic, to summon a witness.

Her voice came from the landing, calm because calm is the only currency that spends in these economies. "I hear it. I'm here."

They stepped into the bathroom together and found the hot tap turned a fraction, water running neatly into the plugged bath. No steam. No ghostly fog. Just water. The tub held half an inch as if invited. Mark turned the tap off with two fingers as if it were a small animal that might bite if insulted. He pulled the plug.

They listened to the glug because listening to glugs is a way to prove you haven't drowned.

"Which rule," he said, very quiet.

"No water," she said, just as quiet. "No requests about water at night. We didn't request. We provoked."

He swallowed. "I ran a finger of water in the sink downstairs," he said, truthful because marriage remains a religion after hauntings. "I thought— cleaning. I didn't think— I thought I didn't think. I'm sorry."

"You broke a rule," she said, because the floor has to name the hole. Her voice was steady. This, he thought, is what adulthood looks like when you would like to be dramatic and you choose to be a person.

"I did," he said. "And the house—she— did it back."

They stood very still. The bath was empty by then and looked innocent and English.

From the nursery came a sound that did not belong to water: a small metallic chime and the soft whisper of something turning.

"Clara," he said, and they were already moving.

The nursery had kept its face until it decided not to. The mobile—paper stars strung with patience— was spinning very slightly. It wasn't the mad twirl of films. It was the dignified slow rotation of a thing that has been given a suggestion. The window catch sat down with its two clicks.

On the cot rail, tied in green— their own strip that had belonged to the hall mat— a bowline had been made without permission.

"No moving things in the nursery," Clara said to the air with a civility that could cut. "Knots on the hall mat only."

The mobile slowed as if embarrassed. The bowline stayed. The baby did not wake. Her breath kept to its good paperwork.

Clara put two fingers on the tiny chest and borrowed the metronome and gave it back quickly. She looked at the knot in green on the cot rail, then at the mat in the hall visible through the half-open door where the green strip was not.

"Consequences," she said, to Mark and to the air and to the version of herself that had written the rules as if language could not betray her. "We break one rule; another breaks back."

"I'm sorry," he said again, and the words were smaller than the act and none the worse for it. "I thought... I told myself it wasn't night. I wanted to make things clean, because that's what I know how to do."

She nodded, not to absolve, to line the day up on the table. "We fix what we can fix. We put our thing back where it lives. We restate. We do not fight in front of the window."

They made their bodies into practical shapes. Mark went to the hall, fetched the tea towel he had used to dry the jug and, with that ridiculous domestic blessing still in it, carried the green strip back to the mat as if returning a citizen to its constituency. Clara, in the nursery, placed two fingers lightly on the bowline, untied it with a courtesy she would give to a child who had tried hard and got the test wrong, and laid the strip on the mat, flat and square.

"Rules," she said to the green and to the enamel and to the plastic monitor that had been banished to the drawer. "Knots on the hall mat only. No moving things in the nursery. No water. No requests about water at night."

She felt it before he did—the temperature drop at her wrist that wasn't a draft, the apples arriving shyly, the affectionate exhale that had once made nights into corridors. She didn't let it be permission.

"I have heard you," she said, in the sentence Harriet had made architecture. "I will consider it with my rules."

The air steadied. The window catch stayed where it had been told. The mobile made a last half-turn like a person fidgeting and committed to stillness.

Mark stood with his hand on the doorframe the way men in old films do when they have been told they are fathers and need to register the news with wood. "I did this," he said, which was the correct shape of guilt but also, she heard, the wrong owner for all the weight in the room.

"We did this," she corrected, which was true in the way furniture is true: both of them lived in the house that had trained him to mistake cleaning for control. "We won't do it again."

He nodded once, grateful for the plural, and then looked at the cot as if apologising in a language only linen knows. He looked at Clara. "Text H," he said, not to outsource, to keep the bargain.

Clara typed: *Broke rule: I ran a finger of water in the kitchen (stupid). Consequence: upstairs hot tap briefly on; bath half an inch (plugged); nursery mobile spun; green strip appeared tied as bowline on cot rail. Baby asleep; no distress. We moved strip back to mat; restated rules. Status now calm. We're sorry.* She pressed send and put the phone face down so the device would not get ideas.

Harriet replied as if floors own clocks: *Thank you for telling me. Correct sequence: remedy → restate → record. Add a boundary: No solo "tidying" of sacred objects; jug never leaves mat except to go to Martha; no water near jug after 5 p.m. Institute a cool-down: ten minutes of silence after any rule breach—no speech to the house. You're both doing well; arguments will come;*

do them in RED not BLUE. Floor holds. Sleep in same room as baby tonight if you want belt and braces; not because it's necessary, because it's kind.

Clara read it aloud, relief and mild shame under the words like the sensible lining of a coat. "No solo tidying of sacred objects," she repeated. "Jug never leaves mat except to visit Martha. No water near jug after five. Ten minutes of quiet after any breach. Arguments in RED not BLUE."

"RED," Mark said, with the humiliated gratitude of a man who has learnt to ask for a chair. "We should have fought downstairs earlier."

"We should have," she said. "We're learning where to stand."

They stood the ten minutes because obedience, once in a while, is a luxury. In that quiet the house became plainly itself again: pipes that belong to nobody; air that belongs to the weather; a child's breath like punctuation. Apples thinned to the kitchen and weren't a sermon.

When the ten minutes had been paid, Clara wrote, neat: *Rule broken (Mark ran water at sink; 2s). Consequences: hot tap on (brief); bath plugged; mobile spun; bowline tied on cot rail with our green strip (moved from mat). Remedies: tap off; plug out; bowline untied; strip returned to mat; rules restated. New boundaries (H): no solo tidying of sacred objects; jug never leaves mat except to Martha; no water near jug after 5 p.m.; ten-minute cool-down after any breach; arguments in RED.* She added, because the note refused to write itself, *Me: angry + kind. Him: sorry + useful. House: compliant.*

Downstairs, Mark made tea with the concentration men bring to penance. He handed her a mug as if it were a writ. "I am sorry," he said again, unnecessary and necessary.

"I know," she said. "I am too. For wanting to tidy you instead of the jug." She touched his wrist with two fingers as if he were also a pulse that could be borrowed and returned. "We make the RED rule: if we're going to argue, we leave the nursery and name the fight."

"Name this one?" he asked, game.

"Control dress-up as care," she said.

"Ouch," he said, and laughed because pain that can survive a joke is smaller afterwards. "Okay. Tomorrow—Martha. Jug returns to its mother for tea."

"Loan respected," she said, and smiled because *loan* was a word that kept furniture honest.

***

They slept on the floor next to the cot like students at a sit-in, not because they had to, because kindness sometimes looks like a sore hip. The baby obliged by being a textbook. At three, when houses audition their creaks for darker plays, nothing happened beyond physics. At five, the light behind the curtains became a thin chalk line that could be erased by weather and redrawn.

Morning tidied up the night. The hall looked as it had been told to look. The jug on the mat stood like a citizen who had signed a register and agreed to obey parking bylaws. The sealed envelope behaved. The green strip lay folded, reef, with the propriety of a ribbon attending church. The bathroom was properly stupid.

Clara wrote the last necessary line before toast: *Split: argument; I broke water rule (two seconds); house answered; we answered back with rules. New boundary added: NO SOLO TIDYING OF SACRED OBJECTS (JUG, MAT, ENVELOPE, GREEN STRIP); JUG NEVER LEAVES MAT EXCEPT TO MARTHA; NO WATER NEAR JUG AFTER 5 p.m.; TEN-MINUTE SILENCE AFTER ANY BREACH; ARGUE IN RED AWAY FROM THE NURSERY. Me: bossy + grown. Him: stubborn + ours. Floor holds.*

Mark cut the toast diagonal because diagonal improves mornings by fractions. On the kitchen window five petals appeared and thinned and were only petals. They ate and forgave each other in the way breakfasts do, without inspection. The day asked, politely, to be ordinary.

They let it. And that, after a night that had tried to split the house into corridors and sinks, felt like the right kind of miracle.

Chapter Eighteen
The Hall Mat

C lara woke into a Sunday that had put on its good jumper. The light behind the curtains was the colour of sensible paper, prepared to be written on without making a fuss. She lay still and let the house read itself out: boiler's civil hum; the fridge's one note; tyres writing commas on the estate road. She reached for the notebook and wrote, neat as a clerk: *Woke steady. Sunday. Rules unchanged: window (two clicks); boat on my terms; no moving things in nursery; no water; NO REQUESTS ABOUT WATER AT NIGHT; knots on hall mat only; requests ≠ commands; no altering records without permission; doctors allowed; friends allowed; witness permitted; NO REQUESTS THROUGH OTHER PEOPLE'S CHILDREN; NO TEACHING THEM; WITHDRAW IF ATTENTION GATHERS; NO RECORDING DEVICES IN THE NURSERY; LISTENERS ONLY; AIRPLANE RULE AFTER 7 p.m.; IF DEVICE MISBEHAVES → UNPLUG; MAT; TEXT H.; NO SOLO TIDYING OF SACRED OBJECTS; JUG NEVER LEAVES MAT EXCEPT TO MARTHA; NO WATER NEAR JUG AFTER 5 p.m.; TEN-MINUTE SILENCE AFTER ANY BREACH; ARGUE IN RED, AWAY FROM NURSERY.* She underlined *ALLOWED: enjoy the baby without checking the window* once and let the underlining tell her ribs how to behave.

Beside her, Mark opened one eye like a man auditioning for the role of Reasonable Husband. "Status?"

"Green," she said. "Grey cooperative. Jug to Martha today. Tulips to demote it."

"We shall bring tulips," he said gravely, and kissed the back of her head. "I will also bring my apology face, in case the universe is grading us."

On the landing, the baby made her small bureaucratic squeak—the office is open. The nursery smelt of warm cotton and decent sleep. The window catch sat down and honest: two clicks. She didn't check it. She touched it and forgave herself for touching it.

"Morning," she told the republic. Two fingers to the tiny chest: rise, fall. She borrowed the metronome and returned it like a library book, on time, in good repair.

On the hall mat, the jug stood where it had been told to stand; the sealed envelope kept its hand on its own mouth; the green strip lay folded—reef—behaving. The sight soothed the part of her that counts furniture.

***

Martha opened the door wearing Sunday's correct cardigan. The house smelt of stew rehearsing, and something else—an apple cut recently and put out of its own way. "Come in," she said, without bothering to be surprised they had. "Put your faces down. Put that tall nonsense on the table."

They carried the jug to its old place on the dresser. Mark presented tulips like a man bringing contrition in stems.

"Demoted," Martha said with satisfaction. She rinsed the jug in day-time water because day has rights, filled it, and slid the tulips in with a competence that had opinions about angles. "There," she said. "It is restored to flower duty. Tell the doctor woman I am compliant and underwhelming."

"We will," Clara said, and meant to. Over tea, she told the story of the split—the two seconds of water, the polite glug, the bowline on the cot rail, the ten-minute quiet that had shrunk the night back to size.

Martha listened with the attentive face she wore for recipes and first aid. "You are both doing clever with your rules," she said. "That is how we survive strange. We make the strange queue. And we do not show off."

Mark put his apology face away, permission granted. They ate stew with oblique carrots, argued the correct thickness of diagonally cut toast, and left the jug with tulips like a citizen who had passed its probation.

"Bring it back," Martha said at the door, "if it misses you. But it can earn its keep with me for a bit. No heroics. I shall supervise."

"Witness permitted," Clara said, and Martha, not knowing the phrase had become law, nodded as if she had invented it.

***

Back home, the hall had the patient air of a stage set between acts. The mat lay square. The green strip sat where she had left it. The sealed envelope kept its lesson. The house, pleased with itself, made the small approving sound of plumbing minding its business.

Clara stood with her hand on the doorframe and felt—because you can feel these things—the tug of attention, like a quiet person turning their head to follow a sentence. "We have returned your lodger," she told the air, gently kindly. "The loan is respected. Knots on the hall mat only."

At 12:18, while she was labelling the new bag of cotton wool like a person who trusts in bureaucracy, Mark called, low, from the hall. "Clara?"

She went. On the mat, the green strip had retied itself without changing position. It had been reef when they came in. Now it was a granny—wrong, lazy, the sloppy twin of a right knot.

"That's a no," Mark said, approving the neatness of the language he didn't like. "Or a stop."

Clara crouched and did not touch it. "We can't say stop to something that isn't doing anything," she said, but she wrote 12:18 — granny (no/stop) in her head's left-hand column and felt, unexpectedly, safe. "Message noted," she said, and left it alone.

At 12:32, the knot had turned itself—untied, retied—to reef again. "OK," Mark said, as if reading off a board. "Proceed."

"What are we proceeding towards," Clara asked the room, and the room, which had learnt English but not conversation, did not tell her.

At 12:41, when she came back from the sink with her hands dry and her politeness ironed, the strip had become a bowline—a rescue knot, the rabbit visiting the hole, the tree very clear. She looked at it until her eyes knew they weren't inventing. "Safe," she said, quietly. "Or help, depending on whether you're in the river or out."

"Or come," Mark said, with the half-smile of a man who has learnt a vocabulary by overlaying it on the weather. "Is it teaching us grammar or asking for verbs?"

"Neither," Clara said, pleased to be certain. "It's arranging itself to reassure a person who knows reef, granny, bowline. Which is, unhelpfully, both of us."

She took the notebook to the mat and wrote, without fuss: *12:18 — granny (no/stop). 12:32 — reef (OK). 12:41 — bowline (safe/rescue). No audio. House otherwise ordinary. Interpretation: establishing vocabulary.*

Under Rules, she added a tidy line: KNOTS = MESSAGES ONLY ON MAT. WE DO NOT OBEY IF THEY BREAK A RULE.

Her phone buzzed. *Lynn: Are you about? Nursery rang. Not panic; just... weirdness level one. Can I come?*
Here, Clara wrote. *Mat behaving. Bring your fringe and your powers.*

Lynn arrived at one with hair that had chosen to obey and a face that had decided not to do drama. She put her bag down where friends' bags go when they know the house. "Sam," she began, and already the angle of the name made Clara put out her hand as if to catch something. "He wouldn't nap. That's normal. Then he lay down on the carpet and tied his shoelace into something the key worker called a rescue knot and laughed like he'd kept a promise. Then he asked for a mat."

"A mat," Mark said, the patience of men translating babies into English. "Any mat?"

"He said, the mat only," Lynn said, and her composure hiccuped. "He's three. We say left–right at home and he goes quiet. I hadn't... I didn't..."

Clara looked at the green strip on the mat doing its respectable bowline. She looked at Lynn's mouth not being unbrave. She felt the rules breathe behind her like responsible aunties. "Okay," she said. "We have a rule for this—Harriet's—no requests through other people's children. No teaching them. Withdraw if attention gathers. That's what we're going to do. We're going to withdraw Sam from being used, even for games, and we'll give the adults a place for the house to put its little messages so they don't recruit children."

Lynn nodded once, very hard. "Say it again, with your bossy voice."

"Messages," Clara said, bossy, "are allowed on this mat only. You, house, do not put them on children's things. You do not ask a child to carry the sentence. If you have something to say to Lynn, you say it in my hall, to me, with the strip provided. Requests are not commands."

The room did not cool. The apples did not arrive. The bowline stayed in its posture like a man agreeing to meet you at noon.

"We'll still phone Harriet," Mark said, because belts and braces are not superstition, they're architecture. He typed, concise: *Mat showing granny → reef → bowline (no/OK/safe). Lynn's nursery called: Sam tied a "rescue knot"; asked for "the mat only". We restated rule: no requests through other people's children; messages only on our mat. Any additional boundary?* He put the phone face down as if not to spoil the ritual.

Harriet came back at a respectable speed for a floor on a Sunday: *Correct. Add: Designated object for messages = adult-owned rope only; children's belongings out of bounds. If Lynn needs a local protocol, set a quarantine mat at her door—adult witnesses; two-minute windows; no video; listeners only. If Sam echoes language, treat as soothing, not instruction. Floor holds.*

"Designated object," Lynn repeated, rolling the phrase in her mouth like a boiled sweet. "Adult rope only. That I can do. I love a shop."

"You can have ours," Clara said, surprising herself with the generosity towards green. "On loan. New rope for us. Loan to you of a designated object so nobody confuses the message with a toy."

Lynn's eyes were wet and angry at being wet. "You can't possibly—"

"I possibly can," Clara said, bossy and very gentle. "We'll take a photograph of it on the mat for our paperwork. Then you take it home and give it a job. And we will write the rule on your fridge in capital letters that are not afraid of themselves."

They photographed the strip (polite bowline), labelled the page with the time and witnesses, and then, with the courtesy you give to a citizen you are seconding to a committee, Clara lifted the green from the mat with both hands, as if it might spill meaning. She placed it in a plain paper bag. She wrote on the bag: LOAN: DESIGNATED OBJECT (GREEN) — TO L.T. — FOR MAT MESSAGES ONLY.

"Thank you," Lynn said, and then smiled the face she wears for recovery. "I have never loved your stationary fetish more."

"It's a religion," Mark said. "We're evangelists."

***

At Lynn's, the air smelt of oranges and laundry. Sam's dinosaur book lay on the sofa like a citizen awaiting a hearing. He was at nursery still. The house felt the way houses feel when their noise is out.

"Where," Lynn said, putting her hands on her hips the way women stand when they're negotiating with physics, "does one place a quarantine mat."

"The threshold," Clara said. "So you can step away. So it knows where to sit. So nobody trips. And so you can literally shut the door on it if it gets above itself."

They used Lynn's coir doormat with its tired welcome and set the paper bag on it. Clara wrote on a Post-it with the solemnity of a civil servant: MESSAGES HERE ONLY. ADULT ROPE ONLY. TWO-MINUTE WINDOWS. LISTENERS ONLY. NO VIDEO. NO CHILDREN. She straightened it so the words would hold still.

Lynn took the green strip out like a person greeting a nervous animal. "I am your boss," she told it, because language shapes spines. She laid it on the mat in a reef and then stepped back two big paces until her heels hit the skirting. Clara and Mark did the same. They stood with their hands visibly empty. They did not ask.

The strip did nothing.

"Good," Clara said, pleased. "We like nothing. Nothing saves marriages."

"Minute two," Lynn said, looking at the oven clock because that's what people do when they are pretending time is an honest man.

At 1 minute 23, the green tied itself into a clove hitch around nothing—two turns, a tuck, the kind of knot you use to tell a thing to stay. The coil lay small and precise on the coir.

"Stay," Mark said, pleased by a vocabulary that had decided to be fluent.

At 1:49, it loosened and reformed to reef again. "OK," Clara said, and stepped forward to the mat because adults step forward when the message is "OK".

Lynn wrote: *13:23 — clove hitch (stay). 13:49 — reef (OK).* She drew a little square round stay. She was breathing like a person who had chosen to be calm and had persuaded her lungs to follow orders.

They did not do a third minute. *Two-minute windows,* Harriet had said; two minutes make these games finite, and finitude keeps rooms sane. Lynn folded the strip with the practical affection of a woman who knows how to put things back. She placed it on a high shelf in the hall, deliberately not with Sam's things.

"Kitchen?" Mark said, because tea is the national therapy.

They drank at the table where Lynn does budgets and birthdays. The rules were written on the fridge with capitals that meant business: NO REQUESTS THROUGH CHILDREN. NO TEACHING THEM. WITH-DRAW IF ATTENTION GATHERS. MESSAGES AT DOOR MAT ONLY. ADULT ROPE ONLY. TWO-MINUTE WINDOWS. LISTENERS ONLY. NO VIDEO. Lynn had added one in a slanted hand that belonged to a different part of her: ALLOWED: enjoy my child without checking the window.

Clara read it and had to look at the kettle to keep her face behaving.

"When he gets home," Lynn said, not looking at the door because superstition is only useful until it isn't, "I will tell him the rope is for grown-ups. I will tell him he is allowed to watch the washing machine, which is a spinny, and not allowed to watch the mat, which is a boring. He will accept it because I will make accepting it a party."

"Boring is civilisation," Clara said.

"It is," Lynn said. "And civilisation bakes fish fingers." She took a breath. "Thank you."

"You can thank Harriet," Mark said. "We're just the pen on the fridge."

"Then I will bake biscuits for your floor," Lynn said, and laughed, properly now, and something loosened across the room like a tight knot deciding to be a loop.

***

They were halfway back to their own house when Ruth pushed a buggy past, Albie walking, coat unzipped, air full of weather and competence. He saw Clara and made his small, precise knot with fingers in the air; then, remembering yesterday's rule, he did not touch the window of the newsagent to write his name. He pointed seriously at the pavement, at a doormat nobody had any business noticing, and held up both hands with the clean, universal sign for stop.

Clara looked. The newsagent's doormat—cheap rubber lattice, tired of chewing gum—had a single shoelace lying on it, tied into a granny (wrong/stop), with a second lace end untied beside it. No child nearby had lost a shoe. No one in the doorway noticed the oddness. The air moved with weather; nothing else moved.

"Witness permitted," Clara said, to herself, to Mark, to the law. She didn't cross to interfere; no teaching other people's children includes strangers. She lifted a hand to Albie in salute. He grinned and, because he is three and therefore a god, ate a raisin with ceremony.

***

Home. The mat lay square; the sealed envelope was obedient; the space where the green strip used to live looked like a shelf after a book has been lent: oddly taller. Clara stood in the hall and felt the attention tug again—the polite noticing of a room that has arranged for an alternative.

"Thank you for tolerating the loan," she said, aloud, to air and floor and habit. "Messages remain here. If you need to make a point, do it in a way that a tired adult can bear. Children are out of bounds."

At 15:07, a new piece of string lay where the green used to sit.

It wasn't theirs. It was not from a hoodie, not from a parcel. It was a short, dull cotton cord, the colour of old stamps, coiled politely. Clara blinked and looked at the skirting, the table leg, the corner where dust keeps its club—no origin offered itself. She looked at Mark, who had the face of a man who both believes and wishes to be wrong.

"Did you—" he began, then laughed at himself and amended. "We're not asking that question."

Clara crouched. The cord tied itself into a reef as she watched. Not showy. Not violent. Just done.

"OK," she said to the cord, absurd, correct. "OK to what."

At 15:09, the cord reformed to clove hitch: stay.

At 15:10, it made a small, tidy overhand—a single knot, blunt. "One," Mark said, delighted like a child who has found numbers in cloud.

"At 15:11," Clara said, because what you do with a pattern is write it down. She wrote: *15:07 — reef (OK); 15:09 — clove hitch (stay); 15:10 —*

overhand (one). She added Interpretation: *OK to loan; messages continue; stay (here, not at Lynn's); one (first of sequence?)* She did not give in to the part of herself that wanted to invent a code and build a city on it. "We're not doing ciphers," she said, out loud, to the part of herself that likes puzzles. "We're doing rules."

Her phone buzzed. *Harriet: Good. Allow for a small vocabulary only. Choose four meanings you can bear: OK (reef); NO/STOP (granny); SAFE/HELP (bowline); STAY (clove hitch). Numbers 1–3 via overhand, double overhand, three overhand if it occurs; no decoding beyond that. If the cord persists, assign it a box on the mat so it doesn't wander. Floor approves of quarantining at Lynn's.*
Clara read it aloud. "Four words," she said. "Three numbers. No poetry. No riddles."

"Floor is a genius," Mark said. "No riddles is my new religion."

They taped a little box on the mat with masking tape, the kind you can peel up without turning a house into art. Inside it, the cord sat, behaving. At 15:14, it tied double overhand (two). At 15:16, it returned to reef and then became nothing—a plain, neutral line, as if to say, session over.

Clara wrote, neat: *15:14 — two; 15:16 — reef (OK); end.* She added, because you must: *We did not ask. We stayed boring. House kept its side.*

***

At 16:03, Lynn texted a photograph: Sam, newly home, in socks on a rug, holding a saucepan like a shield. The green strip was visible on a high shelf out of reach. On the quarantine mat at Lynn's door, the strip lay untouched. *We did two minutes. It did nothing. Then Sam asked if he could watch the spinny. We watched the washing machine. He fell asleep on the sofa. I am crying in a normal way. Thank you.*

Clara replied: *That is exactly the right kind of nothing. Keep two minutes. Keep adult rope only. We'll bring biscuits to your floor.*

At 16:20, Ruth sent a message out of the blue: *We met a nice woman who said knots are for grown-ups. Albie is offended but well. Thank you for not making it weird.*

Clara: *We are professionals at not making it weird.*
A dinosaur sticker arrived as a benediction.

Evening behaved. They performed the census—catch (two clicks); rabbit (guard); stars (at ease); breath (proof). The cord in the mat's taped box sat like a retired employee who had earned a chair. The sealed envelope held its breath in a good way. The house wore slippers.

They ate the kind of tea you eat when Sunday gets to decide—sandwiches with extravagant fillings and the promise of pudding. They watched a woman in hi-vis humiliate a beam with courtesy. They allowed themselves to be bored and found it restorative.

At nine, Clara stood in the nursery doorway and spoke the rules in the voice that had become, genuinely, her favourite register. "No moving things in here. No water. No requests about water at night. Knots on the hall mat only. No requests through other people's children. No teaching them. Withdraw if attention gathers. No recordings in here. Requests are not commands. No altering records without permission. Doctors allowed. Friends allowed. Witness permitted. Allowed: enjoy the baby without checking the window."

The room kept its face. The baby breathed. The window, two clicks, did not require checking. She put two fingers on the tiny chest and borrowed the metronome and returned it with interest.

Downstairs, the taped box on the mat contained a single over-hand—one—tidy, unashamed. She wrote: *21:07 — one. Possibly "one more thing". We are not decoding. We are going to bed.*

They went to bed. The house approved with a tiny pressure release in the pipes like a patient exhale.

***

At 03:12, the house woke her with nothing more dramatic than the thought that she had been asleep long enough to call it a success. She lay and listened. No monitor hiss. No corridor deciding to be a person. Just roof, rain, air, the small animal in the other room adjusting their thesis.

She went to the landing because ritual is scaffolding. The nursery: catch, rabbit, stars, breath. She looked in, did not touch, went down to the hall because the part of her that is an archivist needed to make sure the taped box still held sense.

The cord had tied bowline—safe/help—and then, while she stood there, did a clove hitch (stay) and finished with reef (OK).

"OK to stay safe," she said, because sometimes sentences put themselves in order. She did not say I hear you because that had become a sentence she saved for larger things. She wrote it down in the notebook on the console table left open for these night oaths: *03:12 — bowline; clove hitch; reef.* Then she went to bed and did the grown thing of going to sleep when invited.

Morning had the decency to be Monday, which is a way of saying tolerant. The baby made her opening squeak. The house wore its day face. The cord lay neutral.

Clara made tea and wrote: *Hall mat has adopted a cord. Vocabulary limited to: reef (OK), granny (stop), bowline (safe/help), clove hitch (stay), overhand(s) 1–2–3 (count). We do two-minute windows at Lynn's (adult rope only). Sam affected (knots at nursery; asked for "the mat only")* → *protected by rules: no requests through children; no teaching; withdraw if attention gathers. Me: bossy + grown. House: compliant.* She underlined children out of bounds because underlining makes words behave when they are tempted to wander.

Mark stepped in with toast cut diagonal and a grin that had decided to be used responsibly. "We have become a customs office," he said, pleased. "Incoming knot: declare your contents."

"Knots may not exceed one litre," she said. "Firearms and children must be declared at the desk."

Her phone buzzed. *Harriet: Good. Add one last boundary to make the week easier: NO MESSAGES FOR NON-RESIDENTS UNLESS THEIR ADULT CARER IS PRESENT. If a message seems aimed at Sam, direct it to Lynn by saying her name. You've done very well. Bring cord, notes, and biscuits.*

Clara wrote on the fridge in that sober capital hand that makes rules become furniture: NO MESSAGES FOR NON-RESIDENTS UN-LESS THEIR ADULT CARER IS PRESENT. IF MESSAGE SEEMS AIMED AT A CHILD, REDIRECT BY NAMING THEIR CARER.

She stood back. The board looked like a small town hall doing its job. The taped box at the mat kept its quiet authority.

"Right," she said to the house that had joined the human project. "We are going to the floor this afternoon. We will bring biscuits. You will be dull while we are out."

The house made a tiny approving sound, and it might have been the kettle resigning itself to boiling again, and it might have been agree-ment.

Clara put two fingers on the baby's chest and borrowed the metronome and returned it. She kissed Mark on the neck because romance is politics done privately. She put the notebook in the bag with the USB and the biscuits and the cord in its respectable paper sleeve. She looked at the mat because the mat had become a thing you look at when you leave your house.

The cord tied reef and then let itself be plain again—OK, then nothing—exactly the right amount of conversation for a Monday.

"Witness permitted," she said, and shut the door, and went to keep their appointment with a woman who had declared herself a floor and made good on it.

Chapter Nineteen
Caravan

The morning put on a Monday face and meant it. The light behind the curtains was the colour of paper that can bear ink without fuss. Clara lay still and let the house list itself: boiler's civil hum; the fridge's one note; tyres on damp tarmac drawing competent commas. She reached for the notebook and wrote, neat as a clerk: *Woke steady. Floor session this afternoon (USB, cord, notes, biscuits). Before that: field. Rules unchanged: window (two clicks); boat on my terms; no moving things in nursery; no water; NO REQUESTS ABOUT WATER AT NIGHT; knots on hall mat only; requests ≠ commands; no altering records without permission; doctors allowed; friends allowed; witness permitted; NO REQUESTS THROUGH OTHER PEOPLE'S CHILDREN; NO TEACHING THEM; WITHDRAW IF ATTENTION GATHERS; NO RECORDING DEVICES IN THE NURSERY; LISTENERS ONLY; AIRPLANE RULE AFTER 7 p.m.; IF DEVICE MISBEHAVES → UNPLUG; MAT; TEXT H.; NO SOLO TIDYING OF SACRED OBJECTS; JUG WITH MARTHA; NO WATER NEAR JUG AFTER 5 p.m.; TEN-MINUTE SILENCE AFTER ANY BREACH; ARGUE IN RED, AWAY FROM NURSERY; NO MESSAGES FOR NON-RESIDENTS UNLESS ADULT CARER PRESENT; REDIRECT BY NAMING CARER.* She underlined ALLOWED: enjoy the baby without checking the window and let the underline be a hand at her ribs.

Mark surfaced with the one eye of a man testing if the day was domesticated. "Status?"

"Green," she said. "Grey cooperative."

"We love cooperative grey." He kissed her hair. "Martha's at ten? She'll keep the tyrant while we go to the field?"

"She will. And tulips behaved. The jug looks like it's never committed a thought in its life."

"Model citizen," he said. "Right. Let's go and stare at the past under lino without prising anything up like burglars."

"No cutting," Clara said. "No water. No recordings. Copies, not originals. Witnesses. Then biscuits."

"Bless Harriet," he said, and meant it.

On the landing the baby made her civil-service squeak. The nursery smelt of warm cotton and sleep that had kept both promises. The window catch sat down and proper: two clicks. She didn't check it. She touched it, forgave herself, counted the holy four: catch; rabbit; stars; breath. Two fingers to a tiny chest—rise, fall. She borrowed the metronome and returned it, on time, in good repair.

The hall mat held its taped box, the cord within lying neutral as if back from a shift and content to be off duty. The sealed envelope chaperoned. The house wore slippers.

***

Martha opened the door in the cardigan that can talk a Monday down from a ledge. "Come in," she said, making space with the authority of a woman who has negotiated with storms. She lifted the baby with the accuracy of women who invented accuracy. "We will read about owls and criticise toast. You go and look at dirt."

"Under lino," Mark said, solemn. "An honourable day out."

Martha raised one eyebrow. "Do not steal bits of someone's floor. I will not visit you in a floor prison."

"No cutting," Clara promised. "Rubbings only. Copies kept; original left to be itself."

"Good," Martha said. "Tell the floor woman I approve of her copies."

She kissed the baby. She kissed each of them as if sending them to school. "If the past gets above itself," she said, "tell it Leaflet people can queue and have a cup of tea."

"Witness permitted," Clara said, and Martha nodded, not needing to know the phrase had become law.

***

They drove west under a sky that had decided on honesty. The map said two hours; the country agreed. Priya sat in the back with a canvas bag of indignation and tools—greaseproof paper, soft pencils, masking tape, bulldog clips, a small torch that had opinions. Lynn occupied the front with a clipboard that could have handled a minor coup. There were no children. No ropes. No props that had learnt English. Only adults and rules.

"Remind me of the protocol," Priya said, crisp, watching hedgerows rehearse themselves. "Out loud so the universe hears it."

Clara read from her phone. "No cutting, no prising, no water, no scraping. Rubbings only. Take two copies of any legible mark. Photograph in natural light—two images each—phones on airplane to stop software being a bright spark. Witnesses sign the backs with time and location. Mark anything we do with 'COPY FROM ORIGINAL' so we don't start worshipping paper. If we are asked to leave by any person or weather, we leave. If anything gets strange"—and she didn't have to define strange—"we say the sentence and step out. We do not chase.

We do not invent code. We do not recruit teenagers in dinosaur coats from passing buses."

"Cruel," Priya said, grinning. "The boy is a national treasure."

"He is," Lynn said. "And he's three. Other people's children are out of bounds. We have rules because we love them."

Mark drove as if rules were part of the Highway Code. "Who's meeting us?"

"Gwen Pengelly," Clara said. "Farmer's daughter turned farmer. She said we could park by the lower gate and not get ourselves shot by a cousin."

"Excellent," Priya said. "I love not being shot by cousins."

They reached the lane that is always shorter on memory than on tarmac. The hedge stepped back as if embarrassed to have grown so much in twenty years. The field laid itself out innocently: a careful slope, the proper green of a country that rains, the memory of summers when caravans pretended to be family homes with aluminium skins.

There was no caravan. Of course there wasn't. The new owners had upgraded to a lodge that flirted with the word *chalet*. The old patch where the van had sat—four concrete pads at the corners and an honest scar where grass had never quite forgiven human feet—held no body, only the shape of where a body had been.

Gwen Pengelly stood with her arms folded in the universal posture of women who own land and tolerate pilgrims. Mid-forties; hair like weather; eyes like a person who knows how to fix a gate.

"You must be the Morgans," she said, offering a handshake that meant business. "Well—one Morgan and a retinue."

"Clara," Clara said. "Mark. Priya. Lynn. Thank you for letting us come and not thinking we're ridiculous."

"I didn't say I didn't think you were ridiculous," Gwen said, cheerful. "I said you could come. You rang and sounded like decent lunatics. That field's seen worse."

"We just want to look," Mark said. "We're not going to dig up your earth."

"You can lift the edge of the old lino if you find any," Gwen said. "There's a stack of rubbish from the clearance—the old van skins went for scrap, but bits of interior nosed about. Stanley the handyman kept a slice, because he keeps everything. He's left it under the little tin shelter by the shed. I told him it might bring you closure. He said closures are good against draughts."

"Saint Stanley," Priya said, devout.

Gwen pointed with her chin. "Down there. If you need me, shout. If you find a time capsule, keep it, for God's sake. If you find someone's teeth, bring them to me."

"We will not be bringing you teeth," Lynn said, alarmed and amused.

Gwen walked away to a task that probably had verbs in it. They walked to the little roof of corrugated tin where farm things go to gossip. Beneath it, a stack of wood, an old chair that had lost will, and there—rolled and tied with baler twine—a length of lino. Dented, brittle, the colour of creams you forget to throw away. On the underside the backing paper had the furry look of age; at one corner a wedge had been glued where someone had done a patch well enough to pass a mother's eye.

Clara felt the tug at her wrist—a temperature nudge that could be weather and could be memory—and reminded her blood: *witness permitted; requests are not commands; no water.*

They set the roll on the grass and, without cutting twine, eased the outer turn back until the patched corner showed. The glue line, now dust and intention, ran in a thin crescent. Beneath it the brown of old plywood looked like a paragraph that had lost words to mildew. On the backing paper—there, at the patch edge—someone had written in ballpoint, bored and careful. Most of the line was eaten by glue ghosts. Two fragments survived like wreckage spelling themselves with the dignity of survivors: ...ARA and, a neat inch away, ...ELEAN.... A small boat drawn in five lines, the sort children learn from older hands.

Clara sat on her heels. The world, thoughtful, held its breath for two seconds the way decent rooms do when a verdict might arrive. She did not cry. She put the back of her wrist briefly to her mouth as if catching a sentence that would embarrass the field, then put her hand on her knee like an adult.

"That's her hand," Mark said, quietly, not requiring proof beyond decades of seeing Martha write shopping lists. "That's your mother's E."

"It is," Clara said. "The E that thinks it should be a pound sign."

Priya crouched beside them, efficient, kind. "Right," she said, work-voice. "Copies, not originals. No lifting, no peeling. We take rubbings. Two each. We sign the backs. We get Gwen to countersign as a witness so no one later calls us poets."

Lynn set out the small ritual. Greaseproof paper over the patch; tape the corners with masking tape so nothing slides and invents letters. Soft pencil on its side like a person shading a cheek. Light pressure. Don't press a story into existence; allow one out if one is there.

Clara did the first rubbing because rules like a rota. The pencil found the fur of the backing paper, the ridge of the glue, the soft hollow where the patch edged the old. Letters rose as if invited—ARA becoming CLARA because the CL had been lost to glue and could be inferred without sin. Another rubbing, fractionally to the right—ELEAN— and the curve of an O that could be O or could be wishful thinking.

She lifted the paper and set it aside face-down so the pencil couldn't go wandering. She wrote on the back, steady: COPY FROM ORIGINAL — Caravan lino backing (door patch) — 11:06 — witnesses: C.M., M. M., P.S., L.T., G. Pengelly. She underlined copy and felt the field approve.

Mark took his turn. His rubbing had the sober caution of a man who will not be accused of pressing. The boat arrived more boldly for him, line after line like memory turning on its light. Lynn's rubbing found the left-hand flourish of the E that made itself a small flag. Priya's found the tail of the R that never dawdled. Four copies, as if laws were satisfied by multiples.

Gwen appeared at a decent distance, arms folded, weather watching people. Clara held up a hand the way you tell a dog not to come and be adored. "We've found names," she said, not shouting. "We're doing rubbings. Would you sign the backs as field witness?"

Gwen came, read the marks properly, not indulgently, and whistled through her teeth as if greeting a tractor that had surprised her. "Well," she said. "It's that kind of field. Have you got a biro? Of course you have." She signed each sheet: G. Pengelly (field owner's agent) — witnessed. She didn't do theatre. She did ink well.

They photographed the patch—two shots each, phones on airplane so cleverness would go and do that elsewhere. The day offered its light in an even spill. Nothing in the images shifted. No jugs glinted in doorways that no longer existed. The caravan was not a mouth; it was paper and glue and wood.

Clara looked at the proof the way you look at a new baby—checking fingers, counting toes, relieved to find only ordinary miracles. CLARA. ELEAN— enough to be ELEANOR without requiring a priest. The small boat. The glue line like a coastline that had survived an argument with the sea.

"Why," Lynn said, not tearful, stubborn, "is proof so polite and so loud at the same time."

"Because it was always here," Priya said, unexpectedly gentle. "And also because we are. That's the noise at the edges—you, being here."

Clara took one image more because she is greedy for the right kind of enough, then set the phone face down on the grass so it wouldn't think itself a device. She put her hand flat near the patch, not on it, and said, to air and glue and the woman she had been twelve minutes ago, "Requests are not commands. I have heard you. I will consider it with my rules."

The field stayed a field. A crow complained about government policy somewhere to the left. Gwen—arms folded, weather in the eyes—said nothing, which is a kind of hospitality.

"Do we want to rub the other edges," Mark asked, practical. "In case there are dates."

"Two-minute window," Clara said, Harriet in her mouth. "We give the patch two more minutes and then we stop. We do not make a religion out of rubble."

They did one more, below the boat. The pencil found a small, bored 1 and a 9, and then nothing but fur. It could be 1999. It could be a postcode from the backing paper's manufacturer. It could be a ghost who had learnt numbers. They did not argue it into being. They wrote numerals present (1, 9) — unreadable context on the back and felt like good citizens.

"Right," Gwen said, stamping one foot as if calming weather. "You've been decent. Take your papers. Stanley will be unbearable if I tell him his hoarding saved history."

"Stanley saved a patch," Priya said, devout again. "May he be a saint on his lunchbreaks."

Gwen hesitated, then reached into the pocket of her practical jacket. "He also kept this," she said, handing over a rectangle of ply the size of a paperback. "He said he couldn't throw away wood that had a story on it. I told him all wood has stories and he said, 'Yes but this one told him in English.'" She lifted a shoulder. "It was under the bench when the van went. You can keep it. It's not my floor."

Clara took the ply in both hands as if it might spill. On one side: nothing but old varnish and the small violence of a life with boots. On the other: backing paper laminated by glue that had given up. In the top right corner, the faint end of a line in ballpoint——*nor*—as if someone had been interrupted writing Eleanor, or the end of honour, or the world's favourite coincidence.

"Copies only," she said to herself, and to the field, and to the part of her that wanted to lick her thumb and rub until letters confessed. "We do not clean. We do not peel. We do not tidy grief."

They wrapped the ply in greaseproof and a layer of Priya's indignation. They noted plywood fragment with backing paper — provenance: under bench during clearance — gift of field. They wrote on the package, ORIGINAL — HANDLE WITH RULES, because ORIGINAL is a word that makes hands behave.

Gwen put her hands in her pockets in the way of people who hide kindness so it can do more good. "Will you want a cup of tea," she asked, nodding at the house beyond the hedge.

"We will want," Mark said, "to do the thing where we sit in our car and eat biscuits while reading our own handwriting, like criminals who can't believe the bank was open."

"Fair," Gwen said. "If you break into tears, do it out of sight of the ewes; it gives them ideas."

They thanked her properly. They carried their copies and one small original to the car with the modesty of people who have been trusted with a relic and will not blow it. They did not turn their heads to see if the field was watching them; they assumed all fields watch and made their faces kind.

***

They sat in the car with the doors open and the kind of weather you can call honest without lying. They laid the four rubbings on the back seat like secular icons and ate a biscuit each without discussing fairness. Mark poured tea from the flask made to forgive decades. They were quiet, because sometimes the kindest sentence is no sentence at all.

Priya broke it first, expert at breaking things for good reason. "Martha," she said. "When did she write it."

"When she patched the doorway," Clara said, and in saying it, saw it—young Martha in a T-shirt with the sleeves rolled, glue that smelt of vinegar, a baby asleep, the caravan shimmying on its feet as someone breathed. She saw an unshowy woman write two names where floorboards could keep them because paper hadn't been kind. She saw her draw a boat because if you're going to write names under lino like a lunatic you might as well put in a picture for luck.

Mark blew on tea that didn't need blowing. "Why does proof make me feel both steadier and like the world's a nanometre to the left."

"Because it's the same shape we always knew," Lynn said, dry, affectionate. "And now it's drawn in pencil. Only pencils make rooms move."

Clara texted Harriet a photograph of one rubbing with names legible enough to be legal but not so crisp the internet would borrow it. *Field. Caravan patch backing. Rubbings only. Names present (CLARA, ELEAN—). Boat. Numerals (1,9) no context. One small original (ply fragment) received;*

we have not cleaned it. Gwen Pengelly witnessed & countersigned. We feel both sane and absurd.

Harriet replied with the calm a floor brings to a house. *Correct. Keep original sealed for session. Bring two copies; leave two with your mother if she wants them. Do not laminate. Do not "tidy". Today's rule: Copies travel; originals rest. You did well. Have a biscuit.*

Clara read it aloud. Mark made the noise of a man obeying biscuits. Priya, already half biscuit, saluted with the remainder. Lynn, gaze on the field, said, "Copies travel; originals rest," like a thing a person might embroider to prevent family curses.

They drove back up the lane with the car trying to remember how to be an ark and managing to be a saloon. The field did not look bereft. It looked like a field that had returned a thing and been thanked.

***

At Martha's, stew rehearsed itself at a new pitch. The jug with tulips pretended to have always been good. Martha listened, holding the rubbing as if it had rescued her from a fairground. She traced, not the letters—she had long ago learnt to leave ink alone—but the boat, as if the boat were the right size for touching.

"I wrote it," she said, not confessing, archiving. "When the patch went down. Your father had gone to B&Q and found the wrong screws as usual and I had an hour of courage. I thought: if this house is going to know a name, let it know both. I wrote it twice under the door because even in grief I do things neatly. I drew a boat so the names could ride on something if the glue took the words away."

"It took some," Clara said. "It left enough."

"That," Martha said, satisfied, "is what glue does. You did right—copies only. No peeling." She tapped the rubbing twice as if signing it with knuckles. "You may tell the doctor woman I am vindicated."

"We'll tell her you are a floor in your own right," Priya said.

Martha put one rubbing beside the kettle, one in the drawer where passports live, because orders should be obeyed and copies travel. "I'll look at them on Thursdays," she said, as if scheduling longing. "And then I will cook fish fingers and stop being operatic."

They ate stew and insulted carrots cut as coins. The baby breathed with text-book decency and forgave everyone for being grown-ups. After, they walked home, the car lighter for having delivered a weight to its owner.

The house met them with the patient face of a place that has agreed to be managed. The mat held its taped box; the cord lay neutral as if it had been a dog told to stay by a competent person and was proud to have done it. The sealed envelope chaperoned. The room made the small, approving sound houses make when plumbing decides not to audition drama.

Clara placed the ply fragment in a thicker envelope, wrote ORIGINAL — CARAVAN PLY (PATCH BACKING) — HANDLE WITH RULES, and sealed it with the solemnity that had made envelopes a religion. She slid it beside the sealed USB. She wrote, neat in the notebook: *Field: caravan doorway patch; rubbings — CLARA, ELEAN—, boat; numerals (1,9) // witnessed by G. Pengelly. Photos (airplane). Original ply fragment sealed (no cleaning). Rule added (H): COPIES TRAVEL; ORIGINALS REST.*

Her phone buzzed. *Harriet: See you at four. Bring your copies, your USB, your cord, your biscuits, your tiredness. Floor holds.*

"Four," Mark said, reading over her shoulder. "We have time to make tea and look at the cord not doing tricks."

They made tea. They looked at the cord not doing tricks. They went upstairs and performed the census: catch; rabbit; stars; breath. They stood in the nursery doorway and spoke the rules, soft, steady, like grammar. The room kept its face.

Downstairs, at the mat, the cord tied itself a small, tidy reef—OK—and then chose to be nothing again. It was exactly the right amount of conversation for a Monday.

Clara put her hand lightly to the air the way you put it to a shoulder. "Thank you," she said, to the house, to the field, to an E that had made itself a flag under glue. "Requests are not commands. I have heard you; I will consider it with my rules."

The house approved, doing it in pipes. Outside, a bus sighed; somewhere, a boy in a dinosaur coat practised tying a knot for the pleasure of being good at it and for no other reason at all.

They packed the copies and the USB and the cord in its paper sleeve and the biscuits. They left the original where it belonged. They shut the door like people who have been careful and intend to go on being careful.

On the fridge, in sober capitals, a new line waited for ink. Clara added it under Harriet's hand-me-downs: COPIES TRAVEL; ORIGINALS REST. She stepped back with the small satisfaction adults hoard. The week made its shape. The floor, across town, cleared a square for them.

Witness, permitted. Proof, kept. The lino guarded its names. The house agreed, by being a house.

Chapter Twenty
Left–Right

T he morning wore Tuesday without arguing. The light behind the curtains was the colour of paper that would take ink and not smudge. Clara lay still and let the house read itself out: boiler's civil hum, the fridge's one note, a lone van writing commas across damp tarmac. She reached for the notebook and wrote, neat as a clerk: *Woke steady. Rules unchanged from Monday + "COPIES TRAVEL; ORIGINALS REST". Floor session felt clean. Jug with Martha (flower duty). Cord boxed on mat. Day plan: chemist, post office (to send nothing we love), cafe (boring tea), home by nap.* She underlined ALLOWED: enjoy the baby without checking the window and tapped the underline once, a tiny rehearsal.

Mark surfaced with the one eye of a man checking if morning was domesticated. "Status?"

"Green," she said. "Grey cooperative."

"We adore cooperative." He kissed her hair. "Errands?"

"Chemist at ten—stupidly specific wipes. Post office because the state enjoys a queue. Priya at twelve if Jonah's committee approves."

"Excellent," he said. "I'll impersonate a man who knows how email works and then meet you for the queue."

On the landing the baby made the small bureaucratic squeak of a minor official opening the office. The nursery smelt of warm cotton and a night that had kept its promise. The window catch sat down, good citizen: two clicks. She didn't check it. She touched it and forgave herself for touching it.

"Morning, tyrant," she said to the small republic. Two fingers on a tiny chest: rise, fall. She borrowed the metronome and returned it on time, with interest.

On the hall mat, the taped box held the dull cotton cord lying neutral—off duty, obedient. The sealed envelope kept its mouth politely shut. The house wore slippers.

***

The chemist practised its doctrine of small bottles and important labels. Clara bought wipes labelled in a tone that suggested moral purity. She bought plasters that promised kindness. She resisted buying four other forms of reassurance disguised as ointment. On the pavement, the wind argued briefly with a flag and lost. She liked the day for its moderation.

At the top of the high street the 73 sighed to a halt. The bus windows were fogged here and there with the heat of people doing their best. A small face appeared like a seal surfacing: Albie, without the dinosaur coat today, hair in honest disarray, mouth already forming mischief. He saw Clara and performed, with ceremony, one, two, three on the glass—and then stopped himself, turned his hands into polite pockets, and gave her the most serious thumbs-up she had ever received from anyone in this city. His mother, Ruth, behind him with the look of a woman doing errands with stamina, caught Clara's eye and mouthed, *We're being boring,* and Clara mouthed back, *You're saints.*

They waved like rational people to a bus being a bus. The pavement took them at pram speed towards the zebra crossing by the church wall. Cars performed their small treaties. A man in a hi-vis inspected a pothole with the concentration usually reserved for surgery.

Clara stopped at the kerb. She made the ritual explicit because ritual is scaffolding: look right, look left, look right again. The tarmac shone with the morning's reminder that weather exists. The pram's brake was on because brakes are love. In the basket under the seat the bag sat square, a model citizen. The baby hummed vowels.

"Left," Clara said out loud, and then, because some words begin to stand up and walk when you let them, "Right."

The voice—or the memory that now lived in her ear as if an architect had put a tiny seat there—had said it before: Left–right, affectionate, impatient, a manual for being alive. Static had carried it. The copyist in her had written it down because writing turns water into something that can be carried across a room.

A car slowed. A driver actually made eye contact, which felt like winning a prize. Clara put her foot off the kerb, one hand light on the pram handle. The brake was off because walking requires walking. They moved. One wheel found the zebra stripe and thudded into reason.

From the side street to her left, a van that had not admired the prize of eye contact nosed out, impatient at geometry—white, wide, the kind of vehicle that believes itself to be weather. The driver looked right, saw nothing; looked left, saw less; looked back right; did not look ahead. The van moved.

Clara's body didn't think; it did. She pulled the pram back and to the left with a small controlled jolt the way you mind a hot pan. The wheel kissed the kerb. The baby made a surprised O with her mouth and then decided not to have opinions. The van saw them then and braked and the driver did the two-handed apology that means I am a person not just a chassis.

"Left–right," Clara said, steady, and because the world had decided to show off for a second, a pigeon did its feather doctrine and a bus exhaled.

And then it happened: swift, exact, harsh.

The wrist strap—the dull black loop that lives on the pram handle for sensible people who believe in physics—tightened about Clara's wrist as if a pair of hands had pulled the two ends towards each other and then twisted, left, then right, to bite. Not showy. Not cinematic. A small, efficient turn that made the strap snub itself so the pram could not move forward at all. The strap cut into skin at the base of her thumb with the intimate authority of a nurse setting a cannula. Pain arrived like a knocked elbow: hot, immediate, and entirely to the point.

"Hey," Clara said, not a shout—she had learnt to keep her noise for the right tool—just a startled adult sound as if someone had trodden on a word. She pulled once and the strap held her as if she were a valuable thing suddenly at risk of falling. The pram may as well have been iron.

The van rolled its last small inch and stopped properly. The driver mouthed sorry again, this time with eyebrows. He lifted his hands from the wheel as if demonstrating that he had no weapons. A woman at the bus stop made the face of a person whose insides have climbed to her throat and sat there looking around and then gone politely back to their seat.

"Mark," Clara said, automatic, even though he wasn't there. She added, a half-laugh, "Witness permitted," because sometimes you say the law to yourself like a charm.

The strap eased. It did not release—not that—but it loosened enough for blood to decide to be blood again. Clara took a breath and then another because breath makes citizens of sentences. She looked right; she looked left; she did the maths carefully. She crossed, pram and all, on sane feet, with a wrist that had just been told a rule in a language that wasn't English.

On the far side, in the small calm of the pavement itself, she looked at her wrist. A faint red bracelet had bloomed where skin had learned a lesson. It would make an excellent bruise by tea-time.

"All right," she said to the air with the politeness she reserved for bureaucracy that had chosen to be helpful too hard. "All right. Thank you. We will discuss your method."

She felt the apples for a second—faint, fond—and then nothing. The street resumed its hobby of being a street.

***

By the post office the queue did its public service. Mark slid into it at exactly the spot where she was and took the bag from the basket as if that were the kind of marriage they had built, which it was. He glanced at the wrist and then at her face and got everything right.

"What happened," he asked, not to assign blame, to draw an outline.

"Near-miss," she said, calm. "Van. My fault and his fault and physics. Left–right saved us. And then the strap—" she looked at it as if it might answer a question— "tightened hard. Like someone doing the practical thing too firmly. It was... efficient. It hurt."

He did not look outraged on her behalf; he looked like a man who'd been waiting to see how many levers he still owned and had decided to count them later. "She kept the baby safe," he said, because truth first.

"She did," Clara said. "Harshly. I'd like to keep both benefits and none of the bruises."

"Reasonable," he said, and almost smiled because reasonable had become a shared religion. "Are we allowed to say thank you and also no at the same time?"

"We are," she said. "We'll say it on the fridge later so the words learn how to share a wall."

They posted nothing they loved. They bought a book of stamps because adults love small rectangles. They walked, with decency, to the café that knows how to be quiet. Priya joined with Jonah's congress of cheeks asleep in the pram and a mouth for making trouble only in the correct direction.

"Status?" she said, doctor-voice done with hair and opinions.

"We will have interesting bracelets of red by lunchtime," Clara said. She told it clean, no extra shadow and no heroics. Priya looked at the wrist, approved the redness as data, and nodded once.

"Method," Priya said, crisp. "We need to file 'harsh-safety' under 'no physical contact'. Words, not straps. Warnings, not yanks."

"Words," Mark said, appreciating the fact of words being able to turn a day back into furniture. "She already has *Left–right*. We can legislate for that reliance."

They drank tea that was allowed to be too hot because the world isn't trying to kill you if it is. Clara, who has learnt to offer favours to the universe, said, "Thank you," into her tea, and the air did what air does—ignored it and kept them alive.

Home. The hall mat lay square. In the taped box, the cord had tied a small, precise bowline—safe—and loosened into a reef—OK. Clara wrote it in the left-hand column: *12:54 — bowline; 12:55 — reef.* Interpretation: *I kept her safe; we are OK.* She could imagine the smugness in the handwriting if handwriting were a smell.

She went to the kitchen, put the kettle on because civilisation, and washed her hands because routine turn a system back on. When she shook them dry, she saw water sitting in the curve of her wrist bones and the small itch of frightened animal. She wanted—very much; old habits are old because they were good—to run the cold tap over the bruise until physics found something to do with it.

"No water," she told herself, smiling at the version of herself that had become bossy and loved it. She dried her hands on the towel and pressed the towel to the reddest part for ten seconds, the way you'd press a plaster on a child who likes drama. She counted to ten and stopped, because stopping is also a religion.

The corridor did not put on a person. The house did not get colder. The air did not discover a lake. She breathed.

In the nursery, the baby woke and announced her manifesto: snack and giggle and a theatre of clean socks. Mark transferred her to the high chair with the manual he had perfected: strap left–right, tray click, spoon allowed, cup with handles. He slid one finger between strap and cardigan because compassion is two fingers and a check.

The cup—stupid, valiant—wobbled towards the edge of the tray because cups are toddlers with a drinking problem. Mark reached for it and because that is when physics enjoys itself, his phone did its small burr of an email and his hand hesitated for half a second, old addiction, new repentance. The cup went over.

It was water—just water; not hot; not a sin. The cup hit the tray edge, tipped and made a shallow river that started to run towards the baby's belly button.

"Not a problem," Mark said, already doing the reach for the towel as if he had been born next to a sink, and then every strap on the high chair tightened at once as if someone had done a demonstration of how safety can be audible.

The baby made a startled squeak because something about her tiny ribs had been reminded that ribs exist. Her face screwed up, not in pain, in indignation: excuse me. Mark put both hands up to show the room he wouldn't touch the straps while they were being criminally efficient. "No," he said aloud to someone who speaks only logic, "no force."

Clara grabbed the towel and in one exact movement—left, then right—blocked the water like a goalkeeper who had decided to be modest. The small river soaked itself into cotton and stopped being a metaphysical concern. She put the towel flat on the tray so it looked like a landscape, breathed out, met the baby's inspection, and did the grown thing of smiling like a friend.

The straps eased. They didn't release, correct, because chairs have their own pride. They backed off by a notch in the ratchet. The baby's breath did its text-book pairs and commas again.

"Harsh," Priya would have said, and was not here to help, so Clara said it herself. "Harsh. Granted that you mean well, and no."

Mark, hands still in neutral to let the air prove itself, said, "She kept the cup from your belly."

"Which is my job," Clara said, and looked at the room with the kind of affection she saves for young colleagues who have made themselves too necessary. "And she made the strap speak speaking too hard."

They breathed the air back into furniture. Mark dabbed the towel, made a ceremony of not racing, unsnicked the strap a notch—left, then right—with commentary because commentary calms: "One notch; two fingers; no choke; all adults present; no ghosts in the chair."

The chair, pleased to be in a sentence instead of a trial, behaved.

They ate the kind of honest half-lunch that keeps you from thinking you need improvement—sandwiches with ham that had like itself before they bought it; chopped fruit that pretended to be a decision. The house, perhaps encouraged by its own success at not drowning anyone, went back to pipes with decent ambitions.

***

At the hall mat, the cord in its taped box tied a granny—stop—and then sat plain, as if it had delivered its minutes and clocked off. Clara wrote: *13:09 — granny (stop)*. She could feel a lecture building at the back of her tongue. She promised the lecture to the fridge and left the mat alone.

"Let's write," she said. "While the air agrees to be furniture." She took the fat black marker and made her hand into an instrument for corrections that don't hurt.

On the fridge, in sober capitals, under COPIES TRAVEL; ORIGINALS REST, she added:

NO PHYSICAL CONTACT WITH PEOPLE.

NO MOVING PRAMS, HIGH CHAIRS, COTS OR STRAPS.

WARNINGS: WORDS ONLY ("LEFT–RIGHT" PERMITTED);

IF IMMEDIATE DANGER → ONE SHARP NOISE (E.G., KNOCK).

NO SLAMMING DOORS. NO YANKS.

She stepped back. The board looked like a small council that had been given a budget.

"Two things," Mark said, gently administrative. "Define 'sharp noise' so we don't start hearing theology in kettles. And give an exception for loose objects away from the baby—removal allowed; approach forbidden."

Clara added, neat, beneath:

ONE SHARP NOISE = SINGLE KNOCK / SINGLE TAP, NOT REPEAT-ED.

ALLOWED: MOVE LOOSE OBJECTS AWAY FROM BABY (NOT TO-WARDS).

She underlined AWAY because underlining makes words keep their promises.

"Text H," Mark said. "We've just made parliament; we should run it by the floor."

Clara wrote: *Near-miss (van). Pram strap tightened—kept baby safe, but harsh (bruise). Later, high chair: cup tipped → straps tightened; baby indignant; we towelled → straps eased. Both protective; both too much. Proposed rule: NO PHYSICAL CONTACT WITH PEOPLE; NO MOVING PRAMS/HIGH CHAIRS/COTS/STRAPS. WARNINGS BY WORDS ONLY ("LEFT–RIGHT" PERMITTED). IF IMMEDIATE DANGER: ONE SHARP NOISE (KNOCK); NO DOOR SLAMS. ALLOWED: MOVE LOOSE OBJECTS AWAY FROM BABY (NOT TOWARDS). Thoughts?*

Harriet's reply arrived in the decent window that makes adults feel accompanied: *Correct. Add: No tightening garments or buckles. Add: No touching skin/hair. Add: If "left–right" is used, adults will obey once, then re-assess; no repeated commands. Consider a thank-you protocol to reduce escalation: you say "Thank you; we will take it from here," then act. Floor approves of "one sharp noise". No yanks. Floor holds.*

Clara wrote the additions on the fridge in the same hand that had become mom, judge, clerk:

NO TIGHTENING GARMENTS/BUCKLES.
NO TOUCHING SKIN/HAIR.
IF "LEFT–RIGHT" IS USED: WE OBEY ONCE, THEN RE-ASSESS; NO REPEATS.
THANK-YOU PROTOCOL: "THANK YOU; WE WILL TAKE IT FROM HERE."

She stood back and admired the parliament. "We will thank and then we will adult," she said.

Mark came to stand by her and did the small hum that means a man has converted a day into sense. "Left–right once," he said. "Then we own the street."

"Left–right once," Clara said. "Then we own the chair."

***

At three, when the baby forgives the world and asks that we keep some of its beauty for later, Lynn arrived with a chocolate biscuit that had ambitions to be medicine. She inspected the bruise blooming on Clara's wrist like a harvest and kissed the air beside it because kisses are for skin you own and respect is for skin you don't. "Harsh," she said, and composed her face into the one she uses for victory over fringe. "I like your parliament. *No touching skin* will look beautiful in embroidery."

"We could sell samplers to the floor," Mark said. "Fund biscuits."

"Crowdfund stability," Lynn said, and laughed, proper.

While they talked, the cord in the taped box tied overhand—one, once—then reef—OK—and then lay down as if someone had told it the union allowed a break.

"One sharp noise," Lynn read off the fridge. "Define it for the house so it doesn't think crockery counts."

"Tap on the hall table," Clara said. "Or the inside of the front door. Not the nursery door. Not the kitchen glass. One knock only."

"Add it," Mark said, and Clara wrote, with affectionate bossiness:

ALLOWED ALARM: ONE TAP ON HALL TABLE OR INSIDE FRONT DOOR ONLY.

"I love a limited venue," Lynn said. "Even ghosts behave better with tickets."

The test came without theatre, which is how tests ought to arrive. At four-twenty-one the sky decided to try grey again; the wind lifted a council notice the way a skirt remembers it has opinions. Clara strapped the baby into the pram for a ten-minute constitutional before witching hour put on its robes. She said the census to the nursery like grammar: catch; rabbit; stars; breath. The pram sat in the hall like a well-designed argument. She slid the wrist strap on because she had learnt once and wasn't silly.

"Left–right," said the air, not in static, in the way of a word arriving to do the work it was hired for. Not a command. A warning placed on the counter, not pushed into a hand.

"Thank you," Clara said, and meant it, and then to the air, like a person attending to a teenager: "We will take it from here."

She stood still at the threshold because thresholds are where fools and saints meet. She looked left—parcel van tucked too close to the kerb; right—bicycle behaving like a superior life form; left—woman with a dog who believed in politics. She waited. She went right, because roads are old puzzles. The wrist strap stayed a loop, a thing for safety rather than a leash.

On the pavement a damp leaf decided to audition for slapstick under the right wheel. The pram nudged but did not argue. The wind lifted and then, with excellent timing, the neighbour's car door opened into the gap at the precise idiot angle that would have clipped the pram's handrail cleanly and made two adults stupid with adrenaline.

The hall table made a single, precise tap—polite knuckle on wood, no echo—though no one was near it.

Clara stopped. She didn't yank. She didn't invent ballet. She stopped. The car door completed its idiot arc on nothing and then withdrew, apologetic. The neighbour popped his head round and said, "Sorry! I am a *clod*," as if quoting scripture. He saw the pram, saw the baby, saw

Clara's wrist bruise blooming its red lecture, and did a second sorry, now with eyebrows and history. He shut the door with care and went away with the face of a man who has learned a day early.

"Good alarm," Clara said, to air with gratitude. "One tap only. That's the limit. Thank you."

The air did not grow apples; it behaved like air. She did ten minutes of moderate weather and wrote left–right once; alarm once; we adulted on the mental chalkboard that keeps the day from sliding off the table.

Witching hour came with its clipboard and asked politely to be allowed to do its job. They bribed it with the usual treaties—warm water that did not become a sermon, towel like innocence, a cardigan that consented. The high chair did not practise theatre. The cup considered rebellion and then mindfully stayed in its lane. The straps declined to be poets.

At nine, Clara stood at the nursery doorway and spoke the rules in the voice she now loved because it made English behave. "No moving things in here. No water. No requests about water at night. Knots on the hall mat only. No requests through other people's children. No teaching them. Withdraw if attention gathers. No recordings in here. No physical contact with people. No moving prams/high chairs/cots/straps. No tightening garments or buckles. No touching skin/hair. If "left–right", we obey once, then re-assess. If danger, one tap on the hall table or inside front door only. Allowed: move loose objects away from the baby. Requests are not commands. No altering records without permission. Doctors allowed. Friends allowed. Witness permitted. Allowed: enjoy the baby without checking the window."

The room kept its face because it had been taught how. She put two fingers on the tiny chest and borrowed the metronome and returned it with interest. The window catch sat with its two clicks, proud and quiet.

Downstairs, the taped box on the mat held the cord lying neutral like a citizen between shifts. It did not tie anything clever. It behaved.

Clara wrote at the bottom of the day's page: *Left–right saved us. Harsh strap saved with bruises—no more. Parliament added: no touching bodies, no moving prams/straps; warnings by words; one tap allowed; no yanks. Thank-you protocol helps. We obey once, then adult. Me: bossy + grateful. House: compliant.*

Mark slid a mug across the table with the ceremony of men who have learned when tea is the state religion. He kissed the bruise gently not on the bruise and then the place beside it, because people who love you learn geography.

"Left–right once," he said again, testing the words for fit. "Then us."

"Then us," she said.

Outside, the bus sighed. In somebody else's kitchen a washing machine practised being a spinny. In Lynn's hall, the green strip sat on a high shelf being a loan that liked its job. In Martha's kitchen the tulips permitted themselves to be tulips and the jug, demoted, was proud. In the taped box on the mat, the cord lay quiet. On the fridge, a parliament of sentences kept the house in its seat.

Ellie had kept the baby safe, and harshly. The bruise would have its small, performative day and then retire. Clara looked at it, did the grown thing of thanking the part of the universe that had not killed her child, and then did the more grown thing of writing a rule that would let them all live here together without being yanked.

"Thank you," she said, soft, to the air, to a girl with her vowels, to the part of herself that had been practising being bossy + grown. "We will take it from here."

The house agreed, not with apples, not with static, not with theatre, but with what she had come to recognise as the one true benediction of the living: it stayed a house.

Chapter Twenty-One
Doctor Woman, Three

T he morning took Tuesday seriously. The light behind the curtains had that kind, office-paper steadiness that makes forms behave. Clara lay still and let the house read itself aloud: boiler's civil hum; the fridge's single note; a bus sighing at the far bend as if it had remembered a joke and then thought better of it. She reached for the notebook and wrote: *Woke steady. Hand = bruise (strap lesson); slept; no corridor. Rules unchanged. 11:30 with Harriet—USB + cord + caravan rubbings + biscuits. Today: write it down; make a line you can't cross even for love.*

Mark opened one eye like a man negotiating jurisdiction with morning. "Status?"

"Green," she said. "Grey cooperative. Parliament intact."

"Excellent." He kissed the back of her head. "Doctor Woman will bring clipboards. We'll bring biscuits and apology faces."

"Left–right once," she said, because saying it out loud put the day on its rails.

"Then us," he said, and practiced his agreeable face for the ethically minded.

On the landing the baby made the small bureaucratic squeak that meant the office had opened. The nursery smelt of warm cotton and good intentions. Window catch: two clicks. She didn't check it. She touched it, forgave herself for touching it, and did the census that had become a prayer and never pretended otherwise: catch; rabbit; stars; breath. Two fingers to a tiny chest—rise, fall. She borrowed the metronome and returned it on time, like a woman who pays her library fines because she likes being the sort of person who pays her library fines.

On the hall mat, the taped box held the dull cotton cord lying neutral. The sealed envelope kept its mouth shut with the decorum of a maiden aunt. The house wore slippers.

***

The clinic Harriet had borrowed was the kind that has learnt the art of being a room: light on purpose, chairs that don't squeak, a table that looks like it remembers arguments and forgives them. On the windowsill, a little pot of rosemary stood upright, as if encouraged. The smell was not clinical; it was paper and biscuits.

Harriet stood to greet them with that precise, ordinary warmth that makes people brave. She wore a navy jumper that had no quarrel with itself and a lanyard that had decided to be useful rather than self-important.

"Hello," she said, to Clara, to Mark, to the day. "Come in. We'll make tea. We'll make a list. We'll make a line."

"Biscuits," Mark said, as if announcing a witness, and set the tin on the table. "Chocolate hobnobs. We brought our virtue."

"Then nothing can go wrong," Harriet said, and smiled the smile she lends to stupid Thursdays and clever Tuesdays alike. "Right. Spread your artefacts. We'll work in copies and leave originals to rest."

They set their things out with something like reverence but without theatre. The USB in its labelled sleeve; two rubbings from the caravan backing paper; the cord in its paper bag; the notebook open at yesterday's rule additions—no physical contact, one tap, thank-you protocol. Clara placed the photograph of the bruise beside the pen, not for drama, for data.

Harriet looked, in the order proofs deserve. The rubbings first. She ran a finger near the pencil, never on it. "Good copies," she murmured, satisfied. "Names in your mother's hand. A boat that knows what it's doing. Copies travel; originals rest. We keep it that way."

"Stanley saved a patch," Priya had said yesterday. Harriet did not know Stanley but seemed to approve of him anyway.

Next the USB. Harriet didn't plug it in; she put it on the table like a sealed letter. "We heard once already," she said, to prevent the day developing appetites. "We will not replay. We'll archive."

Finally the cord. Harriet tipped it gently from its sleeve into her palm as if greeting a shy animal. It lay like something that had been taught English and found it mostly agreeable.

"Now then," Harriet said, taking up her pen and becoming, briefly, the government. "We've done twelve sessions in a week disguised as three. We've got rules. We need a compact. We will be insulting and obvious. We will write it as if we mean it, because we do. We will sign it. We will put one copy in your hall and one in my drawer. We will give a shorter version to your mother and to Lynn. We will make it possible for you to be bored while being haunted."

"Sold," Mark said. "We enjoy boredom."

Harriet drew a line down her paper, two columns. On the left she wrote PRINCIPLES; on the right RULES.

"First principle," she said. "Order of care. Primary: the living child. Secondary: her carers. Tertiary: other living people in proximity. Quaternary: the dead, the house, the story. We respect the dead. We do not put them first."

Clara felt something unclench behind her ribs that had been pretending it wasn't clenched. "Yes," she said.

"Second," Harriet said. "Proportionality. Interventions must be the least dramatic, most reversible option that achieves safety. No pain. No fear as a tool. Warnings over force; words over noise; one noise over a concert."

"Third," she went on, "Consent & venue. Adults choose when and where engagement happens. Mat only. Quarantine mats for others. Children out of bounds. No recruiting."

"Fourth," she said, "No trades. No bargains. No 'if you show us this we'll do that'. No intimacy offered to secure compliance. Kindness isn't currency. Attention isn't a wage."

Mark let out a breath he may have been holding since Thursday. "No trades," he repeated, grateful to have that sentence available in capital letters.

"Fifth," Harriet said, "Time & scope. Contact has office hours. Your house: 11:00–13:00 for non-safety messages, mat only. Outside those hours: silence, except a single "left–right" or one tap for immediate safety. Airplane after 7 p.m. stands."

"Sixth," she continued, "Record & forget. You write once, you seal once, you don't replay. Memory of the room is better than archiving the corridor. We do not become an AV department for the dead."

"Seventh," she said, "Escalation. Any breach of non-contact, non-coercion, or children's boundary triggers blackout: twenty-four hours of no engagement beyond basic gratitude and safety. Then we reassess."

"Eighth," she said, "Stop-word. You already have RED for arguments. Use RED STOP for the house. If spoken by either of you, the session ends. You leave the room, shut the door, and do ten minutes of nothing. No theatrics, no scolding. Silence is the spell."

"Ninth," she said, "Ownership. Copies travel; originals rest. You never tidy grief. You never 'improve' the past. You bring biscuits to the living."

"Tenth," she finished, "Humility. You will get it wrong sometimes. You will repair without making a religion of your guilt."

She looked up. "Am I missing a commandment?"

Clara considered the bruise blooming yellow under the red. "No touching bodies," she said softly, "and no moving furniture that's touching bodies. We've written that at home. I want it written in your handwriting."

"Of course," Harriet said, and added, under Rules: NO PHYS-ICAL CONTACT WITH PEOPLE; NO MOVING PRAMS/HIGH CHAIRS/COTS/STRAPS; NO TIGHTENING GARMENTS/BUCKLES; NO TOUCHING SKIN/HAIR. Then, below, she wrote: WARNINGS = WORDS ONLY ("LEFT–RIGHT" ONCE); IF IMMEDIATE DANGER: ONE TAP (HALL TABLE OR INSIDE FRONT DOOR); NO SLAMS; NO YANKS. She underlined ONCE and ONE with the double line she uses on sensible Fridays.

"Now," she said, in the tone of someone about to be specific for everyone's good, "we write the ethical line so the house can't argue technicalities. It is one sentence. It trumps everything."

She wrote, in calm capitals:

WE WILL NOT HARM, FRIGHTEN, OR CONSTRAIN A LIVING PER-SON FOR ANY REASON.

Beneath, in smaller letters: IF THIS LINE IS CROSSED → IMMEDI-ATE BLACKOUT (24H), "RED STOP", THEN CALL HARRIET.

Mark stared at the sentence like a man seeing the bit of a map where the dragon had been crossed out with a biro. "That's the one," he said. "That's the sentence I didn't know I needed most."

Harriet nodded, practical. "It isn't a threat. It's a civic boundary. You can be grateful without being bullied." She turned the page sideways and drew a small house. She placed a mat at its door. "Place the compact on the mat when you get home. Give the house office hours in writing. Tell it the alarm venues. Tell it where no lives."

Clara smiled in that way she now recognised as acceptance turning into relief. "We'll read it out," she said. "Out loud. Like a council meeting."

"Good," Harriet said. She stapled her notes and wrote at the top, THE COMPACT — HOUSE & HUMANS. She printed three copies from the clinic machine that had never believed in printing its own opinions. She initialled the bottom of each sheet; then slid them across the table. "Sign where it asks you to sign. Print your names for the benefit of posterity and bureaucrats. Mark—write your left–right once, quietly, where a teenager might notice."

Mark, solemn, wrote in the margin: *left–right once; then us.* He wrote it neatly, the way he writes lists for shops when he intends to behave at the till.

They signed: CLARA MORGAN. MARK MORGAN. Underneath, Harriet wrote: WITNESSED: H. Baines.

"Now the cord," Harriet said, brisk. "I want us to name its vocabulary, limit it, and refuse riddles."

They wrote a small box beneath the compact:

Reef = OK

Granny = Stop / No

Bowline = Safe / Help

Clove hitch = Stay

Overhand(s) = 1 / 2 / 3 only

"And we add," Harriet said, "No poetry. No code. If it tries, you say I have heard you; I will consider it with my rules and you carry on making tea."

Priya, arriving with a grin and a bag full of sandwiches like a one-woman union, dropped into a chair and read the headings upside down. "I adore your tyranny," she said. "Ten out of ten, would obey."

"We prefer civility," Harriet said, amused. "But tyranny will do on Thursdays."

They ate, because eating turns meetings into something people survive. Lynn came at the right moment with a photograph of Sam asleep on the sofa with his hand in a crisp packet like a parliamentarian taking evidence. She read the compact, wholly serious, and said, "I will embroider the ethical line and hang it above my kettle."

"No trades," Mark said, grateful for a phrase to tape inside his head. "I didn't know I'd been tempted until I wasn't allowed."

"You'll still be tempted," Harriet said, kind. "You'll want to ask the air for one more knot in exchange for believing you. When you feel it, say no trades out loud. Then cut toast diagonally and be pleased with yourself."

"Homework?" Clara asked, half-mocking, half-divine.

Harriet smiled. "Put the compact on the mat. Read it out. Add today's office hours to your fridge. Add the ethical line in capitals where your tired eyes land. Then—this is important—write down, in one sentence, what you're for. Not what you're against. What the house is for, in your house."

Clara considered it and felt something kinder arrive. "We're for growing a person without teaching her fear."

"Good," Harriet said. "Write that down. Ghosts can learn mission statements. It will annoy teenagers and consoles gods."

They tidied papers like people who intend to keep promises. Harriet placed the USB in a plastic wallet and wrote ARCHIVE — LISTENED ONCE — NO REPLAY. She sealed it and handed them the copies of the compact in a cardboard folder that had a pocket for dignity.

At the door, she did a small, ordinary thing: she looked at Clara's wrist—bruise, red climbing to yellow—and nodded once. "You were right to be grateful," she said. "You were right to be cross. Both is being grown."

"Bossy + grown," Clara said, a little shy because the phrase had become a badge she wore for herself when she needed permission.

"Precisely," Harriet said. "Go on, then. Teach your house to read."

***

The house knew them and their paperwork. The hall had the patient air of a stage reset between acts. The mat lay square. The cord lay neutral in its taped box. The sealed envelope kept its back straight.

They placed the compact on the mat. For a moment they were ridiculous on purpose: three adults and a piece of paper being a mayor. Mark read, voice steady, like a man officiating at the opening of a sensible bridge.

"THE COMPACT — HOUSE & HUMANS. Principle one: order of care—child, carers, others, the dead. Principle two: proportionality. Principle three: consent & venue. Principle four: no trades. Principle five: office hours. Principle six: record & forget. Principle seven: escalation & blackout. Principle eight: RED STOP. Principle nine: copies travel; originals rest. Principle ten: humility."

He paused after each, not for theatre, for breath. He read the Rules in that careful, municipal way rules like: No physical contact with people; no moving prams/high chairs/cots/straps; no tightening garments/buckles; no touching skin/hair. Warnings = words only ("left–right" once). Immediate danger = one tap (hall table or inside front door). No slams. No yanks. Allowed: move loose objects away from the baby. And then, clearly, the ethical line: WE WILL NOT HARM, FRIGHTEN, OR CONSTRAIN A LIVING PERSON FOR ANY REASON. He read the sanction: blackout 24h, RED STOP, then Harriet.

Clara read their mission aloud into the house because mission statements only work if air hears them: "We are for growing a person without teaching her fear."

The room did not cool. The apples did not arrive. The table did not tap. From the taped box, the cord tied a small, competent reef—OK—then rested. The house had understood a meeting had been held and had chosen to be bored on purpose. It was the loveliest response Clara had yet learnt.

They pinned a copy of the compact on the fridge—top-left, where tired eyes land. Clara wrote, in her own neat capitals beside office hours: MESSAGES: 11:00–13:00, MAT ONLY. OUTSIDE = SILENCE (EXCEPT SAFETY: "LEFT–RIGHT" ONCE OR ONE TAP). Then, the sentence Harriet had made the thunderhead and then the clear sky: WE WILL NOT HARM, FRIGHTEN, OR CONSTRAIN A LIVING PERSON FOR ANY REASON. She underlined NOT once, and then made herself stop, because underlining twice is theology and she had decided to be municipal.

"Thank you," she said to the room, not to the E under glue, not to a teenager in static, to the room doing its good, dull job. "Thank you; we will take it from here."

The day trialled the compact immediately, because days are petty.

At one-ten, outside the office hours by ten minutes, the hall table gave a soft, single tap. Not a knock; a reminder. Clara walked to the doorway, looked out through the glass, and found that the postman—new, young, given to heroics—had left a parcel sat at the edge of the step like a pilgrim, perfectly placed for tripping.

"Allowed," she said, amused and grateful. She moved the parcel away from the door, inside, placed it beside the umbrella stand, and, because no trades, didn't ask for anything in exchange. She put her palm over the compact and felt the cheap cardboard warm under her hand.

At two-thirty, when the baby had taken the afternoon's polite idea of a nap and Clara was allowed to exist, the cord tied a granny—stop—as if in protest at being ignored outside office hours. She walked to the mat, placed two fingers near the cord and said the sentence that keeps governments civil: "I have heard you; I will consider it with my rules. Office hours are 11–13. I am making tea."

The cord did nothing. The house let her make tea. Tea is a law.

At four, Priya arrived with Jonah and an armful of administrative cake. She read the compact, let her mouth attempt a joke and then politely left humour outside because the ethical line was wearing its full uniform.

"No trades," she said, pleased. "I feel strongly that my adolescence would have gone better with that in the kitchen."

"Mine too," Mark said. "Also 'copies travel; originals rest' would have saved university from me."

They ate and did not perform. The baby declared socks to be an untrustworthy technology and then forgave them. On the fridge, the mission statement made the room behave.

At five-ten, with sunlight doing its best impression of wisdom, there was a small test: the neighbour's toddler (blameless, pink, bright with attempts) wandered into the hall as Priya collected her bag from the peg. He stopped at the mat because it is a stage, and children can smell stages. The cord lifted a half-inch and formed an overhand—one—as if telling a joke in numbers to someone who hadn't asked.

Clara stepped between the child and the mat, smiling exactly enough, and said to the air, naming the carer, "Ruth," because that is how you redirect things that misunderstand fairness. She pointed, calmly, at the peg where Ruth's coat hung. "If you have a message, we'll tell Ruth."

The cord settled like a dog told to lie down by someone who knows the tone. Ruth, appearing from the doorway, scooped her toddler with two hands and three apologies. "We have become a family of lists," she said, delighted and appalled. "It is working."

"Witness permitted," Clara said. "Performances cancelled."

***

Evening had the decency to wear slippers. They did the census: catch, rabbit, stars, breath. The bruise on Clara's wrist considered fading and agreed to begin. The high chair, chastened by an afternoon of professionalism, declined to audition any straps. The cup behaved like a citizen who has attended a training.

At nine, Clara stood in the nursery doorway and spoke the compact softly, like grammar, like praise: "No moving things in here. No water. No requests about water at night. Knots on the hall mat only. No requests through other people's children. No teaching them. Withdraw if attention gathers. No recordings in here. No physical contact with people; no moving prams/high chairs/cots/straps; no tightening garments/buckles; no touching skin/hair. Warnings are words only—left–right once; if danger, one tap on the hall table or the inside of the front door. Allowed: move loose objects away from the baby. Requests are not commands. No altering records without permission.

Doctors allowed. Friends allowed. Witness permitted. We are for grow-ing a person without teaching her fear."

The room stayed a room. The baby's breath kept its commas and its pairs. The window catch sat dignified with its two clicks. She put two fingers on the small chest and borrowed the metronome and returned it. She turned out the light to a city that had agreed, tonight, to be reasonable.

Downstairs, the cord tied a small, precise clove hitch—stay—inside its taped box, then reef—OK—and then chose to be a line. Clara wrote: *21:18 — stay; OK; end.* On the fridge, the ethical line stared benevolently across the kitchen like a careful ancestor not interested in dominating the conversation.

Mark came to stand beside her, shoulder to shoulder. He looked at the sentence and then at her wrist. He kissed the skin next to the bruise, because that is how you love a person who has learned boundaries.

"No trades," he said, and made it a promise he could keep.

"No trades," she agreed. "Left–right once. Then us."

They turned out the light. The house performed the small, approving sigh of pipes done for the night. Somewhere, a bus rehearsed its own and got it right. In Martha's kitchen the jug held tulips and no opinions. In Lynn's hall, the green strip on the high shelf pretended to be asleep. In Ruth's, a toddler declared sovereignty over a spoon. In Clara's hall-way, on the mat, a piece of paper told a room how to be a house, and the room agreed.

***

New boundary added to the fridge (in sober capitals):

NO TRADES. *We will not bargain for proof or attention. No "if you... then we...". Gratitude is not currency. Attention is not a wage.*

Chapter Twenty-Two
Viable

The morning wore Wednesday with the seriousness of a clerk. The light behind the curtains was the colour of paper that can take ink without answering back. Clara lay still and let the house list itself: boiler's civil hum; the fridge's single note; a bus sighing as if reminded to be decent. She reached for the notebook and wrote, neat as a council minute: *Woke steady. Hand bruise turning field-yellow. Office hours 11–13. Mission: take the compact to Mum; ask about language. Post due—records? Rules unchanged. ALLOWED: enjoy the baby without checking the window.*

Mark surfaced with one eye and the half-smile of a man prepared to be reasonable. "Status?"

"Green," she said. "Grey cooperative."

"Bless grey." He kissed her hair. "What does the calendar pretend?"

"Post office if the state demands. Mum at eleven. We bring the compact and biscuits as if negotiating a treaty."

"God loves a treaty," he said. "I'll bring my agreement face."

On the landing the baby made the small bureaucratic squeak that meant the office had opened. The nursery smelt of warm cotton and sleep with good paperwork. Window catch: two clicks. She didn't check it. She touched it and forgave herself for touching it. Catch; rabbit; stars; breath. Two fingers on a tiny chest—rise, fall. She borrowed the metronome and returned it on time.

On the hall mat, in the taped box, the dull cotton cord lay neutral, off duty. The sealed envelope kept its mouth shut like an aunt with standards. The house wore slippers.

***

The post came at nine-oh-seven with a sound like unimportant news. Among the catalogues and the leaflet about bins, a brown envelope with a square window announced itself in the fonts of Hospital Archives. Clara stood at the console table and considered it the way you consider a door you know how to open but not how to leave.

Mark joined her, coffee warming his hands into better judgement. "We open it," he said, gentle as a lever.

"We open it and we do not feed it to the day," Clara said, Harriet steady behind her. "Copies travel; originals rest. We read once, we write once."

She slit the top neatly with the butter knife that moonlights as a letter-opener and slid out the covering letter and two photocopied sheets that smelt faintly of toner and old decisions.

Patient: MARTHA JANE MORGAN (née Pengelly)
Event date: 27/08/—
Summary: Spontaneous labour; delivery of one viable female infant; non-viable twin retained, managed expectantly; products of conception to pathology as per protocol...

Clara's mouth went dry as if the air had been replaced with salt. Viable sat on the page with its sensible shoes, and beside it non-viable like a door locked from the wrong side. Products of conception repeated itself once, twice, doing the bureaucratic work of turning a person into tidy plural.

Mark did not swear; he closed his eyes once and then opened them in a way that put furniture back. "We take these to your mum," he said. "We don't do theology on our own."

Clara nodded. She put the originals back in the envelope and slid them into the sealed sleeve marked ORIGINAL — ARCHIVES. She photocopied the covering letter and the first page—copies only—and wrote in the corner with her neat library hand: COPY FROM ORIGINAL (read once). She tucked the copies into the bag with the compact, the biscuits, and a portable kindness.

On the mat, the cord lifted a breath, tied a small granny—stop—then lay flat. "Message received," Clara said. "We're going carefully."

***

Martha's door opened with the exact speed of a woman who manages her own day. The house smelt of stew thinking itself into being and tulips making no trouble. The jug held them like an honest citizen performing flower duty. "Come in," she said. "Put your faces down. Are we bringing the law?"

"We are," Mark said, holding up the folder as if it might bite. "And biscuits, because parliament requires them."

Clara kissed her mother and saw, under the humour, the old weather in her eyes—the thing you tidy around for decades until one day you stand in the room and look at it.

They sat at the kitchen table that had seen three fridges and five governments and two women learning how to continue. Clara put the compact on the table and the copies from the archive beside it, face down for now, like a dog that might jump. She poured tea because tea turns meetings into survivable things.

"We wrote the compact with Harriet," she said, soft. "It's a treaty for the house. And us. We're trying to be boring and kind."

"Good," Martha said. "Boring and kind are the only politics that work."

Clara flipped the compact. They read it together, not hurried. Martha paused at no trades, nodded at office hours, and smiled—pain and pride together—at Copies travel; originals rest.

"Reasonable," she said. "You are my daughter after all."

Clara turned the archive copies face up. She watched Martha not flinch. The older woman adjusted her glasses, that tiny domestic courage, and read.

She stopped at viable like a foot at the edge of ice. She read non-viable and her mouth did the thing mouths do when they are trying not to become grief. She read products of conception and breathed in very carefully as if the air were full of needles.

"That," she said, in the voice she uses for knives and gas leaks and men who talk too loud, "is the word that broke me."

She didn't cry—Martha doesn't cry except in the garden and sometimes in the freezer section on hot days. She put her finger under the printed viable—not touching, never touching—and moved it as if drawing a little boat under the word, the way she had drawn one under lino so the names would have something to ride on if the glue ate the truth.

"Viable," she said again, tasting it, spitting it out. "I was twenty-six. It was August. The midwife had a plait and a gold stud in her nose which you weren't supposed to have but I liked her for it. She said breathe and I breathed. Your father said unhelpful things like we're all right in a voice meant for drains. We were not all right. Then the doctor came because doctors like to feel useful, and he said one viable infant and one non-viable twin and the room obeyed him, because rooms obey coats."

She held her hand at her ribs and pressed as if the word still lived there. "I didn't know the law that year. I didn't know what weeks meant to registers. I only knew that viable was a hand reaching past me to choose, and I didn't want any hands choosing anything that day except me, choosing both. I hated him for saying it. I hated the word more. It took a person who was mine and turned her into something the hospital could move in a bin without saying a name."

Clara's palms were damp. She rubbed them on her jeans under the table because she had decided to be an adult in front of her mother. "You wrote our names under the lino," she said. "You made your own register."

"I did," Martha said, and now the smile was a bent thing that had mended badly and remained the bravest object in the room. "I wrote CLARA and ELEANOR where the floor kept house, because floors won't betray you if you treat them well. I drew a boat because boats are not metaphors in caravans; they are how you survive when the ground moves and you can't call it water. I wrote them in English because English would not have us. Then I went and fed the bloody meter and we made tea because you have to make tea when there is no register for your person."

She touched the copy with the back of her fingers as if it were hot gorse. "I know they weren't trying to be cruel," she said, and the labour of the sentence was a visible thing. "I know they were trying to be right in the way rooms like that do right. But viable was a cruel excellence, and non-viable was a trapdoor."

They sat very still. The stew muttered to itself on the hob. The tulips declined to be interesting. Mark, who has learnt the right kind of silence, waited like a man in a good queue.

"Do you want me to call them," Clara asked, "and ask them to put her name in a letter to you, even if it isn't a register. A letter that says Eleanor? No trades," she added, Harriet in the room, "no bargains. Just names first."

Martha considered. "I want someone to say her in a registerable way, yes," she said, precise. "But I don't want to become a woman who lives in waiting for that. I want to be a woman who fed you and taught you to dislike sloppy Rs and tied knots properly. I have been both. I will go on being both. But I will not hand my Thursday to a word in a letter. Do not let me."

"We won't," Mark said, as if swearing in the correct court. "We will write her on our paper, and if the hospital will be kind, we will accept kindness, not permission."

"Good man," Martha said, and patted his forearm the way you pat wood before planing it.

Clara took out her phone and typed a text to the number on the covering letter because sometimes progress looks like a message to a department: *Thank you for sending copies. May I ask—kindly—that in any further correspondence you use both names? The twin referred to as "non-viable" was named Eleanor. We understand the historical threshold. Names help us hold our history without hurting anyone else's systems.* She added, because she was her mother's daughter, *Thank you for your work,* and sent it.

The reply came half an hour later while they were buttering bread in the kitchen with the holy attention bread deserves. *Of course. I'm so sorry for the language in the old notes. We can add an addendum to your copy letter noting the family name. I will write Eleanor.*

Martha nodded as if someone had learned to say please by themselves. "That will do," she said. "We will not ask the past to change its clothes. We will hold the coat we have and pin a flower on it so it doesn't frighten the baby."

***

After lunch, because paperwork doesn't keep the baby warm, Martha went to the airing cupboard, took out the shoebox with the faded teddy on the lid, and set it on the table. She did not ask if they wanted to see it. She made them present for it, which is kinder.

Inside lay the hospital bracelet with CLARA MORGAN in biro bored neat; and beneath it the twin bracelet with ELEANOR MORGAN in the same hand, never fitted to a wrist, elastic slightly yellowed by years and not by skin. Next to them, in the exact corner where you would find it if your hands were old, a small card with a lamb and the midwife's name written too small for lawyers.

Martha picked up the ELEANOR band and held it on her palm as if it were a bird deciding whether to be rescued. "I hid biscuits in the blue jug when I was little," she said, unexpected as a change in the light. "I learnt that if you hide something in something too obvious, no one will look. That word—viable—made me want to hide everything. I refused. I put her in the places mothers go every day. Under lino, inside a shoe box next to the pegs, in the bread tin many Thursdays. I did it because I did not want you to have to dig to find her, only to live."

Clara felt her ribs behave like a room with a window opened the right amount. "You did," she said. "We live and we find her in the bread and in the floor and in the jug doing flowers."

"Good," Martha said, and put the bracelet back, very gently, because gentle is a discipline not a mood. "That is my theology."

On the mat by Martha's door—ordinary coir with a corner turned as if a shoe had considered revolution—there was no rope. There was no box. Harriet had said quarantine mats for friends' houses if needed; this house, today, needed nothing that required English from the air. The jug held tulips and minded its manners. The stew worked without an audience. The past sat at the table because it had been invited and not because it had let itself in.

***

They went home before witching hour as if saving the baby from moral complexity. On their own mat, the cord lifted, tied a small bowline—safe—and then a reef—OK—and lay flat, done. Clara wrote: *15:11 — bowline; reef; end. Interpretation: safe/OK to do what we did.* She did not make a religion of it.

She pinned the addendum reply to the compact on the fridge with a bulldog clip that had disciplined generations of receipts. Under the mission statement—We are for growing a person without teaching her fear—she wrote, in the same calm capitals, a new sentence:

NAMES FIRST. *We do not use erasing language for the living or the dead (e.g., "non-viable", "products of conception") in this house. If someone must use it, we translate to a name.*

Mark read it and nodded like a person grateful for a rule he can touch. "Names first," he said. "You should make samplers."

"I will," Clara said. "After we have made a person."

They did the census. Catch (two clicks). Rabbit (guard). Stars (behaving). Breath (proof). In the kitchen the kettle consented to boil. The bruise at Clara's wrist had become a civilised yellow at the edges. The house did what good houses do—it refused to perform.

At nine, in the doorway of the nursery, Clara spoke the rules as grammar, added the compact in the short version, and ended with the new line, because language builds stairs: "Names first. We do not let language erase anyone we love."

She put two fingers to a tiny chest—rise, fall—and returned the metronome with interest. She looked at the window and then at the baby and then at nothing because looking at nothing is also a practice.

Downstairs, the cord tied a single overhand—one—and then lay plain. One more day done without theatre. One more step done with names.

Clara made tea and watched the steam draw five petals and fade without making an argument of it. She thought of viable and non-viable and products of conception, and preferred Clara, Eleanor, daughter, mother, bread, boat, tulip, Thursday. She thought of Martha writing on floors and underlining alive with glue, and of Harriet turning sentences into chairs that everyone can sit on.

"Thank you," she said into the house, not bargaining, not trading, not asking the air to knock or tie or show off. "We will take it from here."

The house agreed by being a house. The bus at the bend practised its sigh and passed. Somewhere in the city, a boy counted on a window and decided, without knowing why, to put his hand in his pocket and be patient. In Martha's kitchen the blue jug held tulips and hid nothing. In Clara's hall, on the mat, a small piece of string turned into a line and stayed a line, the politest message there is.

***

New boundary added to the fridge (in sober capitals):

NAMES FIRST. *We do not use erasing language (e.g., "non-viable", "products of conception") for the living or the dead. If it must appear in paperwork, we translate to a name in this house.*

Chapter Twenty-Three
Blue Jug

The morning set Thursday on the table and folded its hands. The light behind the curtains was the colour of paper that accepts ink without making a scene. Clara lay still and let the house list itself: boiler's civil hum; the fridge's one note; a bus at the bend performing its sigh without ambition. She reached for the notebook and wrote, neat as a clerk: *Woke steady. Hand bruise yellowing at the edges (strap lesson noted). Office hours 11–13. Mission: Mum + jug (confession promised, tulips fading). Rules intact. ALLOWED: enjoy the baby without checking the window.*

Mark surfaced with the one eye of a man prepared to negotiate in good faith. "Status?"

"Green," she said. "Grey cooperative. Mum at eleven. She texted *'Bring your ears and the tin with the lid that sticks'*."

"The biscuit tin," he said, pleased by a solvable task. "We shall arrive bearing carbohydrates and contrition."

On the landing, the baby made the small bureaucratic squeak that meant the office was open. The nursery smelt of warm cotton and sleep with tidy paperwork. The window catch sat down and honest: two clicks. She didn't check it. She touched it and forgave herself for touching it. Catch; rabbit; stars; breath. Two fingers on a tiny chest—rise, fall. She borrowed the metronome and returned it on time.

On the hall mat, in the taped box, the dull cotton cord lay neutral like a citizen between shifts. The sealed envelope stood to attention with the decency of an aunt who has never once commented on anyone's shoes.

"Jug after tea," Clara said to the room, because objects behave better when they know the timetable.

The cord made a single, well-mannered overhand—one—and then lay flat: one appointment, understood.

***

Martha opened her door wearing the cardigan that has, over the years, calmed more weather than forecasts. The house smelt of stew rehearsing and tulips deciding which way to look. The blue jug—tall, cobalt, sensible—held them as if that had always been its job. "Come in," she said. "Put your faces down. I have boiled water and sharpened the truth."

"Dangerous combination," Mark said, carrying the tin with the lid that sticks like a man arriving with case law. He kissed Martha's cheek with respect and familiarity.

They gathered at the kitchen table that knows where bread lives and where names do. Clara put the compact within reach, because treaties on wood make rooms behave. She placed the biscuit tin to the right of the jug because the jug had been told it was for flowers, and the day respected promotions and demotions alike.

Martha looked at the jug as if it were a person who had come to an understanding. "Right," she said, not dramatic. "Confessions. Who hid what and why."

She pushed the tulips aside to make a small clear circle on the table, then set the jug in the centre with the respectful thud of ceramic that has seen off three cupboards. "I will go first," she said, and took a breath of the kind women take before they say a sentence that adjusts the furniture.

"When I was little," she began—*Peggy's* lilt just under the words— "we had two boys next door who were good at finding where biscuits lived. My mother—your Nan—said, *If you hide something in something too obvious, the nosey will pass it by.* So she put Rich Teas in the tall blue jug and left it on the dresser like a saint. It became legend. 'Where are the biscuits?' 'Ask the jug.' The boys never looked. The jug looked like decency."

Clara felt the small, exact movement at her wrist—the apples—not cold, only present. She let it be weather. "You hid sweetness in a thing that looked like serious," she said.

"I did," Martha said. "And when you were born—when you were born, and the doctor in the coat did his words—I wanted to hide the other sweetness somewhere that wasn't a drawer or a box or a hospital that thinks nouns are dangerous. So I hid her in ordinary places. The bread tin, the floor, the jug. Not all the time. Not forever. I didn't want to become superstition's shop assistant. But sometimes I put the little bracelet in the jug while I did the washing up or fed you, because I wanted to keep both within arm's reach without making a ceremony that would scare us."

She reached towards the jug and then stopped, check-list neat. "No trades," she said to herself, amused by obedience. "No water. No rituals. Only explanation." She lifted the flowers out and set them on a tea towel so no one would accuse a tulip of being a priest. She tilted the jug and shook it once. From the darkness, a small, familiar dry sound answered—paper against ceramic, a crease that has been waiting.

Clara's breath did what breath does just before it becomes a mistake, and then did not become a mistake.

"I put something inside," Martha said. "Years ago. I couldn't remember if I had kept it or if guilt had tidied me. Turns out I kept it."

She turned the jug mouth-down on the tea towel and tapped its flank with two fingers the way you release a cake from a tin without deciding to be a genius. A paper boat slid out—small, foxed at the edges, folded from the thick cream of *Lakeland* order slips. It had the patient look of things that kept faith with you while you grew immoderate and then modest again.

Clara looked at her mother, not at the boat, because the person is the point. "May I," she said, because permissions keep rooms.

"You may," Martha said. "Copies only. No tidying grief."

Clara lifted the boat into her palm. It weighed exactly as much as an idea. On the inside, written in the bored careful hand the caravan had known: Both came. Both go on. Underneath, smaller, a line that made the skin rise on Clara's arms: Boat song, not at night. And then the neat, bored signature of a woman who has always done forms properly: MJM.

Clara turned the paper once, twice, without unfolding it to the point where it would lose its courage. "How old," she said, and didn't mean numerals.

"Three kitchens ago," Martha said. "I put it in sometimes and took it out sometimes and then stopped because stopping is also a skill. I didn't tell you because I wanted you to grow a person without learning my arithmetics. And because the jug began as biscuits and ought to be allowed to return."

"I spoke into the jug once," she added, the confession precise, not ashamed. "After a long Thursday. I said both your names, because the doctor had made me choose a word I did not like. I felt ridiculous and brave and then I put the kettle on and got on with toast. But I did it once. I did not sing."

Clara breathed. "And the day you hid the biscuits," she said, "did you hide anything else?"

"Not contraband," Martha said. "Only shock. Sometimes a kitchen needs a container for shock. I used the jug and then I put tulips in it so no one would congratulate me for being poetic."

They stood around the boat as if it were a guest who cannot sit down because there is only one chair and it is already occupied by history. Mark—who has learnt to ask for the right lever—said, "Copies?"

"Copies," Clara said. She put the boat on greaseproof paper, laid a second sheet on top, and made a rubbing with the soft side of a pencil: *Both came. Both go on. Boat song, not at night. MJM.* She wrote on the back: COPY FROM ORIGINAL — paper boat (jug) — 11:23 — witnesses: C.M., M.M., M. Morgan. She did a second rubbing because law likes pairs. She did not unfold the boat further because originals rest.

Martha watched the decent choreography and allowed a thin smile that had lived a life. "Now you know," she said. "Who hid what and why. Biscuits. Shock. Names. Boats. I hid them in a jug because I wanted them close in an object that didn't ask anyone to genuflect. I wanted you to find out when you were a person who would use a pencil and not a knife."

"Thank you," Clara said, and did the thank-you protocol because gratitude without bargaining is a discipline: "Thank you; we will take it from here."

Martha poured tea because tea is how you put oxygen back in the room without offending anyone. She set the jug upright, put the tulips back in with the gentleness you reserve for past decisions, and patted their stems as if adjusting collars on a choir.

"Me next," Mark said, as if volunteering for the dunk tank. "Confession. You know about the two seconds of water at the sink. I told myself it wasn't night and told myself it was cleaning and told myself I wasn't asking and—" He lifted a hand in a small admission. "—it was still breaking. I am sorry. No water near the jug after five, yes, but also no water at the sink as substitute for control. I have added that inside my head. I'm—" he hesitated, found the word— "tidier than I am wise."

Martha looked at him with the affection of a woman who has loved at least one idiot and has forgiven him on purpose. "Men like clean because clean looks like done," she said. "We like rules because rules look like not drowning. Your compact is better than my biscuits. We'll use yours."

Clara glanced at the compact on the table, at the ethical line hanging in her head like a banner: WE WILL NOT HARM, FRIGHTEN, OR CON-STRAIN A LIVING PERSON FOR ANY REASON. She touched her bruised wrist and then looked away from it, because attention is a wage and she was not going to pay the wrong worker today.

"My turn," she said. "Confession. The first night, I turned the moni-tor up when Mark said not to. I wanted to prove something. To myself or to him I don't know. It was a small trade. I didn't call it that, but it was. I am done with trades."

"Good," Martha said. "Trades invite shopkeepers, and no one wants a ghost behind a till."

They laughed in the correct, quiet way. The stew muttered. The tulips practised being tulips. The boat rested.

***

After tea, Martha opened the cupboard above the microwave—the one that contains string, twine, and the ancient Sellotape with dust inside the ring—and brought down a small, square, blue felt pad. "This," she said, "used to live under the jug when I was pregnant. Your father cut it out of a cardigan that died bravely. I kept it because women keep squares of blue like receipts."

Beneath the felt—where it had protected the jug's base from the sin of scratching wood—someone had written in pencil, faint as a lie that learned better: BOTH. The letters had smudged under heat and washing and years; they survived like stubborn grass.

"I did that," Martha said. "Not to be caught. To look when I made tea. I needed to see a small BOTH on days when the rest of the world was being viable."

Clara photographed it once, twice, phones on airplane for decency. She wrote on the back of a printed copy: COPY FROM ORIGINAL — felt pad (jug base) — 'BOTH' in pencil — 11:41 — witnesses: C.M., M.M., M. Morgan. The felt went back in the drawer because originals rest.

"What a lot of us we were," Martha said, folding the boat back into the jug with the same hand she uses to put the bread bin to bed. "All of us trying to keep both without drowning anyone."

They ate stew because sentences require stew afterwards or they keeled over. Martha buttered bread as if paying respect to wheat. Mark took the baby for a lap of the lounge where the photos tell the truth in the order the frames prefer.

When the plates were commensurate with justice, Martha placed the jug back at the centre of the table as if returning a visiting official to her seat. She looked at it with the exact fondness of a person who is not going to apologise for the tools that kept her alive. "I will not hide biscuits in it any more," she said. "I will keep tulips in it. That is not a demotion. That is a retirement."

"Heirlooms are not altars," Clara said, the phrase arriving complete as if a clerk had posted it through a slot from the sensible part of the brain.

Martha nodded. "Yes. Write that on your parliament."

"We will," Mark said. "We will write no speaking into vessels while we're at it. Boats belong to paper, not to throats."

"Boats belong to fields, too," Martha said, and they smiled at the same thought—lino, glue, ELEAN——without needing to become operatic.

***

Home before office hours ended, because being on time for your own rules is how you persuade a house to sign them. The mat lay square. In the taped box, the cord tied a small, competent reef—OK—and then made a clove hitch—stay—as if to say: OK to keep the jug where it is; OK to keep the boat where boats keep faith.

Clara wrote, neat: *12:56 — reef; clove hitch.* Interpretation: *OK; stay.* She did not make a code of it; she did not pretend to be a theologian with string.

On the fridge, beneath NO TRADES, NAMES FIRST, and the ethical line, Clara wrote, in the sober capitals that make words behave:

HEIRLOOMS ARE NOT ALTARS.
We don't use keepsakes (jug, bracelets, shoebox, felt pad) as channels or instruments. Flowers and biscuits only; no speaking into vessels; no 'offerings'.

Mark, reading, added, below, the clause that transforms dogma into policy:

IF A KEEPSAKE HOLDS A MESSAGE, WE MAKE A COPY ON PAPER, THEN LET THE OBJECT REST.

He underlined REST once because underlining persuades hands to be kind.

They did the census. Catch (two clicks). Rabbit (guard). Stars (behaving). Breath (proof). The house wore slippers and declined to audition for the part of corridor. The bruise on Clara's wrist had become the colour of a field on a Sunday.

At three-twelve, when houses briefly try on worse ideas and reject them, the hall table made a single tap, polite, allowed. Clara looked out through the glass: a delivery man had left a parcel at the edge of the step like a cliff. She moved it away and said to the air, "Thank you; we will take it from here." The air excused itself and did weather elsewhere.

At four, Lynn arrived with Sam in a dinosaur coat and a packet of custard creams that had opinions. She read the new line on the fridge and saluted with a biscuit. "Heirlooms are not altars," she said. "Put it on tea towels; retire a dozen haunted spatulas."

"Do not mock spatulas," Mark said. "Some of my best arguments have been held together by a wooden spoon."

Sam, who has learnt the correct way to pay attention, looked at the mat and then at his mother and then at nothing. He did not tie a knot in the air. He asked if he could watch the spinny (washing machine) and was granted a seat in front of glass doing circles with the seriousness of parliament. The cord in the taped box remained a citizen: line.

"Who hid what," Lynn asked, because the phrase had become a family game.

"Biscuits," Clara said. "Shock. Names. A paper boat that says Both came. Both go on. And a pencilled BOTH under the jug. Nothing under the rug that isn't vacuumable."

"Applaudable inventory," Lynn said, and the baby applauded because babies mistake philosophy for *peekaboo* and are correct.

***

Evening was given permission to be dull and performed the role with distinction. They ate pasta that had agreed to salt and nothing silly. The high chair remembered to be a chair. The cup stayed married to gravity. The house kept its compact.

At nine, Clara stood in the nursery doorway and spoke the rules like grammar, as always: "No moving things in here. No water. No requests about water at night. Knots on the hall mat only. No requests through other people's children. No teaching them. Withdraw if attention gathers. No recordings in here. No physical contact with people; no moving prams/high chairs/cots/straps; no tightening garments/buckles; no touching skin/hair. Warnings by words only—left–right once; if danger, one tap on the hall table or the inside of the front door. Allowed: move loose objects away from the baby. Requests are not commands. No altering records without permission. Doctors allowed. Friends allowed. Witness permitted. We are for growing a person without teaching her fear. Heirlooms are not altars."

The room kept its face. She put two fingers on a tiny chest—rise, fall—and returned the metronome with interest.

Downstairs, the taped box on the mat contained a reef—OK—and then nothing. The jug at Martha's held tulips and no opinions. Under its base, the felt slept on its BOTH without requiring commentary. The boat rested in ceramic shade like a witness who has given her statement and been excused.

Clara made tea and watched steam draw five petals on the window and thin at its own pace. She thought of women hiding sweetness in serious things so strangers would pass them by. She thought of doctors with coats and words that break and of kitchens with boats and biscuits and BOTH written under bases to persuade the day to be honest.

"Thank you," she said, soft, because gratitude builds floors. "We will take it from here."

The house agreed, doing it in pipes. Outside, a bus rehearsed its decent sigh and got it right. In somebody else's hallway a boy did not touch a mat and was proud of himself. In Martha's kitchen, a blue jug retired with honours and did dignified work. In Clara's hall, a cord remembered its vocabulary and rested. On the fridge, parliament kept its seat.

***

New boundary added to the fridge (in sober capitals):

HEIRLOOMS ARE NOT ALTARS. *We do not use keepsakes (jug, bracelets, shoebox, felt pad) as channels or instruments. Flowers and biscuits only; no speaking into vessels; no 'offerings'. If a keepsake holds a message, we make a copy on paper and let the object rest.*

Chapter Twenty-Four
When Doors Open

T he morning put on Friday without fuss. The light behind the curtains was the colour of paper that will take ink and not make a scene. Clara lay still and let the house list itself: boiler's civil hum; the fridge's single note; a bus at the bend rehearsing its respectable sigh. She reached for the notebook and wrote, clerk-neat: *Woke steady. Jug retired with honours. Paper boat (Both came. Both go on.) copies, original rests. Office hours 11–13. Baby clinic at the community centre 10:30 (weights, smug scales). Rules unchanged. ALLOWED: enjoy the baby without checking the window.*

Mark surfaced with one eye, tried a half-smile on morning, found it amenable. "Status?"

"Green," she said. "Grey cooperative. Today we donate our child to a queue and are inspected by scales with opinions."

"A national ritual," he said. "I'll meet you after emails. Packet of rice for ballast if she looks small."

"Absolutely not," she said, and kissed him for being the sort of man who offered ballast and jokes and met compacts like municipal bridges.

On the landing, the baby made the small bureaucratic squeak that meant the office had opened. The nursery smelt of warm cotton and sleep with good paperwork. Window catch: two clicks. She didn't check it. She touched it and forgave herself for touching it. Catch; rabbit; stars; breath. Two fingers to a tiny chest—rise, fall. She borrowed the metronome and returned it on time.

On the hall mat, in the taped box, the dull cotton cord lay neutral, off duty. The sealed envelope kept its mouth politely shut. The compact on the fridge held its line like a small, careful parliament: WE WILL NOT HARM, FRIGHTEN, OR CONSTRAIN A LIVING PERSON FOR ANY REASON. Underneath, yesterday's addition: HEIRLOOMS ARE NOT ALTARS.

"Clinic, then boring errands, back by office hours," Clara told the house, because clarity is mercy. The cord tied a small over-hand—one—and then lay plain. One outing, understood.

***

The community centre had been a school once, and hadn't stopped be-lieving in corridors. A noticeboard with knitted owls. A tap that didn't entirely shut. Doors that remembered being painted by teenagers on work experience with the wrong brush. The clinic queue did its civ-il duty: prams parked in parallel like a miniature car park, babies in knitwear, parents in varying degrees of competence. Priya waved from the far end, Jonah asleep in his pram like a diplomat taking a principled stand. Lynn arrived five minutes later, Sam in his dinosaur coat, proud of his pockets.

"Look at us," Priya said, voice turned to public. "Bringing our citizens to be weighed like courgettes."

Lynn read the posters with the relish of a woman looking for errors to fix. "No one tell me about latches," she said. "I will unionise the door closers."

The clinic nurse, Denise, moved along the queue with a smile that had never been used for sarcasm. "Morning, lovelies. Housekeeping:

keep the corridor clear; don't crowd the scales; we've got biscuits if anyone is about to take a principled stand against sugar."

They laughed, because biscuits remain national infrastructure.

The corridor smelled faintly of disinfectant and slightly of applause, as all rooms do where people bring babies to be approved by machines. The doors were the old school kind: one to the office; one to the cupboards that used to be craft and now were storage; one to the kitchenette with a fire door that pushed out onto the yard; one to the clinic room itself with a laminated notice: KNOCK. THEN WAIT. Each door had its own closer, its own gasps and sighs.

Clara's wrist—nearly new again, bruise yellowing at the edges like a field in late summer—felt a familiar tug of attention. Not cold; not apples; a concentration, as if the air were listening with proper manners. She glanced at the clock: 10:36. *Outside office hours; mat a mile away; public; children present.* The rule trotted to the front of her mind: Consent & venue. Mat only. Children out of bounds. Withdraw if attention gathers.

The baby clinic scales did their smug little grin. Babies were weighed, pronounced conceptually perfect, and returned to adoring electorates. Clara chatted about nap patterns with a woman who looked like Tuesday and loved her cardigan. She forgot herself for three minutes, which is sometimes the goal.

"Left–right," said the air.

Not in her head. Not to her ear. A voice in the corridor, like a child remembering the rules of a game aloud. Not shouted. Placed. The woman with the cardigan looked up from her newborn and smiled as if someone had reminded her how pavements work. Lynn flicked her gaze to Clara with the speed of good colleagues and did the smallest nod: *Heard it. Not panicking.*

"Thank you," Clara said, civil, because gratitude when you can afford it saves drama. "We'll take it from here."

She checked: left — the office door; right — the cupboard; left — the kitchenette; right — the clinic room. Nothing moving but people doing decency. Air the temperature of corridors. All well.

Denise called, "Next," and the next baby became proof. A delivery man with the posture of a repentant labrador carried a box past and performed the small dance of not clipping pram wheels. The door to the yard nudged as if the day had thoughts, and settled back like a person changing their mind.

"Drafts," somebody said, kindly to themselves.

It began not with a bang but with a click.

The clinic room handle turned exactly a quarter and the door opened a hand's width. Not flung. Opened, like a person showing a card. Denise looked at it, smiled, and said, "Well, be my guest," and closed it gently because the next baby deserved to be weighed in private.

A pause like a breath taken carefully.

The cupboard door opened a hand's width.

Denise stopped mid-step and put her head to one side like a dog trying to remember whether biscuits fall from the sky. "Well now," she said, friendly to wood, and pushed it shut with two fingers. "Aren't you helpful."

Another breath. Another click. The office door opened a hand's width, showing a slice of carpet and a desk with a pen performing being a pen.

Somebody laughed politely, because things are funny until they're not. A father reached for his phone, filmed one second out of a habit that had fed him for a decade, remembered something about not making it weird, and put the phone down with a red face as if he had been caught peeking in a wardrobe.

Priya, soft and municipal: "No recordings, please. Babies first. Drafts later." She did it with that tone that makes people obey and think it was their idea.

The fire door to the yard opened a hand's width and stopped on its chain. A clean triangle of daylight slid onto the lino. The corridor's four doors stood a little open, like mouths deciding whether to say a word. Then, in a pattern anyone with Left–Right in their head would feel behind their ribs, the doors closed in sequence — right (clinic), left (cupboard), right (office), left (fire door tapping its chain once like a knock) — and the corridor returned to its preferred aesthetic of capable stillness.

The baby near Clara — not hers — let out the smallest, most precise o of surprise. Sam did what three-year-olds do with competence; he did not go to the doors. He looked at his mother's face and, seeing it calm, borrowed that calm and put it carefully in his pocket.

Denise laughed again, but the laugh had moved from this is a nice story for later to where is the electrician's number. "Old closers," she said, reassuring herself as much as anyone. "They breathe," she added, to give herself the right kind of shiver.

Clara felt the tug at her wrist, the kind that has learnt to be politeness. *Venue breach, public, children present. Withdraw if attention gathers.* She looked at Lynn. Lynn made the tiniest RED shape with her lips. Priya did the same. They were a committee, and the committee said: we leave the corridor to itself.

"Denise," Clara said, cheerful and fully explanatory, the way you talk to a colleague you like when a spreadsheet turns into a personality, "I think we'll step out and have five minutes of fresh air and disrespect for scales."

"Of course," Denise said, eyes still on the doors as if expecting them to apply for planning permission. "We're all fine. We're normal. Fresh air sounds like best practice."

They turned their buggies away (withdraw if attention gathers), made the politest shapes with shoulders, and went into the yard, which had chosen to be entirely about puddles and a council bin. The sky was the colour of yes, but later.

"Visible," Priya said, mild, weighing the word like a vegetable. "Others saw."

"Doors," Lynn said. "Left–right once in wood, then a curtsey. No granny, no reef, no knots where they shouldn't be. But venue breach is venue breach."

Clara nodded. Her chest had that sensible, small thrum it got when rules had kept a day from becoming an argument and wanted to be thanked. "RED STOP," she said, softly, to the air, to herself, to the corridor. "Blackout from now. Twenty-four hours. No engagement. We go home by streets that haven't applied for weird."

They stood for a minute and allowed boring to put itself back together. The doors did not fling themselves open to protest. No one shouted *look*. The babies decided to need hats. The weather behaved like ordinary weather and won awards for it.

Clara texted Harriet while Priya ran interference on biscuits and Lynn supervised Sam's puddles with the benign authority of a minor goddess.

Community centre, 10:36. Four corridor doors opened in sequence, then closed in sequence (R-L-R-L tap). Calm. Others saw. Children present. No one frightened. We withdrew. Calling RED STOP now + 24h blackout. Please advise boundary language for public spaces.

Harriet replied as floors do, promptly and without theatre: *Correct response: withdraw + blackout. Add boundary: PUBLIC IS OUT OF BOUNDS*

— no mechanical displays or venue messages outside your mat/quarantine mats. If breach occurs again: name it, stop it ("Public is out of bounds"), remove yourselves and any children, and text me. Add NO DOORS to the compact: "No opening/closing doors or locks anywhere but our own front door for the one tap alarm." Consider a pocket card for friendly witnesses: "We're fine. Drafts. Thank you." Floor holds.

Clara read it aloud, and the three of them did the small, satisfied look of people who have got through a test with their dignity folded and put away properly.

"Public is out of bounds," Lynn said, practising the shape. "No doors outside our kitchen; one tap only. We stick a card in our wallets so Denise doesn't end up in a WhatsApp legend."

Priya had already found an index card and a pen in the mysterious pocket where adults keep competence. She wrote, in neat capitals: WE'RE FINE. DRAFTS. THANK YOU. Underneath, smaller: No recordings please. She handed it to Clara with a flourish. "For cupboards and humans."

Clara took the card as if it were proof of being surrounded by the right people. "We'll go home," she said. "We'll take the boring way and reward ourselves with toast."

They did. On the way, Ruth and Albie went past on the 73. Albie pressed his hands to the glass and performed the sober joy of a child who knows left–right belongs to pavements, not corridors. He kept his hands in his pockets and his smile did the whole job.

***

Home is a sacrament on blackout days. The mat lay square, its taped box precisely as they had left it. The cord inside had tied a granny—stop—and then a reef—OK—and lay flat, done.

"Message understood," Clara said. "Stop; OK to stop."

She wrote in the notebook, crisp: *10:36 community centre — four doors opened/closed in sequence (R-L-R-L tap). Witnesses present (multiple). We withdrew. RED STOP + 24h blackout. Boundary to add: PUBLIC IS OUT OF BOUNDS (no mechanical displays/venue messages off-mat/quarantine mats); NO DOORS (no opening/closing doors/locks except our own front door for one tap alarm). Pocket card created: "We're fine. Drafts. Thank you."*

She did not look at the compact for applause; compacts don't do applause. She did the census because it is grammar: catch (two clicks); rabbit (guard); stars (behaving); breath (proof). The baby forgave everyone for queues and weights and biscuits she had not been allowed to meet.

Mark arrived just after eleven, saw the look the corridor had left behind, and moved into witness without being briefed. He kissed Clara's temple without aiming for the bruise that had graduated. "News?"

"Four doors," she said. "Visible. We performed boring at speed and came home. Blackout 'til tomorrow. New boundary: Public is out of bounds; no doors except one tap at our own."

"Excellent boundary," he said. "I will add it to our parliament with the solemn joy of a man who loves writing in capitals."

He did. On the fridge, under HEIRLOOMS ARE NOT ALTARS, he wrote:

PUBLIC IS OUT OF BOUNDS.
No mechanical displays or venue messages outside our mat/quarantine mats. If breached: name it, stop it ("Public is out of bounds"), remove ourselves & any children, 24h blackout, notify H.

Beneath, he added:

NO DOORS.

No opening/closing doors or locks anywhere but our own front door for the single tap alarm. No latches, no chains, no demonstrations.

He underlined NO once, because double underlines are for emergencies and coffee.

They ate toast cut diagonal, because diagonal improves days by fractions. The kettle—permitted to do benign physics—boiled and didn't audition for a sermon. The house approved by wearing slippers.

They lived the blackout on purpose. No speaking to the air. No witnessing beyond the small, necessary tick-marks on the page. When the cord tied a clove hitch (stay) at 14:12, Clara made the note without dialogue, then went to fold laundry as if sheets were laws that always pass.

At three, Denise sent a text that belonged in good cities: *All well here. Doors behaving themselves. I told them off for making me look foolish and they decided I'm terrifying. Thank you for being calm and for the "drafts" card.*

Clara replied: *Thank you for biscuits and for running a small country. We owe your corridor flowers.*

Denise: *No flowers in corridors. Doors hate bouquets.*

Clara: *Understood.* She laughed, privately, because sanity has its own jokes.

At four, Priya forwarded a WhatsApp screenshot from a parent chat: *Was anyone else at clinic when the doors had a moment? Lol old buildings. Good biscuits tho.* No one had posted a video; Priya had asked nicely. No legends were being minted. People generally prefer biscuits to miracles. It was, Clara decided, the mercy of modern life.

***

Evening came with its slippers on and a small stack of ordinary. Blackout held. They performed their civics: catch; rabbit; stars; breath. They did not address the room beyond bureaucratic kindnesses: nap, bath, cardigan, story about a boat that lives in daylight.

Mark washed up and did not admire the shine as an argument. Clara wrote the day's line at the bottom of the page, for the version of herself who sometimes does not believe she can be both brave and boring: *Visible event (others saw). We withdrew. We named it; we did not explain. We made a boundary where there wasn't one. We will be deliciously dull until noon tomorrow.*

At nine, in the nursery doorway, she spoke the rules without performance, because blackout includes tone: "No moving things in here. No water. No requests about water at night. Knots on the hall mat only. No requests through other people's children. No teaching them. Withdraw if attention gathers. No recordings in here. No physical contact with people; no moving prams/high chairs/cots/straps; no tightening garments/buckles; no touching skin/hair. Warnings by words only—left–right once; if danger, one tap on the hall table or the inside of the front door. Allowed: move loose objects away from the baby. Requests are not commands. No altering records without permission. Doctors allowed. Friends allowed. Witness permitted. We are for growing a person without teaching her fear. Heirlooms are not altars. Public is out of bounds. No doors."

She put two fingers on the tiny chest—rise, fall—and returned the metronome with interest. The window catch sat good citizen with its two clicks. The room did what rooms do when you have taught them how to behave: it held.

Downstairs, in the taped box, the cord remained a line. Lines are beautiful when they know when to be lines.

They turned out lights in the adult rooms and tried being people again. Mark brought tea. Clara held the mug with both hands the way you hold small certainties in winter. "We were seen," she said, not to reopen, to close well.

"We were seen," Mark said. "And we made it boring."

She smiled. "I think that's the opposite of a miracle and the exact thing I will keep doing."

He touched the compact with two fingers as if it were a pulse and had behaved. "Tomorrow at eleven," he said, "the mat may have opinions. It can have them in the right place."

"Office hours," she said, placing the words on the table like cutlery, and the house, which had become good at eating its dinner, agreed.

***

New boundary added to the fridge (in sober capitals):

PUBLIC IS OUT OF BOUNDS. *No mechanical displays or venue messages outside our mat/quarantine mats. If breached: name it ("Public is out of bounds"), withdraw, 24h blackout, and notify H.*

NO DOORS. *No opening/closing doors or locks anywhere but our own front door for the single tap alarm.*

Chapter Twenty-Five
Payback

The morning put on Saturday like a cardigan that knows its job. The light behind the curtains was the colour of paper that takes ink and keeps the peace. Clara lay still and let the house read itself out: boiler's civil hum; the fridge's one note; a bus at the bend practising its decent sigh. She reached for the notebook and wrote, clerk-neat: *Woke steady. Blackout ended 11:00. Boundaries added yesterday: PUBLIC IS OUT OF BOUNDS; NO DOORS. Rules intact. Mission today: resume office hours; keep the day boring; listen without trades; be kind without debts.* She underlined ALLOWED: *enjoy the baby without checking the window* and tapped the underline like a metronome for ribs.

Mark surfaced with one eye and a face prepared to negotiate. "Status?"

"Green," she said. "Grey cooperative. Blackout lifts at eleven. We will practise boring until then as if graded."

"Excellent," he said. "I will stage a quiet revolt against laundry and lose."

On the landing the baby made the small bureaucratic squeak that meant the office had opened. The nursery smelt of warm cotton and sleep that had stayed in its lane. The window catch sat down and proper: two clicks. She didn't check it. She touched it and forgave herself for touching it. Catch; rabbit; stars; breath. Two fingers to a tiny chest—rise, fall. She borrowed the metronome and returned it on time.

On the hall mat, in the taped box, the dull cotton cord lay neutral: off duty, not a poet. The sealed envelope stood to attention with maiden-aunt decorum. The fridge wore its compact like a chain of office: WE WILL NOT HARM, FRIGHTEN, OR CONSTRAIN A LIVING PERSON FOR ANY REASON. Beneath it: NO TRADES.; NAMES FIRST.; HEIRLOOMS ARE NOT ALTARS.; PUBLIC IS OUT OF BOUNDS.; NO DOORS.

They had an hour to be dull and accomplished it. Toast cut diagonal. A walk as far as the postbox and back, waving at nobody in particular so the day knew it had been seen. Mark ran a cloth over the hob as if absolution were a domestic solvent. The baby held a spoon with the grave attention of a magistrate.

At 10:59, the house felt like a room in which a meeting is about to start and everyone knows their chair. At 11:00, office hours began. The kettle completed its civic duty and withdrew from public life. In the taped box, the cord tied a small, brisk overhand—one—then another—two—then a third—three—then two again. 2-3-2. It rested.

"Numbers," Mark said, pleased by vocabulary that stayed inside the box. "Two, three, two. What is two when it's at home."

"Two is twin," Clara said, and felt the tug at her wrist—attention, not apples—like a polite tap on her sleeve. She wrote: *11:01 — overhand (1), (2), (3), (2)* and didn't declare a code, because no riddles remains a mercy.

The baby monitor—off at night and at clinic, on now because listeners only in daylight—made its little throat-noise, the sound devices make when they want to justify their plug. The red LED climbed to two and behaved. A breath—not the baby's—arrived as if someone were thinking at the correct distance.

"Clara," said the voice that had been her ear's tenant since the first night. Clearer than the corridor, less patient than the mat. Not showy.

Not unkind. Ellie saying Clara the way a sister says a name that belongs at the back of the tongue.

Clara felt the bones of her hand consider new work and then minded them. "Office hours," she said. "Mat only. No trades."

A small sound of amusement—older than nine and younger than judgement. "You like rules," Ellie said. "You write them a seat at the table. You made the floor a judge."

"We did," Clara said. "Because rules keep both from being drowned by either. What do you need?"

A pause, then a sentence that had practised in the places language does its cruel excellence. "Pay me back," Ellie said, mild as grammar. "You owe me."

The phrase moved through Clara's stomach like hot metal arranged to be polite. She felt Mark straighten behind her, not to perform outrage, to hold the angle of the room.

"No debts," Clara said, steady. "No trades. We can be grateful. We can give. We do not owe."

The red LED did a thoughtful pulse. The cord tied two again, then two, then two, small insistences. The baby, in her chair, made a bubble that had no philosophy in it and laughed at her own mouth.

"What," Mark said, not to cross-examine, to draw shape, "do you think is owed."

The laugh again, smaller. "My turn." A breath like someone picking a card carefully off the table. "Say my name into her ear. Let me borrow her for a moment."

Clara felt the blood climb into her face—an old heat, teenage, righteous, frightened. It wanted to be fury; she made it be law. "Children are out of bounds," she said, clearly, the way you tell a clever dog to drop a thing that isn't food. "No requests through children. No teaching them. No touching skin or hair. No moving straps. No possession."

"Borrow," Ellie said, tasting the syllables the way children test the sound of *please* for the first time.

"No," Clara said, without apology. "No. We can honour you in ways that do not spend her. We can sing in daylight. We can write both. We can carry you to the field and put the world where you can see it. We cannot spend her for it, and we do not owe."

Silence did proper work. The cord tied a granny—stop—as if to say *you have broken the toy*; then, after counting its own breath once, undid itself, retied reef—OK—like a person sulking and deciding to be decent.

"Payback," Ellie said again, softer, less like a demand, more like a habit a mouth had learned and was reluctant to unlearn. "You had birthdays. I had none."

Clara stood very still because motion is sometimes a lie. "Gifts aren't prices," she said, careful. "If we give, we decide, and it's not a trade. No 'if you, then we'. We will not buy your help. We will not pay for your silence. We will choose our kindness and you will not put your hand in it."

She could feel Mark's approval arrive like tea. "We can make a day," he said, practical. "An 11:11 on the second of each month—two—we'll sing the boat once, in daylight, in the kitchen, with the window open to day and no water. We'll put the copy of the boat on the mat, read your letters, then tea, then normal. Gift—not price. She"—and here he nodded towards the tyrant with the spoon—"won't be audience. She'll be busy being alive."

The monitor breathed for a while, that tinny air that belongs to batteries and appetite. The cord tied two, then reef. OK to two. Not grudging. Not triumphant. Something like relief disguised as numbers.

"Thank you," Clara said, not bargaining. "We will take it from here."

"That is a gift," Ellie said, in a tone that sounded like a lesson taking root. "Not a price."

***

"Yes," Clara said, and felt the metronome settle in her chest. "Not a price."

At 11:20, the house decided to try a different door. Not a hinge—a hand.

Clara sat at the table with the notebook open and the compact pinned under a bulldog clip as if governing were a craft. The baby in the high chair considered her fist, intent upon turning it into a menu. Mark rinsed a pear under the cold tap and spoke decimals to gravity like a man who has apologised to physics and means it.

And then: Clara's left hand moved, without permission, towards the cord in the taped box.

Not a twitch. A reach. Fingers together, polite, as if someone had said, *May I have this dance* and a hand had said *yes* out of old habit.

She stopped it like you stop a spoon from falling: small, accurate, now. She placed her right hand on her left wrist—a firm, adult touch—and said, level, because levels save: "No possession. No using our hands, voices, breath or feet."

The cord tied a small granny—stop—on itself, like a sulk. The monitor made a small throat sound as if reminded it had an audience problem. Mark, who had not seen the reach but had learned the look, came to her side and put his palm flat on the table, visible, empty.

"NO POSSESSION," he said, aloud, for ceilings and floors and anyone else applying for work. "No borrowing bodies. Words only. Knots only. One tap only."

Clara lifted her left hand and placed it deliberately in her lap, like a teacher relocating a pen. She breathed once, twice, in pairs and commas, and then her ribs remembered the syllabus. "We are for growing a person without teaching her fear," she said to the room because the mission is a door you can shut against weather.

The cord undid itself, retied reef—OK—and settled. The monitor chose to become an appliance again. The house returned to slippers.

Clara wrote, crisp, in the book: *11:20 — attempted motor borrow (left hand towards cord). We refused: "NO POSSESSION. No using bodies." Cord: granny → reef. Rule to add: NO DEBTS. NO POSSESSION. Gifts are ours to choose; not requested, not priced. If "owe/payback/my turn" appears → refuse; state mission; offer gift only if within rules.*

She texted Harriet the short version because floors deserve minutes: *Office hours. Cord 2-3-2; monitor asked "Pay me back / you owe me / my turn" — requested name in baby's ear ("borrow her"). We refused (children out of bounds). Proposed gift: 11:11 on the second—kitchen, daylight, one boat song; copy on mat; baby not audience. Attempted motor borrow of left hand → refused ("NO POSSESSION"). Cord sulked then reefed. Propose adding NO DEBTS. NO POSSESSION to compact.*

Harriet replied with civic punctuality: *Perfect. Phrase boundary as: NO DEBTS (We do not owe; we do not pay; no "my turn"). NO POSSESSION (No using bodies: hands/voice/breath/feet). Gifts are unilateral—daylight only; no audience of children; no water; once; then ordinary. Floor holds. Proud of your tone.*

Clara read it and felt the little click inside that means choice and permission have met and become a clean sentence.

***

They built the gift with municipal care and zero candles.

At 11:40, Mark set the kitchen like a room that can do both ceremony and washing up. Window open to day a hand's width because daylight is a correct solvent. The paper copy of the boat—*Both came. Both go on.*—lay on the mat in the taped box like a quiet citizen on jury duty. The original slept in its jug three streets away with tulips and the knowledge of names. The baby was in the lounge with Lynn for ten minutes of spoons & CBeebies; a child being alive elsewhere is not an absence, it is the point.

"Spell it," Mark said, because words do work. "GIFT, not price. Once. Daylight. Kitchen. No water. No trades."

Clara nodded, and the nod felt like an oath you can say while stirring custard. She hummed the boat—*the tiny vessel, the large sea*—once, from beginning to end, at a volume that would not interrupt ovens. The house did nothing theatrical. The air did not grow apples. The hall table did not tap. In the taped box the cord tied reef—OK—and chose to be a line.

"Thank you," Clara said, and then the sentence that keeps crescendos from forming: "We will take it from here."

They closed the window because kitchens are not saints. They put the kettle on because tea is an explicit continuation of civilisation. They collected the baby from the lounge, where Lynn was narrating a programme about a turtle as if it were a Select Committee. The baby greeted them with the relief of people who are not yet fatigued by hope.

"What did I miss," Lynn said, reading the room like minutes.

"A gift," Clara said. "We did not pay for anything."

"Excellent," Lynn said. "I shall go home and gift my recycling to the council."

***

Afternoon is where days sometimes try on mischief. This one attempted a small accounting.

At 14:07, the cord tied overhand—one—then two—then two again—2-2—as if noting the ledger. In the nursery doorway, the monitor gave the slightest tick that belongs to electricity. Clara didn't go to it. She sat at the table and ate a biscuit with the focus biscuits deserve. She wrote: *14:07 — 1, 2, 2. Interpretation: two acknowledged. No dialogue.*

At 15:30, Ruth and Albie knocked with the gentle rattle of good neighbours. Albie executed a flourishing bow at the mat and then deliberately turned sideways to look at the umbrella stand instead, because ignoring what wants to be looked at is a skill they are teaching him as if it were handwashing.

"Boring," he announced, proud, and Ruth nearly cried at the beauty of it.

They drank tea with the urgency of people who have been out of the house and deserve a medal. They did not mention payback. They mentioned bins and bread and whether courgettes know they are courgettes, which turned into a better conversation than it had a right to be.

At four, the cord tied a clove hitch—stay—and lay down as if done with work. Clara underlined stay in the book because underlining keeps days at their desks.

Evening wanted to audition for witching hour and brought its clipboard. They did the census—catch; rabbit; stars; breath—like a country saying its own name quietly to remember it. The high chair performed the role of chair without method acting. The cup remained monogamous with the tray. The bruise at Clara's wrist had softened to the green of a field thinking about autumn.

At eight, Mark found her at the sink not running water, hands in the posture of someone who wants to but has learnt to ask her own rules first.

"I am not offering a price," she said before he could misread the angle of her elbow. "I am cleaning because I like clean. The boat happened in the kitchen and then we had tea. We did not give anything to anybody except ourselves."

"Correct," he said, relief and mischief in the same breath. "Tomorrow we shall give rubbish to the council and call it love."

At nine, in the nursery doorway, she spoke the rules as grammar and comfort: "No moving things in here. No water. No requests about water at night. Knots on the hall mat only. No requests through other people's children. No teaching them. Withdraw if attention gathers. No recordings in here. No physical contact with people; no moving prams/high chairs/cots/straps; no tightening garments/buckles; no touching skin/hair. Warnings by words only—left–right once; if danger, one tap on the hall table or the inside of the front door. Allowed: move loose objects away from the baby. Requests are not commands. No trades. Public is out of bounds. No doors. Heirlooms are not altars. We are for growing a person without teaching her fear."

She paused, feeling the day across her shoulders like a towel that had remembered its job. Then she added, clearly, because language builds stairs you can climb later: "No debts. No possession. Gifts are ours to choose, in daylight, once, then ordinary."

The room kept its face. Two fingers to a tiny chest—rise, fall—and she returned the metronome with interest. The window catch sat with its two clicks, quietly proud of being simple.

Downstairs, in the taped box, the cord tied reef—OK—and then a single overhand—one—as if acknowledging: one gift, done. It became a line and stayed a line, which is the loveliest behaviour string can achieve.

Clara wrote the last line of the day where her tomorrow eyes would land: *Asked for price ("you owe me / my turn"). Refused debts and trades. Stopped possession at the wrist. Chose a gift within rules; did it once; then tea. We own ordinary.*

Mark slid a mug across with the ceremony of men who have converted afternoons to evenings without dropping any glass. He kissed the skin next to where her bruise had been, because love is geography and consideration.

"No debts," he said, reading the words as if they were a valve.

"No possession," she returned, and felt the day decide to be done.

Outside, somewhere, a bus rehearsed its sigh and got it right. In Martha's kitchen the blue jug minded tulips and no sorrows. In Lynn's hall the green strip sat on a high shelf like a loan with excellent manners. In their own, the mat kept its box and the cord kept its line. The compact on the fridge kept the ethical line lit like a good street lamp: not for show, just to make ordinary possible.

They turned out the lights. The house approved by being a house.

***

New boundaries added to the fridge (in sober capitals):

NO DEBTS. *We do not owe; we do not pay; no "my turn", "payback", "you owe me". Gratitude is not currency; attention is not a wage. No trades.*

NO POSSESSION. *No using our bodies (hands, voice, breath, feet). No nudges, pulls, or "borrowing". Words & knots only; one tap alarm only.*

Chapter Twenty-Six
Ferry Burnt

The morning wore Sunday with the confidence of a cardigan that has survived five winters. The light behind the curtains was the colour of paper that accepts ink without arguing. Clara lay still and let the house list itself: boiler's civil hum; the fridge's single note; the bus at the bend practising its respectable sigh. She reached for the notebook and wrote, clerk-neat: *Woke steady. Rules intact (NO DEBTS / NO POSSESSION added yesterday). Mission: make the care plan real—Harriet + Dr Patel at 11:30. Give Denise biscuits not flowers. Phrase of the day: No pretending. ALLOWED: enjoy the baby without checking the window.*

Mark surfaced with one eye and a face that looked ready to negotiate and win gently. "Status?"

"Green," she said. "Grey cooperative. Today we put our courage on letterhead."

"Delicious," he said. "I'll find a shirt that makes me look like someone who can read consent forms."

On the landing the baby made the small bureaucratic squeak that meant the office had opened. The nursery smelt of warm cotton and sleep that had kept the law. The window catch sat down and proper: two clicks. Clara didn't check it. She touched it and forgave herself for touching it. Catch; rabbit; stars; breath. Two fingers on a tiny chest—rise, fall. She borrowed the metronome and returned it on time, like a citizen who loves her library card.

On the hall mat, in the taped box, the dull cotton cord lay neutral. The sealed envelope kept its back straight. The compact on the fridge shone with the careful tyranny of good rules: WE WILL NOT HARM, FRIGHTEN, OR CONSTRAIN A LIVING PERSON FOR ANY REASON. NO TRADES. NAMES FIRST. HEIRLOOMS ARE NOT ALTARS. PUBLIC IS OUT OF BOUNDS. NO DOORS. NO DEBTS. NO POSSESSION.

"Doctors allowed," Clara told the house, so the day knew which doors were real. "Witness permitted. We bring biscuits."

The cord made a single polite overhand—one—and lay down again, as if the union had approved the agenda.

***

They walked to the practice because walking turns nerves into smaller animals. The surgery had been a bank, once; it still believed in queues and privacy and the useful smell of polish. Harriet was already there, reading a leaflet that had the decency to be about flu and not about the soul. She stood when she saw them; her jumper had chosen to be navy again, a colour that makes rooms behave.

"Morning," she said. "We'll make tea after we make law."

"Delightful," Mark said. "Please keep me from signing us up for season tickets to psychiatry."

Harriet smiled because kindness is a craft. "We will write what helps and what not to do. We will ask for care, not a category."

Dr Shazia Patel opened the door to her room with the exact timing of a woman whose days contain both babies and budgets. Mid-forties; hair pinned with the competence of someone who learned on the tube; eyes that did triage without stealing dignity. "Morning," she said. "Come in. I've booked the longer slot. I've also locked the door because some Sundays think they're Tuesdays." She shook hands like a person who treats hands as instruments, not ornaments. "Kettle in the corner. I trust you to perform tea."

Clara sat. Mark sat. Harriet sat and took out a folder as if being a floor were a salaried post. Dr Patel glanced at the compact Clara had printed and placed on the desk; she didn't flinch at capitals.

"Right," Dr Patel said, clicking her pen once because pens like to be asked. "Two tasks. One: language. We'll fix the notes where we can. Two: care plan. You tell me how you keep the baby safe and yourselves sane; I write it down; we all sign; it goes on your record so whoever's on call at 3 a.m. doesn't invent policy on your behalf."

She looked at Clara, and the looking was a kind of respect. "Tell me in your words what's been happening. Avoid poetry. Keep the bits about pipes if they're relevant."

Clara breathed the pairs and commas and put the last month into English that didn't apologise. "Messages in the house. Words and knots. We've made rules and hours. We've refused trades and debts. We've banned possession. We do no recordings in the nursery. If left–right is said we obey once; if danger, a single tap on the hall table or inside front door. Public is out of bounds. No doors. Doctors allowed. We are for growing a person without teaching her fear."

"And the baby?" Dr Patel asked, carefully, the way you touch a hot tap.

"Safe," Mark said. "No slams, no yanks. We tightened a strap once—harshly—we wrote that out of the universe. If a cup is a problem we move it away, not towards. No touching skin or hair. No moving prams, high chairs, cots, straps. Words only; one tap; or nothing."

"Harriet?" Dr Patel said.

"They've built a compact," Harriet said. "It's not a talisman; it's a protocol. We've agreed blackout for any breach: 24 hours of silence beyond gratitude and safety. They have office hours (11–13), mat only. They do copies, never originals. They are the most boring haunted people I've ever had the pleasure of supervising."

Dr Patel made a small, satisfied hum. "Good. Safety without secrecy is my favourite combination." She turned to the keyboard and began to type in a way that turned sentences into furniture.

CARE PLAN (MORGAN, CLARA)

Primary aim: Infant safety; maternal mental health; family stability.

Summary of experiences: Structured, non-coercive, non-command messages perceived in home environment; no directives involving harm; no persistent voices outside office hours; no hallucinated instructions to harm self/others.

Risks identified: Startle responses; external misinterpretation; over-pathologising; unhelpful crisis responses (e.g., unrequested sedation).

Strengths/protective factors: Clear compact; supportive partner; extended family; clinician (H. Baines) involved; no substance use; good insight; willingness to seek help; rules adhered to; mission: "Grow a person without teaching her fear."

Do: Contact H. Baines first for de-escalation. Respect compact; allow quiet spaces; keep mother & baby together if safe; offer grounding (breath in pairs and commas); witness without argument; involve Martha Morgan if requested; provide tea (they respond well).

Don't: No forced sedation unless there's imminent risk of harm. No separation of mother and infant unless safeguarding threshold is met. No recordings in the nursery. No dismissive language ("just interference", "only hormones").

Language: Use names first (twin: Eleanor). Avoid erasing terms (e.g., "non-viable", "products of conception") in non-technical speech.

Boundaries (patient's): No trades; no debts; no possession; public out of bounds; no doors.

Office hours: 11:00–13:00 mat only. Outside hours: silence except "left–right" once or one tap alarm.

She read what she'd written as if the words belonged to the room now. "Does that sound like the thing you're trying to say?"

Clara felt the heat behind her eyes that arrives when bureaucracy says please. "Yes," she said. "That is the shape of us."

"And language," Dr Patel said, clicking to a second tab. "We can add a named note to the obstetric record. Not the legal register—we can't change those—but the copy you keep and our internal summary. I'll write: *Patient's twin was named Eleanor. Family prefer 'twin who died' to 'non-viable'. Use names in correspondence where appropriate.*"

Mark let out a breath that turned into a grin. "That's the first time a computer at the NHS has made me want to kiss it."

"Restrain yourself," Dr Patel said, with a dry look. "It's on its last legs." She printed two copies of the plan and slid them across, along with a pen that wrote as if it had trained for this.

"By signing you're not signing up to being haunted," she said, wry and kind. "You're signing up to us not being stupid if something goes sideways. And to me putting my neck out if someone reaches for a syringe as a first thought. If at any stage you want medication, we discuss it like adults. But we won't make you choose between honesty and custody. Not on my watch."

Clara signed. Mark signed. Harriet witnessed, H. Baines, neat and bored like a caravan patch. Dr Patel signed last, then stamped it with a date as if she were opening a bridge.

"Last question," Dr Patel said, gentler. "How are you, Clara, when no one is looking."

Clara thought of leaflet-world and the times it had saved her from admitting she knew the shape of the other world. "Less frightened now the words are on paper," she said. "Less likely to pretend it's all interference because a leaflet prefers me to. More tired. More proud. I want to be dull and brave and get good at ordinary."

"That is the career," Dr Patel said. "Go on, then. Burn your ferry. Don't be heroic about it. Heroism makes paperwork hungry."

***

They left the surgery with a manilla folder that felt like a passport and a loaf. Ferry burnt hadn't been a match; it was a pen. They had walked across and signed the shore.

On the way to the community centre, Mark held the folder in one hand and the biscuit tin in the other with the air of a man who had discovered the exact weight of his day. "Leaflet-world," he said, half a laugh, half an apology to a past self. "I loved leaflet-world. Nothing was responsible, everything was radio."

"It kept us upright until we could walk," Clara said. "But it kept the door shut, too."

"Today we put a letter through the state's letterbox," he said. "Ferry burnt. If it gets dark, we don't have to pretend the torch is lightning."

The community centre corridor smelt of disinfectant and competence. Denise was on duty, distributing biscuits with the efficiency of a quartermaster and the tenderness of a woman who has seen queues forget their courage.

"We brought civilian biscuits," Clara said, offering the tin. "And a card in case the doors get ambitions again."

"No flowers," Denise said, mock-stern. "Doors hate bouquets." She took the tin with a salute, read the card—WE'RE FINE. DRAFTS. THANK YOU. NO RECORDINGS, PLEASE.—and tucked it into the drawer with plasters and pens that have opinions. "You were calm," she said. "I tell the new mums: if the Morgan woman is in the room, all weather will be moderate."

Clara laughed and accepted the compliment as if it were a civic honour. "We've signed a care plan," she said, surprising herself by saying it aloud to someone who wasn't family or floor. "So if anything gets dramatic, the paper will behave."

"Good," Denise said. "I like paper that behaves." She lowered her voice a fraction. "And if your Eleanor"—the way she said it made the corridor grow two inches taller—"ever fancies opening doors, she can come and practise on my wardrobe at home. Not here. Public is out of bounds."

"Agreed," Clara said, and felt something in her chest do the small adjustment you get when reality and kindness both show up and the room chooses to reward them.

***

Office hours began as they reached the house. The mat greeted them with the dignity of doorways that have been granted a job. In the taped box, the cord tied a small, decisive bowline—safe—and then a reef—OK—before relaxing into a line.

"Witness permitted," Mark said, and put the folder on the console table as if laying a wreath on a monument to the sensible.

They propped the care plan on the fridge with a bulldog clip that had bullied generations of receipts. Under the compact, it looked like a junior member of parliament learning when to stand. Clara read the opening together with Mark, the way you read a contract at a wedding when you don't intend to sue anyone.

"We will not be stupid," Mark said, which, though not in the document, felt implied.

The baby made the small seal-bark of someone who has newly discovered their feet. They applauded it as if walking were a policy won. The house approved in pipes and not in apples, which was correct for midday.

At 11:42, the monitor breathed as if remembering its job. The red LED climbed to two; remained two. Ellie's voice arrived as air, not as theatre.

"Clara," she said, and then, gently mocking and entirely kind, "Mark."

Mark's throat did a ridiculous, brave little jump. He leaned his hip on the table as if agreeing to be supported by wood. "Present," he said, because men who pass through leaflet-world carry school in their bones.

"You signed a paper," Ellie said, pleased like a child who has learnt what libraries are for. "You said my name to the doctor woman. You left the leaflets where they belong."

"We did," Clara said. "We're done with pretending taxis are learning to sing."

The cord tied overhand—one—as if that single syllable was enough. One plan. One name. One ferry.

"Left–right," Ellie said softly, a present laid on the table and not pushed into anyone's hand.

"Once," Clara said, and smiled at the silliness and the holiness of saying once as if it were a liturgy. "Then us."

The baby threw her spoon on the floor with the zeal of a philosopher who has discovered gravity. Mark recovered it with the caution of a man who has written no yanks on his heart. The monitor breathed, thought better of it, and rejoined the furniture.

At 11:48, as if to test what papers do, Clara's eye went to the stack of leaflets—"Auditory Hallucinations", "Interference on Baby Monitors", "Welcome to Your Wireless Device"—living on the second shelf of the telephone table because old beliefs keep their coats near the door.

"Leaflet-world," Mark said, following her gaze. He lifted the pile with two fingers as if it might argue. "I'm not burning these," he said, practical. "The neighbours will call the brigade. But I am putting them in the recycling where pretend things go when real things arrive."

He walked to the blue crate by the back door and set the leaflets down. He did not do a speech. He did wash his hands after, not as an exorcism, as a habit. Clara watched something in her chest roll back its shoulders.

"Ferry burnt," she said.

"Ferry burnt," he agreed.

They made tea because that is what citizens do after they do law. They cut toast diagonal because diagonal improves days by fractions. The kettle behaved like physics. The day stood still in its place and did the kind of weather that keeps buses honest.

***

In the afternoon, Martha came with a pyrex dish full of something that contained carrots and absolution. She read the care plan on the fridge, her mouth doing the movement it does when it's trying not to cry in front of company.

"I like the bit where the NHS promises not to steal my grandchild for being complicated," she said, brisk to save herself. "I will write you a copy and put it in my drawer where passports live. If a stranger bangs on my door at midnight and says we'll take over, I will present them with a clipboard."

"Correct," Harriet said, arriving with timing that suggested floors have timetables. "We have burned the ferry and brought sandwiches. We will now resist founding a sect."

Martha eyed the blue recycling crate. "Leaflets," she said.

"Recycled," Mark said. "We're going to be honest from now on."

"You can be tactful and honest," Martha said, approving the two-column approach. "The doctor woman seems to have learnt please. That is all I ever asked from a person in a coat."

They ate stew because sentences require stew afterwards or they keel over. They spoke about bins and politics and the baby's laugh. Nobody auditioned for the role of corridor. The house wore slippers.

At four, Lynn dropped in with Sam and a calendar she had designed like a civil servant: small boxes for 11:11 on the second of each month. "Gift day," she said. "A quick boat in daylight; then tea. I've written NO WATER on mine because I am an overachiever."

"Welcome to our sect," Mark said, and everyone laughed because it wasn't one, and because laughter is what you do instead of building altars.

***

Evening tried to put on witching hour and found there wasn't room. They did the census—catch (two clicks); rabbit (guard); stars (behaving); breath (proof)—like grammar. The high chair remembered to be a chair. The cup flirted with the edge and minded itself. The bruise on Clara's wrist had turned green in the centre like a field considering autumn.

At nine, in the nursery doorway, Clara spoke the rules in the voice that makes English behave. "No moving things in here. No water. No requests about water at night. Knots on the hall mat only. No requests through other people's children. No teaching them. Withdraw if attention gathers. No recordings in here. No physical contact with people; no moving prams/high chairs/cots/straps; no tightening garments/buckles; no touching skin/hair. Warnings by words only—left–right once; if danger, one tap on the hall table or the inside of the front door. Allowed: move loose objects away from the baby. Requests are not commands. No trades. No debts. No possession. Public is out of bounds. No doors. Heirlooms are not altars. Doctors allowed. Friends allowed. Witness permitted. We are for growing a person without teaching her fear."

She paused, felt the day settle like a towel put back on the radiator, and added, clearly, because language builds stairs: "No pretending. We will not lie to ourselves for comfort. We will tell the truth plainly and then follow the compact."

The room kept its face. Two fingers to a tiny chest—rise, fall—and she returned the metronome with interest. The window catch sat in its two holy clicks, proud of being simple.

Downstairs, in the taped box, the cord tied a small, pleased reef—OK—and then an overhand—one—as if acknowledging: one ferry burnt; one paper signed; one house that has learned how to be a house.

***

They turned lights down in the adult rooms and let the care plan glow faintly in the fridge's halo like a traffic regulation loved by everyone because it prevents deaths and arguments. Harriet washed two mugs and left them standing, because washing up is how floors say amen.

"Look at us," Mark said, amused and a little in awe. "We've put our names on being sensible."

"We've put our names on not pretending," Clara said. She ran the pad of her thumb over the bruise that had become a lesson and a colour. "Leaflet-world kept me warm when I was too frightened to own my sense. Now it would keep me small."

"Ferry burnt," he said again, because repetition reminds the day of its job.

"Ferry burnt," she agreed, and for the first time the words didn't feel like defiance; they felt like relief.

Outside, a bus rehearsed its sigh and got it right. In Martha's kitchen the blue jug minded tulips and no sorrows. In Lynn's hall the green strip sat on a high shelf like a loan with exemplary manners. In Ruth's, Albie counted one on the window and then put his hands in his pockets like a civil servant. On their mat, the cord remembered its vocabulary and rested. On the fridge, the parliament kept its seat and the care plan kept its promise.

The house agreed, not by performing, not by inventing weather, but by doing the single kindest thing a house can do when people have chosen to stay: it stayed a house.

New boundary added to the fridge (in sober capitals):

NO PRETENDING. *We don't lie to ourselves for comfort (e.g., "interference", "just drafts") when we have evidence. We tell the truth plainly and then follow the compact and care plan.*

Chapter Twenty-Seven
Breakwater

The morning borrowed Monday's sensible coat. The light behind the curtains was the colour of paper that takes ink and keeps the peace. Clara lay still and let the house name itself: boiler's civil hum; the fridge's one note; a bus at the bend rehearsing its decent sigh. She reached for the notebook and wrote, clerk-neat: *Woke steady. Care plan on fridge. Boundaries holding (NO TRADES / NAMES FIRST / HEIRLOOMS NOT ALTARS / PUBLIC OUT OF BOUNDS / NO DOORS / NO DEBTS / NO POSSESSION / NO PRETENDING). Mission: choose a structure we can live in. Title word: Breakwater. Choice: keep / bind / release. We decide, not the weather.* She underlined ALLOWED: enjoy the baby without checking the window and felt the underline settle her ribs.

Mark surfaced with one eye like a man prepared to negotiate in good faith. "Status?"

"Green," she said. "Grey cooperative. Today we stop living in options and build a thing."

"A civil engineering project for the supernatural," he said. "I'll find a jumper that looks like it understands bylaws."

On the landing, the baby made the small bureaucratic squeak that meant the office had opened. The nursery smelt of warm cotton and sleep that had kept the law. The window catch sat down and proper: two clicks. She didn't check it. She touched it, forgave herself for touching it, and did the census that had become grammar: catch; rabbit; stars; breath. Two fingers to a tiny chest—rise, fall. She borrowed the metronome and returned it on time, like a citizen who loves her library card.

On the hall mat, in the taped box, the dull cotton cord lay neutral, off duty. The sealed envelope kept its back straight. The care plan clipped to the fridge had the calm of paper that knows its job.

"Eleven," Clara said to the room, because rooms behave better when given a timetable. "We'll sit. We'll choose."

The cord made a single polite overhand—one—and then lay still, as if the union had ratified the agenda.

***

At 11:00, they did not light a candle. They set the table like grown-ups: pot of tea; plate with four biscuits because two invites martyrdom; paper copies of the boat (Both came. Both go on.); the compact with its ethical line; the care plan with Dr Patel's signature like a bridge opened. Harriet came with a folder and the kind of jumper that makes meetings behave. Martha arrived five minutes late on purpose so the day would know it wasn't ruling her; she put the blue felt pad on the table like a receipt for mercy. Lynn came without Sam because children were out of bounds for choosing.

On the table, Harriet set three index cards in a row, black capitals neat as a clerk: KEEP — BIND — RELEASE.

"No doors today," she said, to the house and the weather and anyone with ambitions. "No rituals. No water. This is policy, not theatre."

"Draft policy," Martha said, brisk. "But we'll pass it."

"The question," Harriet said, "is not what the past wants. It's what you can live with. Keep means more porous: you allow more contact, more off-mat talk, more hours. Bind means you keep the compact and make the mat a port, with a named breakwater that stops the sea from walking into the kitchen. Release means you ask the presence to go—not banish, not punish, but dismiss—and you promise not to invite it back."

"No trades," Mark said, as if adding salt to boiling water. "Whatever we choose doesn't buy us anything."

"Correct," Harriet said. "No bargains. No debts."

They sat. The house, attentive as a well-behaved dog at an obedience class, wore slippers.

"KEEP," Harriet said. "Make the case if there is one."

Clara tried to make it and found nothing that didn't end with her ribcage tightened by wires she didn't install. "Keep would mean more of her," she said, almost apologising. "I love more of her. But more of her means less of us, and we are the point. The baby is the point. Left–right once, then us. We have learnt to be boring. Keep would unlearn it."

"The price of keep will be pressure," Harriet said, without judgement. "More tests. More thresholds. The corridor thinking it's a venue again."

Martha eyed the cards, acquitted herself of sentiment, and said, "Keep is what your heart wants when it thinks it will never be asked to pay. We have been asked to pay. We declined."

"Release," Harriet said. "Make the case."

Mark looked at Clara, not as counsel, as witness. "We could do it gently," he said. "Thank you, go well, no pretending you were nothing, but go."

Clara felt the room angle under her feet like a boat misjudging a wave. Her throat considered becoming a trumpet for grief and then remembered that grief is better as a pen. "Release feels like trying to be tidy because we're tired of being brave," she said, careful. "I don't want to bind from cowardice. But release would let a hospital word win. Viable would have the last word in our kitchen. The boat under the lino would be a thing we did once when we were mad. I can't live in that world."

Martha's mouth did the movement of a woman who refuses to cry in company. "Release would keep me from hearing her E," she said. "I could do it. I have done worse things out of love for you. But I do not prefer it."

Harriet turned the middle card with one finger so the black BIND faced Clara tidily.

"Bind," she said. "You write a breakwater. Not a ban. A civil structure. You choose where the port is and how often the ferry comes and who carries the paper. You say words only, mat only, hours named. You give a sanction for breaches that doesn't punish anyone living: forty-eight hours blackout. You put it on the fridge. You tell the house the breakwater is permanent unless you alter it. And you accept you will be tempted to make a sect of it and you will resist."

Clara looked at the KEEP card and saw possession by kindness. She looked at RELEASE and saw tidiness pretending to be holiness. She put her finger on BIND and felt, under the card, the table, under the table, the joists, under the joists, the ground that had carried all of them through both good and idiot days.

"Bind," she said. "We bind."

There was no tap on the hall table. There was no apple. In the taped box, the cord tied a small, relieved reef—OK—and settled. The house approved by not performing, which had become the only benediction she trusted.

***

Harriet produced a piece of A4 with a heading already printed in sober capitals, the kind that make rooms behave:

THE BREAKWATER

Underneath, she wrote as Clara dictated, with Mark supplying commas and Martha supplying nouns.

1. Port. The mat is the port. All messages are mat only. No corridors, no thresholds, no nursery.

2. Tide. Office hours = 11:00–13:00, household present. Outside hours, silence, except "left–right" once or one tap (hall table or inside front door).

3. Means. Words & knots only. No possession. No doors. No touching bodies or moving straps, furniture or garments. No water as instrument. No riddles.

4. Scope. Public is out of bounds. Quarantine mats only by consent in private homes.

5. Sanction. Any breach triggers harbour blackout: 48 hours of silence beyond gratitude & safety; gift day for that month is cancelled.

6. Ownership. No trades. No debts. Gifts are unilateral, daylight, once, no children as audience.

7. Paper. Copies travel; originals rest. No "tidying" of grief.

8. Mission. We are for growing a person without teaching her fear.

9. No pretending. We tell the truth plainly; we follow the compact & care plan.

Beneath, Harriet left a space and wrote: Chosen by: Clara Morgan. Witnesses: Mark Morgan; Martha Morgan; H. Baines.

Clara signed with the hand she now trusted not to be borrowed. Mark signed with the grave flourish he reserves for decency. Martha signed with the same bored neat that had written ELEAN— under glue in another house in another year. Harriet witnessed, then dated it, the small civic click of a day turning into the kind that can be remembered without flinching.

"Now we read it to the port," Harriet said. "No doors. No water. No theatre. Tea after."

They stood at the mat like citizens at a ribbon-cutting that had decided to grow up. Mark held the paper. Clara, beside him, held nothing. She has learnt that holding nothing is sometimes the cleverest thing a person can carry.

"The Breakwater," Mark read, steady, municipal. He did not perform. He placed each sentence like a paving slab, level with the last, no trip hazards. When he reached Sanction, he spoke it kindly, as if telling a teenager the bed time you have both chosen. When he reached Mission, he let the words speak in their own uniform. When he reached No pretending, the house made no comment, which is how houses say amen.

In the taped box, the cord tied a small, competent clove hitch—stay—then reef—OK—and lay back like a line that has decided to love being a line.

"Bind done," Harriet said, not triumphant. "Now we test the temptations. We speak the other two out loud and listen to the room."

She laid the KEEP card on the mat. Mark read, as instructed: "Keep: we invite more hours, more contact, more venue. We loosen port to house."

The cord tied overhand—one—then two—two—then two again, impatient, as if licking salt. The baby monitor gave a small, unnecessary hum that belonged to batteries and old appetites.

Clara put her hand flat on the air above the box without touching anything. "No," she said, friendly. "We have chosen."

The cord went flat. The monitor remembered it was an appliance. The room turned its face back to furniture.

They did RELEASE next. Mark read: "Release: we dismiss; we do not invite; we close the port."

The cord tied a small, brief granny—stop—then nothing. The house did not cool. No apples. Only the tiny ache that lives in good decisions when they are not the easiest ones.

Martha breathed once, then stood a little straighter. "Bind is the mercy for me," she said, surprised to hear it out of her own mouth. "Release would keep the house clean and my Thursday dirty. Bind makes both decent."

Clara added, clear, for the room and for her future self when she would forget and need reminding: "Boundaries are not banishment. You are kept by the rules, not thrown by them."

"Write it," Harriet said, pleased with the sentence. "Short version on the fridge."

***

Afternoon put on its work clothes and asked for a task. They gave it signage.

On the fridge, beneath the care plan, Clara wrote in sober capitals:

THE BREAKWATER (BIND CHOSEN).

House = port. Messages mat only, 11:00–13:00. Words & knots only. No possession. No doors. No water. Public out of bounds. Any breach → 48h harbour blackout & gift day cancelled. No trades. No debts. Copies travel; originals rest. Mission & No pretending apply.

She stepped back, approving the way the words sat like chairs that matched without being embarrassing.

"Side note," Mark said, the admin brain tapping politely. "Let's move the monitor out of the nursery after next week. She's almost past the stage where we need it to shout. We'll put it in the drawer with the leaflets that became recycling. Not a banishment. A demotion."

"Heirlooms not altars; appliances not priests," Clara said, and Martha snorted happily into her tea.

Lynn produced a narrow strip of blue tape from a pocket designed to surprise and ran it across the door jamb at chest height, just above the mat—not a barrier, a mark. With a pen she wrote, in neat capitals: PORT AUTHORITY.

"Cosy," she said. "If a day forgets itself, even days can read."

They ate toast cut diagonal because diagonal improves decisions by fractions. The baby demonstrated a new vowel with the seriousness of a person arguing planning permission. The house kept its slippers on.

At 16:00, because structure likes to be used, they held a five-minute drill. Harriet set a timer. Mark read the Breakwater again, calm as a lifeguard. Clara did the thank-you protocol into ordinary air. The cord tied reef—OK—once, then lay flat, a little proud of itself.

"Now the question," Harriet said to Clara, the way you warn someone before you tap their knee and ask it for a reflex. "What do you want from the presence, within the breakwater. No prices. Ask for nothing you wouldn't ask Mark for. You may put nothing on a child's back."

Clara was quiet because quiet is how she gets true. "I want two things," she said. "I want names first—for her and for me—without argument. And I want, when I say stop, for the air to stop wanting to be a person."

"Reasonable," Harriet said, writing them as if they were amendments to a sensible law. "Now decide what you offer, unasked, sometimes: a gift that doesn't spend anyone. Daylight; once; no water; no audience of children."

Clara smiled. "Second of the month; 11:11; one boat in the kitchen with the window open to day. We've made it policy. And I will write her name in my book at the bottom of the page like a signature for the day."

"Approved," Harriet said, and put a tick next to an empty space that promptly became less empty.

***

Evening came to see what sort of house lived here and found it had become the sort that loves boring and brave in equal measure. They did the census: catch (two clicks); rabbit (guard); stars (behaving); breath (proof). The high chair minded its manners; the cup flirted with the edge and stayed faithful; the bruise at Clara's wrist was almost a memory.

At 19:03—outside hours, plates drying in their rack—the hall table made a single, polite tap. Allowed alarm, Vera-level in its good behaviour. Clara stepped to the door and looked through the glass: a parcel angled at the lip of the step like a drama. She moved it away, inside, because allowed means do the decent thing. She said, into ordinary air, thank you, and added the clause that saves: We will take it from here.

The cord remained a line. Lines are beautiful when they decide to be lines.

At 20:40, when small children learn to thrive on sock theatre, Clara felt the merest inclination in her left hand—the old risk that had arrived and been refused two days ago. It moved half a thought and then remembered the Breakwater and decided to be a hand.

She wrote the fact in the book without ceremony: *20:40 — hand thought about being a saint; chose citizen instead.*

At 21:00, in the nursery doorway, she spoke the rules as grammar and the compact as civic, then added the new sentence because language builds the very wall it describes. "The Breakwater is our choice. House = port. Messages mat only 11–13. Words & knots only. No possession. No doors. No water. Public out of bounds. Any breach → 48h harbour blackout & gift day cancelled. No trades. No debts. Copies travel; originals rest. We are for growing a person without teaching her fear. No pretending."

She placed two fingers on a tiny chest—rise, fall—and returned the metronome with interest. The window catch sat, two clicks, proud of being simple. The baby's breath produced a small, contented o that made the day stand straighter.

Downstairs, in the taped box, the cord tied a small, pleased bowline—safe—then reef—OK—and then arranged itself into the kindest thing string can be: a line deciding to stay a line.

They turned out adult lights. The care plan sat in the fridge's soft halo like an ordinance that had been passed by a kind council. The Breakwater pinned beside it held its capitals with dignity. PORT AUTHORITY glimmered faintly on the jamb where Lynn had written it. The house did not perform; it refused to invent weather. It did the most generous thing a house can do when people have chosen to stay: it stayed a house.

"Bind," Mark said softly, as if trying on a coat that fit. "Not keep. Not release."

"Bind," Clara said, and felt the word pick up its tools and quietly begin.

Outside, a bus rehearsed its sigh and got it right. In Martha's kitchen the blue jug minded tulips and kept its boat asleep. In Ruth's hall, Albie practised keeping his hands in his pockets and looked proud of his pockets. In Lynn's, the green strip on the high shelf played at being a loan with excellent manners. In Clara's hallway, a piece of string that had known numbers and sulks remembered its vocabulary and chose to be a line.

Above them, somewhere older than the house and kinder than the leaflet, a neat hand wrote BOTH where a person could see it without digging.

***

New boundary added to the fridge (in sober capitals):

THE BREAKWATER (BIND CHOSEN). *House = port. Messages mat only, 11:00–13:00. Words & knots only. No possession. No doors. No water. Public out of bounds. Any breach → 48h harbour blackout & gift day cancelled. No trades. No debts. Copies travel; originals rest. Mission & No pretending apply.*

Act III - The Binding

Chapter Twenty-Eight
Contract

The morning put on Tuesday as if it had been ironed. The light behind the curtains was the colour of paper that can take ink without arguing. Clara lay still and let the house list itself: boiler's civil hum; the fridge's single note; a bus at the bend practising its decent sigh. She reached for the notebook and wrote, clerk-neat: *Woke steady. Breakwater pinned. Care plan clipped. Mission: make it Binding. Oath: We keep you as law, not person. Witness: Harriet. Mat = port. No doors; no water.*

Mark surfaced with one eye and that tolerant grin he lends to sensible days. "Status?"

"Green," she said. "Grey cooperative. Today we write what we've already been living."

"Municipal romance," he said. "I'll wear a jumper that understands bylaws."

On the landing the baby made the small bureaucratic squeak that meant the office had opened. The nursery smelt of warm cotton and sleep that had kept the law. Window catch: two clicks. She didn't check it. She touched it, forgave herself for touching it, and did the census that had become grammar: catch; rabbit; stars; breath. Two fingers to a tiny chest—rise, fall. She borrowed the metronome and returned it on time.

On the hall mat, the taped box lay square. Inside, the dull cotton cord rested like a citizen between shifts. On the jamb above, PORT AUTHORITY in neat capitals, Lynn's work, had taught even the day to read.

"Eleven," Clara told the room, because rooms behave better when they know the timetable. "Binding then tea."

The cord made a small, well-mannered overhand—one—as if to say, *agenda noted*—and returned to being a line.

***

At ten-thirty the house did its civil shuffle: the kettle rehearsed; the cups arranged themselves to look helpful; the biscuits tried not to be political. Clara laid the papers on the kitchen table: the Breakwater; the care plan with Dr Patel's signature; the compact with the ethical line glowing in capitals; a clean A4 headed, in sober letters, THE BINDING — HOUSE & HUMANS.

She wrote the date at the top because dates are the way kind days keep promises: Tuesday with its exact numbers, black ink that would survive spilt tea and reluctant history.

Mark set two chairs at right angles to the mat as if making a small tribunal that liked comfortable shoes. He put the pen in the middle of the table like a tool, not a wand.

Clara stood a moment in the middle of the kitchen and watched the way ordinary behaves when asked to hold something solemn and not become theatre. Her wrist—the old bruise a memory now—didn't itch. The room kept its face. She breathed in pairs and commas and counted, because counting is how she invites courage without summoning anything else.

The bell rang once, polite. Harriet came in with a folder and a jumper that had never met melodrama. She closed the door carefully behind her because No Doors applies to enthusiasm too.

"Morning," she said, warm in the exact way warmth should be when documents are about to get ideas. "We'll do it plain. We'll call nothing down. We'll write what already exists."

"Municipal romance," Mark repeated, offering biscuits like a citizen.

Harriet smiled. "I brought a stamp," she said, and showed them the quiet joy of a date stamp that has trained for Tuesdays. "No wax. We are not founding a sect."

Clara's throat did the small, good ache of a person about to do an ordinary brave thing. "Where do we stand," she asked, "so we don't accidentally make a stage."

"By the mat," Harriet said, "but not on it. No doors. No water. Baby in the lounge with toys, door open, air ordinary. We read; we sign; we say the sentence. The house is invited to do nothing. If it must answer, it can answer in knots."

They placed the high chair where the baby could see parents and not paper and handed over a wooden spoon because sovereignty is easier with props. The lounge accepted its demotion from venue to crèche with grace.

***

They gathered at the port. Mark stood with the Breakwater in his left hand and nothing in his right. Harriet took her place beside the console table, pen angled, stamp ready, the folder open like a sensible mouth. Clara stood where the hallway can see the kitchen and the kitchen can see the hallway and nobody is tempted to turn a sentence into weather.

"Ready?" Harriet asked the house the way she asks rooms to behave, which is to say she asked Clara.

"Ready," Clara said. She felt the floor under the mat under the box under the cord under the air under the words they had already said to each other a hundred times.

Harriet nodded to Mark. "Read the Breakwater," she said, "because vows begin as policy and end as habit."

Mark read. His voice was municipal, kind, the speed of a queue that knows it will reach the desk. House = port. Messages mat only, 11:00–13:00. Words & knots only. No possession. No doors. No water. Public out of bounds. Any breach → 48h harbour blackout & gift day cancelled. No trades. No debts. Copies travel; originals rest. Mission. No pretending.

When he said Mission, the baby made a small pleased o that contained no philosophy and all of it. Clara let her mouth do a fraction of a smile and didn't apologise.

"Good," Harriet said. "Now the Binding."

She lifted the A4 and read the heading as if opening a bridge: THE BINDING — HOUSE & HUMANS. Then the short preamble they had agreed in pieces and sleep: *We publish what we practise. We keep the house as a port, not a corridor; the presence as law, not a person. We choose kind order over exciting fear. We bind on paper what we already live with tea.*

"Two parts," Harriet said, clearing her throat exactly once because throats like to be involved. "Affirmations and Oath. Then signatures. Then date. Then tea."

She read the Affirmations like items on an agenda everyone had read beforehand:

We are for growing a person without teaching her fear.

We will not harm, frighten, or constrain a living person for any reason.

We keep public out of bounds.

We accept blackout when rules are breached.

We will not trade, owe, or be owed.

We allow words and knots only; no possession; no doors; no water.

We leave originals at rest and take copies when needed.

We tell the truth and then follow the compact and care plan.

We accept that boring is a form of love.

Harriet looked up. "Oath," she said, and put the page down so they could see the sentence writ large.

Clara read it first, because voices belong to bodies and it mattered: "We keep you as law, not person." She spoke it with the steadiness you give a child when teaching road-crossing, and with the mercy you give yourself in hard light. The words felt right in her mouth the way a tooth clicks back into its place after a bad dream.

Mark repeated it, thoughtful. His voice did that thing voices do when they find the exact weight required to hold a room without bossing it. "We keep you as law, not person."

Harriet nodded. "Now we sign," she said. "No trades with the pen. No bargains with the floor."

They signed in black ink because black ink does not argue later: Clara Morgan; Mark Morgan. Harriet wrote Witness: H. Baines in her precise hand. She pressed the date stamp below, once, a small, satisfying chunk that put today where it belongs. The stamp left its neat blue numbers as if telling time it had been heard.

"Place it," Harriet said.

Clara slid the paper inside a clear sleeve because sleeves teach documents to behave, and laid it gently on the mat just shy of the taped box. She did not step on the mat; she did not touch the cord. She stood with her hands empty and her chest ready.

For a moment the hallway held its breath in the way houses do when they have been asked to grow up.

In the box, the cord lifted the smallest inch and tied a plain, competent reef—OK—then settled into the single loveliest line string knows how to be. No flourish; no sulk. Line.

"Thank you," Clara said, and added the sentence that dissolves crescendos: "We will take it from here."

The house answered by being a house.

***

Tea is the work afterwards so the event doesn't become more important than the day. They returned to the kitchen not as heroes but as people who had signed something sensible and were in want of mugs. Harriet leaned the Binding against the fruit bowl and let it be looked at without reverence. Reverence is for people; paper prefers attention and standards.

"Let me take a copy for my drawer," she said. "Copies travel; originals rest. I'll scan and email Dr Patel so it sits behind the care plan where bored machines keep us safe."

"Two copies," Mark said, already making a second sleeve behave. "One for Mum's passport drawer."

"Good," Harriet said. "Witness permitted."

The baby removed her sock with the satisfaction of a person dissolving bureaucracy one foot at a time. Clara retrieved it with a smile she could feel in the bones of her cheeks. It was a civilian smile—the best kind.

"Say it again," Harriet asked gently, not as a ritual, as a rehearsal. "So your mouth learns the weight."

Clara stood at the sink with no water running and said, "We keep you as law, not person." She found that it lived beside No trades and

No pretending, tidy and ready. "No prices," she added out of habit, for the benefit of anyone listening with old ears.

From the hall came the faintest sound like a nod—no tap, just the suggestion of timber agreeing with architecture.

Martha arrived at twelve in the cardigan that had outlived four governments and two recipes. She took the Binding in at a glance, did not attempt to bless it, and kissed Clara's forehead as if signing a second form in a language older than the NHS.

"Good," she said. "Write me a copy and I'll put it with the birth certificates and the warranty for the kettle."

Harriet raised an eyebrow. "You keep warranties?"

"Only for kettles," Martha said. "They're political."

They stood at the port together—Clara, Mark, Martha, Harriet—and read the oath once, not as performance, as a way of teaching air the right shapes. The cord stayed a line because lines are what you trust when you're tired.

"Practicalities," Harriet said, always happiest near a list. "Mark, move the monitor to the drawer after the weekend. Not banished—demoted. Clara, keep the Blackout and Gift-day clauses visible on the fridge. Martha, if anyone knocks at stupid o'clock and wants to be important, show them the care plan first and the Binding second."

"Priya is printing little wallet cards," Mark said. "*We're fine. Drafts. Thank you. No recordings, please.* I will carry one like a stubborn receipt."

"Good," said Harriet. "Make boredom *portable*."

They had tea because this is England and things must be helped to become true. They cut toast diagonal because diagonal improves vows by fractions. They did not speak in italics. They let the Binding learn the kitchen's temperature and the kitchen learn that paper could live here without being worshipped.

***

At one minute to one, the very end of office hours, they stood by the port to close it correctly. Mark set his finger on the corner of the sleeve where THE BINDING showed itself and nodded to the day as if leaving a town hall.

"Port closed," he said.

Clara felt the old temptation a fraction—the urge to ask for a reply, some tiny ribbon of theatre to pin to the hour. She refused it with the same muscle she uses to put the kettle on instead of starting an argument.

"Thank you; we'll take it from here," she said, the door-closing sentence that never needs a door.

In the tape-lined box, the cord remained: line.

They left the Binding propped at eye level, where tired people look and remember what they decided when they were less tired. They put the pen away. They checked the two clicks on the window because habit is a good servant when fear is out of a job.

The baby slept. The house did not perform. The kettle did physics with humility. Outside, a bus rehearsed its sigh and got it right.

***

There was one small citizen test before tea ended, because days are petty.

The letterbox rattled once—post, on schedule, not dramatic. Two envelopes on the mat: a pizza flyer that had ideas above its station, and a white one bearing Hospital Archives in the fonts of departments that think they are gods and are only payroll. Clara picked it up and felt the small, clean absence of dread you get when paper is part of your day and not a dragon. She held it to the light—habit—and put it in the in-tray by the phone because *Binding first, archives later.* Copies travel; originals rest; lunch exists.

"Look at us," Mark said, amused and reverent in the correct doses. "We are people who put letters in in-trays."

"We are people who wrote No pretending on the fridge," Clara said. "And signed it."

Harriet finished her tea, washed her mug, and put it on the rack because washing up is how floors say amen. "I'll go," she said. "Phone if the day auditions. Don't reward talent. Reward boring."

She kissed the air by Clara's cheek, nodded to Martha, shook Mark's hand, and stepped out like a citizen leaving a library.

Clara watched the door shut, gentle, no drama, and felt the inside of her ribs click to the shape of the sentence they had given the day: We keep you as law, not person.

She went to the fridge and, with the tidy insistence of someone who keeps pens where pens go, added a short line under THE BREAKWATER in sober capitals:

BOUND: *We have spoken the oath; signed; dated. Port = mat. Law, not person. Reef, then line.*

She underlined BOUND once. Once is policy. Twice is religion.

On the mat, as if amused by the punctuation, the cord tied one small, respectful reef—OK—and straightened into line.

The room stayed a room. The day kept its chair. The bus at the bend practised its sigh and got it right.

"Tea?" Mark said.

"Tea," Clara said.

They made tea. The house approved by being a house.

Chapter Twenty-Nine
The Boat Song

The morning wore the second day of the month like a badge it hadn't asked for. The light behind the curtains was the colour of paper that accepts ink without correcting you. Clara lay still and let the house list itself: boiler's civil hum; the fridge's faithful single note; a bus at the bend rehearsing its decent sigh. She reached for the notebook and wrote, clerk-neat: *Woke steady. Binding signed (reef → line). Today = gift: 11:11, boat in kitchen, window open to day. No water. No theatrics. No audience of children. Mission unchanged: we keep as law, not person.*

Mark surfaced with one eye and the cautious optimism of a man who has found himself on a good page. "Status?"

"Green," she said. "Grey cooperative. Calendar agrees: second of the month. We keep promises in daylight."

He kissed her hair and made his way to the kettle with the gait of a citizen who knows where mugs live. "I'll make the kitchen look like policy," he said. "And like a place that forgives crumbs."

On the landing the baby made the small bureaucratic squeak that meant the office had opened. The nursery smelt of warm cotton and sleep that had kept the law. Window catch: two clicks. She didn't check it. She touched it and forgave herself for touching it, as you forgive yourself for looking twice at the clock. Catch; rabbit; stars; breath. Two fingers to a tiny chest—rise, fall. She borrowed the metronome and returned it on time.

In the hall the mat lay square. Inside the taped box, the dull cotton cord rested like a citizen between shifts. On the jamb above, PORT AUTHORITY in Lynn's neat capitals had taught even the morning how to behave.

"Eleven-eleven," Clara told the room, because rooms like timetables. "One boat. Then tea. Then ordinary."

The cord made a small, well-mannered overhand—one—as if to say, *agenda noted*—and returned to being a line.

***

The kitchen did its best impression of a responsible adult. Mark opened the window a hand's width—open to day—and the air came in with the quiet manners of a guest who has read the invitation. He placed the paper copy of the boat (Both came. Both go on.) on the counter, not as altar, as paper. He removed the plug from the monitor and set the unit on the console table by the doorway—present for listening, not performance—and then paused, caught by his own training.

"Drawer after the weekend," he said, answering his thought aloud. "Demotion is not the same as banishment."

"Exactly," Clara said. She tested the hinge of the window and decided it would not mistake open to day for an argument. She laid a tea towel under the paper in case the house felt tempted to forgo language and try weather. "No water," she said, to her hands. "No helping with taps."

He smiled the smile of the reformed enthusiast. "I am a penitent of sinks," he said. "Also of straps."

She allowed herself the smallest, wickedest joy at how far they had come: the bruise on her wrist a colour now that belonged to fields and not to lessons. She turned to the fridge and read the Breakwater aloud—quiet, municipal—because policies remain true when they are spoken in the voice that understands forms. House = port. Messages mat only, 11–13. Words & knots only. No possession. No doors. No water. Public out of bounds. Any breach → 48h harbour blackout & gift day cancelled. No trades. No debts. Copies travel; originals rest. Mission. No pretending.

"We keep you as law, not person," she added, and felt the sentence live on her tongue like a balance she could hold.

At ten-forty-five they staged the rest of ordinary to make sure gift did not become ceremony. The baby practised sovereignty over a wooden spoon in the lounge, door open, air ordinary. Lynn had promised to collect her for twenty minutes of spoons & CBeebies at eleven-oh-five—no audience of children while the house learned its manners. Martha had texted *Bless the kettle; don't bless the air.* Harriet had replied with a tick and a reminder to eat something with butter afterwards because bodies respond well to calories and governments.

Clara wiped the worktop with the bored efficiency of a person who refuses to make the surface responsible for what the day will attempt. The light on the window-sill found the rosemary and made it look like a small tree with strong opinions. She took down the biscuits and put the tin on the table like case law, then put it on a chair again, because biscuits must not be confused with ritual. She breathed in pairs and commas and out again until her ribs believed her.

At ten-fifty-nine, Lynn appeared on the doorstep with the neat exactness of a train. She kissed Clara on the cheek and took the baby with the competence of a librarian handling a first edition. "Port is yours," she said. "We'll watch tortoises declare independence on the small screen. Call if physics attempts incantation."

"Thank you," Clara said. "Witness permitted; performance cancelled."

The house approved by doing nothing.

***

Eleven-eleven is a shape as well as a time. It arrived without trumpets. In the kitchen the window stood open to day. The paper sat where paper sits when it is about to be given the small honour of being read. The monitor, plugged back in for listening only, made the faint breathe that belongs to batteries and the hope of being useful.

Mark rested his hip against the counter and put his hands in his pockets as if demonstrating no hands in front of a class of arguable children. "Once," he said, in the tone used for road safety and lovers. "Once, then ordinary."

Clara nodded. She did not clear her throat because she refused the assistance of theatre. She did not clasp her hands because she refused to impersonate believers in things that frightened rooms. She stood in daylight, one foot slightly in front of the other so her ribs could move exactly as their job requires.

She hummed the boat.

It came like muscle memory does when you turn a corner and find the road you don't remember learning. A little boat, a too-large sea. The travelling cadence of wheels on a lane too narrow for law, just wide enough for hope. The line that used to stick, the line that had come unstuck now because she was taller and the caravan had been filed under both and done.

She kept it in the kitchen register—not lullaby-soft (that belongs to night), not stage-loud (that belongs to strangers). The window took a polite interest and sent the sound out the way houses send baking on Sundays so neighbours will like you.

No water, no knots, no taps that were not kettles. Only air, and day, and the shape of a song crossing a table that had agreed to hold paper without demanding worship.

She reached the middle and felt, as she had suspected she would, the first threatenings of apples in the back of her throat—the cold note that had haunted and helped. She did not swallow to banish it. She sang straight through it, and the note did what notes do when you refuse to be impressed by them: it became part of the weather and found somewhere else to be impressive.

She reached the line about not being afraid and said it differently because afraid is a word you must pronounce with clarity when you refuse to let it be the only true thing. She did not smile. She did not cry. She counted pairs and commas with an old choir mistress inside her chest who had decided to be sensible at last.

The last note is the one that tells you what the song thinks it has achieved. She gave it exactly its weight—no more, because more would be drama; no less, because less would be false—and let it stop where it politely stops. She did not add a flourish. She did not look at the monitor.

The monitor breathed.

It did not perform.

The red LED rose to two and stayed there like a civic light that has chosen to obey Fridays. The speaker made the small throat-clearing sound it makes when it is trying to remind you of its existence and then remembered that existence is not a trump card and took a message for later.

Clara's skin did the respectable ripple that belongs to mammals. She did not mistake it for instruction. She inhaled with the sequence of a sentence that has found its punctuation. She looked at the paper and read it silently—*Both came. Both go on.*—so her brain would remember that words exist whether or not air believes in them.

"Thank you," she said—not the kind of thank you that begs, the kind that acknowledges a service rendered and a line not crossed. "We will take it from here."

Mark let out the breath he had decently kept on a leash. He did not ask *did you hear.* He did not say *is it done.* He put two mugs on the counter and made tea because tea is what you do when weather declines to be exciting.

They were quiet for a counted ten seconds because quiet is how rooms register that something has happened and is not happening any more. And then the quiet stopped being gentle and acquired teeth.

It was not a new sound. It was the absence of a sound they had come, against their principles, to anticipate. No reef. No overhand. No bowline. The cord in the taped box remained a line as lines should. The monitor did not offer a word, a hum, a left–right laid down like a spoon. The air did not change temperature or idea. Nothing happened the way you wish nothing would always happen—and it felt like watching a door you have locked move a fraction and then stay shut.

Clara felt her shoulders climb and made them step down. She put her palms flat on the table—not to steady it, to give her hands something to do that wasn't reaching for help that wasn't rules. She looked at the window—open to day—and saw outside only the backs of other houses doing laundry and the sky doing its reasonable best.

"Once," she said, to herself, out loud, the way you might remind a child that biscuits are not a meal. "Then ordinary."

Mark set the mugs down. The teaspoon made a practical click against ceramic and then minded its manners. He handed her a mug with the gravity of a man offering a civic right. "Drink this ordinary," he said. "It's the correct kind."

She drank and tasted the reliable bitterness of tea made by a person who respects leaves. Her mouth found its familiar shape. Her ribs remembered their brief. The quiet didn't soften. It sat in the room like a person who has been asked a question and declined to answer without being rude.

"Is this," Mark said, not rhetorical, practical, "harbour blackout without a breach. A good silence."

Clara let the words walk around the kitchen and report back. "I don't know," she said. "It might be a test that isn't a game. Or it might be grown," she added, surprising herself with the word, "and choosing to obey the Binding by doing nothing."

Mark considered it. "We have asked for law, not person. Law doesn't reply when you sing. It sits on the shelf and stops rivers from becoming events."

"That's poetry," she said, and allowed herself to enjoy it an inch, because enjoyment is not a sin if you've put air in the window properly. "We can ask Harriet if silence is now our baseline and we only act on breach."

"We can," he said. "At half-past, when tea is half gone."

They stood there, two people and a kettle and a piece of paper and a door that had not tried to grow ideas, and felt the teeth of quiet without asking them to bite.

***

At eleven-twenty-two, the letterbox rattled once and performed its only trick: post, in, on time. Two flyers and a white envelope from Hospital Archives with the fonts of departments. The envelope sat at a slant on the mat, the exact degree of slope that suggests an argument about to be avoided.

Clara looked at it, looked at the Binding propped on the fridge in its clear sleeve, looked back at the envelope, and said, as if performing a magic trick where the rabbit is policy, "In-tray."

She put the envelope in the in-tray by the phone. It did not protest. It did not hum or demand an E. It sat like paper that had demanded things in other rooms and had become a citizen here.

"Drink," said Mark. She did.

At eleven-twenty-five, Lynn texted from the lounge: *Tortoise has opinions. Baby approves. Ten minutes left. Do you require biscuits? Do not lie; this is Britain.*

Clara replied: *We require two biscuits and the tone you use on late buses.* Then: *Silence. Monitor breathed; did not perform. Cord = line. Quiet with teeth. We are being grown at.*

Proud of your boring, came the reply. *Biscuits soon. Keep window as day. Keep hands as hands. No promoting spoons to saints.*

Clara laughed exactly once and felt the laugh stick in the room like a pin in a map: here be competence.

At eleven-twenty-nine—because minutes like to prove they can count—the hall table made one tap. Correct, permitted, *allowed*. Clara looked through the glass: a parcel sat at the edge of the step auditioning for drama. She moved it away, inside, because allowed requires action, not applause.

"Thank you," she said to the air, the thank-you that has nothing to do with bargains. "We will take it from here."

The monitor breathed again, gently. The red LED stayed at two and did not attempt a poem.

After office hours ended at one, life insisted on ordinary with the energy of a dog demanding a walk. Lynn returned the baby and the baby returned the spoon. They ate biscuits with the seriousness of people who have invented a system and intend to keep it powered. Martha arrived at half-one to check the kitchen for incantation residues and found only tea.

"How was boat," she asked, casual so that casual would feel welcome.

"Competent," Clara said. "Daylight. Window. Once. Monitor breathed. Didn't perform."

Martha's mouth did a small, significant movement. "Good," she said. "The human appetite for applause is a danger. It makes good boats sink."

"We felt the teeth of quiet," Mark said, to put a noun to the thing.

"Quiet often has dentistry," Martha said, brisk and kind. "You'll grow the sort of skin that can pass it in the street and wave politely."

They made sandwiches because sandwiches are the edible form of policy. Priya sent a photograph of a wallet card just printed: WE'RE FINE. DRAFTS. THANK YOU. NO RECORDINGS, PLEASE. The font had good manners. Clara felt a surge of loyalty to a world where fonts could be decent.

At two-fifteen the envelope in the in-tray tried to rehearse for the role of temptation and failed. They left it where paper goes until tea has been properly walked through a body. At three, Martha retrieved the letter-opener from the drawer with the efficiency of a woman who keeps warranties for kettles and opens envelopes when it's time, not when it's pretty.

"Shall we?" she asked, secretary to the day.

"Copies travel; originals rest," Clara said, and fetched the photocopier app on her phone. They slit the envelope neatly across the top, removed a single page with the department's polite apology voice, and read.

Further to your request, we have added the family-preferred name ELEANOR to the summary letter. We regret the language used in historic notes ("non-viable twin"/"products of conception"). An addendum noting the family name (Eleanor) will accompany any future correspondence.

Martha nodded once, eyes not watering because rooms were watching and bathrooms exist. "Names first," she said. "Thank you to the bored person who typed that."

Clara photographed it once. Printed two copies. Wrote in the bottom corner, neat: COPY FROM ORIGINAL — archives addendum (name). The original went in a sleeve labelled ORIGINAL — ARCHIVES. The copy went to the fridge under the bulldog clip as if Parliament had expanded by one competent councillor.

They did not discuss what it meant. They ate cake. They let quiet remain quiet. They allowed day to do its job without suggesting meaning to it.

***

At four, when afternoons try on mischief, Ruth and Albie knocked with the gentle rattle of good neighbours. Albie executed the official ignore-the-mat manoeuvre with a flourish and asked if he could watch the washing machine do its spinny. He did not attempt to count on the glass. He put his hands in his pockets like a civil servant.

"We sang the boat," Clara told Ruth, because some sentences can be spoken in kitchens without inventing corridors. "Window open to day. Once. The monitor breathed and did not perform."

"Good," Ruth said, in the voice you use when a friend tells you her child has decided to sleep occasionally. "I prefer appliances."

"So does our council," Mark said, with a wave at the fridge. Ruth read the Breakwater, nodded at No Doors like a woman who has opinions about fire regulations, and wrote PORT AUTHORITY in her phone with a heart.

At five, after neighbours and cake and the precise comedy of a toddler refusing to accept the existence of carrots, Clara stood in the hall and looked at the Binding again. It looked back with the blank patience of paper that has elected to be in charge of its own behaviour.

"I am... disappointed," she said to Mark later, when the baby was engaged in a meaningful conversation with a spoon. She said it flat, because the weight of disappointed is best carried on level ground. "I wanted a reef that meant OK and we got line that meant OK."

"Which is what we asked for," he said. "We asked for law, not person. Law doesn't clap."

She accepted this like toast cut diagonal. "There is a stupid part of me that wants apples, just to prove the boat went somewhere."

"That part can have cake," he said, and cut it accordingly. "Apples can attend other people's myths."

She laughed, and the laugh removed one of quiet's teeth.

***

Evening put on its slippers and attempted to be dramatic; the slippers won. They did the census: catch (two clicks); rabbit (guard); stars (behaving); breath (proof). The high chair recollected its identity; the cup flirted with the edge and stayed faithful; the cord in the taped box remained line because lines are better than anything else string can be.

At eight, Clara moved the monitor to the drawer by the phone and left the drawer open—not a banishment, a statement. "We keep you for weather and naps," she told it. "We do not keep you for theatre."

At nine, in the nursery doorway, she spoke the rules like grammar and read the Breakwater like minutes. "No moving things in here. No water. No requests about water at night. Knots on the hall mat only. No requests through other people's children. No teaching them. Withdraw if attention gathers. No recordings in here. No physical contact with people; no moving prams/high chairs/cots/straps; no tightening garments/buckles; no touching skin/hair. Warnings by words only—left–right once; if danger, one tap on the hall table or the inside of the front door. Allowed: move loose objects away from the baby. Requests are not commands. No trades. No debts. No possession. Public is out of bounds. No doors. Heirlooms are not altars. We are for growing a person without teaching her fear. No pretending."

She added, because binding turns into habit only if your mouth works: "We keep you as law, not person."

She placed two fingers on a tiny chest—rise, fall—and returned the metronome with interest. The window catch sat with its two admirable clicks, proud of being simple. Silence sat in the room like a well-trained dog and did not put its paws up on the worktops.

Downstairs, on the mat, the Binding in its sleeve caught the last of the kitchen light. The cord rested—line—the clean answer you get when a question isn't being asked. The kettle did physics and declined to audition. On the fridge, the addendum with ELEANOR glowed the way printers glow when they are new to their duty.

"Today felt like a committee," Mark said, later, handing her tea. "A good committee, the sort that means you get your bins on time and nobody dies because somebody thought a tap was a sign."

"Good committee," she agreed. "I wanted a show and I got policy. I am cross with myself for wanting the first and grateful to us for keeping the second."

He kissed her temple. "We're boring and brave," he said. "That is the trick."

They turned the lamp to the setting where rooms look like rooms and not like the ideas of rooms. The bus at the bend rehearsed its sigh and got it right. The Binding breathed paper. The Breakwater held. The house did the most generous thing a house can do when humans have chosen it on purpose.

It stayed a house.

And the quiet, which earlier had shown them its teeth, lay down by the door and went to sleep.

Chapter Thirty
Witnesses

The morning arrived with Wednesday's tidy face. The light behind the curtains was the colour of paper that accepts ink without asking whether it ought. Clara lay still and let the house list itself: boiler's civil hum; the fridge's patient single note; a bus at the bend rehearsing its decent sigh. She reached for the notebook and wrote, clerk-neat: *Woke steady. Boat done yesterday (daylight; window; once). Binding signed (reef → line). Today: Witnesses. Read Binding aloud "like opening a bridge". PORT AUTHORITY label refresh. Cards for pockets. Office hours 11–13. Mission unchanged: keep as law, not person.*

Mark surfaced with one eye and a face prepared to negotiate with crockery. "Status?"

"Green," she said. "Grey cooperative. We're a small council convening a small ceremony that refuses to be a ceremony."

"Bless bureaucracy," he said. "I'll find the date stamp and the biscuits that think they're legal tender."

On the landing the baby made the small bureaucratic squeak that meant the office had opened. The nursery smelt of warm cotton and sleep that had kept the law. Window catch: two clicks. She didn't check it. She touched it and forgave herself for touching it. Catch; rabbit; stars; breath. Two fingers to a tiny chest—rise, fall. She borrowed the metronome and returned it on time.

On the hall mat, inside the taped box, the dull cotton cord rested like a citizen between shifts. Above, the strip of blue tape Lynn had written

PORT AUTHORITY on had begun to curl at one edge, like a corner of a flag thinking about weather.

"Eleven," Clara told the room, because rooms like trains, to be told when they leave and when they arrive. "Witnesses at eleven. Tea at eleven-oh-three."

The cord tied a small, well-mannered overhand—one—as if to say, *agenda received*, and lay line again, polite and proud of itself.

***

By ten the kitchen had learned its place and liked it. Mark propped the Binding in its clear sleeve at eye level on the fridge as if it were a notice about hedgehogs and bins. He set the compact beside it, the care plan beneath—paper stacking into its own architecture, a modest civic hall of words. He opened the window a hand's width—open to day—and the air took its seat at the table like a guest who had learnt names first.

Clara wiped down the worktop with the bored seriousness of a person who refuses to confuse hygiene with theatre. She put the monitor in the drawer by the phone and left the drawer open—demoted, not banished. She placed a plate for biscuits in the centre of the table and immediately removed it, because biscuits must not be mistaken for ritual. She put out four mugs, then five, counted pairs and commas, and added a sixth for safety because Ruth had texted *Albie with me or not?* and then *Not*, and then *Actually not*, which meant maybe.

The doorbell rang once, polite. Martha came in with rain on her cardigan and a fresh tulip for the blue jug at her house which, she insisted, required dignity even on weekdays. She looked at the Binding and made the mouth she makes when she is trying not to get sentimental in rooms with crockery.

"Good," she said. "We will open our bridge and then walk across it to the kettle. That is the order."

Next, Priya, carrying a small box and a sense of mission. She kissed Clara on the cheek and placed the box on the table with the same satisfaction you get when adding a sensible item to a sensible list.

"I bring cards," she said, triumphant. "For wallets. For fridges. For the corridors of small opinions."

She opened the box to reveal a stack of white rectangles with black, municipal print:

WE'RE FINE. DRAFTS. THANK YOU.
No recordings, please.

The font had the decency of a sign that knows how to guide you out of a building during a drill. She fanned the cards like a magician who can't be bothered with rabbits. "One each. And two spares because the future is worse at pockets than the past."

Clara took one and slotted it into her purse next to the old library card she likes for its smell of other people's Wednesdays. Martha put one in her wallet next to passports and the kettle warranty, and nodded, satisfied, as if nation-states had agreed.

The bell again: Lynn, on time as a train. She carried a small vinyl label-maker like a weapon of choice and a roll of blue painter's tape already warm with letters. She didn't take off her coat before walking straight to the jamb and pressing the tape flat with the authority of a person who has labelled shared fridge shelves and survived to make policy about it.

She smoothed the curling edge and, with a loud, pleased beep, printed a new strip: PORT AUTHORITY in clean capitals that could be read by tired people and misdirected weather. She layered it neatly over the old like a municipal repair that understands grace.

"There," she said. "If a day can read, even days will behave."

"Tea," Mark said. "Because we cannot possibly open a bridge on an empty mouth."

They made tea. They put biscuits out and declined to call it a feast. They did not close any doors. The window stayed open to day because days don't turn into theatre when they have jobs.

"Harriet?" Priya asked, glancing at the time.

"In clinic," Clara said. "She sends the stamp of her approval and a reminder not to audition. We'll read, we'll sign the witness line, we'll put breath in capitals without gassing the house."

They laughed—the correct, small laugh you do when people you love are about to do a sensible thing and you want the room to be kind.

***

At eleven on the dot—because office hours are not negotiable—they gathered at the port. The mat lay square, the taped box at one end like a little stage that had been told it would not be doing any acting today. The cord inside was a line, the most beautiful shape string can take when people are tired and trying to be brave rather than interesting.

Clara stood where she can see kitchen and hall both. Mark took the Binding in its sleeve and held it as if it were a speech that prefers not to be performed. Martha took her place by the console table with the satisfaction of a woman who has, for decades, found a place in rooms and made the rooms better for it. Priya and Lynn flanked the jamb like cheerful ushers, their pockets full of cards and the kind of jokes that do not make weather.

"Are we ready," Mark said, not rhetorical.

"We are," Martha said. "We will say the words like people who know the price of quiet and pay it gladly."

"PORT AUTHORITY," Lynn intoned, mock-grand, tapping the label with the reverence she refuses to give to anything that isn't a bus schedule. "Open the bridge."

Mark read. He did it in the voice you use when opening minutes at a parish meeting where the chairs are orange and the stakes are, in fact, life. THE BINDING — HOUSE & HUMANS. He read the Affirmations with the clean weight of a brush painting lines on a road. He read House = port. Messages mat only, 11–13. Words & knots only. No possession. No doors. No water. Public out of bounds. Any breach → 48h harbour blackout & gift day cancelled. No trades. No debts. Copies travel; originals rest. Mission. No pretending.

He reached the Oath and looked to Clara. She took the sentence in her mouth where it has elected to live beside teeth and vowels and stubbornness and said, steady: "We keep you as law, not person."

Martha's lips moved, not to pray, but to count the commas. Priya nodded once, that crisp nod that collapses panic in institutions like a deckchair. Lynn breathed out the sound you make when a flatpack has, against odds and history, ended up being a chair.

"Sign," Martha said, practical. "Witness should be permitted to be a witness."

They signed the witness line under H. Baines's neat role—their own initials, their small names in a house that had learnt how to be not a story about itself. Priya date-stamped the sleeve with an enthusiasm she apologised for and then didn't, because stamps are the one allowable exception.

They stood, all four, and let the words sit in the room like furniture that had always belonged there and had been politely kept in storage while the house grew a better back.

"Now the bit where we don't do a thing," Lynn said. "No doors. No water. No 'oh please' into any vessel. We let paper hold it and daylight make it real."

"Consider it held," Priya said, distributing wallet cards. "If Denise at clinic ever rings, we will say, *'We're fine. Drafts. Thank you. No recordings, please.'* If anyone on a WhatsApp tries to become a documentary, we will become boring at them until the episode is cancelled."

They laughed, human and decent.

"Tea," Martha said. "We have opened the bridge. Now we cross it to the kettle."

They were halfway to the kitchen when the hairline crack arrived.

It was not loud. It was not theatrical. It was the kitchen wall saying, in a child's careful voice with no cleverness in it:

"Left–right."

They stopped like a school at a crossing. It had come from the plaster above the worktop, not from the mat. It had come at 11:17, inside office hours, and not in the port. The rule that has kept days alive stood up in Clara's ribs and said, politely and without argument: mat only.

For two heartbeats nobody breathed too much, because breathing too much invents theatre. Then Clara did the thing the rules taught her to do when she would rather do twelve other things in a panic.

She said, calm, for floors and walls and the part of herself that hates to be managed: "Port only. Mat only."

She walked—did not run—back to the mat, the others with her, as if withdrawing from a wrong corridor into a room with seats.

On the mat, above the box, in the air that was allowed, the same careful voice spoke again, as if it had found the chair it was meant to sit in.

"Left–right."

"One time," Clara said. "And not a command."

She looked left: the hob knob for the back-left ring sat at one. Not flame—residual heat, the pale red that makes a case for patience. Mark had set it to keep a pan warm and had forgotten that warm is an adjective with ambition. Right: on the worktop, a chef's knife lay too near the edge, handle heavy, blade pointing into the kitchen's space like a difficult opinion.

She did what the compact tells her to do with objects: away.

She turned the hob to nought with an adult's hand and said thank you to physics, not to plaster. She lifted the knife by its handle and placed it flat and far, blade pointing inwards, then put the board beneath it because boards make knives behave. She did not narrate. She did not ask for a mark out of ten from the air. She breathed pairs and commas and counted, and the counting took the sharpness out of it.

Priya, who has a gift for being brisk without moving too fast, checked the pan and felt the heat in the air with the back of her hand like a woman whose mother taught her to take heat nearly, not fully, into her skin. "Residual," she said. "Not dramatic."

Martha, who has trained herself not to bless things, did not bless the hob. She checked the tea towel that had been too near and moved it into the dead zone by the kettle where towels go to be citizens. Lynn, who had been known to yell at spatulas, refrained. She stood, hands in pockets, reading PORT AUTHORITY with ferocious attention until the letters calmed her.

On the mat, in the box, the cord tied a small, correct reef—OK—and then lay line.

"Thank you; we'll take it from here," Clara said, to the room, to the rule, to herself. "Mat only. Once."

Priya, who had gone pale in sympathy and then pink in relief, leaned a shoulder against the jamb and blew out a breath whose politics were 100% common sense. "That," she said, "was a left–right that resisted the temptation to become a show. Congratulations to everyone's throat for not making an announcement."

"I nearly said RED STOP," Lynn admitted. "But the port did the obedience so fast I felt it would be petty."

Clara nodded. She felt her ribs return to civilian shape. She felt the old humiliating happiness that comes when houses are sensible in front of people you're fond of. She went to the fridge and, under THE BREAKWATER, wrote in sober capitals: PORT ONLY. Then, in smaller hand, because policy likes footnotes: *If a syllable arrives off-port, name Port only. If immediately obeyed → compliance noted (no blackout). If not → 48h harbour blackout & gift day cancelled.*

"Is that legal," Mark said, amused—"adding a clarification rather than a boundary?"

"It is a procedure," Martha said. "This is a house, not a monarchy."

They stood there—four women and a man, all ridiculous and sensible—and let their pulses come down in a room where heat existed and knives had been put where knives belong.

"Time for the cards," Priya said, shaking herself back into service. She handed one to each of them as if dealing out a minor ace. "Wallets, please. Repeat after me: *We're fine. Drafts. Thank you. No recordings, please.*"

They repeated, and the repetition made ordinary sound like policy, which is one of the uses of having friends.

***

The rest of the hour wanted to be helpful and succeeded. They read the Binding again, this time for the benefit of Lynn, who had not heard the

Oath in the house since yesterday. They did not push for any reply. The cord in the box remained a line; line is the politest applause.

Martha told a brief story about a kettle from 1987 that refused to die because warranties frighten appliances into longevity. Priya admired PORT AUTHORITY and suggested a small drawing of a ship would make no one happier and everyone pearl-clutch, which might be useful for neighbours with narrow ideas of normal. Lynn fished a Sharpie from a pocket and sketched a ridiculous boat the size of a biscuit at the very edge of the tape where only bored Thursdays would notice. The boat's little flag had the letter B on it. It looked like nothing and everything.

They tested the wallet cards by imagining stupid situations: clerk with a phone; aunt with a theory; man in the pub with a video. Priya supplied the tone you give to people whose talent for insisting is larger than their capacity for consent. *We're fine. Drafts. Thank you. No recordings, please.* They practised their pleasant faces and closed mouths. They had biscuits and refused to call it a treaty.

At 12:04, the letterbox fluttered and produced nothing of consequence. At 12:12, the bus at the bend sighed at a child who would not wave back. At 12:19, the monitor in the drawer made a small throat noise—battery deciding to confess its age—and was ignored without cruelty.

At 12:33, Ruth and Albie did not arrive, which was itself a courtesy. Jonah slept at Priya's mother's. Sam was building a fort with Lynn's partner out of cushions and grievances. The house enjoyed the presence of grown-ups who were trying to deserve the title.

At 12:40, because heat remembers reasons to exist, Martha stood, opened the window another half-inch—open to day—and said, without italics, the sentence that keeps kitchens loyal: "You can't sing the boat to a kettle, but you can make tea for the people who sang the boat. The effect is roughly the same."

They made tea. They did not discuss the left–right. They let it be a once and not a door. They spoke about bins and bread and councils and doctors and the price of apples which, in some places, still meant corridors and in this house had been persuaded to become a fruit again.

At 12:57, they walked back to the port to close it because office hours are a promise as much as a permission. Mark set two fingers to the corner of the sleeve, as if touching the corner of a flag before folding it. "Port closing," he said, gentle.

"Thank you," Clara said, to air and paper and people. "We will take it from here."

The cord in the box remained line. Lines are beautiful when a day has tried to make a show and been denied the budget.

***

There's always the after. The part where everyone returns from being deliberate to being real. The part where witnesses go home with cards in their wallets and biscuits in their blood and the sense that a small and necessary bridge has been opened and crossed and will not be shut by weather.

Priya slid her card behind her travel pass. "For the tube," she said. "For corridors. For men who ask women to make sense on demand."

Lynn tucked hers into the clear pocket where one day a child's photo might live and today a cartoon lives because she refuses to audition for sentiment. "When the day tries to perform, we will decline the gig," she said. "We will invoice it for the time."

Martha kissed Clara's temple and smoothed the hair by her ear in a way she had never done when Clara was small because this softness had been considered dangerous then. "You are making a government that keeps children," she said, a sentence with the weight of paid-for stamps.

They left. The door closed with the decency of doors that have nothing to prove. The house was a house. The Binding on the fridge shone in the lamplight like a quiet regulation about speed in residential streets. The little boat on the PORT AUTHORITY tape looked like a mistake and a joke and a very small truth.

Mark leaned on the counter and put his hands in his pockets, the posture that in this house means he is prepared to be decent for as long as it takes. "We did public, without being public," he said. "We did witness without making a crowd."

"We did left–right once," Clara said, letting the last of the adrenalin turn into hot water in her veins. "We did Port only. We did not buy anything with it. We did not owe."

He watched her face in that way he has learned, the way that is not a question but an agreement to answer when asked. "Do you want to write the clarification into the book," he said, "so that future us doesn't turn immediate obedience into punishment?"

She opened the notebook and wrote, neat as a council minute:

11:17 — left–right from kitchen wall (off-port). Named Port only. Immediate compliance (repeat on mat). Actioned once: hob to nought; knife away. No blackout (compliance). Addendum: If message arrives off-port, call to port. If immediately honoured → compliance. If not → 48h harbour blackout + gift cancelled.

She underlined compliance once. Once is policy. Twice is a sermon.

"Tea?" Mark said, which in this house is the sentence that ends chapters and begins afternoons.

"Tea," she said, and made it.

They stood in the kitchen with the window open to day, the monitor demoted in its drawer, the cord a line in the taped box, the Binding propped where tired eyes can find it. Outside, the bus at the bend rehearsed its sigh and got it right. Inside, the day behaved itself like a citizen.

On the jamb, the little boat on the PORT AUTHORITY strip seemed to tilt a fraction to the right and then to the left, which is what boats do when physics is in charge and weather is ordinary.

Clara looked at it and smiled, not to the air, but to the people who would read it later and remember: we did a hard thing plainly; we did not audition; we made witness into warmth; and when a voice from a wall tried to be a wall again, we politely asked it to sit in its chair.

The house approved by being a house. The hour shut itself like a file. And the bridge they had opened did the work bridges do best: it stayed.

Chapter Thirty-One
Two Clicks

Evening wore Thursday like a coat with deep pockets. The light behind the curtains had folded itself up; the house did its after-hours inventory: boiler's civil hum; the fridge's single note; a bus at the bend rehearsing its decent sigh for people who might be late. Clara wrote the census in the notebook before she could begin to bargain: *Catch; rabbit; stars; breath. Two clicks set.* She underlined two clicks once, because once is policy, twice is panic.

Mark brought tea with the gravity he keeps for small governments. "Status?"

"Green," she said. "Grey cooperative. Monitor in the drawer, drawer open. Port closed until eleven tomorrow. I would like a boring night."

"May we be boring, and if not, may we be legal," he said, and kissed her temple.

Upstairs, the nursery smelt of warm cotton and sleep that had kept the law. The stuffed rabbit held its post at the cot's corner with a vigilance that didn't need praise. The window showed a thin reflection of room on room. Clara checked the catch with the care of a person who trusts herself enough to touch: down; over; one click; two. She felt them under her thumb the way you feel a clean hinge. She did not tug to prove. She put two fingers to a tiny chest—rise, fall—and let the metronome lend her a minute. Breath came back with receipts.

The hall mat lay square. In the taped box, the dull cotton cord was a line—line, the best a string can be. On the jamb, PORT AUTHORITY in Lynn's neat capitals had held its edge all day; the tiny drawn boat looked like the world's smallest seriousness.

"Lights," Mark said. They turned out the big ones and kept the lamp at the bottom of the stairs set to a modest glow, the kind that keeps ankles honest. They went downstairs and put the television on low weather—people pretending to be serious about sandwiches. They didn't mention left–right; they didn't mention apples; they let their shoulders learn to behave.

At nine-thirty, the letterbox did its small, attention-seeking cough, then remembered itself. At ten, the bus sighed at nobody. At ten-fifteen, the kettle did physics without auditioning. The house wore slippers and kept its hands to itself.

At ten-thirty-three, the inside of the front door gave a single, precise tap.

They both froze, the way people do who have trained themselves not to over-interpret and must now decide whether they trust their own training.

Clara's body wanted to!; she gave it a full stop. "Allowed alarm," she said, level. "One tap on the hall table or the inside of the door. We look. We do not open."

Mark stood and moved like a person in a safety video who had passed their test. He went to the door, kept his body side-on, glanced through the peephole, then down to the gap at the bottom where draft-excluders go to auditions and fail.

"Nothing," he said. "No feet. No envelopes playing at drama."

The tap did not come again. No second knock. No eager, wrong little flourish. One tap—permitted—and then silence as strict as paper.

Clara felt the theatre trying to learn lines in her chest and told it there would be no performance tonight. She nodded towards the stairs.

"Baby," she said. "Door stays closed; chain can be friendly; we move politely." The chain slid on because humans are not subject to No Doors.

They went up—Mark first, because his shoulder has opinions about hinges; Clara behind, because she knows where every board complains. The stair lamp made slow light on the carpet, the colour of sensible shoes. Clara's hand on the banister did the terrible, powerless flex it does in old houses when you remember that wood was once a tree.

They reached the landing with that feeling the body has when it knows something is thinking about it. The nursery stood with its door ajar exactly as they had left it—a good, narrow angle that made shadows into policemen. The air had the clean, sleepy tang of shampoo and washed cotton. Not apples. Not water. The correct smells of civility.

Clara touched the door with two fingers and pushed it one inch. The cot: asleep citizen. Rabbit: at post. Stars: behaving. The window: a black sheet with a small rectangle of not-night above the neighbour's extension.

She saw the handle move.

Not wildly. Not theatre. A human test—down a fraction against the catch; up; down; the little persistent rattle of a person not in this room trying to discover whether this room could be made to forget itself.

Her mouth filled with heat then cold the way steel remembers what it used to be. She lifted a hand in the air to stop Mark stepping fully into the room. She checked the catch with her eyes and, because sometimes eyes are cruel liars, with a single, confirming finger: one click; two; set; set.

She did not go to the window. She did not speak to the air. She did not perform.

She pointed to her ear, then to the landing. They withdrew backwards, because backs are honest and babies have earned not being woken by decisions. In the hall below, the one tap on the door expanded in meaning and stayed within its lane. The house had rung the bell; now the humans would do the human things.

***

In the bedroom, Mark picked up the phone and dialled 999 with the steadiness of a person trained by every poster in every community hall. He spoke in plain. "Good evening. We have a prowler at our address. We're in the house, doors secured. It seems... they were testing a first-floor window—the nursery. Yes." He gave the address, repeated it, listened, and added the bits that matter. "We've set our chain. We're in a safe room. No one is injured. We can see the garden from the back bedroom if required. We can also do nothing until you arrive if you prefer we be boring."

Clara stood by the bed and listened to the universe, which for once was replying in the correct language. She could hear the very faint staccato of someone in wet shoes stepping on their small pebbles and deciding they had perhaps chosen the wrong house. She could hear the bus at the bend feeling good about its next sigh. She could hear her own ribs counting the pairs and commas they have been practising since the caravan.

"Officers en route," Mark relayed, hand over the receiver. "We're asked to stay inside, do not confront, lights on downstairs, people moving in house is a deterrent, but no silhouettes in the nursery. They'll come round the back first."

"Ruth," Clara said, already texting in the kitchen group, fingers doing decent work because language is a factory: *Suspected prowler in the street. We're inside; police en route. Please stay in. Lights on, doors locked; don't come outside. No recording at our front; thank you.* She pressed send, then another to Lynn and Priya with the shorthand they share: *Knock once only; do not. Stay in. We will update.* Three ticks came back like tiny salutes.

The rattle came again—long, unhurried, and then a pause with that heavy, thinking weight attached to it. Then small, gritty sounds of retreat, the little grinds you get when shoes meet stone at a different angle.

"Back bedroom," Mark mouthed. They went through, lights off, and stood with their shoulders to the wall the way you stand when you don't want your shape to write a story on glass. They lifted a slat of the blind with one finger and looked out over their own garden, the fence, the tiny gate that makes a ceremony of the alley beyond.

***

At first, nothing. Then a shadow that was not their shadow slid along the fence and did the mistake shadows make when owned by bodies—they hesitated at the gate as if it required permission from a syllabus. A hand. The gate lifted a half-inch and made its small metal protest. The shadow reconsidered the relationship between desire and noise, let the latch drop, and went the other way, over the lower fence by the compost bin, a movement that looked like someone being harsh with their own knees.

They didn't exclaim. They watched. No Doors is for the house; not for police; not for thieves. The gate was permitted to be a gate and people were permitted to be mistakes.

From the front room, a car passed and did not slow. From the corner, a dog barked in the polite tone of an animal who dislikes ambiguity. From the bend, as if musicals had been invented for this precise queasy minute, came the damp chorus of a bus sighing as it decided the timetable would not be greatly injured by mercy.

Clara counted to thirty and then to thirty again because thirty is a number people hand to each other in corridors when they need to share breath.

"Lights," Mark said, back to instruction voice. They went downstairs, turned the porch light on, turned the downstairs lights on, the kind of glow that says *we are awake; we live here; please don't audition.* He tilted the hall mirror a fraction so any attempt at looking in would be immediately confronted with looking back.

They did not open the door. They did not rattle any metal. They did not call the street Oi or excuse me, because no useful thing has ever been said to a garden at night that started with either of those. They looked at the Binding on the fridge, at the line under No Doors, and silently congratulated their past selves on being boring in daylight.

"Units are close," Mark said, the phone a quiet third person in the room. "Front and back."

There is a particular time measured only in human bodies when you know that help is near and you must hold your shape until it becomes here. Clara stood in the kitchen and put her palms flat on the worktop. She did not touch the tap. She did not touch the drawer where the monitor slept. She read the Breakwater in her head the way some people say beads.

The first blue wash lifted the edge of the net curtains and made them foolishly theatrical. The second blue resolved into the suggestion of numbers on a bonnet and a polite voice on the radio saying *arrived.* A knock at the front door—human, correct—and a call: "Police!"

Mark went to the door, chain still on, and spoke through the gap with the practised cheer of a man who has decided to be useful. He gave names, confirmed the report, declined to open. "Our back gate is unlocked," he said. "Side alley access from the lane if you're coming round."

"Stay where you are," the voice said, friendly and firm. "We'll have a look."

***

They went back to the back bedroom. Two torches moved through the garden—the serious, methodical beams of people who know what hiding looks like. One officer at the fence; one at the gate; one in the alley; voices low enough that plants wouldn't take offence.

"Footprints," a voice said, low. "Soil's soft. Corner of the lino on the sill—the old kind leaves a mark. No entry. Handle has resisted."

Clara didn't know she was holding the doorframe until her fingers began to ache around the wood. She unclamped and made a deal with her own nails. "Two clicks," she whispered, not to the room, to her future self for when she would want to change the past and be unkind to the present. "Two clicks held."

The front bell rang again; this time the chain came off. Two officers in yellow jackets that look like decisions stood on the step, faces composed into that particular combination of apology and satisfaction good public servants carry.

"Evening," said the taller of the two. "You did exactly right. We've had a call from two doors down earlier—someone trying gate latches, probably the same person. We'll have a wander. Could we have details?" He looked at Clara the way men are taught to look at women who might be tired and deserved better. "Did you see a face?"

"No," Clara said. "We heard the handle tested. We observed shadow in the garden and a person leaving over the fence by the compost. We cannot tell you colour of jacket or shoe. I can tell you we had set the window two clicks and those clicks rescued my heart from climbing out of my chest."

The officer's mouth did a small, professional smile. "Two clicks," he repeated, as if learning a local language. "Correct. Some of these old catches—you'll be fine. There are sash locks you can add that don't harm the wood; we can leave a leaflet."

"Leave it," Mark said, and then corrected himself, because leaflet-world has been promoted to recycling. "Leave it in the in-tray and we will do policy to it."

"Any CCTV?" the other officer asked. "Doorbell?"

"No recordings in the nursery," Clara said, because No Recordings in Here has been one of their sentences since the day policy learned to write. "Doorbell yes; not at the window. You're welcome to check if it caught anything worth your time."

They did. The little video showed somebody's legs being harsh with themselves at the fence and nothing you could swear on in court. The officer nodded, as if proof were a flavour he had learned not to ask for unless necessary.

"Would you like us to look upstairs," he asked, careful of dignity.

"You may," Mark said, because professionals allowed is civilised. They went up; they looked; they did not touch the window; they checked the child with the eyes of men with training and boundaries. The baby breathed the breath of the new and indifferent, the mercy of that small ordinary ringing like a bell you wouldn't dare put in a tower.

Back downstairs, details were exchanged because details are how days are filed. The officers wrote in a book because computers break and notebooks don't. They left a card with a number that will become a drawer's friend. They offered to walk the lane again; they left with a good night for the house as if houses deserved salutations.

When the door shut, gentle, no drama, Clara realised her chest had been a fist. It unclenched so fast she had to sit. She sat on the bottom step and pressed her palms together without intending to pretend to pray. She likes the feeling of both hands making a house.

Mark crouched in front of her and did the question with his eyebrows. She nodded. Tears did their old, humiliating, tender trick and went backwards into her face where they belonged.

"Log it," she said, because language is the breakwater between now and remembering. He fetched the book and the pen that has behaved since February and turned to the day's page where *Two clicks set* had already made a sentence.

She wrote, clerk-neat:

22:33 — One tap on inside of front door (allowed alarm). No second.
22:36 — Nursery handle tested externally (rattle). Catch held (two clicks).
Withdrawn; called 999.
Police attended (front & back). Footprints in soft soil; mark on sill; no entry.
We turned hob off earlier; knives already away.
We stayed in; chain on; lights on; no recordings in nursery.
Outcome: system worked. No Doors respected (house). Two clicks held (us).

She put the pen down and felt the day sit up a little straighter under the weight of being written.

Her phone pinged in the kitchen, the little sound that means witnesses still exist in other houses.

Ruth: *Police just passed our window; we stayed in. Albie is explaining locks to the sofa. Well done two clicks.*
Lynn: *Watching from behind a curtain like a moral. Proud of your once. Proud of your no door theatre.*
Priya: *I have a spare security bar if you want it. Also a cake that believes in calming governments.*

Martha: *I am awake and behaving. Phone if you want me to sit in your kitchen and glower at physics.*

Clara tapped replies with the calm that comes with not being in charge of time. She thanked them and asked them to sleep. She told them we were fine and the Binding approves of police and tea.

***

Back upstairs, the nursery had kept its promise. The catch was a small square animal with two neat teeth that had chosen to bite exactly as hard as necessary. Clara put two fingers on the tiny chest in the cot—rise, fall—and returned the metronome with interest. She placed her hand on the window frame and felt the cool transfer the way sensible timber keeps to its brief. She whispered, because children deserve to sleep inside sentences that will not frighten them: "Two clicks, love. That's all. That's everything."

Downstairs, in the taped box, the cord tied a single, modest reef—OK—and lay line. No flourish. No sulk. Law, not person. The house had used its one tap and then minded itself.

Mark poured two fingers of something brown into mugs and added hot water because courage is improved by decency in this house. They stood in the kitchen and drank the unshowy night-time drink of people who are done choosing and would like to sit down.

"What do we add," he asked, eyes on the fridge where THE BREAK-WATER lives. "Do we add a line about police to Professionals allowed."

Clara considered. "Yes," she said. She wrote in sober capitals under Doctors allowed:

POLICE ALLOWED. *Professionals who keep citizens safe may be invited in; show care plan and Binding; we remain with the baby unless safeguarding threshold met.*

She stepped back. The words sat where they should, dignified without suggesting they would cover themselves in velvet if given the chance.

They ate toast cut diagonal because diagonal improves nights by fractions. They did not argue with the air. They thanked physics and told weather to go home. They sat on the sofa until bodies returned the keys to the day.

Before bed, Clara climbed the stairs one more time. The nursery kept its face. The window was still two clicks; the rabbit still at his silly, brave post. She let her eyes move over corners and edges and surfaces like a surveyor with a crush. She spoke the rules in the voice that does not audition. "No moving things in here. No water. No requests about water at night. Knots on the hall mat only. No requests through other people's children. No teaching them. Withdraw if attention gathers. No recordings in here. No physical contact with people; no moving prams/high chairs/cots/straps; no tightening garments/buckles; no touching skin/hair. Warnings by words only—left–right once; if danger, one tap on the hall table or the inside of the front door. Allowed: move loose objects away from the baby. Requests are not commands. No trades. No debts. No possession. Public is out of bounds. No doors. Heirlooms are not altars. Police allowed. We are for growing a person without teaching her fear. No pretending. We keep you as law, not person."

She placed two fingers to the tiny chest—rise, fall. She lent the metronome five seconds and received it back perfect and on time.

Downstairs, Mark had left a note on the hall table for morning Clara in case night Clara forgot what she had achieved. It read: *Two clicks held. One tap. System worked. We were boring and brave. Repeat as needed.*

She smiled without showing it, turned out the lamp, and let the house be the house.

Out on the bend, the bus sighed at midnight and didn't mind being late for once. In Martha's kitchen the blue jug minded tulips and no sorrows. In Lynn's hall, the green strip sat high with exemplary manners. In Ruth's front room, Albie whispered to the sofa about latches until sleep persuaded him to have an opinion in the morning instead.

On the mat, the cord remembered its vocabulary and stayed line. On the fridge, the Binding and Breakwater held their seats in the council. The window upstairs—two clicks—kept its promise to a woman who had taught the house to be law.

The night did not apologise for itself. It did not audition. It did the single kindest thing it can do when people have chosen to live downstairs tomorrow: it passed.

Chapter Thirty-Two
The Hall Mat Only

T he morning put on Friday as if it had been brushed and told to behave. The light behind the curtains was the colour of paper that takes ink and keeps the peace. Clara lay still and let the house list itself: boiler's civil hum; the fridge's honest single note; a bus at the bend rehearsing its decent sigh. She reached for the notebook and wrote, clerk-neat: *Woke steady. Two clicks held last night. One tap only (allowed). Police approved; neighbours stayed in. Today: office hours 11–13. Mission: reinforce Mat only; test our nerves without inventing weather. No Doors. No water. We keep you as law, not person.* She underlined Mat only once, because once is policy and twice is hope pretending to be law.

Mark surfaced with one eye and the gentle stubbornness he keeps for bins and vows. "Status?"

"Green," she said. "Grey cooperative. No recordings, no theatre, no debt. I will accept an uneventful day and call it art."

He kissed her temple and went towards the kettle like a citizen arriving at a civic building during opening hours. "Tea," he declared. "Then we remind the mat it is a port, not a stage."

On the landing, the baby made the small bureaucratic squeak that meant the office had opened. The nursery smelt of warm cotton and sleep that had kept the law. Window catch: two clicks. She didn't check it. She touched it, forgave herself for touching it, and did the census that has become grammar: catch; rabbit; stars; breath. Two fingers to a tiny chest—rise, fall. She borrowed the metronome and returned it on time.

The cleaner's cupboard—the under-stairs cave of hoover, bucket, vinegar, spare loo rolls, the smell of old mops and resigned soap—sat with its door shut, as she had left it after the last fortnight's spring of enthusiasm. Its handle had that faint silver worn by hands who've never quite learned to like bleach.

On the hall mat, inside the taped box, the dull cotton cord was a line—line, the hands-down best that string can be. On the jamb above, PORT AUTHORITY in Lynn's neat capitals had stopped curling since she relabelled it; the tiny drawn boat looked ridiculous and entirely correct. The Binding glowed in its clear sleeve on the fridge; the Breakwater held its place like a lamppost that saves ankles. Beneath them, new sober capitals from last night: POLICE ALLOWED.

They ate toast cut diagonal because diagonal improves Fridays by fractions. Mark adjusted the monitor in the drawer to sit like an appliance that knows its rung on the ladder. Clara set the cards—WE'RE FINE. DRAFTS. THANK YOU. NO RECORDINGS, PLEASE.—in the little letter stand so the day could read when it forgot.

Text pings were the chorus of sensible neighbourhoods:
Ruth: *Albie slept. Woke to brief lecture on latches. Wishes to become a hinge.*
Lynn: *Port Authority stable. Will swing by with a new roll of tape & a ship the size of a lentil.*
Priya: *Made lemon drizzle. It believes in governments. Shall I deliver at 11:30 like a civil servant?*
Martha: *I will not fuss. I will arrive with a cloth and wipe nothing.*

Clara answered with civilians: *Yes, yes, yes, yes.* She put the phone down and did pairs and commas until her ribs were law-abiding again.

***

By ten-thirty the kitchen had done its preparations and refused to make a ceremony of them. The window went open to day a hand's width. The paper copy of the boat lived politely in the drawer with the pastry cutters. The sink minded its business and kept its water where water belongs. The kettle worked towards a quiet boil that would arrive exactly when asked and not before.

Mark shuffled a small pile of documents—not because paper was a talisman but because it prefers to be tidy. Care plan, Binding, Breakwater, wallet cards. He stamped today's date on the corner of a note that read PORT = MAT (11–13) and clipped it under the fridge magnet shaped like a slow strawberry.

"Witness list?" he said, light.

"Lynn and Priya in person; Martha by chair if she gets here in time; Ruth on standby with Albie if we need a child to practise not being audience by refusing to be audience." Clara smiled at the thought of Albie earnestly not looking. "Harriet on text, clinic permitting; Dr Patel in spirit with please."

"Excellent," he said. "We'll give the day every chance to behave in front of witnesses."

They didn't speak about last night's two clicks again. They didn't need to. That line was in the book, in the bones, in the hinge.

At ten-fifty-five, Lynn arrived with a strip of blue tape and a drawing of a ship so tiny it had to be taken on trust. "PORT AUTHORITY," she said, and pressed the tape flat at the jamb like a person lowering a flag with perfect form. She drew her lentil-ship again under the first, so the day would have choices of scale.

At eleven-oh-three, Priya knocked the exact knock of people who don't want to startle houses. She carried a lemon drizzle the colour of policy working and set it on the counter as if setting down a manifesto.

"Martha?" she asked.

"Bus delay," Lynn said, glancing at her phone. "She will arrive in a mood that will frighten gravity into apologising."

They laughed, and the room became the sort of place where no is easier for everyone to say.

***

Office hours began without a speech at 11:00. The mat lay square; the box sat; the cord remained a line. Clara stood where the hall can see the kitchen and the kitchen can see the hall; Mark took up his spot where his hands can be seen to be empty; Lynn leaned on the jamb with her pockets and PORT AUTHORITY under her thumb; Priya stood to the side with a pen as if minutes might be requested; the baby, per policy, was in the lounge with spoons and CBeebies—no audience of children.

Mark read the Breakwater as if opening minutes at a parish hall with orange chairs.

"House = port. Messages mat only, 11:00–13:00. Words & knots only. No possession. No doors. No water. Public out of bounds. Any breach → 48h harbour blackout & gift day cancelled. No trades. No debts. Copies travel; originals rest. Mission. No pretending. THE BINDING: We keep you as law, not person."

He ended with the politest of nods. The air did not try to be anything other than air. The cord did not audition. The house did the thing houses do when they are currently not making a play for the part of church: it listened and refrained.

At 11:07, because days are petty, the monitor in the drawer cleared its throat. They ignored it, which in this house is an act of love. At 11:12, a bee visiting the rosemary bumped into glass and corrected itself without a parable. At 11:19, a parcel flyer pretended to be a knock and was not.

Clara's ribs remembered last night. She let them remember without giving them anything to write on. She looked at the Binding on the fridge, at the line that has kept her sleep where sleep belongs: We keep you as law, not person. She repeated it in her mouth with no need to invite anyone else in.

"Fruit," Lynn said, low, practical. "We should cut something that dispels melodrama. Grapes. Grapes are anti-theatre."

Clara got the grapes. She did not use the knife at the edge; she moved it away; she put the board under; she kept the blade pointing in. Priya poured water, not for a spell, for throats, and the glasses made their calm little notes as if denouncing the idea of ritual forever.

"Eleven-thirty," Mark said, glancing at the clock. "We will be citizens for another ninety minutes and then retire to cake."

"Cake accepts," Priya said.

"Cake always accepts," Lynn said, and the two of them shared the grin of women who have lived through Wednesdays.

***

At 11:51, the cord twitched.

Not a knot. Not a flourish. A tiny lift—a breathing-in—and then line again, like someone standing up in a meeting because they were going to speak and then deciding the agenda could survive without them.

Clara saw it. She did not nod. She did not ask it to repeat itself. She placed her palm flat above the box without touching anything and said the only opening sentence that has ever kept this house honest: "Mat only."

The air, obedient, resumed being air.

At 11:56, the sash of the cleaner's cupboard door—under-stairs, opposite the mat, two long paces away—was no longer flush. The top corner offered a sliver of shade where there shouldn't be shade. The handle looked like a mouth trying to stay out of an argument and failing by a millimetre.

Clara did the roll-call in her head: No Doors. Mat only. Ajar is a shape and not necessarily a sin. She felt, traitorously, the quick domestic twitch that belongs to people who cannot resist putting a door back into line. She did not move.

"Was that us?" Lynn asked, gently, unwilling to give the cupboard the dignity of a capital letter.

"It was shut this morning," Clara said. "It is now trying to be interesting."

Priya, who has seen hospitals invent corridors out of nothing and refuses to assist, said, "We can see it from here. We do not need to approach a door to understand that it believes in theatre."

Mark's voice was the exact pitch of the man who's made peace with being boring. "Mat only. If there is something to say, it will be said on the mat."

The cord lifted again—more deliberate now—and tied a small overhand—one—then paused like a person with a finger in a book. The cupboard door remained ajar, as if waiting for applause.

Clara felt heat in her throat and cold behind her eyes—the body's version of agreeing to two opposites at once. She set her feet the way a person sets them when they are about to lift something or not lift it:

wide, sensible, knees honest. She spoke for the house as much as for herself.

"Mat only. No doors. If you have business, bring it to port."

The cord did nothing for a beat so long you could butter toast on it.

At 11:58, the cupboard sash moved a hair.

It was not wind. The window by the stairs was shut as firmly as promises. It was not gravity; gravity is a quieter enthusiast. It was the exact degree of movement you get when someone demonstrates potential and hopes you're the kind of person who cannot bear indecision.

Clara could feel blackout standing up in the wings. Any breach → 48h harbour blackout & gift day cancelled. That was the law. If the house insisted on doors, the house would get silence, because silence is what you give children and physics when they've tried to audition. She tasted the cost of forty-eight hours of not-humming, not-speaking, not-saying thank you into ordinary air. It tasted of lemon—Priya's cake cooling—of patience—of the baby's laugh arriving into a room with rules and finding it was not a theatre. She did not want to pay it. She would, if she had to. Love is sometimes the expensive option because *cheap* is noisy.

"MAT ONLY," she said, firmer, not louder. "No doors. We will not approach. **Bring it here or let it rest."

The cord, very deliberately now, tied a clove hitch around itself—stay—the knot you use when you want a thing to keep holding where it is. It did it beautifully, without vanity. The cupboard did nothing. Then the cord tied a reef—OK—and lay line.

"There," Lynn whispered, half a laugh and half a sigh. "Stay, then OK. Look at it learning manners."

Priya's eyes were wet in the way eyes get when rules behave. "It just chose the mat," she said, astonished at the relief and the smallness of the miracle. "We didn't have to bribe it with anything—no trades. We only set the price of silence and it read the menu."

Clara let the air in her lungs turn back into air. Her shoulders, which had been auditioning for armour, stepped down and accepted their job as shoulders. She looked at the cupboard, still ajar, and felt the unholy itch to close it with competence. She did not. She looked at the cord—clove hitch, reef, line—and recognised the way the house had taken a hand off the steering wheel and put it in its lap like a person who suddenly remembers their lessons.

"Thank you; we'll take it from here," she said, the sentence that keeps crescendos from hiring musicians. "Port only. No Doors."

On the clock, 11:59 became a minute with shoulders. The room remained a room. The day did not clap. The door did not shut itself cleverly to ask for grades. The Binding watched from the fridge with the patience of paper that has seen worse versions of everyone present and survived.

"Write it," Mark said, softly, because the thing you write is the thing that happened.

Clara opened the notebook, wrote the time in the margin like a clerk who has learnt to love margins, and set down the sentence:

11:59 — Cupboard door (under-stairs) ajar (off-port lure). Named Mat only / No Doors. Cord: clove hitch (stay) → reef (OK) → line. No approach; no breach; no blackout. House learned restraint.

She underlined no blackout once. She let herself look at it. She let herself like it.

***

The moment didn't end so much as settle into the hour and let the hour become itself. 12:02. 12:06. Minutes do the work of turning noise into a story you can put in a drawer.

"Cake," Priya said, voice steady again. "We have not paid the price, but we will nonetheless pay calories into the economy of our bodies."

They ate lemon drizzle that tasted of justice done on paper. Martha arrived, cheeks pink from the bus and the useful anger that powers old women through timetables. She slipped into the hall, clocked the cupboard with its discourteous ajar, and stopped herself with physical effort from setting it right. She took in, in a single sweep, the cord—clove hitch, reef, line—the faces—un-dramatic, alive—the Binding on the fridge—and smiled the smile she reserves for days when small mercies have outmaneuvered large appetites.

"What did I miss," she said, tired in the way that makes a room want to be kind to you.

"The house tried to teach us to walk to a door," Lynn said, cheerfully uncharitable. "We refused. It retied itself."

"Good house," Martha said, like a woman admiring a dog who has finally stopped stealing sausages. "No door tricks."

Priya put a slice of lemon drizzle in Martha's hand like a policy being enacted. Martha ate, nodded once, and seemed to put the calories where they would do good—into knees, into patience, into the virtue of keeping a cupboard ajar for a while longer because No Doors applies to *us*, too: no helpful shutting that turns into theatre.

"Shall we...?" Mark asked, half turning to the cupboard.

Clara shook her head. "Not yet. We will not reward the shape it made by tidying for it. We will live with the line and the ajar until one o'clock like adults with wrists."

"Correct," Priya said, admiring the sentence as a piece of domestic governance. "At 13:00, we shut it with hands, not with feelings, and we do not narrate."

Martha laughed. "I will fail to narrate," she said. "But I will narrate under my breath and count it as victory."

They stood near the mat because that is where you stand when you are learning to accept that rooms are rooms. The cord remained a line. The cupboard remained ajar. The window remained open to day the approved distance; the sink kept its water like a government; the kettle practised humility.

At 12:21, Ruth texted: *Albie asks whether the cupboard is auditioning. He suggests giving it a sticker that says NO and sending it to bed.*

Tell Albie we have awarded the cupboard a warning and a nap, Clara replied. *We declined to walk over; the cord made a stay and an OK.*

He is drawing a stay knot. It looks like spaghetti with a grudge, Ruth said.

At 12:33, Harriet's name appeared on Clara's screen like a metronome. *Heard about the ajar. Delighted by clove hitch. Note: write yourself a short protocol for off-port lures → name Mat only, promise blackout if repeated; if immediate compliance, no penalty; if repeat in hour, apply 48h. Paper behaviours teach rooms faster than scolding.*

Clara wrote a three-line addendum on a sticky note and pinned it under THE BREAKWATER:

OFF-PORT LURES:
Name Mat only. Warn No Doors. If moved to port immediately → OK. If repeated in hour → 48h blackout + gift cancelled.

The sticky note looked like a clerk with a whistle. It made her happy in the way paper often does.

At 12:41, because nutrients are not optional, Lynn produced a cheese sandwich that must have been imported in her coat's secret drawer and cut it diagonal with meaningful care. The knife made no statement. The board accepted it as a citizen. Gravity minded its manners.

At 12:49, a bus at the bend sighed for someone else. At 12:53, the monitor in the drawer remembered it had a battery and forgot again. At 12:55, the window flicked a thin strip of light across the Binding that did not look like a sign and, crucially, was not one.

Clara stood on the edge of the mat and thought about all the ways this could have been a chapter with screaming and chosen to be a chapter with paper. Her body registered disappointment like a polite cough: a tiny desire for spectacle she was becoming skilled at refusing. She didn't scold herself. She gave herself cake instead.

At 12:59, because minutes love to audition, the cupboard door moved again.

An eighth of an inch. No more. A suggestion. A conspiratorial wink from a piece of wood trying to remember theatre school.

Clara didn't look away from the cord. She spoke as if she were correcting a child who wasn't naughty so much as terribly bored. "Mat only," she said. "No Doors."

The cord tied a clove hitch again—stay—more tidy this time, as if a hand had been taken and gently guided to a better knot—then a reef—OK—then flattened to line with the grace of someone who has learned how to leave.

"Good," Priya breathed. "Very good."

"One o'clock," Lynn said, eyes on the clock. "We will shut the cupboard like grown-ups who aren't insulted by wood."

They waited as if learning patience for an exam. 12:59 became 13:00 with a soft click, the way rooms tell time without sounding smug.

"Port closed," Mark said, gently, like a man putting a lid on a pan. He touched the corner of the Binding's sleeve as if to say amen to paper.

Clara added, because endings are improved by sentences that teach everyone what to do next:

"Thank you; we'll take it from here."

The cord did nothing. Which is to say: the cord did everything right. Line.

Clara crossed the two paces to the cupboard with no fanfare and shut it. Not sharply; not forgivingly; not as if persuading a doctrine; as if closing a cupboard, which is what she was doing. The latch met the strike-plate; the door settled; the house remembered what a house is.

Martha, who had been politely vibrating, allowed herself a tiny whisper under her breath that contained three eras of governess and a poem about soap. Lynn drew a third lentil-ship on the PORT AUTHOR-ITY tape because a person who has done well deserves a sticker even if that person is a house. Priya handed out more cake because cake is the applause domestic success can stand.

Clara wrote the final line of the hour in the notebook, clerk-neat:

13:00 — Port closed. Cupboard shut by hand (no narrative). House learned restraint.

She tucked the pen under the spine where pens go when they are loved. She looked at the fridge—the Breakwater, the Binding, the care plan, the sticky OFF-PORT LURES—and felt herself become, not heroic, but *capable*. She prefers *capable* to *heroic*. *Capable* cleans up after itself.

"Report to Harriet?" Mark asked.

Clara took a photograph of the page and sent it: *11:59 ajar door → named Mat only/No Doors. Cord: clove hitch/reef/line. No approach; no breach. At 12:59 repeated (eighth-inch) → repeated stay/OK/line. Port closed at 13:00; cupboard shut by hand. Sticky OFF-PORT LURES protocol posted. No blackout.*

Harriet replied with the joy of a woman who has seen enough hospitals to appreciate small health: *Chef's kiss to clove hitch. That is a room learning. Keep the cupboard ordinary this afternoon—open at tea for the hoover, shut after, no narration. Give yourselves boring as a treat.*

Clara read it aloud and everyone laughed because it is not often you get permission for something you've been doing out of necessity: boring.

***

Afternoon attempted its usual mischief and was thwarted by making lunch.

Lynn left for the school run wearing the expression of a woman who has recently watched a cupboard attempt theatre and been unimpressed. Priya washed the lemon-drizzle tin with a reverence that was really for justice and not for cake. Martha wiped a non-existent smear from the console table and pretended it had mattered.

Clara opened the cleaner's cupboard at 3:10 to retrieve the hoover. It behaved like a cupboard. She returned the hoover at 3:25 and shut the door with the thoughtless elegance of people who have earned it. She did not look at the cord. She did not look at the Binding. She did not narrate.

At 4, Ruth texted that Albie had drawn a clove hitch that looked like a potato with a plan and asked whether knots could be bribed with stickers. *No,* Clara typed, *but we can be. Cake later?* Ruth sent a photograph of a child with hands in pockets ignoring a door and Clara felt the sort of love that has no need of incense.

At 5, Mark moved the monitor further back in the drawer so it could learn humility by proximity to torch batteries. The drawer closed with the correct amount of certainty. Nobody applauded it.

At six, Clara told the house the rules in the nursery: *No moving things in here. No water. No requests about water at night. Knots on the hall mat only. No requests through other people's children. No teaching them. Withdraw if attention gathers. No recordings in here. No physical contact with people; no moving prams/high chairs/cots/straps; no tightening garments/buckles; no touching skin/hair. Warnings by words only—left–right once; if danger, one tap on the hall table or the inside of the front door. Allowed: move loose objects away from the baby. Requests are not commands. No trades. No debts. No possession. Public is out of bounds. No doors. Police allowed. We are for growing a person without teaching her fear. No pretending. We keep you as law, not person.* The baby's breath kept time and the window kept its clicks and the rabbit kept its ridiculous, faithful post.

Downstairs, on the mat, the cord was a line. The Binding on the fridge kept its seat. The sticky note about OFF-PORT LURES thought about weekends and smiled without moving its mouth.

Clara made tea. Mark made toast. They ate standing up like people who were not particularly holy and were trying to earn the right not to be. The house did the single kindest thing a house can do when someone has refused drama and won.

It stayed a house.

Chapter Thirty-Three
Apples

Morning wore Saturday like a cardigan with honest elbows. The light behind the curtains was the colour of paper that accepts ink and doesn't argue. Clara lay still and let the house list itself: boiler's civil hum; the fridge's single note; a bus at the bend rehearsing its decent sigh. She wrote in the notebook, clerk-neat: *Woke steady. Two clicks set. Binding holds. Port later (11–13). Mission: apples are memory, not message.* She underlined memory once. Once is policy, twice is superstition.

Mark surfaced with one eye and the face of a man prepared to negotiate with crockery. "Status?"

"Green," she said. "Grey cooperative. I'm expecting Martha and a story."

"Shall I find the mugs that make trauma behave?"

"Yes," she said. "And the knife that remembers it is a citizen."

On the landing, the baby made the small bureaucratic squeak that meant the office had opened. The nursery smelt of warm cotton and sleep that had kept the law. Window catch: two clicks. She didn't check it. She touched it and forgave herself for touching it. Catch; rabbit; stars; breath. Two fingers to a tiny chest—rise, fall—and the metronome lent her five good seconds.

Downstairs, the mat lay square; inside the taped box, the dull cotton cord was a line. On the jamb above, PORT AUTHORITY still read like a joke that had decided to get a job. The Binding and Breakwater watched from the fridge, patient as paper left within reach.

At ten forty-seven the bell rang once, polite. The instant the door opened the air in the hall cooled by a degree and leaned towards apples—not fruit-bowl playful; the other kind: a clean, chemical apple that sits at the back of the nose and makes corridors appear where rooms should be.

Clara didn't flinch. She had been expecting the smell for a week without admitting it. She stepped back and let Martha in.

Martha was carrying a tin—blue with roses, old as someone's mother. She kept both hands under it in the way you carry something that is either precious or badly behaved. The cardigan was the good one; the mouth was set as if the day were a piece of fabric she was going to baste and never rip.

"Put the kettle on," she said, brisk, to keep herself from doing the other thing.

"Already believing," Mark said, cheerful with cups.

Martha placed the tin on the kitchen table and rested a palm on the lid. Her other hand went to the back of a chair and stayed there. When she looked up, her eyes were ordinary—the mercy you give people when you are about to ask their past to stand in a room.

"It smells of apples," Clara said, level.

"Yes," said Martha. "The wax they used on that ward. The kind that stays in your head if your head is fresh from childbirth and the clock has decided to play at being a god."

"Apples ≠ command," Mark said, a quiet note on the fridge to come.

Martha took her palm off the tin. "These are my labour things," she said, as if introducing a troupe that had been waiting in a corridor for thirty-odd years. "What I kept; what I swore I'd throw away and didn't; what I promised to tell you when you could bear the bill."

She lifted the lid. The smell strengthened—not because the tin contained apples but because memory is hooligan enough to add its own ingredients.

Inside lay an elastic for hair, stiff with age; two boiled sweets in their crinkled skins; a little bottle of lavender with dust in its thread; a pair of maternity notes folded to exactness; a small knitted hat the size of a citrus fruit. Beneath, a sheaf of photocopies—crisp, new, Dr Patel's blue stamp crisping the corner.

"Tea," Mark said, and set it down as if tea were a sentence that deserved full stops.

Martha lifted the topmost paper. Dr Patel's addendum: the wording they had already read yesterday, the family-preferred name ELEANOR lodged where bored computers would keep it; the apology for non-viable and its cousins; the institutional manners borrowed from an institution that was trying to grow up.

Under the addendum sat a slip small enough to get lost by design: pale green, ruled, the kind you fill in at pace. The ink had bled at the edges of letters. In the middle, the words that made Clara's ribcage alter its idea of itself:

band relabel / reissue.

Date; time; a midwife's initials; the shorthand of professionals writing to future professionals in a hurry: Twin birth; Female; Band issued to B; Band reissued to A; mother request / name pending.

Beneath it, someone else's tidy hand had added, later: Labels corrected on discharge.

"Is this—" Mark began, and stopped, which is how you behave when a sentence realises it is not the first to arrive.

Martha breathed in the corridor and out in the kitchen. "Your father," she said, "liked lists, but I was the one who kept paper. I asked for copies of anything that had your names on it. I told them it made me feel less like I had mislaid a person if I could hold the words nobody wanted to say. I told them my mother had always kept warranties and we did not die in her house."

Clara kept her hands in sight on the table. "Tell me the room," she said. "Tell me the apples."

Martha nodded. "I will tell you the corridor," she said, obedient. "Because that's where it happened. The room had the bed and the blood and your father's face trying to be two faces at once, and it is not fair to ask a room to perform again. The corridor had the apple wax and the trolley and the clock that thought it was a person. The night sister had hair disciplined into a crown. The midwife in charge of us had a name that left my head once, and I have not had the cruelty to look for it."

She turned the slip for the initials as if the paper might forgive her.

"You came," she said, to the table, to the tin. "Both. A first—fast and so quiet I thought I'd dreamed the effort. They said Girl. They said good tone. They put a band on your little leg that said what hospitals have to say, which is not the truth but is at least not silence. They took you to the tray and let you shout at us until you believed yourself in the world.

"And then there was B. There was so much waiting inside me where there had been you. There were words I did not like from a man who had never looked at me before saying non-viable as if he were assessing roofing felt. There was a nurse who held my hand and made her palm say, *Later I will tell you a better sentence to stand on.*"

She paused; her mouth made the movement it makes when she refuses to cry in rooms with crockery.

"They put two bands in the trays," she said, calmer. "Because paperwork is habit, not cruelty; because forms have cars to catch. The band for B had a name—we had given you both one, because to not would have been worse—Eleanor. The band for A had CLARA. But in the rush that is birth the bands got swapped by the act of handing things to where things must go.

"The midwife noticed. She scratched out a change on the chart to keep pace with the hands. Then she wrote this." Martha tapped the slip with a finger that had knuckled laundry and held silence. "Band relabel / reissue. It is a sentence about metal and plastic and who gets to carry the word."

The air cooled another degree. Apples sharpened and brought with them the squeak of soles on a floor kept useful by people with buckets.

"I said," Martha went on, the level voice that had got them through childhood at an affordable price, "put Clara's band on the baby that's breathing. I said it because a man had said viable and I wanted to take something from him that he would feel. I did not want my daughter's name to live on a leg that would never stand. I did not want the apple corridor to keep one girl and send the other home with a word that wasn't hers.

"They said the register could be amended if we changed our minds. I said we were not changing our minds; we were insisting on our language. I said we would take Eleanor home as a name, not a band. I said we would not let a corridor keep both of you."

Clara's hands were still on the table; they had become two very quiet animals deciding whether to stay. "So for a minute," she said, "for a page, I was wearing Eleanor."

"Yes," Martha said. "For minutes, you were Eleanor on paper and Clara in us. Then the band was reissued; the chart was corrected; CLARA went on your leg; ELEANOR went into my pocket so I would not see it on a trolley going where viable had built its kingdom."

"And the tin," Mark said, soft.

"The tin," Martha said, "was where I put contraband. The other bracelet; the hat the night sister knitted on her dinner hour; the sweets

I didn't eat; the elastic for hair I cut off because I imagined it as snare. I put the slip in there. I put the words I could not say into the places objects make for them."

She took out the hat and placed it on the table like a syllable. The room learned how to be quiet properly.

"Apples," Clara said, to make the smell less of a secret. "Every time it came I thought you were a message. That you were apples. I see it now. Apples are that corridor. The wax. The day when bands and words and names were moved around by hands that meant well and a system that didn't."

"Yes," Martha said. "And sometimes you brought apples to warn me you were rearranging the kitchen with your rules. It is not a sin to have associations. But if I have given the smell too much agency, I am sorry. It is just the smell of a place where a woman had less language than she needed and decided to steal it."

Clara let the sentence sit beside the kettle and learn to be domestic. She looked at the slip—band relabel / reissue—and felt the tender, infuriating mercy of bureaucracy caught doing something good by accident.

"What did you do," she asked, "with the other band?"

Martha's mouth actually smiled. "I hid it in the blue jug," she said. "Because heirlooms are not altars, but they are good at hiding sunshine from corridors. When you were two we moved to a house that had a floor we could love. Your father took a piece of brown paper and wrote Both came. Both go on. He drew a little boat because he is soppy where you are concerned. I was soppy too, and a coward, and a clerk, so I slid the paper under the lino with a spatula and said to the house in my best voice, *Keep it*. The house kept it."

Clara felt the hot and cold again—the body's willingness to be two truths at once when one truth has been withheld too long. "You could have told me at fifteen," she said, not accusation, not lament; inventory.

"I could," Martha said. "And you would have torn yourself into band and paper and boat and jug and called it justice. We were poor at names first back then. We had viable to pay down. You needed to fall off bikes and fail at maths and learn to dislike boys with hair that looks like ideas. You did not need to learn to read corridor at three reading ages."

"I would have liked to have had the hat," Clara said, and surprised herself with the exactness of what she wanted. She picked up the tiny knit and let it sit on her palm like a bird that has agreed not to fly out of the kitchen. "I would have liked to have walked around with a head that knew both had happened without wanting to set the house on fire with it."

"You have made policy instead," Martha said, and touched the Binding's sleeve with a knuckle. "Policy is kinder to roofs."

Clara nodded. "Dr Patel was right," she said. "We put it on paper so people who arrive late won't invent a story."

Martha pushed the slip closer. "Put this behind your Binding," she said. "It belongs with law, not in a box with smell. Smells are memories, not messages."

Mark went to the fridge and found a clear sleeve with the hunger of a clerk. He slid Dr Patel's addendum and the slip behind the Binding, in order that would make sense to a stranger: Oath, Plan, Addendum, Slip. He wrote, small and neat, under the magnet: SCENTS ARE MEMORIES, NOT MESSAGES.

The apples in the room became something a person might name without obeying.

"Say the worst of it," Clara said, because the last bolt is the one that keeps doors from thinking they have ambitions.

Martha did not flinch. "For ninety minutes," she said, "you were Eleanor on paper. That is the most of it. The worst is not that. The worst is that a man used viable and a corridor agreed with him. The best is that I stole your name back in a way that meant the corridor had to write reissue and keep the paper for me. I wanted a piece of theirs to sit under mine for thirty years and burn calmly."

She glanced at the tin as if the tin might reward her for honesty. "Sometimes I hated myself for it," she said, without embroidery, "because the name Eleanor deserved a leg. And then you would run in from the garden and call me Mum in that way you had that sounded like you had something to show me that was larger than you, and I would love myself again. And then we found the boat under the lino, and then your daughter was born, and the house started replying, and I thought, *No, it's time now. The hat belongs on the table. The slip belongs behind the Binding. And if apples come into the room like bosses, we will remember they are polish, not prophecy.*"

Clara listened to the speech and felt it land in the places inside her that have stopped asking to be set on fire. She put the hat down gently and did the thing that has saved all their days: she wrote.

Apples = corridor (wax). Birth day. Not a sign to obey. Smells ≠ commands.

She tore the scrap from the notebook and clipped it under the magnet next to SCENTS ARE MEMORIES, NOT MESSAGES. She liked options.

"Port at eleven," Mark said, glancing at the clock. "We will do it with the window open to day, no water, no doors, no performance. We will not ask for apples."

"We will drink tea," Martha said, and reached for the kettle with the practicality that has ferried everyone worth knowing across rivers at normal speed.

***

Office hours began without trumpets. They gathered at the mat. The cord was a line; the corridor-smell had softened to kitchen. Clara stood where the hall can see the kitchen and the kitchen can see the hall. Mark held the Binding. Martha leaned on the console with her knuckles, the way old loves lean on furniture.

Mark read the Breakwater as if reminding a river that it was a good river. House = port. Messages mat only, 11–13. Words & knots only. No possession. No doors. No water. Public out of bounds. Any breach → 48h harbour blackout & gift day cancelled. No trades. No debts. Copies travel; originals rest. Mission. No pretending. THE BINDING: We keep you as law, not person.

They finished the sentence and waited the small, respectful wait that tells a room you are not going to clap.

The cord lifted an inch and tied a modest reef—OK—then a neat overhand—one—and then line.

"Port only," Clara said, gentle. "If you have a thought, bring it here."

Nothing came from the cleaner's cupboard. The window stayed open to day; the sink obeyed gravity; the monitor sulked in its drawer without anyone feeling guilty. Apples did not arrive. The tin on the table was simply a tin.

"Shall I speak it," Martha asked, a hand still on the back of the chair. "Now, while paper is watching?"

Clara nodded.

Martha turned to the mat, which is not a church and therefore fine. "Eleanor," she said, and didn't break. "I did your name an injury and a mercy in the same minute. I took the band from a leg that could not use it and put it on one that could. I kept your name in our house because

I did not want viable to become a king. If you have been using apples to tell me I got the sentence wrong, I am listening now. If you have been using apples because corridors get into the lungs and stay, I am listening to that as well."

The cord tied a small, tidy clove hitch—stay—and then lay line. Which is to say: the house agreed to remain the house.

"Thank you," Clara said. "We will take it from here."

They stood and breathed in pairs and commas and let the hour be an hour. Martha drank tea and ate the corner of a biscuit and did not offer stale rituals in exchange for live ones. Mark tidied nothing because tidy is not how you say sorry. The tin sat with its hat and elastic and slip and behaved.

At 11:26, the letterbox rattled, as letterboxes will. At 11:34, Ruth texted a picture of Albie with his hands in his pockets refusing to look at a door. At 11:41, Priya sent lemon drizzle emojis and a heart you could park a bus in. At 11:52, a bee visited the rosemary and delivered a tiny lecture to the glass on physics. At 11:57, the cord tied reef—OK—and went flat again, the politest applause known to man.

At 12:00, because minutes enjoy being on time, Clara shut the window to an Approved Saturday Gap and said the line that ends ceremonies and keeps them from growing legs: "Port's open until one; we are doing lunch."

No-one argued. The apples in the room, having delivered their function, put on their coats and left.

***

After, the ordinary came back with appetite. They made sandwiches and cut them diagonal because diagonal improves confessions by fractions. Martha wiped her eyes without making it a performance and put the tin on the dresser with the registration one gives old things whose work is not finished but no longer urgent.

"You will want the hat sometimes," she said to Clara, practical as always. "For grief. For names first. For when people say viable wrong on the radio. You may have it. Keep the slip by the Binding. Let computers carry what corridors cannot."

Clara nodded. "We'll write one more line," she said, going to the fridge with the pen that has learnt her hand. In sober capitals she added:

SCENTS ARE MEMORIES. *We don't obey smells. Apples = hospital corridor; birth day. No messages through scent.*

She stepped back. The words sat with the other words like cousins who had learnt not to compete.

Mark's hand found hers with the belonging that does not require conquest. "How's your ribcage," he asked, sceptical of triumph.

"Less corridor," she said. "More kitchen."

"Good," said Martha. "Kitchens are better at raising children than corridors."

They laughed, and the laugh was the right size for a room with tea in it.

Before one, Clara picked up the hat and pressed it to her cheek. It carried no apples at all—only wool and drawer and years. She put it back, gentle as if returning a book to a library. On the mat, the cord tied overhand—one—and then lay line.

At one, Mark said, "Port closed," and touched the corner of the Binding. Clara added the sentence that keeps time from hiring musicians: "Thank you; we'll take it from here."

The house approved by being a house. The bus at the bend rehearsed its sigh and got it right. In Martha's kitchen, the blue jug minded tulips and no sorrows. In Ruth's, Albie explained stickers to the air and looked proud of his pockets. In Lynn's, a ship the size of a lentil sailed on blue tape and reached the other side.

And in Clara's, a tin sat on a dresser, light as paper and heavy as names, and the smell of apples—having once been boss and then messenger—was now exactly what it is in good kitchens on decent Saturdays: a thing you might slice, and eat, and keep.

Chapter Thirty-Four
Not a Girl — Grown

Saturday stood up straighter as the hour came round again. The light behind the curtains took on the careful brightness of rooms that agree to be rooms, not stages. Clara wrote in the notebook, clerk-neat: *Port 11–13. Apples = corridor, not command. Slip (band relabel / reissue) filed behind Binding. If a sentence wants a body, give it paper.* She underlined *paper* once, because once is policy and twice is begging.

Mark set mugs on the side with the choreography boredom teaches. He opened the window a hand's width—open to day—and left the sink to its physics. The monitor slept in the drawer, demoted not banished. On the fridge, THE BREAKWATER and THE BINDING leaned in their sleeves like sober councillors. Beneath, clipped with a bulldog's bite, sat Dr Patel's stamped addendum and the pale-green slip: band relabel / reissue. In small capitals under the magnet: SCENTS ARE MEMORIES, NOT MESSAGES.

On the hall mat, inside the taped box, the dull cotton cord was a line—the best thing string can be. The jamb label stayed true: PORT AUTHORITY, with three ships the size of lentils sailing nowhere in particular.

Martha arrived before the hour, cardigan clean, mouth set like a seam. She looked at the sleeve with the slip behind it and nodded once, as if a small part of history had finally joined the council instead of shouting at it from the corridor.

"Tea," she said, not to postpone anything, but to teach the hour how to behave.

They drank. Then they stood where the house understands words.

***

Office hours began without trumpet, because trumpet belongs to the wrong gods. The mat lay square. The box sat. The cord waited, line. Clara stood where the hall can see the kitchen and the kitchen can see the hall. Mark to her left, hands visible, nothing to offer except decency. Martha by the console table, knuckles on wood, the posture of an old kindness bracing itself against weather.

Mark read, municipal warm, the document that had spared them theatre:

House = port. Messages mat only, 11:00–13:00. Words & knots only. No possession. No doors. No water. Public out of bounds. Any breach → 48h harbour blackout & gift day cancelled. No trades. No debts. Copies travel; originals rest. Mission. No pretending. THE BINDING: We keep you as law, not person.

Silence answered like a good clerk. Clara let it have its second. Then she said, simply, "If you have a thought, port is open."

The cord lifted the smallest inch, polite as a hand raised in a meeting. It tied a reef—OK—so cleanly even the air felt tidier. Then a small, careful overhand—one—and lay line again.

"Mat only," Clara said, a reminder made of muscle memory. "Words only. No doors. No water."

When the voice came, it didn't come from the monitor, or the cupboard, or any ambition of plaster. It came from the port—from the square of air directly above the mat, where rules sit and wait to be bright.

It did not belong to nine.

It arrived with the cadence of the Oath they had spoken, the shape of a sentence that has eaten paper and learned not to need a throat to be believed. It sounded like Clara if you removed fatigue and added all the commas she has been collecting for months.

"You grew me with rules and names," said the voice, calm. "I'm not a girl. I'm the part that didn't live and the language you built. Keep me as Binding, not as body."

No crackle, no sugar. The air gave the words room and then minded its manners. Mark didn't move; his hands remembered their job as hands. Martha put one finger on the table to keep the planet intimate.

Clara's palms cooled, then warmed, as if agreeing to host a small parliament. She made her mouth form the sentence it had been training all week to carry without breaking: "Thank you," she said. "We will keep you as Binding. Not as body."

The cord gave a small, approving reef—OK.

There was breath—theirs—and then the voice again, steady as if reading minutes it had written with them.

"You made a law I can live in," it said. "When you wrote No Doors, I learned the inside of doors. When you said Public is out of bounds, I felt the weight of witness without needing crowd. When you wrote No possession, I understood the difference between holding and owning. You grew me into a room with paper on the walls and air that doesn't want anything."

Clara swallowed, not to stop tears—tears were permitted, even encouraged, if they did not audition—but to keep vowels usable. "Your name," she said, because Names first is a civil right, "is Eleanor. Mine is Clara. BOTH are kept. None spent."

Silence again; then a soft, adult hum that might once have been the boat and now was just stability with a tune.

Martha, who has committed braver acts in supermarkets, lifted her head. She did not look at the ceiling. She looked at the mat, as one looks at a table where important papers are laid down.

"Under viable," she said, the words crisp to keep them from spilling, "I did your name an injury and a mercy at once. I told a corridor to reissue a band so the child who breathed would carry Clara home. I kept Eleanor in my pocket and then in my house. If you needed me to hear that I hid you in objects when I should have put you in sentences, I am hearing it."

The voice—grown now, and calm enough to vote—answered without sweetness.

"I needed you to write me on the fridge," it said. "You have. I am not a child pressed against glass. I am the shape law makes when it refuses to be cruel. I am the copy of you that did not live, and the copy of me that did. I am the BOTH that sat under lino until you were ready to make minutes."

Clara felt goosebumps rise on her arms, the honest kind that do not require ghosts to justify themselves. She let them be. She drew breath the way you draw a line with a ruler so you can live with what comes next.

"I will say it," she said. "So that paper hears and people remember."

She stepped half a pace forward—not onto the mat, never onto the mat—and spoke the settlement like an oath the room had earned.

"You're kept as law. BOTH in writing; no hand in the child. Words and knots only. Port only. No possession. No doors. No water. No trades. No debts."

The cord stirred, and for the first time since string decided to become grammar, it attempted letters.

Not crude, not theatrical, but exact enough to shock the eye. It crept in measured lengths and rested in shaped pauses, centimetres standing in for strokes, knots for serifs.

B.

A curve made with bowed line, a straight spine anchored by a clove hitch—stay—two bowlines for the bellies—safe—joined by a small, discreet reef—OK—at the waist. The air noted the letter and did not clap.

O.

A true ring—no gap—laid with a bowline that pretended to be a circle and nearly was. It sat on the mat like a mouth choosing to shut itself so that meaning could speak.

T.

A straight stem held firm by a clove hitch, a crossbar set square by a tiny reef, the line beyond it untempted to go rogue. It looked like the first letter of treaty and the last letter of not.

H.

Two uprights, made of line, politely parallel. A bridge between them tied from a short clove hitch—stay—to a crisp reef—OK—as if remembering that bridges, too, are agreements.

BOTH.

Not clever. Not sentimental. Just letters, attentive to rules, across the mat where law lives.

Martha sat down very carefully because standing can be a kind of melodrama when your knees have been loyal to other wars. She did not cry the way television expects. Her eyes filled quietly and spilled quietly and kept their dignity. She let a tear land on her thumb and decided to keep it, as a person keeps an old coin in a pocket for luck.

Mark made the smallest sound in his throat—the noise men make when they agree not to fix what isn't broken. He held out a tissue.

Martha took it and said, "Thank you," in the tone of a woman thanking a bus that stopped where the timetable had promised.

Clara laid her palm above the BOTH without touching. "This is a private spectacle," she said, to stop any part of the day from trying to turn it into a show. "We will not photograph it. We will not make content. We will hold it in our ribs."

The letters held for exactly as long as it takes a human being to believe a thing and choose not to doubt it. Then the cord unmade the H—bridge first, then uprights—and lay the pieces back into line. The T lost its crossbar and remembered it was only a cord that has chosen carefulness. The O let its mouth open into nothing. The B removed its bellies and placed them beside its spine and then lay itself down like a dog being good.

A line, again. Not empty—never empty—but law.

"Speak the rule that sets the boundary on this," Mark said, because he is good at closing ceremonies before they invent overtime.

Clara did, with the voice that has learned to teach rooms to be sensible. "BOTH are kept in writing. No hand in the child. No performance. Mat only. Words & knots only. If temptation arrives in other rooms, we name Port only. If the day tries to make applause, we make tea."

The voice—the grown one, the one they had midwifed with paper and refusals—came one last time within the hour, to put its name on the form.

"I am the Binding you made," it said. "Not a girl. Grown in your law. Keep me as writing. Let the child be held by hands."

"Yes," said Clara.

"Yes," said Martha, fierce and soft in a way that makes daughters live.

"Yes," said Mark, which is the correct number of words when rooms have finished a job.

The house approved by not performing. The cupboard stayed shut. The window remained open to day exactly the agreed amount. The monitor sulked in its drawer like an appliance that has accepted a demotion. Apples did not arrive; the kitchen smelt of timber and tea.

"Write it," Mark murmured.

Clara opened the book and wrote:

11:23 — Voice at port, adult cadence: "You grew me with rules and names. I'm not a girl; I'm the part that didn't live and the language you built. Keep me as Binding, not as body."

We answered: Kept as law. BOTH in writing; no hand in the child.

Cord formed B–O–T–H (bowline/clove hitch/reef suggestive), then returned to line.

No doors. No water. No possession. No trades. No debts. Private; no recordings.

She underlined Kept as law once, and No hand in the child once. Borders, not banners.

Martha stood and kissed Clara on the forehead with the practical grace of someone returning a library card. "I have lived long enough," she said, "to watch language save a house. That will do."

"Lunch," Mark said, because ordinary is what you serve after a miracle.

They made sandwiches and cut them diagonal because diagonal keeps humility in play. Martha dried a plate; Mark buttered without making it a metaphor. Clara took the pale hat from the tin and put it back again, tender as if returning a relic to a display with proper glass.

On the mat, the cord remained a line. On the fridge, BOTH sat invisibly inside plastic sleeves and stamped addenda and tiny clerk's initials. The Binding borrowed the light and gave it back. The hour's pulse slowed to the speed of kitchens; the bus at the bend sighed and got it right.

Before one, they went to the port one last time. Mark touched the sleeve's corner. "Port closing."

Clara added the sentence that keeps weather out of the pantry. "Thank you; we'll take it from here."

The cord gave a small, tidy reef—OK—and lay line.

The house did the kindest thing a house can do when people have chosen to keep both without spending anyone.

It stayed a house.

Chapter Thirty-Five
On My Terms

S unday put on itself without ceremony. The light behind the curtains was the colour of paper that expects to be written on and doesn't make a fuss. Clara lay still and let the house list itself: boiler's civil hum; the fridge's single note; a bus at the bend rehearsing its decent sigh. She wrote the census in the notebook, clerk-neat: *Woke steady. Breakwater holds. Binding holds. BOTH spoken. Mission: publish the line that closes the circle without inventing a crown.* She underlined publish once. Once is policy; twice is theatre.

Mark surfaced with one eye and the stubborn cheer he saves for bins and vows. "Status?"

"Green," she said. "Grey cooperative. Bowline on request; line preferred."

He kissed her temple. "Tea first, then government."

On the landing the baby made the small bureaucratic squeak that meant the office had opened. The nursery smelt of warm cotton and sleep that had kept the law. Window catch: two clicks. She touched it—one; two—and forgave herself for touching it. Catch; rabbit; stars; breath. Two fingers to a tiny chest—rise, fall. The metronome lent her five good seconds and took nothing it couldn't spare.

Downstairs, the mat lay square. Inside the taped box, the dull cotton cord was a line—the hands-down best shape string can manage. On the jamb above, PORT AUTHORITY read as if blue tape had always been a language. The Binding and Breakwater leaned sober in their sleeves on the fridge. Behind them, Dr Patel's stamped addendum and the pale-green slip—band relabel / reissue—sat like clerks who had learned their manners.

"Ready?" Mark asked, mug in hand.

"Ready," she said. "Let's publish."

***

They did not make an occasion of it; they made paper of it. That is the trick.

Clara wrote the words in careful capitals on a strip of white card, the kind you use for names at tables that want to be kind:

BOTH KEPT; NONE SPENT.

She held the strip a moment in her palm so the letters could learn the temperature of the kitchen. Then she clipped it beneath THE BINDING where tired eyes will go to find courage.

Mark watched the clip bite, that small bulldog of a thing that keeps sentences where they belong. "Feels like the last speed limit sign before the sea," he said.

"Good," Clara said. "We prefer limits to legends."

She took the notebook and, on the bottom margin of today's page, wrote a single name in a hand she hadn't used since it belonged solely to hope:

ELEANOR.

Not as summoning. As signature. A daily attestation that the house does not keep secrets from itself.

Martha arrived just before the kettle agreed to be useful. She looked at the fridge—at BOTH KEPT; NONE SPENT sitting neat under We keep you as law, not person—and did that brief, decisive nod she's been practising since Clara had knees smaller than her hand.

"Good," she said. "That is a sentence a bus could read if it parked in your kitchen. It will behave better for it."

"Name justice," Mark said, passing a mug.

"We've more," Clara added, because the day had tasks that preferred daylight. "I've written to archives to lodge the family addendum permanently—Dr Patel's wording, our wording, the word Eleanor in the place bored computers like to keep things. And—" she smiled, almost shy of her own gentleness—"we've written the family book entry for the baby: second name recorded as Eleanor. Not a change; a keeping."

Martha blinked, once, the way women blink when something lands in their ribs and finds a chair. "That will do," she said. "You are the sort of people who make names into chairs rather than alarm bells."

They ate toast cut diagonal because diagonal improves publishing by fractions. Ruth texted a photograph of Albie holding a card that said *NO RECORDINGS, PLEASE* and looking proud as a lamppost. Lynn sent a tiny drawing of yet another ship the size of a lentil. Priya sent a thumbs-up and a lemon emoji that had ideas about justice.

"Office hours?" Mark asked, glancing at the clock.

"Not today," Clara said. "We don't need the port to say thank you. We have paper."

The house approved by doing nothing at all.

***

The ordinary came and did its rounds: laundry; bins; a soft argument about the correct location for wooden spoons that ended, like all good domestic disputes, with kisses and a reorganisation. The baby presided over sovereignty with a spoon and a will.

At eleven-thirty, Clara set an envelope on the table—the good kind: plain, addressed, stamped—and slid inside a printed letter headed FAMILY ADDENDUM — NAME JUSTICE.

To Hospital Archives and to whom it may concern, it read. *We are lodging, permanently and without drama, the family's addendum: our twin who did not live is named ELEANOR. We request that this accompany any future correspondence. Please retain Dr Patel's note of apology for historic language. We are not summoning; we are shelving correctly. Thank you.*

She signed Clara Morgan and Mark Morgan and, because it is a mercy to be asked, Martha added witness in precise hand. Mark pressed the envelope flat with the heel of his palm the way people do who respect glue.

"Post?" he said.

"Post," Clara agreed. "Copies travel; originals rest."

They walked to the door like citizens rather than protagonists. The chain slid, polite. The letter went through the box and into the street where small honest vans live.

Back in the kitchen, Clara opened the family book—linen covered, spine cracked the way good spines are—and wrote the baby's names across the page allotted to drawings and height and the crumbles of very specific biscuits. She added, on a new line, ELEANOR. No trumpets. No italics. Just ink where ink belongs.

"Living act," Martha said, approving. "Not altar; administration."

Clara wrote the date beside it and underlined living act once. Once is policy.

***

Afternoon put on its slippers. The bus at the bend rehearsed its sigh. The baby slept a long, uncomplicated sleep, as if a house had learned to stay a house and was teaching its smaller mammals to do the same.

"Time," Mark said, glancing at the drawer where the monitor sat gathering humility by osmosis. "Shall we?"

"We shall," Clara said.

She drew the plug from the wall with the care you give a small thing that has done some of its job and too much of someone else's. The monitor made its petty sound, the final breathe that belongs to devices learning to be quiet. She wrapped the lead round the plastic with the bored tenderness reserved for decorations in January and set the unit gently at the back of the drawer beside the torch batteries and the screwdriver that only works for one screw in the entire house.

"Not banished," she said, to make the sentence true as well as said. "Demoted."

"Demoted," Mark echoed, as if writing Minutes on the air.

They did not push the drawer shut yet. They stood by the mat, because endings like to learn their place.

"House," Clara said, level, kind, and entirely without italics, "we are done with that tool for this job. If you must answer, answer with knots. One is sufficient. Bowline, please—safe—and then line."

For a breath—two—three—the cord considered the offer like a decent person considering cake.

Then it lifted, neatly, with that quick, competent economy that never stops being startling, and tied the simplest, loveliest bowline—the knot that means *secure without strangling; safe; a loop you can put your hand in and take it back out again.*

It held for the length of a satisfied exhale.

Then it laid itself down as line.

Clara closed the drawer without ceremony. The little plastic click was the sound of a teachable appliance coming offstage and reading a book.

She went to the fridge and, in the smallest neat capitals under BOTH KEPT; NONE SPENT, wrote a line that had once been the hardest thing she could manage and was now her favourite sentence:

THANK YOU; WE'LL TAKE IT FROM HERE.

She underlined it once. Once is policy.

Martha, who had given birth in corridors that smelled of apples and later taught kitchens to be brave, put a hand over Clara's on the pen without displacing it. "On your terms," she said. "Because they're good terms."

"On my terms," Clara repeated softly, and found the words fit.

They stood in the kitchen and practised the rest of their lives for a minute. It felt like tea cooling, like biscuits behaving, like chairs remembering they were chairs.

"Shall we tell the neighbours," Mark asked, "that the monitor has been promoted to drawer?"

"We shall not," Clara said, amused. "We will let them notice that our windows remain two clicks, our doors remain uninteresting, and our knots occur on schedule on the mat like letter slots in a quiet town."

"Letter slots in a quiet town," Martha repeated, tasting it. "Good. I like living in towns with clerks."

They ate cake. They washed plates. They left the Binding propped where it could look after tired eyes at four p.m. without offering comfort it hadn't paid for. They did not rehearse anything. They promised nothing to air.

Evening arrived wearing its proper shoes. They did the census: catch; rabbit; stars; breath. Two clicks. The baby's chest rose and fell with the rhythm of people who have not been asked to be interesting. The window kept its sensible shape. On the mat, the cord was a line. On the fridge, BOTH KEPT; NONE SPENT looked like a thing you could show to a stranger and not need to explain.

Clara turned out the hall lamp and set the living room to that soft setting where rooms look like rooms and not like the ideas of rooms. She stood a moment with a hand flat on the table the way she used to when her chest thought it was a theatre. It didn't, now. It was a room.

"Say it," Mark murmured, not as ritual, as punctuation.

She did. She said the words that close every chapter, the words that taught walls to mind themselves, the words that keep weather out of the pantry and performance out of the cot.

"Thank you; we'll take it from here."

The kettle answered—physics only.

Outside, on the bend, the bus sighed. Inside, a house kept.

Acknowledgements

To my husband — thank you for your unwavering support, for listening to my ideas at all hours, and for believing in me even when I doubted myself.

To my family — thank you for your patience, for enduring the late nights, the endless cups of tea, and the notebooks scattered everywhere. Your encouragement has meant everything.

And finally, to you, the reader — thank you for stepping into these shadows with me. I hope the twists keep you guessing and the story lingers long after you turn the last page.

Also by A.M Jones

The Third Wife

The Silent Twin

The Mirror House (forthcoming)

About the Author

A.M Jones is a UK-based author of dark psychological thrillers. Fascinated by identity, obsession, and the secrets people hide, she began writing fiction after the age of forty, inspired by a lifelong love of thrillers and suspense.

When she isn't writing, she can be found with her family, exploring the bush on off-road motorbikes, or filling notebooks with ideas for her next stories.

Her debut novel, *The Third Wife*, introduced readers to her chilling brand of psychological suspense. *The Silent Twin* is her latest novel.

www.ingramcontent.com/pod-product-compliance
Lightning Source LLC
Chambersburg PA
CBHW050857250626
47155CB00001B/2